W9-ALN-085

THE DEAD

HOLLYWOOD

MOMS

SOCIETY

THE DEAD

HOLLYWOOD
MOMS

SOCIETY

LINDSAY MARACOTTA

WILLIAM MORROW AND COMPANY, INC.   NEW YORK

It is the policy of William Morrow and Company, Inc., and its imprints and affiliates, recognizing the importance of preserving what has been written, to print the books we publish on acid-free paper, and we exert our best efforts to that end.

Library of Congress Cataloging-in-Publication Data

Maracotta, Lindsay.
    The Dead Hollywood Moms Society / Lindsay Maracotta.
        p.   cm.
    ISBN 0-688-14498-5
    1. Women detectives—California—Los Angeles—Fiction.
    2. Hollywood (Los Angeles, Calif.)—Fiction.   I. Title.
    PS3563.A6225D4   1996
    813'.54—dc20   95-52210
                                                        CIP

Printed in the United States of America

    2   3   4   5   6   7   8   9   10

BOOK DESIGN BY BONNI LEON-BERMAN

ACKNOWLEDGMENTS

I'd like to express my infinite thanks and gratitude to all those who not only returned my phone calls but were more than generous in sharing their expertise: Dr. Jeffrey Kotchner, Candace Allen, Detective David Simon, Jane Ruhm, Sergeant Ray Verdugo, Peter Graves, the Academy of Motion Pictures Animation Department, and the remarkable ladies of the Montecito Public Library.

THE DEAD

HOLLYWOOD

MOMS

SOCIETY

ONE

1

NEEDLESS TO SAY, WHEN JULIA Prentice began to cast her huge, hazy eyes in the direction of my husband, I should have snapped to immediate attention. But at the moment I was too distracted thinking about her breasts.

The reason I was so fixated on her anatomy was because of something I'd recently heard—that Julia had had *two* sets of breast implants, the first having developed some sort of peculiar bubbles in the silicone, making it appear she'd sprouted a second pair of nipples (a condition that actually exists, I happen to know. It's called polythelia and isn't even that uncommon). So, back to her surgeon Julia sashayed, and had herself repadded, in the process bumping herself up from a 36B to a C; and I found myself staring at the bib of her flowy Romeo Gigli blouse, wondering what this fabulous bosom could possibly *look* like after all that tinkering.

"I can't tell you how much I admire the two of you," Julia was saying.

"What?" I forced my attention back to her cinnamon-painted mouth.

"You and Kit. You've been married practically forever, haven't you?"

"I wouldn't call it forever. Going on twelve years."

"Twelve years." Julia repeated this as if it were some vast, possibly geologic, time span. "Of course, you've always been perfectly happy, haven't you?"

"Oh, we've had our ups and downs. Every marriage has its thin patches. There've been lots of times we've really had to work at it." I heard myself starting to sound like Ann Landers and quickly stoppered my lips with my glass of Chardonnay to keep further platitudes from springing from them.

Julia's eyes scanned the mob of people congregated on her terrace and zoomed in on Kit, cornered against a huge stone urn by what looked like a preteen in a Raiders cap, but was probably either an agent or a studio exec. "I can see why you'd work hard to keep him," she murmured. "He's very attractive. Terrific ass. He must be great in bed."

I gave a startled laugh. "The earth moves, the angels sing. Every time is as magical as the first."

Julia didn't laugh. Rather, she regarded me as solemnly as if I'd quoted some rare and insightful passage of the *Kama Sutra.* "You don't know how lucky you are, Lucy," she said. "Most men in Hollywood are lousy at sex. It's like, while they're doing it, they're still listening for the phone to ring."

I searched for another jokey comeback, as I usually did when I felt unsure of myself, but I was beginning to realize that Julia was one of those beautiful women who'd never felt an urgent need to cultivate a sense of humor. So I opted for saying nothing, staring instead beyond the Prentices' gardens to the broad band of Pacific Ocean sparkling in the sun.

The occasion for our little tête-à-tête was a party Julia was throwing, a Sunday afternoon bash to mark the first anniversary of her return from China with an infant girl—a round-faced, button-nosed little thing named Quanxi. "I'd heard how they were murdering baby girls over there and knew I couldn't live with myself if I didn't try to rescue at least one!" she had breathlessly confided to John Tesh on *Entertainment Tonight.* "Her name means *snow before the dawn,* and no, we wouldn't dream of changing it. We're going to do everything in our power to preserve her magnificent Chinese heritage."

I was surprised we'd been invited. The Prentices had been our across-the-street neighbors in the Palisades for almost four years, but each of our houses was huddled behind an electronically operated gate, and our social contact was generally limited to cheery finger waggles when we passed each other in our environmentally sealed cars. Moreover, Kit and I were no longer what you'd call an A-list couple: Kit, a producer whose last two movies had been resounding box-office flops; me, an animation filmmaker, which set me pretty much out of ranking in the standard Hollywood hierarchy. But invited we were, a card arriving in the mail sprinkled with violet and silver stars, addressed to "The Freers Family," summoning us to an afternoon of "Festive Family Fun."

Family being the present Hollywood infatuation. There were kids everywhere—on sets, crawling through the corridors of production offices, scrambling among the thickets of adult legs at every party and gathering. Pregnant movie stars waddled onto the sets of talk shows. Six-figures-a-year female agents breastfed infants at Spago.

All the Hollywood Wives were scrambling to become Hollywood Moms . . .

And Julia, ever able to sniff the prevailing winds, was Doing Family at this affair with a vengeance. For our Partying Pleasure, we had two Coast Guard–certified scuba instructors dipping teenagers in the pool, while actors costumed as various "Toons"— Roger Rabbit, Daffy Duck—mugged for the toddlers. And on the side lawn, an entire petting zoo, complete with baby llama and boa constrictor, to which my animal-crazy nine-year-old daughter, Chloe, made an immediate beeline, leaving me free to be waylaid on the terrace by our humorless hostess.

Julia, like so many stunning women in town, had started out

as an actress. In fact, just two nights before I'd caught her in an old *MacGyver* rerun, dressed in an eighties power suit, snapping orders at some hunky young guy who proceeded to strangle her with a computer cord. (Dead before the first commercial break—bad news for the residuals.) So now, when she suddenly emitted a sort of gargled cry, it was so exactly like the sound she'd made when the IBM cord tightened around her neck, I gave a start.

"That idiot!" Julia hissed.

I followed her gaze down below us to poolside, where the birthday—or rather, anniversary—girl, tiny Quanxi, was being wheeled through the crowd by her English nanny. She was dressed in a tam-o'-shanter, wee plaid kilt, and emerald leggings (so much for the magnificent Chinese heritage), a vision that sent ricochets of oohing and aahing among the guests.

"She wasn't supposed to bring the kid out until the cake!" Turning abruptly, Julia charged a swath through the crowd from terrace to stroller, and, with a murderous glare at the Englishwoman, proprietarily snatched up the little girl. Julia's TV superstar husband, Woody Prentice, materialized at her side, and together they began to hold court.

"Don't they look divine?" simpered a bony blonde on my right.

I returned a vague smile. *Divine* was exactly right. *People* magazine had recently featured the Prentices on the cover: Julia, wearing something that looked suspiciously like a housedress, gazing with Madonna-like rapture at the black-eyed baby on her lap; Woody, with his saintly shock of white hair, a proud protector behind her. All three were bathed in a kind of radiant, heaven-suggestive glow ... looking, for all the world, like the Holy Family of Hollywood.

"Waaaa!"

The Holy Family was suddenly having a bit of trouble. Little Quanxi had begun to squirm and fret in her mother's arms. Julia, with a rather grim smile, tightened her grip. The baby countered by kicking a smart heel into Julia's taut stomach, then started to howl, which caused papa Woody to hop backward in panic. At which point, Julia thrust Quanxi back into her nanny's care, and the two of them, Julia and Woody, began to lurch rapidly toward a long bar set up against the jacarandas. I laughed out loud. Now, *there* was a shot for *People* magazine.

"What's so funny?" asked Kit, looming up behind me.

"Julia and Woody are experiencing the joys of parenthood. Three minutes of it, and they seem to feel the need for a stiff drink."

He gave a grunt. "I could use a drink myself. I've just spent the last forty minutes being hustled by a twenty-six-year-old ITA agent named Dickie. I feel like I barely escaped alive."

"Poor baby. Why did he zero in on you?"

"I think the word's got out that Sugerman's interested in doing *Willigher*. And just in case it's true, Dickie wants to be my best friend."

In spite of myself, I experienced a quick thrill of excitement. *Willigher* was a script Kit had had in development for several years, a ghost story chock-full of special effects, making it expensive enough that no studio would commit without a major "element" attached, star or director. Recently, miraculously, it had attracted the interest of Jon Sugerman. *The* Jon Sugerman, the director whose last three movies had *each* grossed more than a hundred million, domestic alone. But as I intimately knew, in Hollywood, even the surest thing can vanish in a twinkle: one minute you're whizzing along in a golden coach, then *abrakazam!* suddenly you're just squatting on a pumpkin.

"If the agents think it's worth talking about it, maybe it could actually happen," I said tentatively.

"That kid doesn't know a thing!" Kit snapped angrily. "Except phone numbers. The guy's a walking Filofax."

"Oh," I said. We lapsed into one of the strained silences we'd become so adept at lately. Ironically, amid all the Hollywood family hoopla, our own marriage was not exactly peaches and cream—in fact, we were going through one of those thin patches

I'd just been breezily spouting about. And our sex life was hardly the stuff to make angelic beings reach for their hankies—unless, of course, it was to stifle a yawn. "Listen," I said abruptly, "do you really want another drink? Why don't we grab Chloe and go catch a movie?"

"Now? I think it would be damned rude to the Prentices if we waltzed out now. Besides, there are some major players here. I wouldn't mind circulating some more." He added, a little too smoothly, "It wouldn't hurt you either to make a few new connections."

"Yeah, right. Maybe I should throw myself in with that bevy of starlets over there. I'll bet they could connect me with the best bikini wax in town."

Kit stared at me. He had a broad blond face, like Mr. Sun in the old Raisin Bran ads—at the moment, Mr. Sun under heavy cloud cover. "You know, sometimes I think you actually avoid anything that might help your career. That maybe you've got some screwed-up fear of success."

"That's bullshit!" I flashed back. "I'm the one who got the Oscar nomination, remember."

"Four years ago. And just because you lost is no reason to keep your head stuck in the sand."

I was about to shoot back something zinging in my defense, but People Were Staring, including the bevy of starlets. "I think I'll go find Chloe," I said frostily. "Make sure she's cultivating the right connections. I hear the baby llama's a real power player at MGM."

I swallowed the dregs of my Chardonnay and set the glass down with a plunk on the balustrade. Some instinct made me glance back down at Julia. She had completely recovered her aplomb, and was standing in easy contrapposto, raking her fingers through her rich coffee-colored hair . . .

And gazing hungrily up at my husband.

2

THE FIRST THING YOU LEARN when you shop for a home in any halfway desirable neighborhood in L.A. is that every property comes with a pedigree. Who Used To Live Here is as big a selling point as whether the master bath has a Jacuzzi tub, or whether, if you rip up the grungy pumpkin shag carpet, you'll find maple peg-and-groove flooring underneath.

Our first house, a tiny Craftsman bungalow in Sherman Oaks, had once been occupied (or so we were breathlessly informed by the listing agent) by the sportscaster on Channel 4, the one with the teased blond toupee. After Chloe was born, we moved to a charming, if drafty, miniature castle nestled in the Hollywood Hills, boasting the distinction of having belonged to the ex-wife of a famous English director. But with our present home, we really struck the celebrity-ghost jackpot. Built in the thirties by a producer with the old Metro studios, who'd reputedly dropped dead while shaking up vermouth-free martinis in the breakfast nook. Sold in 1944 to no less than Barbara Stanwyck. *And,* at some point in the freewheeling seventies, leased to Cher.

I admit I relished the idea of Stanwyck pacing our

bedroom, furiously chain-smoking, while some man, possibly Fred MacMurray, sprawled naked and fretting on the bed. But mostly I loved the house for itself—a rambling mock New England farmhouse on a winding, wooded lane. It had a brick hearth in the kitchen, suitable for roasting a pig on a spit; carved mahogany beams that flung mysterious shadows on the whitewashed walls; and a huge ancient spruce that, since the last earthquake, leaned at a Tower of Pisa–like tilt.

When we bought the house six years ago, we were rich. Kit had just produced *Cop Crimes*—brought it in under its eight-million budget, then watched it soar to over sixty at the box office. Money began to shower down on us, a monsoon of fortune. Kit moved into a trailer office on the Fox lot with a development assistant named Giles and a secretary named Amber, and settled plumply back to sort through the dozens of projects now tumbling his way.

But his next two movies were flops. Megaflops. The kind where friends slink out fire exits after screenings rather than risk having to face you. The kind that on opening weekend, the theaters look as if some lethal retrovirus had wiped out the majority of the movie-going population. The money monsoon dried to a sprinkle and had lately become a drought.

As for me, my *succès* was mostly *d'estime*. My short animated films scooped up awards and accolades by the dozen. I'd been flown to Budapest to accept first prize in a Hungarian short-film festival and been honored with a retrospective by the NYU film school. And, yeah, an Oscar nomination—for Best Short Film, Animation Category.

But none of this paid the mortgage.

I was the one who insisted on putting the house on the market. "We're not broke yet," Kit objected. "I've got a lot of stuff in the fire. Three possible green lights. If any of them go . . ."

"If," I cut in. "Hollywood runs on *if*." We were both familiar with the scenario: get a hit, make a small fortune, then spend it as fast as it comes in, because you can't believe it will ever stop.

And when it does stop, you go right on spending because there's always an *if*—right up to the point where the bank repossesses your house and the leasing company demands the keys to your cars. We'd seen it happen to a dozen people we knew. "I, for one, don't feature the idea of being tossed out on the street by some guy in a gray suit from Wells Fargo," I added. "If we sell now, we can still get out with some equity."

So up went the CHAS WHITE REALTY sign, with its tasteful, if geographically baffling, logo of a crescent of Georgian townhouses.

And at eight A.M. sharp, the Tuesday after Julia's party, our real estate agent Marsha Moss-Golson's nails-scraping-a-blackboard voice assaulted my ear over the kitchen phone. "Honeycakes, listen, I gotta couple of sterling buyers on the line. He's a big wheel in marketing over at Columbia, she's an attorney, just had a first baby. They've already unloaded a place in Hancock Park, they've got C-A-S-H, I absolutely know they're gonna flip over your place."

My heart took a thud. It was one thing to stick a FOR SALE sign on the gate, another to imagine the house actually being sold.

"They wanna see it at lunch, say, around one-thirty," Marsha plowed on. "I hate this kind of short notice, but I really don't think we oughta let these people get away." I could hear her, as she spoke, patting on her third layer of foundation and spritzing a membrane of hair spray over her frantic gold do. Marsha had hit upon her look—big hair, important nails, majordomo shoulder pads—in 1987, the year she unloaded a twelve-acre estate in Bel-Air on a Saudi prince and raked in her fabled million-buck commission, and apparently saw no good reason to change it.

"Okay," I agreed reluctantly. "Bring them on by. I'll try to be out of your way."

I hung up, then quickly dressed. My wardrobe was made up almost entirely of vintage items, everything from Edwardian midiblouses to fifties angora twin sets, mostly culled from the flea markets and thrift shops I was forever haunting. I also collected

Fiesta and old Pacific ware, Depression glass, rhinestone costume jewelry—in fact, just about anything made before I was born.

Now I shrugged on a calf-length forties dress, fastened a Bakelite clip in my hair and went downstairs, popping my head into the den, where Kit was engaged in his usual morning routine—gulping a can of Coke Classic while fielding the nonstop carillon of phone calls that began around seven. Producers come in two varieties, those that want to be loved and those that want to be feared. Kit was firmly of the former, caressing, cajoling, always playing the cheerleader. He often worked at home for several hours, sometimes straight till lunch.

"Some people are coming to look at the house at one," I said, sotto voce. "Will you still be here?"

He shook his head vigorously and covered the mouthpiece. "Another hour and I'm gone."

Was a time he'd have pantomimed a kiss and I'd have blown one back, but now he was already back on the phone, hunched into a conversation about whether Danny DeVito would be available in August. Every year a new platoon of killer-eyed young hotshots swarmed into town, ready to make human sacrifice if necessary to oust Kit from his snug Fox lot trailer and install themselves in his place. Kit was running so fast to stay ahead of them, no wonder he had little time left for incidentals like our marriage.

I turned and headed to the stairs and yelled to Chloe. After a dramatic moment, she came sloping down, Little Miss Harper's Bazaar, all trendy layers of denim and lace.

"I'm the only girl in my entire class who doesn't have pierced ears," she announced.

"We've been through this a thousand times. Not till your twelfth birthday." I brushed a stray curl from her forehead, the same Little Orphan Annie red as my own had been before it mellowed into its present dark maple.

"Alwyn Rossner's got two in both her ears, *and* she's got

diamond studs, *and* she's allowed to wear nail polish, even fuchsia if she wants."

"Alwyn Rossner can smoke cigars for all I care. I happen to think kids should act like kids."

"You think nobody should ever grow up so they'll still watch your dumb cartoons."

"You got that right," I said briskly. "Go give Dad a kiss and let's move."

Chloe threw me a sidewise glance before shuffling into the den. I'd long suspected that my daughter felt she was issued the wrong type of mother. What she thought she deserved was one of those Frostee Freeze blond ladies in pastel suits who lunch till four at the Ivy. What she got was a reasonably pretty redhead in crysanthemum-sprigged rayon who looked young for her thirty-seven years—and who currently sported a storyboard under her arm illustrating the adventures of Amerinda, a turquoise flying hedgehog.

Chloe emerged from the den and trailed me into the garage, still cataloging the many hardships of her life. As I backed out my Grand Cherokee, the electric gates across the road creaked open; the Prentices' English nanny sailed out behind the wheel of the biggest of their three Mercedeses, little Quanxi strapped into a baby seat in back. I wondered where the Devoted Mother was. Probably still getting her beauty rest. Or doing her famous hundred-a-day body-toning laps in her fortune-cookie–shaped swimming pool.

Twelve minutes later, I pulled into the line of cars snaking up to the fieldstone gates of The School.

The School was another residue of our being temporarily rich. It was technically named the Windermere Academy for Progressive Education; it resembled the country seat of a dissolute Regency earl, the tuition was a whopping twelve thousand bucks a year and it was the learning institution of choice for the worshiped kids of the Hollywood elite. The story was oft told that one year, for show-and-tell, a fourth grader had brought in Marlon Brando. True or not, I do know the Motion Picture Academy could save a bundle by holding the Oscars at The School's parents' night—the crowd is pretty much the same.

For instance, in the silver Range Rover pulled up behind me was Mattie Ballard, second-highest-paid movie actress in the world. Pale hair scraped back from a makeup-free face, she looked almost nondescript, like any other Hollywood Mom dropping off her seven-year-old.

On the other hand, Francine Palumbo, in the mulberry Jag ahead of me, who *was* a full-time mom, was as glossily done up as any movie queen. Oliver, her son from her first marriage, hopped out of the front seat. He had the flaxen hair, cerulean eyes and peach-down skin of an angel. Chloe waved to him, and he bounced up to her window—and spat, a fat, foamy white glob that slid lazily down the glass.

"Gross!" yelled Chloe, recoiling. "That Ollie Latch is such a creep!"

That's a fact, I silently agreed. Even in a crowded field, Ollie Latch-Palumbo finished a strong first for the title of Local Demon Seed.

"Am I picking you up today?" I asked Chloe.

"Nuh-uh. I've got soccer and then story workshop, and then I'm getting a ride home with Alwyn. Sometimes they send the limo," she added with a disturbing note of awe. Allowing me a quick peck on my cheek, she plunged into the throng of kids. Grade-schoolers with Prada backpacks and PowerBooks and diamonds in their ears: I suddenly wasn't weeping over the fact that we probably couldn't afford to send Chloe back there in the fall.

It took twenty minutes to maneuver my way out of the clot of cars, most, like my own, four-wheel drives that would never navigate any terrain more rugged than Benedict Canyon. Then I headed to the tiny studio space I rented in Culver City. I'd landed one of my rare paying jobs, for a Saturday morning kids' show called *Excellent Science*—a continuing animated segment that each week illustrated another scientific principle. This week was gravity, which was where my flying hedgehog came in. Amerinda goes whizzing around the sky, until a passing Canadian goose clues her in to the laws of gravity, at which point *plop!* down she goes—landing with uncanny luck in the midst of a friendly farm.

Once absorbed in my drawings, I lost all track of time; only the thrashing of rain against the windows made me look up. One of those sudden, drenching downpours that seem to come from nowhere and end as abruptly as they begin—unusual for this late in May. I was starving, it was past lunchtime; I decided to head back home.

The rain had stopped by the time I reached the house; the thick, cotton-waddy clouds were scurrying off to Pasadena, and the meretricious L.A. sun was already sopping up the puddles. Our electric gates were open. Kit was getting damned absent-minded these days, I thought briefly.

I parked the Cherokee in the driveway and went straight into the kitchen, grabbed a fistful of water biscuits and an overripe pear and, munching, hit the playback of the flashing answering machine.

"The deal's closed!" Kit's delirious voice shouted. "Sugerman's committed. He wants Costner or Harrison Ford, Fox says start preproduction immediately, I'm off to Seattle Friday to start location scouting. Dinner tonight at Chinois or wherever you want. And tear down that fucking real estate sign!"

I let out a yell. We were rich again! Our house was saved! My beloved house with its moody beams and tangerine trees and crazy old tilted spruce! Plus now Kit could stop running frantically in place; we'd be a real family again. Maybe even start that second child we used to talk about once upon a time. I started whooping and shimmying around the kitchen, breaking into a sort of Apache war dance as I burst outside.

But then suddenly I was having difficulty getting my feet to move. It was like stomping through mashed potatoes, something thick and oozy sucking at each step.

"Oh, shit," I said aloud. It was mud, a good foot and a half of it spread over the ground.

The rain had caused a slide.

Most of our backyard was formerly a hill that had been terraced into four levels, with steps made of broken brick leading the way up. The pool, a long aquamarine rectangle, was carved into the top level, which—property-value speaking—was considered a flaw: not only couldn't you see it from the house, but before taking a dip you had to huff and puff up four steepish rows. A little stucco casita, which we grandly called the pool house, was built against what was left of the hill. It was from behind here that the mud had cascaded, flowing into one end of the pool, then down in a relentless, winding stream toward the house.

I started up the steps to survey the damage. The Brown Jordan pool furniture had been blown about, one umbrella table knocked completely into the pool. And by the time I reached the second level, I could make out something that looked like seaweed floating in the water.

"A lotta celebrities live in this neighborhood," a voice suddenly intoned.

I glanced down to see Marsha Moss-Golson shepherding a couple out the kitchen door. The Sterling Buyers—I had totally forgotten about them!

"Arnold Schwarzenegger's got a lovely home just a couple a blocks away," the Moss-Golson voice rasped on. "And right across the street, Woody Prentice. Did I mention to you that Barbara Stanwyck used to live here?"

The Sterling Buyers were both whippet thin and wore "I smell cheese" expressions, which puckered even tighter as they surveyed the rivulet of mud. "Looks like a problem here," sniffed the man.

"And that lopsided spruce tree will have to come down," pronounced the woman.

I was going to love telling these folks the property was no longer for sale. Rather gleefully, I skipped up the final flight to pool level . . .

Where I could now see that what I had thought was seaweed were actually long, undulating strands of hair. And that the hair belonged to Julia Prentice, half-submerged in the muddy water, facedown, bottom up.

She was stark naked.

And starker dead.

"You're gonna love living in the Palisades," Marsha was going on. "It's a real family neighborhood. Perfect for kids . . ."

It was all I heard before I started to scream.

3

DETECTIVE TERESA SHOE OF THE Los Angeles Police Department was of medium height, medium build, and walked, toes splayed out, like a duck. Age, fortyish. Hair, mouse brown with silver threads, lopped in a bowl style that, what with her rather round face, unfelicitously called to mind Old King Cole. Poly-blend white shirt, poly-blend taupe slacks, tailored blazer of a browny-gray that made an uneasy marriage with the taupe. Footware, sensible.

In short, she looked like any other overworked, middle-aged American woman, one of hundreds you might see picking through the markdowns in a Reseda Kmart—which was probably why she looked so *un*ordinary tramping through the rooms of our house. In this part of town, even the repair and maintenance people tended to be on the dazzling side. Our pool man, for instance, held three local body-building crowns, light-heavyweight division. The guy who came to fix our cable looked like the Young God of Surfing.

Detective Shoe waddled into my bedroom, cast a summary glance at the sloppily made bed, the painted Mexican wardrobe, the fireplace, which had been blocked up since it had mysteriously started belching a black, tarry substance from its flue. Her eyes lingered longer on the big white goose pull toy, with its three wooden goslings trailing on a string behind it. "This is your room?" she asked in a dubious voice.

"Yes, it is," I said firmly. "I collect vintage toys. Some of these are extremely valuable. That rocking horse in the corner, for instance, is almost two hundred years old."

She produced a noise that was something between a grunt and a snort. I'd already concluded, from other not-so-subtle indications, that she thought me a sorry excuse for a grown woman—this merely confirmed it. She veered to my dresser and planted herself in front of a framed cel from one of my short films, which hung above it. Her brow knit quizzically as she studied the drawing. "What's this supposed to be?"

"It's the Chrysler Building," I said. "It's in New York City, a famous Art Deco landmark."

"It's got a face."

"Yes, well, in the film this was from, all the main characters were buildings. There was the Empire State, and the Sears Tower and the Transamerica pyramid from San Francisco. The idea was that they were unhappy with the way their cities were being run, so they took matters into their own hands."

"They had hands too?"

I smiled uneasily. "Well, figuratively speaking. But I could have given them hands if I'd wanted. You see, that's what animation means, to take something that's not living and bring it to life. Give it a mind, movement, a personality . . ." My voice trailed off. In my nervousness, I had launched into my standard film-festival prize-acceptance speech; but judging from the look Detective Shoe directed at me, this clearly wasn't the happiest occasion to be talking about animating the dead. She turned crisply to my bed table and, with her own gloved hands, began to poke through the clutter on top, searching no doubt for the blunt instrument with which I had bashed in Julia's skull. I stood watching, awkwardly shifting my weight from foot to foot, telling myself to for god's sake keep my mouth shut.

The last few hours were a blur in my mind. I could clearly recall half running, half sliding down the terraced levels from the pool, hysterically yelling that Julia Prentice had drowned, somebody call 911. The Sterling Buyers had goggled at me, at first indignantly, as if I'd just doubled the asking price of the property. "Somebody's dead?" Marsha finally gasped. "I can't get involved in this!" the wife-attorney hollered, and, in her scramble to get away, sat down smartly in the thick of the mud, clear to the waistband of her navy silk Anne Klein skirt. The husband/marketing maven, after only the merest hesitation, manfully sacrificed his own ox-blood Guccis to wade into the glop and yank her out. I somehow made it inside to a phone; as I blurted my story to the 911 operator, Marsha hustled her charges back through the house, shooting me a withering I'll-get-you-for-this look as they surged by.

And then suddenly there were cops. At first two, skidding up to the house in a shrieking, flashing squad car, but then they kept multiplying, like some form of single-cell organism: cops in uniforms, cops in plainclothes, cops with cameras and notepads and measuring devices and technical equipment. Cops with dogs. Detective cops waving a warrant. Cops peppering me with questions, until I had explained a dozen times about the storm dashing the windows of my studio and returning home for lunch, and the opened gates, and the pear and water biscuits, and Marsha and the Sterling Buyers. There was considerable interest in a flowering purple bruise on my cheek, which I must have acquired during my grand slalom down the terraced levels. Detective Shoe in particular kept squinting narrow little glances at it.

I had to identify Julia only once, since these cops all seemed astonishingly starstruck and couldn't wait to inform each other of the corpse's identity: "It's the wife of Woody Prentice, yeah, from *In the Same Boat* . . . Uncle Roy, right . . . 'Shucks, it's a Subaru' . . . Yeah, that's him, lives right across the street!"

And all the time I couldn't wring from my mind the image of Julia bobbing, perfect bottom up, in that murky water.

*   *   *

DETECTIVE SHOE FINISHED HER INVENTORY of the bed table and began snooping in Kit's closet. "Lotta sneakers," she remarked, perusing his jumbled pyramid of running shoes.

"My husband's a jogger. He's always buying new running shoes because he's got unusually high arches and can never really find a good fit."

"Uh-huh." I wondered what she really thought they were for—perhaps an after-hours career of cat burglary. She began thumbing through Kit's jackets and hanging trousers. "Did Mrs. Prentice come over here a lot?"

"No, not a lot," I said. "In fact, never. As far as I know, this was the first time."

"You weren't friends?"

"Not at all," I said emphatically. Then I realized that this could be interpreted to mean just the opposite, that we were enemies, thus giving me motivation to knock her off, so I added quickly: "I mean, we were *friend*ly, in a casual, neighborly way. But that was it. I don't know why she'd come over here. And hey, maybe she didn't," I went on eagerly. "Couldn't it be possible she was killed at her own home and whoever did it brought her here? You know, to throw everybody off the track?" I could tell how idiotic this sounded as soon as the words left my mouth: a murderer hauling a naked body across Caprese Drive in broad daylight . . . staggering up those four steep stair levels with the dead weight . . . then remembering to plant Julia's tangerine-colored terry-cloth robe beside the pool, as well as to hang her Mark Cross canvas bag containing swim goggles, Shiseido conditioner and an *après bain* lotion tidily on a hook inside the pool house.

"At this point, we don't rule out any potentiality," Detective Shoe deadpanned. "When was the last time you saw Mrs. Prentice?"

"They had a party last Sunday afternoon. A birthday party for their adopted daughter. There were about two hundred people there."

"Did you speak to her?"

"Just for a few minutes."

"What did you talk about?"

I suddenly remembered exactly what we had been talking about, and my skin prickled in an unpleasant, spidery way. "You know how it is at cocktail parties, everybody talks kind of tongue-in-cheek, it doesn't mean anything really."

Detective Shoe swiveled to turn her full attention to me. Her face wore an expression that I recalled as having been employed often by a Jungian therapist I had seen in the confused year between my graduating from Swarthmore and entering film school, an expression of mildly sympathetic blankness that said, "I'm prepared to wait as long as it's necessary, much longer than you can hold out, to get to the bottom of all this." Its effect on me now was identical to its effect on me then, which was to make me babble on uncontrollably, and with truth-serum fidelity. "We were talking about being married. Julia said something about how lucky I was to have a sexy guy like Kit and how great it was we'd been together so long. . . . You know, the kind of things you say when you want to be charming."

"She thought your husband was sexy?" Detective Shoe said tonelessly.

The husband that I had left alone here this morning. The husband who now couldn't be found, his secretary Amber declaring she had no idea where he was and there being no answer on his car phone. I let out a tinkly little laugh. "Well, like I said, we were just making party talk. I mean, I find *her* husband sexy too." This wasn't strictly true. Woody Prentice, better known as "the beloved Uncle Roy" of the monster-hit sitcom *In the Same Boat*, was sort of Everybody's Grampa: craggy but kindly of face, twinkling azure eyes, avuncular little catch in his growly voice. And frankly, you could hardly star Everybody's Grampa in an erotic fantasy. "Anyway," I went on, assuming a plucky tone, "it's not as if Julia would be really interested in Kit. She's married to a very famous person, she's got everything she's ever wanted." I realized I had lapsed into the present tense, still trying to reanimate the deceased. What my Jungian Dr. Postro would no doubt have called heavy denial.

The phone beside the bed rang. I moved to pick it up, but Detective Shoe said, "Detective Downsey will get it." Downsey, first name Armand, was her partner, a wiry, purring-voiced black man with a stubble haircut, who seemed to play the role of good cop to Shoe's bad. Downsey and Shoe, it sounded like a comedy magic act—I could picture them headlining Wednesday nights at the Laugh Factory.

A uniformed officer appeared at the door. "Mrs. Freers, it's your daughter wants to talk to you." He sounded skeptical, as if suspecting it wasn't really my daughter but the killer, voice cunningly disguised as that of a nine-year-old girl.

"Mom," piped Chloe. "I'm here with Alwyn."

"At her house?"

"No, we're in the Rolls-Royce, and we're at the corner. But there's TV vans and mobs of people in front of the house and the driver doesn't want to pull up. What's going on?"

I told her there'd been an accident but there was nothing to worry about. Then I had her put the driver on and informed *him* that I was currently awash with police and if he didn't deposit my daughter at her door this *instant*, I'd have him picked up, shackled and hauled downtown for kidnapping a minor.

I slipped out front to wait for her. There was indeed a mob of media and rubberneckers jamming the road, a kind of protean mass that oozed and flowed back and forth between our gate and the Prentices', depending on the latest development. At the moment it was clotted at the Prentices' gate, behind which huddled a bewildered, non–English-speaking Salvadoran maid—who, I knew from my own personal cop grapevine, was the only one currently at home. The sight of a chauffeur-driven Rolls-Royce limousine turning down the block caused near pandemonium.

Woody! The great man himself was arriving! The great protean mass began to boil and heave; the limo pulling up to *our* side of the street left it momentarily confounded, allowing Chloe just enough time to slip out and into my arms without being engulfed.

I hustled her inside the house. The sight of all the milling cops rendered her uncharacteristically speechless. "There's been a bad accident," I lied again. "Julia from across the street was taking a swim in our pool and hit her head and drowned."

Chloe's nose wrinkled in her that's-gross face.

"I want you to go to your room and stay there till I get you. Don't bother any of the policemen, and do not go outside."

"Mom?" she said anxiously. "What's going to happen to the little baby?"

"Quanxi? She'll be fine. She's still got her dad, don't forget."

"But he's old. What if he dies too, and they send her back to China, and she gets her head chopped off?"

"That's not going to happen," I declared. "She's an American now. And there's no reason to think Woody's going to die, at least not for a long time." I hugged her. "It's going to be okay. Go on, I'll bring you a Koala. Kiwi lime, okay?"

"With ice. And an apricot granola bar." She turned and shuffled upstairs to her room.

Both our phone lines had begun to ring frantically now. Julia had adored "coverage," and now she was about to get more than she'd ever dreamed of—maybe even the cover of *People* an unprecedented twice in one year.

Meanwhile, a new battalion of cops had arrived, bearing shovels, with which they started to clear away the river of mud, digging gingerly in hopes of unearthing clues. It was getting on toward dinnertime, and in my addled state I began obsessing about what they'd all want to eat—whether cops would go for the goat cheese and smoked duck sausage pizza from Delucca's, which was about all that qualified for takeout in this neighborhood, or if they'd dispatch one of their ranks on a run for burgers and fries.

Then a fresh roar erupted outside, followed by the sound of a car pulling into the garage. A shaken Kit burst into the kitchen, carrying an enormous bouquet of raffia-bowed copper tulips. "What the hell's going on?" he exclaimed.

"It's Julia Prentice," I said quickly. "I found her dead in the pool when I came back for lunch."

"Jesus!" Kit dropped the bouquet on the table and lowered himself heavily into a chair.

Detectives Shoe and Downsey loomed suddenly behind me. I introduced them to Kit, then busily began pouring cups of coffee.

"What time did you leave the house this morning, Mr. Freers?" Downsey began.

"About ten, quarter to ten."

"Is that a usual time for you?"

"It's not unusual. Julia was here," he blurted.

Both cops instantly assumed my Jungian shrink's I-have-all-the-time-in-the-world expression. Kit took a rather shaky sip of coffee. "She called right after Lucy left. She said her pool was being drained so they could fix a crack on the bottom, and she made some comment about being addicted to doing a hundred laps a day—if she didn't, she said it was like withdrawal, she got cranky and irritable all the rest of the day. So I told her she was welcome to use ours. I was going to leave soon and it wasn't one of the days our housekeeper was here, so she'd have perfect privacy."

"She knew your wife was out?" Detective Shoe still spoke tonelessly, yet the question seemed to sound like a smutty insinuation.

Kit blinked twice. "I guess so. I mean, she asked when Lucy would be back, and I told her probably not till the afternoon. I guess she'd seen Lucy's car pull away."

Detective Downsey said, "How soon after Mrs. Prentice called did she come over?"

"About ten minutes later. I left the gates open for her, then went up to the pool to check it out—to make sure the filter was running and the water wasn't all gunked up with leaves and stuff. None of us use it much this time of year. While I was doing that, she showed up, and we joked a little about her being addicted. And then I showed her where to change, in the pool house."

"What was she wearing?" Downsey pursued.

"A robe. A yellow bathrobe. And those kind of Mexican shoes with ropy soles . . ."

"Espadrilles," I put in. The cops' eyes flicked in perfect tandem toward me, then back to Kit for corroboration. He nodded. "And she had a beach bag, black I think it was, with I guess her bathing suit in it. So then she said thanks a lot and went into the pool house to change. And I picked up some stuff from the house and left."

"And what did you do then?" asked Detective Shoe.

"Drove Mulholland for about an hour and a half." Two pairs of cop eyebrows arched perceptibly. "I had an extremely important meeting at noon. A movie that Jon Sugerman was potentially going to direct—a make-or-break deal for my career. I was nervous as hell about it. So, what I did was go up to Mulholland Drive and I just started driving. All those twists and bends, you really have to concentrate—it's a good way to clear your mind. I took it all the way to the ocean, then back again to where it starts in Hollywood. By then, it was about a quarter to eleven, so I headed on to Universal."

"Where you had this important meeting," Downsey prompted.

"That's right. It lasted about an hour and a half. And . . . well, it was a success. I got a go-ahead on the movie." He let out the same sort of tinkly laugh I'd been producing frequently myself. "Funny, when I saw all those TV people outside, I had the crazy thought that that's what it was all about—that they'd heard about this Sugerman movie and were here to interview me or something." He laughed again, less tinkly, more strained.

The two cops pulled poker faces. "Okay, so an hour and a half, we're at one o'clock," said Downsey. "What did you do then?"

"A few of us went on to Cicada to celebrate. Lunch, a couple of bottles of Cristal . . . We left around two-thirty." When Kit got nervous, he had a habit of touching the thinning spot on his head, the beginning of a tonsure in his sandy thatch of hair. His hand flew up to it now. "And then . . . well, after that, I went and bought a car."

Three heads snapped up in surprise. "What did you get?" I asked without thinking.

"BMW Seven-fifty-i. Green with the parchment leather upholstery," he added rather extraneously.

"That's a pretty fine automobile," purred Downsey. "Sells for about sixty grand, doesn't it?"

"List price. I bargained a few thousand down from that."

Both detectives were silent a moment, no doubt contemplating this "bargain" that probably amounted to pretty near their yearly take-home pay. Bad Cop Shoe said crisply, "This big important deal . . . did Julia Prentice or her husband have anything to do with it?"

Kit gave a startled laugh. "Christ, no. You think . . . That's ridiculous, this had nothing to do with either of them."

Good Cop Downsey nodded reassuringly. "Now, all the time you were driving, did you stop anywhere or make any calls? Or pass anyone you know who could verify your story?"

"No. I just kept driving."

Lovely, I thought. Both of us had spent the morning in total solitude: the uniquely alibiless Mr. and Mrs. Freers, with a body in their backyard. I had a feeling that neither Downsey nor Shoe believed a word I'd said.

And some horrible instinct told me that Kit was not quite telling the truth.

I got up to pour my umpteenth cup of coffee. From the bay window over the sink, I could see that up the hill they were finally removing Julia from the water. I suddenly remembered my stupid preoccupation with her breasts—what they looked like after all that designer surgery—and the macabre thought flashed through my mind that here was the ideal opportunity to find out.

But I stayed where I was. I had already seen more of Julia Prentice in the raw than I ever cared to see.

4

OVER THE COURSE OF THE next ten days, most of what I learned about the case I gleaned from the popular media. The cops who still swarmed over our property were as communicative as stones, opening their mouths only to swallow the fresh-ground Kenyan medium-roast coffee and the Mrs. Gooch's all-natural fruit bars I plied them with in the futile hope of being rewarded with a few facts.

But the local newscasts were a trove of information—though it meant enduring the occasional frazzled sight of myself, usually peering like a startled goldfish through the window of my car. Also, to hearing myself identified variously as a "cartoonist," an "award-winning animation maker" or—most frequently—"the wife of the well-known Hollywood producer."

But I was paid off with some fascinating new tidbits about Julia. That she'd been born Julie Ann Tribble, was a former Miss Idaho State runner-up and Coeur D'Alene Community College dropout, and was thirty-nine, not the thirty-six she'd claimed to be. Also that she'd been married before, to a Nissan dealer in Boise (annulled after six weeks for nonconsummation). And that before her untimely demise, she'd been active in so many charities, fund-raisers and all-around do-gooding, she'd been giving Mother Teresa a run for the money.

The rehashing of Woody's career was less informative. How he'd first come to fame in the early seventies as the laconic star of *Bryer, P.I. for Hire*, a tongue-in-cheek whodunit on NBC. How, after it was canceled, he disappeared completely from view—until five years ago, when Nick at Nite began to air *Bryer* reruns, spawning a whole new set of Prentice fans. The year after that, Woody, now fifty-nine and snowy-haired, popped up in a hit sitcom, *In the Same Boat:* crusty recluse Roy Self, camped out on a houseboat on the Cuyahoga, has four orphaned nieces and nephews foisted upon him and—surprise, surprise!—reveals a heart of crusty gold. Then, suddenly, Woody was all over the tube, Madison Avenue quickly glomming to the fact that Everybody's Grampa made a natural pitchman. Click a channel: there was a bemused Woody, a-squeezin' into the backseat of a Subaru already jammed with kids, dogs and sticker-plastered suitcases. Click again: there was Woody, dancing a soft-shoe with a humongous box of Shredded Wheat.

Not much news to me—or, for that matter, to anyone not currently in a coma.

Far more gripping was the info that the police were definitely classifying this a homicide, having concluded that the abrasions on the back of Julia's skull could not have been caused by her diving into the pool and accidentally hitting her head. So that if this were a game of Clue, the answer would be: Julia, on the pool deck, with the lead pipe.

Except that no lead pipe had been recovered. Nor ball-peen hammer, nor brass candelabra, nor any other potential murder weapon; after carefully shoveling away all the mud and trooping over every inch of the ground, all the cops had retrieved from my backyard were Julia's espadrilles (tangerine to match her robe) and a dog-eared paperback of a Zelda Fitzgerald biography I had abandoned by the pool god knows when.

Finally, there did appear one interesting fact about Woody—that at the time of his wife's murder, he'd been filming a miniseries about the Apache Indians and the U.S. Cavalry and been vouched for by others on the set, thereby securing an air-tight alibi.

Which, as far as I could see, still left the Well-Known Hollywood Producer and his Award-Winning Animation Maker Wife as suspects numbers one and two.

KIT AND I SPENT AN edifying two and a half hours in the Century City office of a famous criminal lawyer, whose thousand dollars' worth of advice boiled down to "Keep your mouths shut and refer all questions to me."

Back home, we were exquisitely polite to each other. "Why don't *you* have this last pot sticker?" I'd say, over a dinner of take-out dim sum. "Oh, no, you go ahead," he'd reply. "No, really, I want you to have it," I'd insist. Miss Manners was surly compared to us. At night, we slept with our backs turned, squinched at opposite edges of the bed, carefully avoiding all bodily contact.

And in the meantime, we tried to get on with our lives. Kit rose at dawn to go camp out all day in the haven of his office. I ran the daily gauntlet of the press pack to drive Chloe to school, grateful for once that The School employed more security than the White House. Then I retreated to my studio and tried to concentrate on my flying hedgehog. But I was having trouble with the part where Amerinda has to fall to earth: instead of landing with a funny little plop, she kept going *splat!*

One dead blue insectivore.

THE WINDERMERE ACADEMY HELD ITS commencement on Saturday, nearly two weeks after Julia's demise. Much New Age-y

music and handholding in circles, while we parents cheered ourselves hoarse. The kids had been exhorted to dress in a way that
creatively expressed themselves, The School being very big on
concepts like Self-Expression, which meant lots of props filched
from productions—kids with Uzis, crossbows, phasers. Alwyn
Rossner came decked out as a fairy princess, complete with
gossamer emerald wings that *actually flapped!* and which (I was
sorry to see) made Chloe, who'd just settled for body paint, almost
sick with envy.

After the ceremony, everyone sauntered out to the eucalyptus-
shaded lawns, where paraphernalia for various games had been
set up. The principal, Ms. Baljur, who had last year unsuccess-
fully campaigned to be addressed as Headmistress, darted
through the crowd, pleading, "Badminton, anyone? Anyone for
croquet?" but was roundly ignored, the kids opting for free-form
roughhousing, while their elders clumped in little groups to sip
designer water and shoot the breeze. It was an unspoken rule of
The School that nobody engaged in the usual Hollywood talk.
No discussing deals. No studio gossip. Definitely no networking.
Conversations, by default, revolved mainly around kids. Topic
number one was Nannies—the finding, training and keeping of.
Topic number two was Diet—whose nutritionist had said what
about the virtues of fructose versus sucrose for pre-schoolers.
Topic number three, but moving up fast, was The School itself,
and Whether It Was Going Downhill.

Today, there was also a Topic to Be Avoided at All Costs,
which was the recent unpleasantness in my backyard. And by
extension, it appeared, I was to be avoided as well. The same
people who'd recently been lighting up my phone lines, doing
heavy-mouth breathing in anticipation of the juicy details, now
edged away from me with frosty little smiles, as if my shirt cuffs
were still dripping with Julia's blood.

Kit wandered off with I-vant-to-be-alone body language to go
brood in the shade. I hovered on the outskirts of a group that

•

clustered around the Rossners—David Rossner, head of the powerful International Talent Agency, and his ice-blond wife Summer, uncrowned queen of the Hollywood Mom elite.

"Do you still have that dead lady at your house?" The voice
issued from the level of my elbow. I looked down to see Francine
Palumbo's monster child, Oliver. He was tricked out like a dwarf-
sized drug dealer: hair slicked back, three-hundred-dollar gold-
rimmed Oliver Peoples shades, Armani A/X pullover. One hand
rather daintily held a paper plate stacked high with brownies; the
other, by contrast, was employed in crudely and systematically
cramming them into his mouth.

"No, we don't, Oliver," I said. "That's all over."

"Damn, I wanted to go look at her. And she was nude too,
right? I really wanted to see that. Was it you who killed her?"

"Absolutely not," I snapped.

He tilted back his head: my peeved expression reflected back
to me from the mauve lenses of his sunglasses. "Yeah, but if
you did do it, you wouldn't say so," he declared. "You'd lie your
ass off."

How remarkable, I thought, that no one had as yet smothered
this kid in his sleep.

I tried to move away, but Ollie trailed me like a faithful puppy.
"Guess how much I got for getting promoted to the fifth form?"
he demanded.

"I have no idea. Twenty dollars?"

He gobbled another brownie—I found it interesting to note
that he could chew and sneer at the same time. "You kidding?
You think my mother's cheap? She gave me five hundred dollars,
and I can spend it on anything I want to."

"How nice for you, Oliver," I said.

"So, how much did Chloe get? I bet you only gave *her*
twenty bucks."

"Oliver!" His stepfather, Sandy Palumbo, suddenly, mercifully,
intercepted us. "Why don't you go play with the other kids?"

"Bor-ing," pronounced young Oliver.

"I mean it, Ollie. Get going, and fast!"

With a deliberate motion, Oliver overturned his plate; the unfinished brownies plopped in a fecal-like heap on the grass. Giving an insouciant swing of his hips, he swaggered off. I glanced at Sandy: in his eyes flickered something that was startlingly close to pure loathing. Then it was gone, and he turned to me with his customary easy smile. "Ollie can be kind of a handful sometimes."

"You know how The School encourages self-expression," I said. "Ollie's got absolutely no problem there."

Sandy gave a wry chuckle. "Francie does let him get away with murder. But I can't really blame her for it. As you've probably heard, her first husband ditched her when Ollie was a baby, and she went through a couple of years of terrible poverty. Scraping just to get by—she couldn't give him anything at all. One Christmas, she actually had to accept presents from the Policemen's Benevolent Society. So it figures she's been overcompensating ever since."

I tried to picture the glossy, designer-labeled Francine Palumbo without money. I couldn't. "It was lucky for both of them you came along," I said.

"Like Mighty Mouse." Sandy grinned and sang softly, "Here I come to save the day . . ."

I laughed, wondering, for the hundredth time, how Francine had ever snagged him. Sandy Palumbo, head of Newgate Cinema, was one of those decidedly ugly men—huge nose, slightly protuberant eyes, kinky light hair—who are nevertheless extremely sexy. It was something about his easy grin. . . . Or the way he dressed, a sort of cross between a cowboy and a banker (cowboy boots, faded jeans, custom Turnbull & Asser shirts). Or maybe it was his natural athletic grace: he always seemed to be just on his way to climb a rock, or ski Tahoe, or whup somebody at tennis.

His company, Newgate Cinema, was an "independent," meaning one that produced and financed movies outside the major-
studio system. Sandy's taste ran to the offbeat—his films were
always interesting, occasionally brilliant, rarely profitable; somehow he kept the company afloat through skillful deals and sheer
affability. And that was another thing about Sandy: in an in-
dustry where most people would stab them*selves* in the back
if it could get them ahead, he was universally acknowledged to
be a nice guy.

Nice enough even to broach the Forbidden Topic with me.
"You and Kit must've had quite a time of it this week," he
said sympathetically.

"It's just your basic nightmare." I tried for a jaunty smile.

"Christ, I can imagine. But I guess it's times like this you
really appreciate having each other."

I glanced sharply at him, wondering, in my state of galloping
paranoia, if he were putting me on. But of course not—as far as
anyone knew, Kit and I were still a blissfully matched pair. "It's
been really hard on Chloe," I said evasively. "She's totally
freaked out. We're sending her on Monday to spend a couple of
weeks with Kit's parents. With luck, by the time she gets back,
this whole thing will be over."

He nodded. "Are there any developments? Clues or anything?"

"That's the worst part of it!" I sputtered. "The damned cops
won't tell us anything. You'd think that, since it did happen at
our house, we'd have some right to be kept informed."

Sandy was silent a moment. It occurred to me that, like everyone else, he naturally suspected that I had dispatched Julia. Or
that Kit had. Or Kit and I worked in ghoulish tandem. And it
stood to reason that the police might demur at tipping their hand
to the perps.

"So, I suppose you've got no inside leads on who the cops
think had sex with Julia," he said.

I blinked, startled. "What do you mean?"

He smiled gently. "You didn't catch the news this morning.

It was the hot breaking story—some source at the coroner's office leaked the autopsy results to the press. Apparently, there was semen in the body."

"She was raped?" I breathed.

"They don't know. The reports said there was no physical evidence of a struggle, but that they're not ruling out the possibility."

"My god! Every time I think we've hit bottom, it gets worse."

"Hang on. You'll make it through." As if sensing how wobbly my knees had become, Sandy laid a supportive hand on my arm.

The sudden, high-pitched shouts of children made us both look up abruptly. I turned just in time to catch the entertaining spectacle of my daughter socking Oliver Latch-Palumbo smack in his adorably turned up nose.

WE BEAT A HASTY RETREAT from the reception. At the sight of blood gushing from her darling's nose, Francine Palumbo had thrown herself into a curiously Edwardian-flavored hysteria, demanding a "physician" be "summoned," as well as the "authorities." Fortunately, there were any number of physicians in the crowd, including a pediatrician, Rhonda Perlmutter, who diagnosed a simple nosebleed, nothing a little ice wouldn't fix straight up. While everyone was hanging on her words, Ma Barker and her gang, otherwise known as the Freers family, were able to effect their getaway.

"He was being such a turd," Chloe declared petulantly as we pulled into our garage. "He kept saying that Mom killed Julia by shooting her in the guts. And he didn't even care that's not the way it *hap*pened! She wasn't shot, she got bashed in the head."

"Just because someone acts like a jerk doesn't mean you have to act like one too," Kit pontificated. "Especially not by hitting them."

"*He's* always hitting people, or kicking them, or spitting on them, and he tells lies too. I don't see why you guys are taking his side. I'm glad I'm going to Grandma's. I can't wait to get away from here!" Quivering with indignation, Chloe burst from the car and stomped into the house.

Kit let out a long sigh. "I'm going to hit the Stoly. Do you want one?"

"Thanks, no. I've got the beginnings of a monumental head-ache. I think I'll go lie down for a while."

I went upstairs, passing Chloe's room. She was making an eloquent statement by blasting gangsta rap, a tape undoubtedly obtained from Alwyn Rossner, who seemed to possess the entire inventory of Tower Records. I heard a *cunt*, a *fuck*, something that sounded like *iron-bitch pussy*, then another round of *fucks*, but this didn't seem like the optimum time to get tough. Instead, I inched open her door and tried the reasonable approach. "Listen, sweetie. I know this has been a weird week, but all this stuff will be over soon, and then everything will go back to the way it was before."

"Yeah, right," she snorted.

I suddenly had no strength to argue. I carefully reshut her door, then staggered on to my own bedroom and threw myself in a tragic posture on the bed.

The phone rang twice, then stopped. Kit, I presumed, had picked it up downstairs. Fine, let *him* deal with the media creeps. Aimlessly, I clicked on the TV, killing the sound. On-screen appeared Woody, softshoeing it up with the box of Shredded Wheat.

The phone rang again, and I reached for it.

"Woody Prentice here." The voice was low, barely audible.

"Oh, hello," I said with a start.

"You tell that husband of yours if he did it, I'll kill him."

"What?"

The TV Woody was do-si-do—ing with the giant cereal box. The telephone Woody breathed harshly in my ear, "I'll kill him myself. You just tell him that." He hung up.

Stunned, I lay gripping the receiver, still staring at the television screen, which had segued into a laxative ad. I didn't notice Kit come in until he spoke.

"That was Detective Downsey on the phone," he said. "They want me to come downtown and take a blood test. He said they're collecting blood samples from everyone related to the case to compare them to some biological evidence they found. They're so fucking vague. Why doesn't he just tell me what it's for?"

"They found semen in the body," I said. "At the autopsy. Apparently it's been all over the news—that somebody had sex with Julia just before she died." In a light tone, I added, "I just had a rather interesting call from Woody Prentice. He seems to think it might be you." I glanced up at Kit. His face was starched a dead white. My stomach turned over. "*Was* it you?"

"No," he said. He issued a heaving sigh. "But it could've been."

"What do you mean, 'It could have been'?" My voice came out high and squeaky, much like I had intended Amerinda's, my flying hedgehog, to be. "Are you telling me that things didn't happen exactly the way you told the cops?"

"No. I mean, mostly they did. Up till the part where I showed her where to change in the pool house." He sank into a wing chair, pressing the back of his head into the tufted fabric.

"Go on," I said tersely.

"She hung up her bag on the hook, and kicked off her shoes. I said something like 'See you later' and was about to leave, when she called my name. When I turned, she took off her robe. And, well . . . she was totally naked underneath."

"Ah," I said. "And then?"

"Well, naturally I was startled. And I guess aroused. I mean, a beautiful woman suddenly standing in front of you naked, it's a turn-on. So I guess maybe I grabbed her. But I didn't *do* anything. I mean, Christ, her breasts felt like Styrofoam."

Of course they felt like Styrofoam. They *were* Styrofoam—or at least a close chemical relation. "But you did touch her breasts," I said slowly. "And if they hadn't felt like Styrofoam, if they'd felt like melons or meringue or downy pillows, then you'd have screwed her brains out?"

"Look, she took me totally by surprise. But the important thing is that nothing happened, isn't it?"

"What *did* you do?"

"I said something about it not being a good idea, and backed away from her. At which point she started to get really nasty. She called me a faggot, and said she was sick of castrated men, and if I couldn't get it up, she'd call a real man who could. Shit, she was practically screeching! I just wanted to get away as fast as I could. So I did. I ran back down to the house and grabbed up my stuff, and then I jumped in the car and got the hell out of here."

Something snagged in my mind: how could Julia have called someone else? She hadn't used any of our phones—all the records had been checked, as had the phone records of the Prentices.

I said, "Why didn't you tell this to the cops?"

"Because of *Willigher*. I didn't want to screw up the deal. As it is, I've done nothing for the past couple of days but work on damage control. Sugerman's a fanatic about privacy and family and all that. I mean, Christ, he just took the last six months off to hole up with his kids in Montana. He's the king of family values. I've been jumping through hoops to convince him I'm totally clean, I had nothing at all to do with this, it was just a horrible accident that happened in my backyard."

"Shouldn't you have thought of that before you started feeling up Mrs. Prentice?" I snapped.

His mouth set in a prissy way. "For god's sake, Lucy, do you have to be so crude?"

I stared at him in astonishment. But before I could reply, he stood up with a let's-get-on-with-things briskness. "I'd better get going. I told Downsey I'd be there within an hour." He gave a lame chuckle. "I don't want him to get suspicious."

"Is there anything else, Kit?" I blurted. "Anything else you've neglected to tell me?"

"No. I swear, that's exactly the way it happened."

"I mean *ever*. Has any other woman ever 'taken you by surprise'?" Out came my flying-hedgehog voice again: "I mean, goddamnit, have you ever slept with anyone else since we've been married?"

He lowered himself back down onto the chair in a way I hated.

"Once," he said, with another long sigh. "It was while we were shooting *Finally Yours* up in Vancouver. Everyone already knew it was going to be a dog. It had the smell of a flop all over it. I could see my career heading straight for the Dumpster. And meanwhile, there you were in Budapest, accepting awards, being wined and dined. . . . I guess I felt a little resentful."

My mind raced back five years ago to skim the cast list of *Finally Yours.* . . . It couldn't have been Winona Ryder, she was just a kid . . . certainly not Jessica Tandy . . . "Oh, my god!" I gasped. "You had an affair with Mimi Rogers!"

"Of course not." He glared at me reproachfully. "It wasn't anybody with the production. I'd never be that unprofessional."

Adulterous, lying and deceitful, yes. Unprofessional, never. Shivering, I drew my knees tightly to my chest. "Who was it, then?"

"A reporter from *Vanity Fair,* who came up to the set to do a story on Winona. Jean somebody. I can't even remember her last name."

But I remembered that article. I remembered it referred to Kit as "the winsome, keenly creative producer, Christopher 'Kit' Freers." I remembered proudly sending a copy of this item to my father, even though he'd already sunk too far into Alzheimer's to read it, and to my two stepsisters in Minnesota, who got a kick out of their Hollywood connection. "Let me tell you about Budapest," I said slowly. "It was cold, blood-freezing cold. You couldn't get warm anywhere. The hotel was a fleabag, and I had to sit through endless speeches in Hungarian. I resented *you* back there on your glamorous movie set, with central heating and edible food. And let me tell you too—I had plenty of opportunities to take out *my* resentment with other men." One, actually—a fellow award-winner named Stefan, who looked like the young Franz Liszt, if the young Franz Liszt had chain-smoked Kents. He kept telling me I had "beautiful soles," which at first I'd taken to mean he had a foot fetish before realizing he was referring to my inner spirit.

"What can I say?" Kit muttered coldly. "You were right, I was wrong." He didn't, I noted, sound overwhelmingly contrite.

"What about now?" I said.

"What *about* now?"

My teeth were chattering, almost preventing me from getting out the words. "If you were so ready and able to have a go at Julia, what about the next one? Whatever starlet or reporter or goddamn script girl next makes goo-goo eyes in your direction."

"For godsake, Lucy, this is hardly the time to go into all this. I've really got to go." He stood up again and this time I let him retreat out the door.

After he left, I sprawled facedown on the bed, my nose buried in the pillow, fat tears plopping onto the Star of Bethlehem quilt. My husband was a secret philanderer. My daughter was turning into a brawling thug. My home, which had once seemed such a haven of peace and security, was now a featured stop on the Celebrity Death Line Tour—a refurbished hearse pulled up to the gate every day at precisely four-fifteen P.M. and disgorged a blotch of gawking, photo-snapping tourists.

And everything was going to go back to the way it was before. Yeah, right.

There was a framed picture on my bed table. Kit, me and Chloe at two and a half, on some rocky beach, all tangled up in each other, laughing, almost giddy with happiness. There was one thing I knew for sure: as long as Kit and I were even remotely suspected of Julia's murder, there wasn't a chance on earth we could get back to being that tangled-happy little family.

Okay, then, I told myself, sitting bolt upright. If clearing our names was what it would take, stop wallowing in self-pity and start doing something about it.

5

EARLY MONDAY MORNING, WE PUT Chloe on a Delta jet nonstop to Atlanta, where she would be collected by Kit's parents. Walter Freers was an internationally famous horticulturist, currently developing a new hybrid of pecans for the Southeastern Pecan Growers Association; he always seemed rather mystified by Kit's choice of career, perpetually asking, "Now, just exactly what is it that you *do*?" His mother, Stacey, however, a bubbly Scotch-Jewish Southern belle, subscribed to *Variety, The Hollywood Reporter* and *Buzz,* and regaled her golf partners with insider talk of gross points, turnarounds and whether Johnny Depp was as bankable as Brad Pitt. Both adored Chloe and would spoil her rotten while they had her, and hopefully it would help her forget her Freddy Kruegerish past two and a half weeks.

At first light on Tuesday, a studio limo arrived to whisk Kit to LAX. His blood test had apparently passed muster with the LAPD; Armand Downsey had given him sanction to leave town, requesting only that he "keep his whereabouts known"; and off he was to Seattle to begin location scouting for *Willigher.* "Don't do anything to rock the boat while I'm gone," he warned me as the black-capped driver tossed his bags into the trunk. "Sugerman and his people are still skitterish as hell. They could still back out of this at any time."

I gave a haughty nod. We stood for a moment, eyes carefully averted. Say something, I silently pleaded. Just one word of reassurance, however small. Any hint that your family is even remotely as important as making a movie with Jon Sugerman. Just one little indication that we come first, and I'll forgive your fling with Ms. *Vanity Fair*, I'll trot back into the house and throw myself into creating the world's most lovable flying hedgehog, and not give a damn whether we're prime suspects in every unsolved murder of the year.

But then the driver closed the trunk with a brusque slam, and Kit glanced up with undisguised relief. "I'll call you tonight," he said, planting a formal kiss on my cheek. He slid into the plush backseat of the car. It glided off, and I was on my own. Even the paparazzi had finally disappeared, except for one die-hard fat photographer from the *Enquirer*, who kept a lonely vigil at the Prentices' gate; and even he could no longer muster enough interest in me to give me more than a passing and dismissive glance.

I stood gazing at the Prentice house. It looked eerily still. There had been no sign of Woody for days—nor of the nanny or little Quanxi. Even the help seemed to be staying away.

The Prentices' automatic sprinklers spurted on. One broken jet sent an Old Faithful spume up and over the gate, spattering Mr. Fat Paparazzi, who muttered a pungent oath and lumbered off to his parked Mustang. I watched him roar off, then turned back and went into my house.

Time, I thought, to start rocking the boat.

IN THE KITCHEN, I RANG up the Santa Monica office of Chas White Realty, and asked for Marsha Moss-Golson.

"It's Lucy Freers," I announced when she picked up. "I'd like to come over and talk to you."

There came a sound like air escaping from a punctured tire. Marsha was about as interested in talking to me as she was in letting her hair grow out gray. I had caused her no end of grief: not only had I withdrawn my house from her listings, but her ultimate showing of it had cost her the custom of the Sterling Buyers.

"Please, Marsha," I pleaded, "it's really important. There are some things I've got to know about Julia."

"Look," she snapped, "I had a couple of cops here last week demanding to know the names and confidential phone numbers of my clients. I said, 'Whatta you think, that *they* were the ones who knocked off Julia and then planted her body in the swimming pool, so's to have more leverage in the deal?' I said, 'They didn't even *see* anything, for Chrissake, we got outta there as soon as we heard something was the matter.' But would our asshole boys in blue listen? Not a chance. They went right ahead and interrogated my clients, who naturally proceeded to change brokers as fast as they could dial up Fred Sands. So I don't want anything more to do with this, thank you very much."

"I'm sorry about all that, Marsha," I said. "But you know, once this murder has been cleared up, we'll probably be putting our house back on the market. And now that Kit's on this Sugerman film, we'll be able to afford something much bigger. Beverly Hills, maybe, or even Bel-Air."

I could sense Marsha's tizzy as she weighed the possibility of future fat commissions against her instinct to avoid me like a virus. "Okay," she said grudgingly. "You can come by my place. I've got my decorator coming at two, so I'll be there all afternoon. But I'm not promising anything."

IT WAS A TRUTH UNIVERSALLY acknowledged that Marsha Moss-Golson was rich enough to buy and sell most of her celebrity clients; that she had untold millions squirreled away in some tax-free paradise like Tasmania or Grand Cayman.

In the early sixties, she had married Jerry Moss, the silken-voiced, dumpy-bodied Vegas lounge singer and Rat Pack hanger-on; and when, in 1976, he dumped her for a Lufthansa steward-ess, Marsha made a clever, even inspired, move: instead of fi-nancially eviscerating the bastard in the way favored by most discarded wives, she Stayed on Good Terms. Accepted a nice, but by no means ball-breaking, settlement, made no demands on his cars and diamond rings, and continued to check in with him every day to schmooze about his dog-track losses and his hemorrhoids and the latest skullduggery on the part of his book-ing agents. She even threw the newlyweds a luncheon at the Polo Lounge, toasting *mazel tov!* with vintage Dom Pérignon.

The upshot being that she retained something more valuable than Jerry's bookie-drained bank account—to wit, possession of the show-business friends. Nobody had to be afraid of asking Marsha to a party or wedding or bar mitzvah to which Jerry and his bride were also invited—in fact, Jerry seemed more relaxed with Marsha around—so that when she made the plunge into real estate, she brought with her a fabulous network of potential clients: agents, crooners, actors, club owners—all in possession of gaudy mansions in the highest-priced neighborhoods. Right from the start, heavy commissions rolled her way.

But it was also common knowledge that Marsha's really big dough came from the canny buying and selling of foreclosures. At the first whiff of a bankruptcy, there would be Marsha hov-ering like a turkey vulture, ready to swoop down at the final croak. Often she'd get the furnishings thrown in with the home as well; then she'd move in, treat the place to a hasty makeover, slap an inflated price tag on it and toss it back on the market.

Because of her constantly shifting residences, I never knew what kind of habitat I'd find her in: Tudor, Mediterranean, Forties Moderne . . . 15201 San Lopito turned out to be a contempo white box in the Palisades, crammed anomalously into a block of modest pastel stucco bungalows. One of the double-height double doors opened a crack as I came up the walk. Marsha

peered out, her eyebrows lowering ominously at the sight of me.
Before she could change her mind, I pushed past her into the
foyer.

Except there was no foyer. It was one of those houses with no
interior walls, just one gargantuan white-on-white space. A few
black leather and chrome couches floated adrift on a sea of arctic
wall-to-wall carpeting. The size, the sparsity of furniture, the
blinding whiteness of it all, gave me the feeling of having wandered into a lunatic asylum in some antiseptic near-future—an
impression underscored by six large streaks of paint slashed on
one huge wall in varying shades of pinky-brown.

A woman who could have been Marsha's tinier, bulimic sister
was scrutinizing the slashes through a kind of periscope made
of her interlocked fingers.

"Lois, Lucy. Lucy, Lois," intoned Marsha, by way of introduction.

"Pleased to meet you," Lois said, lowering periscope. "Marsh,
I've made a decision here. I wanna go with Desert Dawn." She
aimed a crimson fingernail at the paint slash on the farthest right.

"It's got too much pink," Marsha declared.

"That's cause you're seeing it compressed. Once it's spread
out over the entire wall, you're gonna see it's a true earth tone."

"You're gonna see it's a true pink. The idea's just to warm
up the place a little, not turn it into a giant womb."

"You gotta trust my eye," said Lois.

"Fine. I trust your eye. But if your eye fucks up, your eye
pays for the cost of repainting."

Hot X rays of hatred shot from Lois's pupils, only to bounce
impotently off Marsha's invulnerable back.

"Want a beer?" Marsha said to me and, without waiting for
my reply, led the way into the kitchen. Another dazzlingly all-
white space, like the lab of the mad, if exceptionally tidy, scien-
tist who experimented on the asylum inmates. Marsha pulled two
bottles of Pilsner Urquell from the refrigerator, popped the tops

and, shoving one into my hand, sat herself down on a stool at the breakfast bar. I perched more gingerly on another.

"I talked to Woody last night," Marsha said, after a quick chug. "What that poor, poor man has been through! He's absolutely shattered!"

"I haven't seen him at his house," I said.

"No, he can't bring himself to go back there yet. He's checked into a bungalow at the Bel-Air Hotel. And tomorrow he's taking Julia's remains up to Boise for a private family burial. Which is strictly confidential, by the way. He doesn't want that to get out."

In which case, he'd have done better to publish it on the front page of the *L.A. Times* than breathe a word to Marsha Moss-Golson.

"Poor little Quanxi," I remarked. "She must be really upset."

Marsha gave a puzzled squint. "Oh, the kid. I don't know, Woody doesn't have her. She's with some relatives."

"Up in Boise?"

"Yeah, probably up in Boise." Marsha took a deep swig of the Pilsner. I joined her in a convivial sip.

"So, Marsha," I said, dabbing my lips, "tell me about Julia."

Marsha gazed down at her own set of crimson nails, frowned and—to my utter disconcertion—slowly peeled one off. "Look at this. Ninety bucks, plus I tipped her a twenty, and the goddamned things didn't even last a week. I'm gonna kill that broad." She flung the nail into the sink, where it lay like a drop of blood in the white basin. "What about Julia?"

"Well, everything. When did she come to L.A.?"

"When she was about twenty-two. Tooled down from Boise in this crappy VW bug, got a pad in Silverlake with about a dozen roommates." Marsha leaned closer, evidently forgetting her reluctance to talk to me: as I'd counted on, she couldn't resist the opportunity to dish. "And fleas. She said the place was crawling with fleas."

"And then what?"

"Then she does what they were all doing in the eighties. She drops half her life savings for a new hairdo at Jose Eber, hangs out at Nicky Blair's and those Brat Pack coke parties in the hills, maybe goes to bed once or twice with Warren Beatty . . . and in her spare time, tries to become a star."

"But never quite made it."

Marsha gave an eloquent snort. "Ever see Julia act?"

I nodded. She was, to put it plainly, lousy: once a camera rolled, her face simply refused to keep still—eyes popped, nostrils flared, lips twitched in a series of moues, pouts and "I'm in agony" grimaces; all actually rather riveting in a way.

"She was good-looking enough to get some work," Marsha went on. "A couple of B movies, guest-star shots on cop shows, that kinda thing. But after she turned thirty and the guest-star shots started to get few and far between, she made herself a real hardheaded decision—quit the acting career cold and marched her gorgeous derriere into a seat at the Chas White training program. Which is where I took her under my wing."

"Right, I'd heard she'd once been a real estate agent. Isn't that how she met Woody?"

"Yeah. He'd just made his big comeback, so naturally he wanted to move up to a swanky neighborhood. The first place he looked at happened to be Julia's very first listing."

"And he bought it. Great luck for Julia."

"Luck, schmuck. She had a surefire sales technique. They've already seen the whole home, right? So, now she leads him back to the kitchen, points out once again all the desirable features— Sub-Zero fridge, double oven with overhead microwave, glazed terra-cotta floors. . . . Then she kneels down, right on the terra-cotta, which has gotta be hard as hell. And she unzips his fly and gives him a firsthand demonstration of just what a good time cooking here could be."

I glanced at her, startled. Marsha chuckled grimly. "You know, Woody sprang for the full asking price of one-point-six million. And you remember what that place looked like? A dump. The roof leaked, the landscaping looked like Mars, everything painted the color of Doritos."

"What I do remember," I said, "was that when they moved in they were already married."

"Yeah, a week after escrow closed, Julia became the third Mrs. Joseph 'Woody' Prentice. *Sayonara* real estate career. She now goes to town redoing the place head to toe—new roof, new landscaping, new paint job. Crams the house with a hundred thousand bucks' worth of shabby chic. And now she's ready for her *true* life's work, which is climbing her ass up the social ladder."

"I guess she saw that the quickest way would be to join the ranks of the Hollywood Moms."

"Huh?"

"I mean, going the kids-and-family route."

"Yeah, that's exactly it. Julia wanted to cash in on the whole kid status thing. There was just one problem, though. . . ." Marsha paused for dramatic effect. "Woody'd had a vasectomy."

"Really?" I wondered how the tabloids had missed this interesting detail.

Marsha nodded. "He had the Big Snip. Which didn't stop Julia for one tiny second. She hops a plane to Shanghai and comes back a week later with this squawling infant. And the very next *day* she's already on the talk-show circuit." Marsha issued another snort. "Remember how she made it sound like this big cloak-and-dagger adventure? Running through back alleys, rescuing the kid from certain death just in the nick of time?"

"So it wasn't true?"

"Please. She went through channels. The kid came from a perfectly normal government orphanage. All she had to do was fill out the papers."

I was silent a moment, pulling at a damp corner of the beer label. "Listen, Marsha," I said. "As far as you know, was Julia having an affair with anyone?"

She drained her own bottle. "Was Julia schtupping anyone?

You want the absolute truth? I don't know. But I can tell you
one thing. If she was, she'd've made damned sure it was someone
who'd keep it quiet. Some family guy, devoted to his kids. Someone with as much to lose as she had if it got out."

Someone, for instance, like my husband. I couldn't help feeling
a little spurt of relief that Julia had seen Kit as a devoted family
guy—that the rift between us wasn't as nakedly obvious as I'd
thought. Unless, of course, Marsha had it wrong . . .

"Maybe Julia was getting ready to leave Woody," I suggested.
"She might have been shopping around."

"No way. Woody was her ticket to what she wanted more than
anything else in the world, which was to be a Hollywood queen
bee. She wanted to become just like Summer Rossner. To play
in Summer Rossner's crowd. All those babes who head up the
big committees and ski Aspen with the Costner family and have
little dinners with the Eisners." She now inclined so close to
me, our noses practically touched. "Didja know Julia once made
a big play for David Rossner?"

"No," I said eagerly. "I didn't."

"It was just before she started at Chas White. She still had
some last-ditch hopes for her acting career, and she'd wrangled
herself an invitation to Swifty Lazar's Oscar party at Spago, the
last one before he croaked. Naturally, the Rossners were there.
*Every*one was there. At some point, Julia corners David and
makes him some very creative proposition. But, you know, David
Rossner worships that ice-cube wife of his. Not only does he
turn Julia down, but he runs right back to Summer and reports
the whole thing. And Julia shoots immediately to number one on
Summer Rossner's very lengthy shit list."

I took a thoughtful sip of my beer, smothering a belch. "So,
Summer had reason to hate Julia."

"You bet. Especially since, once Julia snagged Woody, she
started moving heavily into Summer's territory. Got involved in
all the right causes and joined all the right charities. There was

even talk that she would ace out Summer as president of the Magic Wand Foundation."

"But wasn't it Summer Rossner who founded Magic Wand?"

"Yeah. But there's a lot of people who think she's become a royal pain in the ass and would love to see her take a dive. And Julia was a genius at cultivating friends. Besides which, what could Summer do? She certainly couldn't snub Mrs. Woody Prentice. So she had to be all kissy face and bosom buddies with Julia, at least in public."

I mulled all this over for a moment. "Let me ask you another thing," I said. "How did you know about . . . well, about the way Julia first attracted Woody?"

"You mean about the blow job on the kitchen floor?" Marsha narrowed her chartreuse lids. "What do you think, I was watching through a keyhole? She told me about it, naturally."

"And she also told you about having to get her breasts done twice."

"So?"

"So it seems like she confided in you about very intimate things. Wouldn't she have let you know if she was having an affair?"

Marsha shrugged. "We weren't in touch that much over the last year. Anyway, she never told me everything. With Julia, it was like she'd dole it out to you, just as much as she'd want you to know."

Lois came sashaying in, an industrial tape measure in hand, a triumphant smile beaming from her fleshless face. "I just measured the guest room, and I was absolutely right, it *is* only twenty-two by sixteen. Which means the stripped-pine armoire that *you* went right ahead and put down the nonrefundable deposit on is gonna look like King Kong in there."

"You're crazy," said Marsha. "It's at least ten feet more."

"You wanna measure it yourself, be my guest."

Marsha stood up. "I gotta deal with this," she said to me.

"Fine," I said. "Thanks for talking to me. And thanks for the beer." I let myself out, back through the ice floe of carpeting, Marsha and Lois's squabbling voices accompanying me out to the car.

I HAD A LOT TO occupy my thoughts on the way home. First of all, about Julia herself. Julia, always calculating, never uttering so much as a cough without an ulterior motive. Her remarks about Kit at her party made sense to me now. I was supposed to go back and report what she'd said to my devoted hubby—who, being a normal, and therefore temptable, man, would be flattered and titillated and, when she came by for her "swim," waiting with anticipation. In other words, I was to be the warm-up for the Kit and Julia Sexcapades.

But what possible motive could she have had for feeding Marsha, the Hollywood Town Crier, items about herself that were, to say the least, less than flattering? Only one reason that I could think of—to throw Marsha off the track of something else. Something that Julia wanted to keep everyone—particularly her husband and meal ticket, Woody—from knowing.

And what about Woody, suffering in style in a seven-hundred-dollar-a-night bungalow at the Hotel Bel-Air while his baby daughter was stowed with "relatives"?

And then there was Summer Rossner. The Snow Queen, pale of hair, pure of skin, cold of eye—and indisputably at the top of the Hollywood social heap. Even her lineage was, Hollywood-wise, unimpeachable: direct grandniece on her mother's side of Louis B. Mayer. Her clout extended to both the political and the social—every Democrat running for any office higher than crossing guard courted her slavishly. And the membership roster of the Magic Wand Foundation, of which Summer was founder and president, nearly blinded with the glitter of its names.

And yet her exalted position was being challenged by a snippety former starlet, a nobody from nowhere, who just happened to have snagged an important star. It must have eaten at Summer like a disease. Was she cold-blooded enough to have somehow arranged for Julia to be bumped off? I tried to picture it: a hired hitman, looking perhaps like Christopher Walken, staking her out for days, patiently waiting for an opportunity . . . finding it when Kit left the gate open—and, after clobbering Julia's brains out, indulging in a bit of necrophilia before dumping the body in the pool.

Preposterous.

So, what about David Rossner, all-powerful head of International Talent Agency, and Grand Suzerain of Hollywood deal making? I'd rubbed elbows with him from time to time at Windermere functions and, like everyone else in the galaxy, found him irresistibly charming. Chubby, pinchable cheeks, rosy smile, round baby-blue eyes that appeared to widen with delight at your company. Yet his professional reputation was one of utter ruthlessness: it was said that he sprang vigorously out of bed each morning, anticipating just how many people he could crush that day.

What if Marsha was wrong? What if Julia *hadn't* flopped in her attempt to seduce him? What if they'd been carrying on an affair; perhaps she'd called him over for a quick alfresco snack, and afterward, in a spasm of guilt, or fear, or remorse, he'd sent her with a whack into that good night?

But that seemed even more preposterous. I just couldn't imagine David Rossner bolting from a meeting with, say, Clint Eastwood and Tom Cruise in response to Julia's summons, perhaps pausing only long enough to say, "Oh, Clint, could I possibly borrow your Oscar, you never know when it might come in handy to crack a skull . . . ?"

And the thought that had nagged me before nagged me again: how could Julia have called him or anyone?

*   *   *

I PULLED MY CHEROKEE INTO the garage, still not used to the sight of Kit's new car, the green Beemer with the parchment leather, occupying the adjoining space. Rather than go straight inside, I walked around instead to the back of the house, and for the zillionth time I stared up at the pool, trying to see something, anything, I might have missed before.

It was remarkably quiet. The pool motor, with its customary gurgling and rumbling, had been turned off. No cars passed on the street, there wasn't even a breeze to ruffle the foliage. I suddenly realized that I was alone—all alone in a place where a murderer had recently been busily at work.

And now that I thought about it, there was something different in the yard. The canvas lawn chairs seemed subtly repositioned, my pots of impatiens, foxgloves and African irises not quite grouped in their usual way. The skin on the back of my neck began to prickle.

Stop it! I ordered myself. There's nothing changed, you're just doing a damned good job of spooking yourself! The gates were shut, the security system armed; no one could hack through the dense eight-foot hedgerow that fenced us from our next-door neighbors, nor scale the steep cliff behind the pool house.

And I'd just managed to convince myself of all this when something bounded out at me from behind the rhododendrons.

6

I GUESS I'D NEVER REALLY understood how someone could actually die of fright until that moment. My eyes goggled, every vein in my body constricted, my heart felt squeezed by an iron hand for several interminable seconds—until finally my brain managed to register the fact that I was not confronting a crazed killer with a blunt object but a frisking Saint Bernard puppy.

"Hey, pup," I gasped, getting the wind back in my lungs. The puppy, who looked to be about five months old, leaped around me, yapping and madly wagging her tail. "What a good puppy," I crooned. "Are you lost?" She was wearing no collar or tag; perhaps she'd been abandoned. I ruffled her thick coat and let her leap against me, lapping at my face with delirious joy; if no one claimed her, I thought, we could keep her—it would be a terrific surprise for Chloe when she got home. Because of Kit's myriad allergies, Chloe had been allowed no pets except a bright green gecko, inevitably named Gordon, who had taken permanent residence under the guest-room bed, emerging only at rare intervals—usually late at night, when you were least prepared for a mini-stegosaurus head to come popping out at you. Tough for Kit, I decided stubbornly. If the dog made him sneeze, he could go get shots.

There was the vroom of a car gathering speed in the street. The puppy instantly forgot her new mad passion for me and, barking loudly, bounded off toward the front of the house. I heard the car brake with a screech, and then a man's voice called out, "Lola? Where are you, girl?" I followed the dog to the front, and found her pawing at the gate. I opened it. She leaped ecstatically at a guy who came sprinting with equal vivaciousness toward her.

"I guess she belongs to you," I remarked with a little sink of disappointment.

"Yeah, this is Lola." He giggled, trying to keep his balance against the puppy's loving body slams. "I was just about to drive around the neighborhood looking for her when I heard her barking."

"She was in my backyard. I don't have a clue how she got there."

"I think she burrowed under the hedge. I've seen her digging a few times, but never dreamed she could go deep enough to get through. Just shows you how much I know."

He's cute, I thought. Okay, very cute, in his early thirties, with the kind of wolfish good looks I'd always had a weakness for: lean jaw, long straight nose, sardonic, the-better-to-eat-you-with dark blue eyes. Actor, I guessed. But no, his oak-brown hair was just a little too unkempt. An actor might be starving, scraping, inhabiting a cardboard box and dining out of a Dumpster, but his hair is always perfect.

He was probably used to women being tongue-tied at the sight of him, for he continued easily: "I'm Justin Caffrey. I'm shacked up in Doc Pennislaw's guest house next door. He and his wife are in Austria, at some ear doctors' symposium." Devastating smile. "Of course, I know who *you* are."

I shrugged with a flush. "Anyone who watches *Live at Five* these days knows who I am."

"No, I mean who you really are. I'm a huge fan of your work. I saw the short you had at Sundance a few years ago, the one about the children lost in a rainbow. It really knocked me out, visually. You were nominated for that, weren't you?"

"It didn't win," I said, with my usual grace in accepting a compliment.

"It should have. The Academy judges are assholes. And anyway, so what? Most of us would kill for an Oscar nomination, win or lose."

I smiled awkwardly and changed the subject. "How long have you been next door?"

"I moved in ten days ago. I'm a writer, I'm on deadline with a script for Touchstone and I thought this would give me some seclusion and quiet. Little did I know I'd end up with a cop convention right outside my door."

"Did they question you?"

"Hell, yes. They've been fascinated with me, since they found out I was one of the last to see Julia alive."

"You were?" I said eagerly. "Where was that?"

"Right here in the middle of the road. I was just driving back from a breakfast meeting and here was a woman in a bathrobe crossing the street. I recognized her—by coincidence, I'd just been introduced to her a couple of weeks before by a mutual friend. So I pulled up and made some friendly remark. And got a look that said, 'Fuck you, buster,' in return."

"Why, do you think?"

Justin shrugged. "She did have a reputation as something of a bitch in heels. You know," he went on airily, "I've always wanted to do an animation script. I've been playing around with a knights-and-magic story, with Merlin as the main character."

My mind immediately began to fill up with images: swords with eyes, and winged horses, and ladies with spun-silver hair and dragon tails. "It could be wonderful!" I breathed.

He smiled. "Maybe we could collaborate."

I let myself gaze into those midnight-blue eyes and felt a sexual rush so strong it turned my knees to milk. Immediately followed by a strong rush of guilt. Followed by resentment that I should be feeling guilt over a perfectly innocent flash of attraction when my husband obviously had no inhibitions when it came to lunging for boobs.

Fortunately, there was a distraction—the sound of the Prentices' automatic garage door rumbling open. A car backed out into the drive, though not one of the Prentice Mercedeses; it was a dented green Fiat I hadn't seen before.

"It's the nanny!" I exclaimed. The electric gates creaked apart and the Fiat continued to back onto the street. It was definitely the Englishwoman at the wheel: no mistaking the ramrod-straight posture, the pewter skullcap of hair. "I saw her leave the house with the Prentices' baby the morning before Julia was murdered, and haven't seen her since. Or the little girl." The Fiat turned left and rolled up to the stop sign on the corner. "I wonder where she's going."

"Let's follow her!" Justin said. I blinked, thinking for one fuzzy moment that he meant we should go jogging in pursuit. He grabbed my arm. "My car's right here. Come on, we can easily catch her." He whistled for Lola to follow and pulled me toward a black Porsche Carrera crouched in front of the Pennislaws'. Before I could protest, I was in the front seat, the Saint Bernard's hot breath on my neck; I gasped as Justin floored the accelerator, jumping the stop sign. "I always wanted to do this!" he laughed, whipping around a corner. "God knows I've written this scene about a dozen times."

"Okay, if you were writing the script of Julia Prentice's murder, who'd have done it?"

"Oh, you'd be the murderess," he said cheerfully. "But it would turn out you had an excellent motive. She'd have been thoroughly evil in some way. The audience would be cheering you in the end."

"But, then, who did she have sex with before she died?"

"Oh, that would be a red herring. The pool man, or someone who just happened to come along before you did."

"The cops already thought of that. But it wasn't our pool man's day. He works Mandeville Canyon on Tuesdays."

"Okay, then, how about this: it was the nanny, who turns out to be a man. Kind of a Mrs. Doubtfire thing, with a dark edge."

Laughing, we shot onto San Vincente, catching up with the Fiat as it swung left onto Ocean Avenue. The light turned to red, which in no way impeded Justin—he gunned the motor and shot into traffic, nearly clipping a van marked KEN THE KARPET KLEANER KING. The King responded with an eloquent middle finger.

I was suddenly having a great time, breaking every traffic law in a sports car with a terrific-looking guy, the wind whipping our hair, warm sun caressing our faces. The question wandered through my mind why someone with a sixty-thousand-dollar automobile would be camping out in an ear, nose and throat specialist's guest house, but it wandered out again as we skidded onto Santa Monica Boulevard.

There was no sight of the Fiat in the traffic ahead. "How could she get so far ahead of us?" Justin said testily, peering down the street.

"She didn't. She parked." On the next block, the Englishwoman was feeding a meter. Then she turned and began walking briskly up the street. "She's going to the Queen's Guard Pub," I exclaimed.

"A little early, isn't it? Our nanny must be something of a lush." We crept forward. "Looks like she got the last space."

Justin pulled up in front of the tavern, a dark wooden structure festooned with ersatz half-timbering and a flapping Union Jack. "You go in. I'll find someplace to park."

I nodded gratefully, then jumped out of the car and hurried into the tavern.

The Queen's Guard Pub is the unofficial clubhouse of L.A.'s British population, which seems to be vast in number. The English *love* L.A.: take a Brit who's spent childhood, adolescence and young adulthood shivering in some clammy, underheated flat in drizzly North London, set him in a snug bungalow in balmy Santa Monica with a date palm in his backyard and a white-sand beach just a stroll down the road, and he thinks he's died and gone to paradise. Except, once in paradise, he then mysteriously seems to set about trying to re-create a bit of drizzly North London in its midst. Hence the Queen's Guard, a near-perfect replica of a Hammersmith pub, all rough-hewn posts and beams, walls covered with signs for Watneys ale and Player's Navy Cut, Joe Cocker blasting nostalgically from the jukebox. It reeked of old beer and fresh tobacco smoke—so much that my eyes watered as I walked in. I scanned the jolly groups packed at the bar and around the splintery wood tables. No sign of my nanny.

"Lucy, my darling! What brings you to this den of iniquity?"

At first I didn't recognize the man who spoke to me, a huge, pink-faced, fat fellow, throwing darts with two young rugger types. Then, with a shock, I realized it was Philip Weston, who'd been director of photography on *Cop Crimes*—a brilliant DP, top of the heap, two Oscar nominations. I remembered him as a gentle Welsh giant with a taste for off-color ditties and an unfazable temper.

"Phil!" I said, a shade too brightly. "It's great to see you. How've you been?"

"Shitty, my darling. I've been absolutely shitty." He twinkled, his eyes, like currants, nearly disappearing in the pink pudge of his cheeks, and he toasted the dartboard with a foamy mug of beer. "But things aren't all bad. I'm winning this game."

I suddenly remembered hearing about him: his house had burned to the ground a couple of years ago in one of those infernos that periodically ravage the Malibu hills; he'd started drinking uncontrollably, and his live-in girlfriend decamped with an Australian sound mixer. On his last film, he'd been sacked after ten days of shooting.

Phil turned to his fellow dart players. "This gorgeous young thing is Lucy Freers, and her husband is a famous Hollywood producer. Doing a movie with none other than Mr. Jon Suger-man." He directed a wobbly little smile at me. "I don't suppose he sent you 'round to offer me a job?"

"If it was up to me, I'd hire you in an instant, Phil," I said lamely. "But I'm just here looking for someone. A woman about fifty, short gray hair ... I think she came in here a few minutes ago."

"That would be Audrey," one of the rugger types said. "She's just popped into the kitchen. Go on back if you like, no one will care."

As if on cue, a door beside the bar swung open, and the Prentices' nanny emerged from it, holding tiny Quanxi Prentice in her arms.

She stopped dead when she saw me, her features hardening with dismay. I stepped hastily toward her. "Could I speak to you a moment?"

For an instant, I was certain she was going to bolt back into the kitchen. Then Philip opened his arms to the little girl. "Here, I'll mind her, and you two have a good gossip. Come on, darling, come to old Uncle Phil."

Uncle Phil was evidently a favorite with Quanxi, for she gurgled happily, waving her arms. Reluctantly, the nanny handed her over. "We can sit over here," she said crisply to me.

I followed her military back to a round table tucked into a corner. She selected a chair from which she could keep an eye on the little girl, who now had five "uncles" eagerly emptying their pockets for shiny objects to entertain her. "One of the cooks, Ellie, is a great friend of mine," the nanny said. "She minds Shanni when I've got errands to do. And, of course, all the regulars have become very fond of her. It's like one big family for her."

She rummaged in her handbag, a brown leather number with a sturdy clasp, suitable for the queen mother, and drew out a pack of Benson & Hedges. "Mind if I smoke? I gave it up three years ago, but this past week has been rather harrowing."

"I know what you mean," I said. "It's been a bit harrowing for me, too."

"Yes, I suppose stumbling upon a naked corpse would give anyone a bit of a turn. Quite spoil one's afternoon." She took a deep draw of smoke, then exhaled, smiling at me. I smiled back with some relief—I hadn't expected her to have a sense of humor.

She inched the pack toward me. I'd quit before Chloe was born, but my fingers suddenly itched to take one. Reluctantly, I shook my head. "We haven't actually been introduced. I'm Lucy Freers."

"Audrey Huff." She clamped her ciggy rather raffishly between her lips and offered a firm handshake.

"I'm surprised to see Quanxi. I'd heard she was in Boise with Julia's family."

"Huh, that's a good one. Mrs. Prentice had little use for her family. Called them white trash and other things which I can't repeat in polite company. The father disappeared on a drunk years ago. The mother would ring up from time to time begging for a handout, but Mrs. Prentice wouldn't take the call. There's a brother floating around somewhere, but Mrs. Prentice wouldn't give him the time of day either."

"Then, why would Woody be having the burial in Boise?"

The nanny—Audrey—gave a disgusted snort. "For show. Everything those two did was just for show. Especially Her Ladyship. Like adopting that child—as long as eyes were watching, she was the most devoted mum in the world, but in private, she didn't give two hoots for her. She'd parade around the house with one of those little telephones glued to her face, making plans for this committee and that, going on about what la-di-da was going to be at which party, and never mind her own daughter. Unless, of course, there was the chance to make a play date with the child of some movie star or pukka mogul. Then she became a regular Mum of the Year."

"So, I guess Woody wasn't much of a father, either," I ventured.

Audrey shrugged. "I'd say he was more scared of her than anything else. If he chanced to find himself in the same room with her, he'd act as if she were some sort of Martian who'd somehow beamed down into his house." The corners of her broad mouth tightened. "But, of course, even their marriage was just for show. They didn't even sleep in the same bed, you know."

I sat up a bit straighter. This was a fascinating look at the Holy Family At Home.

Fierce chutes of smoke issued from Audrey's nostrils. "Then there was all that charity and Lady Bountiful stuff. More sham. That woman wouldn't lend a penny to a starving man if there was nobody around to notice. And she treated the help like dirt, yelling and carrying on if some poor maid so much as chipped a two-dollar saucer."

"At you too?"

"Huh, she didn't dare. She knew I can give as good as I get." Audrey stubbed out the cigarette, went to shake another from the pack, then, as if exercising an act of will, set the pack down. "There was one time, though," she went on. "My second day there, when I wasn't familiar yet with the layout of the house, I stumbled into her bedroom by mistake. She was just dressing, standing in the middle of the room naked as a jay, holding her knickers. I said, 'Excuse me,' or words to that effect, but she went off like a cannon. Grabbed a vase and, just like in the movies, lobbed it at my head. Narrowly missed killing me, I can tell you."

"Strange," I mused. "I didn't think of Julia as being terribly modest about her body." At least not around other people's husbands, I silently added.

"No, one wouldn't, not from the way she wore those dresses with her bosoms falling out. I suppose what she minded was my getting a look at those scars on her arse."

My brows rocketed up. "What kind of scars?"

"Great, nasty welts. As if she'd had a good caning once or twice in her life." Audrey gave a mirthless smile. "Mind you, there were times I wouldn't have minded taking a birch to her myself."

There flashed unwilled in my mind the gruesome sight of Julia sprawled in the pool, bottom bobbing ingloriously up from the muddy water. Her flawless bottom. "Are you sure there were scars?" I asked.

"Quite. I've got excellent eyes, better than twenty-twenty, they tell me." The excellent eyes glanced at a watch, a sensible item of waterproof steel. "I'm sorry, but you'll really have to excuse me. I was on my way to getting Shanni home for her supper and bath. She can be very cranky when she's hungry."

"You're taking her back home?"

"*My* home. I've got my own wee flat here in Santa Monica." She stood up.

"If you don't mind me asking," I said, "why did you go on working for Julia? You probably could've easily gotten hired somewhere else." This was an understatement. The Grail quest was as nothing compared to a Hollywood Mom's pursuit of a genuine English nanny.

"Absolutely. Before Her Ladyship's body was even cold, I began to get calls from all her 'friends.' " She pronounced the word with an inflection that made it sound worse than *enemies*. "I've got my pick of positions, and I'm asking a pretty penny, I can assure you. But I couldn't leave the Prentices because of that little one." Her eyes traveled back to Quanxi, and her plain features went slack with adoration. "For me, it was love at first sight. There she was, so helpless, with that bitty face so full of love, and the intelligence you could see in her eyes . . . I couldn't just leave her in that house."

"What's going to happen to her now?"

"She's staying with me. I'll let all this murder business shake itself out, and then somewhere down the road, I'll do what's necessary to adopt her." She added fiercely, "Mr. Prentice won't stand in my way."

God help him if he does, I thought, watching her purposefully stride over to collect her charge. I gave a start as Justin dropped into her vacated seat.

"How did it go?" he asked.

"She's an incredible woman. I think we hit it off really well."

"Did she reveal any deep, dark secrets?"

"One thing's pretty clear. Julia was getting her sexual kicks from outside of holy wedlock."

"Big surprise."

"You knew that?"

He shrugged. "It goes with the territory, doesn't it? This is the capital of temptation. You want monogamy, move to Peoria."

I mulled this over a moment. Was I just hopelessly naïve to expect a faithful husband while residing in Temptation's Capital? And what about my own commitment to my marriage vows—did it just mark me as a sucker?

"What else did Nanny have to say?" Justin inquired. I hesitated. He leaned toward me; the closeness of his body to mine, the scent of his hair like sun-warmed earth, sent a tingling through me. "Yeah?" he prompted.

"Well . . . according to Audrey, Julia had scars on her buttocks. As if she'd been badly flogged."

His eyes sparked with attention. "This is getting interesting."

"Yeah, but listen . . . When I found Julia, she was floating face-down in the pool. I got a good look at her buttocks. There were no scars. They were as smooth as . . ."

"As a baby's bottom?" He gave a quick smile.

"They looked normal," I finished.

"Maybe you just didn't notice. When you get a shock like that, you don't necessarily take in all the details."

I shook my head. "I can picture it clearly. Too clearly. I wish I could erase it from my mind."

Justin slouched back in his chair, crossing his arms on his chest. "Then, Nanny's wrong. Or else . . . Julia had the scars removed."

Soft dark hairs lay on his forearms, beneath the pushed-up

sleeves of his denim shirt. I made myself not look at them. "Can you do that?" I said. "I mean, remove scars so there's no trace?"

"Absolutely. I've got an actress friend who had a bad appendicitis scar—ugly purple thing, prevented her from going up for any roles that required her to show her tummy. So she took herself to a plastic surgeon, some hot-shot Beverly Hills guy who worked with lasers, or whatever. A couple of months later she was modeling bikinis."

I felt a disturbingly inappropriate tug of jealousy for the actress whose abdominal scars were familiar to Justin. "One thing I do know about Julia," I said quickly. "She was no stranger to plastic surgeons. She went to Stew Goodrow, the guy who does all the stars—he's always popping up in *Vanity Fair* with some remodeled actress on his arm. Maybe," I added, "I should have a consultation with Dr. Goodrow."

"You mean go undercover, see what you can dig up?"

"Something like that."

"This is getting *very* interesting. And hey, maybe I can help out your investigations. I wrote a cop thriller for Paramount a couple of years ago. Never got made, thanks to the weasel producer, but I developed some pretty good contacts with the LAPD. I could take a couple of guys out, stand 'em a round of drinks and see what I sniff out."

Phil Weston came lumbering toward us on his way to the door. He squeezed my shoulder, said, "Take care of yourself, luv," then continued his laborious way out.

"That was Philip Weston," I whispered to Justin. "You know, the cameraman."

Justin's eyes barely flicked his way. "Real burnt-out case," he said. Cold words. Icy voice.

But his smile, wolfish and wide, was more than warm enough to keep me happy.

*   *   *

WE STAYED IN THE QUEEN'S Guard for a round of dark ale, then bangers and mash and Cornish pasties, and then a nightcap round of tequila shooters, while Lola the puppy romped around the tables in defiance of the board of health, but to the vast delight of the rugger types. Justin gave me an abridged bio. Born and raised in Bloomington, Indiana (a fellow midwesterner!). Majored in anthropology at Williams. Landed a job in a Chicago ad shop. After four years, found himself grinding out copy for adult diapers and cat food, said screw this and lit out for the Coast. Starved for a couple of years, sold some stuff to TV. "Lately I've had some success in features," he said with a lightly dismissive laugh, then deftly turned the subject back to me.

It was after dark and I was slightly tipsy when he dropped me back home. "See ya," he said. Then leaned and lightly brushed my lips with his.

I tensed, pulled away, managed a strangled "Bye," then bolted from the car. I ran directly to Kit's den and took out the *Writers Guild Directory*. Justin Caffrey: I should have recognized his name—he wrote *Irresistible,* a winsome romantic comedy about a guy who can't decide among three glamorous women, then gets swept away by a mousy fourth; it was the sleeper of last summer, played straight through till Christmas, hauled in a fortune . . .

And was co-written by one Nancy Louise Caffrey.

His sister? Fat chance.

Okay, I told myself, he's got a wife. *You*'ve got a husband, if you care to remember, with whom you're supposed to be trying to work things out. Not to mention a daughter who'd no doubt been trying to get in touch with you while you were busy playing footsy with a somewhat too young and far too cocky screenwriter. Penitently, I turned to the answering machine, which seemed to be blinking with reproachful urgency.

First message, Chloe, rhapsodizing over Gram and Grampa's Siamese cat, who just had kittens! Plus, she met some twins named Lily and Evie and they were all going roller-blading in the morning, but please tell Grammy she was allowed to watch *Seinfeld*, it was *not* too racy for her.

Then the producers of *Excellent Science*, worried about the flying-hedgehog segment (as well they should be—I was falling further and further behind).

Then Kit. I stiffened when I heard his voice. He sounded like he always did when he was actually on a movie—pumped up, happy and about fourteen years old. Sugerman was pushing them all like a madman, every minute booked. No use trying to reach him, will try to call again when he gets a chance.

"Rat!" I screamed at the machine. "Insensitive rat shit crumb! Having yourself a ball while I'm stuck here trying to mop up the mess you left behind!"

In my ranting, I almost missed the last message: "Hey, Lucy? Sandy Palumbo here. I just wanted to apologize for Francie's behavior the other day, and Ollie's too. I'd like to make some amends. How about lunch, Wednesday at Morton's?"

I listened to it again. Sandy Palumbo. Bedroom eyes. Bedroom bod. And with an obviously trumped-up excuse to ask me out to lunch.

Suddenly it seemed I had two decidedly sexy men sending signals my way. Was it the Freudian thing, sex and death inextricably bound, making my association with Julia's violent end a turn-on? Or maybe the crack in my marriage was more apparent than I'd realized . . .

And why did I find their interest in me so intriguing?

In confusion, I climbed the stairs to my bedroom, opened the shutters and leaned out into the brisk air. A pair of klieg lights were tracing twin parabolas across the night sky. A dozen years ago, when Kit and I first moved here with stars in our eyes, I'd thought those sweeping lights meant that something unimaginably glamorous was taking place—that somewhere, just over the next hill, Robert Redford and Meryl Streep were stepping from white limousines onto wine-red carpets. Then our neighbor, an old character actor with an Elmer Fudd–like irascibility, set me straight. "You think that's some big movie premiere? Forget it! These days they drag the kliegs out for anything. That's probably the grand opening of a new Baskin-Robbins, thirty-one flavors. Or a tacoria, two guys named Manuel."

But right now, watching those ghostly stalks of light loop and part, loop and part, I didn't care. It didn't matter what they were celebrating; it was suddenly just thrilling to see them there.

7

I HAD A BAD NIGHT, alternating between periods of wakefulness in which I lay frozen, certain I heard an intruder creaking around downstairs, and fretful, paranoid dreams. In one of these, Justin Caffrey was undressing me, slowly peeling layers of Jean Harlowy satin garments from my body while I shivered with pleasure—until I realized with utter horror that Detectives Downsey and Shoe were watching from a partially opened door.

I awoke groggily to a bright morning. And there *was* someone in the house, moving about downstairs—but from the cheerful clinking of pots and dishes, I was reasonably certain it was Graciella, our housekeeper. I had given her a week off to spare her the ordeal of being ripped to shreds in the media feeding frenzy, and now, when I went down, we hugged as emotionally as if we'd been separated for a year. While downing two cups of her mud-strong coffee, I entertained her with a vivid account of the *señora muerta* in the swimming pool.

Fortified, I closeted myself in the den, where Kit would normally be at this time of the morning. The true lair of a movie freak: there were movie posters from the forties and fifties, a scarily realistic head of John Travolta made of some space-age polymer, a blowup of Rocky with Kit's head superimposed on Stallone's, two VCRs, stacks and stacks of movies on video—great ones, lousy ones, it hardly mattered. I swept a pile of back issues of *Premiere* off a canvas director's chair, sat down and, dialing Beverly Hills information, asked for the number of Dr. Stewart Goodrow, plastic surgeon. "That number is unlisted," declared a supercilious male operator.

"Not his home, his office."

"Correct, ma'am, the *office* number is unlisted." Smug bastard. I could actually *hear* him smirk.

Undefeated, I rang up Kit's D-boy, Giles, who required exactly four and a half minutes to muster up the number from his dazzlingly extensive gay network. "It takes *weeks* to get an appointment," he informed me, "*if* you can get one at all. But I know some people who could use some pull for you."

"Thanks, but it's not for me, it's for a friend," I said hurriedly and hung up. I knew the word would immediately be going out on the same network: "*Guess* who's having a little eye work done? I mean, it's about time!"

"Goodrow Clinic, how may I help you?" responded a beautifully modulated voice at the clinic's number.

I countered with a vaguely Irish brogue. "This is Laura Spielberg's personal secretary. Ms. Spielberg would like to schedule a consultation."

A pause. I could sense the receptionist frantically flipping through a mental Rolodex. *Laura* Spielberg . . . mother, sister, sister-in-law . . . ?

"Tomorrow would be very convenient for Ms. Spielberg," I pursued.

Tomorrow! Unheard of! And yet it would be a sensational mistake to piss off Hollywood royalty, even a distant branch of it. "I believe I can make an opening at one P.M.," came the modulated response.

I hung up, feeling a giddy little swell of triumph. Then a new thought struck me: if I were going to play royalty, I'd have to look the part. My thrift-shop-treasure vintage chic might dazzle my friends, but it wasn't likely to impress a surgeon to the superrich and famous. I had another inspiration: hitting the phone one more time, I tracked down my friend Valerie Jane Ramirez, a costume designer, to where she was currently working, on the Warners lot. "Definitely, I can fix you up," she laughed. "I'm on a lousy movie, but we've got great wardrobe. I'll leave a drive-on for you at eleven."

I was almost fanatically pleased with my undercover work so far. But it was a short-lived elation. As I was dressing, the doorbell rang; then a worried-looking Graciella appeared at the bedroom door. *"Policía,"* she pronounced ominously.

It was Detective Shoe. She'd already made herself comfortably at home, bellied up to the breakfast table, knocking back a mug of coffee. There was something different about her. . . . Her hair—it was now shaved boyishly short in the back.

"Morning," I chirped. "Would you like a muffin to go with your coffee? I've got cranberry, bran, granola flake . . ."

"Thanks, no. But I will have another cup."

I peered into the pot—what was left was stewed to the consistency of a petroleum product. But I was fed up with making coffee for cops. Let them drink dregs.

I served her the evil brew. "I see you've changed your hair," I remarked chattily.

She Hoovered a few fingers through it. "Lot easier to take care of. A finger comb in the morning and I'm done." She had, I realized, rather stunning eyes, light golden brown, large, deep-lidded and deep-lashed. "So, here you are all alone," she went on. "You okay with that?"

"Yeah, I guess so. I'm used to Kit being away for long periods of time. Though not, of course, when we've just had a killer on the grounds. And I really miss Chloe. It's the first time I've really been apart from her."

She nodded. "I know what you mean, I've got three of my own. You get used to the racket. I'm gonna hate it when they start leaving home."

This little personal revelation startled me. Detective Shoe, a wife and mother? Yes, on her ring finger was a band of beaten gold, inscribed with what looked like Chinese symbols. Any normal time, I'd have noticed it right away. "How old are your kids?" I asked.

"Eight, six and three." She reached into her shoulder bag hung on the back of her chair and rummaged for her wallet; from its folds, she removed three snapshots and flipped them toward me. Two boys and a girl with Asian features: for a moment I wondered if, like Julia, Detective Shoe had gone on some shopping trips to Shanghai. "This is Sung June, Patrick Tack and Jeong Tae, or Sunny, Pat and Joey." She tapped each face in turn, then tucked the photos tenderly back into her wallet. "Frank, my husband's, Korean. Korean-American, I should say. He's first generation. His folks' name was originally Cho, C-H-O. When they came here from Seoul, they lived in a little walk-up over on Western, on top of a shoe repair. Shoe, Cho, it sounded the same to their ears, so they figured that's the way their name was written in English. And Shoe it's been ever since." She cracked a dry smile. "Being a cop, you can imagine the kind of jokes it's caused me."

I grinned back, totally disarmed by these confidences. Suddenly it seemed we were just two gals yakking over a cup of java. "But you're obviously not Korean," I brilliantly observed.

"Heck, no. Italian-Irish-Scotch-German. Your basic American mutt. Grew up around Fresno. There was a lot of wailing and weeping on both sides of our families when Frank and I got married. My pop fought at Inchon; to him a Korean was something you shot at. And Frank's folks, they acted like he'd come down with a terminal disease. But they all came around eventually. The grandkids helped a lot." She took a businesslike slurp of the muck in her cup. "Now, you two, you're neither of you native Californians, are you?"

I shook my head. "I'm from Minnesota. Little town, the middle of nowhere. I never left it until I went away to college. But Kit was just the opposite, he grew up all over the world. His father's a horticulturist, he's hired by growers to develop new hybrids, so they were always on the move. Once it was a petunia-growing farm in Costa Rica. Then a coffee plantation in Kenya. Then Hawaii, on the big island, as they call it. . . . And a couple of years in Iowa . . ."

I had the sudden sensation that I was babbling, but Detective Shoe looked engrossed. "It must've been a very interesting way to grow up," she said.

"Sure, I guess, but kind of lonely too. Every time he'd make friends, he'd have to pack up and move on."

She made a thoughtful pursing of her lips. "I can see how it must've been tough. A lonely kid, always on the move . . . It must've left a few scars."

I glanced at her warily.

"So maybe this unusual childhood affects him even now he's grown up? Maybe it's left a few quirks to his personality."

"What do you mean?"

"Let's say, for instance, sexually. Is there anything in your husband's sexual behavior you'd consider out of the ordinary?"

A strained chuckle escaped from me. "Not really."

"Not really?"

"Not at all."

"Hey, look, I know these days anything goes. So maybe, from time to time, he's suggested a threesome? Maybe talked about bringing in another man . . . or another girl? Has he ever shown any interest in going to an orgy?"

My skin suddenly felt like Jell-O, shivery and slick. "Nothing like that."

"Is watching his thing? Has he ever wanted you to make it with someone else while he looked on?"

I got to my feet, trying with limited success to keep my voice from slipping into the flying-hedgehog squeak. "If you have any further questions, I suggest you direct them to my attorney, Harvey Tabor. Link, Tabor, Decklestein, in Century City."

She locked her eyes on me. I wondered how I could have thought them attractive; now they looked like an animal's, yellow and cunning. "You have the right to an attorney during any questioning," she said evenly.

I goggled. This was it! She was reading me my rights, after which she would order me to assume the position and slap hand-cuffs on my wrists. The charges: murder, accessory to murder, hampering an investigation, lusting in my heart and serving an officer of the law lousy coffee.

But all she said was, "Thanks for your time, Mrs. Freers." She stood up, hooked her bag over her shoulder. And she was gone.

I sank back down, shaking uncontrollably. How dare she? Cat-eyed bitch, slurping my coffee, feeding me cozy little tidbits of her loathsome domestic life, then spreading the slime of her disgusting insinuations!

But another thought crept insidiously into my mind: Kit had lied to me. He had lied to the cops. How much more could he be concealing? What if he had an entire secret life that he'd kept hidden from his dense-as-a-wall wife?

For the first time since this all began, I started to really cry, great shuddering, racking sobs. Graciella hovered in the doorway, strickenly kneading a sponge in her hand. Then she rushed toward me, wrapped two sturdy arms around my shoulders. *"No te preocupes,"* she murmured. *"No te preocupes de nada."*

A LONG, HOT SHOWER, AND I was able to pull myself together in time to head out to Burbank.

How do I explain Valerie Jane? Simply, that she was like no one else I'd ever met. Over six feet tall and skinny as a boy, with toasted-almond coloring and jet-black eyes. She wore her dark hair in a cheekbone bob; this, with her angular elbows and swishy skirts, gave the impression of a beautiful Olive Oyl. Though I'd known her for eight years, her personal life remained

a mystery: she lived with about a dozen cats in one of those
Hansel and Gretel cottages off Melrose with fake thatched roofs
and wooden shutters; and rumor had it that she was the lover of
a legendary French actress—but since I couldn't find a way to
say, "Hey, Val, I hear you and Jacqueline DePres are an item,"
and since she volunteered nothing, a rumor to me it remained.

We'd met at a gym, a rundown place in North Hollywood that
reeked of mildew and sweat socks, but offered spectacularly
cheap deals to those gypsies—actors, freelancers, the unem-
ployed—who could work out in off-hours. Valerie came exclu-
sively for the treadmill. She was a riveting sight, all flailing
elbows and endless legs, wearing a leopard-print unitard and
colossal silver earrings of her own design. At the time, she was
a lowly set costumer, working on low-budget quickie films. But
she quickly rocketed her way upward, due in great part to a
specific talent—the uncanny ability to disguise figure flaws
through clothes. Under Valerie's magic touch, paunches flattened,
flat chests bloomed into alluringly rounded bosoms, narrow shoulders took on military bearing. Actors, needless to say, loved to
work with her. She was now a full-fledged costume designer, with
a continuous choice of major productions.

At precisely eleven o'clock, I pulled up to the studio gate.
The late-morning sun on this, the valley side of the hills, was
blindingly intense, and the guard in his sentry box squinted in
its glare. "Stage Ten," he said, plastering a pass on my windshield. "Park in any visitor's space." Since all spaces marked
VISITORS seemed to be occupied, I parked in a spot marked MEL
GIBSON, figuring that if Mel showed up, he could stash his Lam-
borghini anywhere he damned pleased and no one would say
boo; then, after wandering five minutes in a circle, I finally stumbled on the soundstage area.

Stage 10 had a green light on, which meant there was no
shooting in progress and it was okay to enter. I shouldered open
one of the ponderous double doors and slipped inside.

It's a spooky feeling to step from the flat, hard glare of the

Burbank sun into the vast gloom of a soundstage—like falling down a well into some dim and enchanted netherworld, filled with monsters and snakes and trolls. Then, after a moment, your eyes grow accustomed to the murk, and what appeared to be monsters are just odd hunks of electrical equipment, and the snakes are long, fat cables and the trolls are just guys. And mostly what the guys are doing is sitting around. Guys with beer bellies and bull necks squatting on camera boxes, thumbing through *Guns and Ammo* magazine. Guys with long hair and satanic tatoos lounging on apple crates. Baby-faced guys in hiking shorts and radio headsets leaning against props, looking bored. Here and there a few women perched on little fan chairs passing the slow-creeping hours with needlework and crochet.

I hovered tentatively for a moment in this shadowland, then made my way, trying hard not to stumble over the cables, toward the craft services table, where I could have a full view of the set, as well as help myself to a bagel and Nova Scotia.

The set was an upper-crust bedroom. King-size bed. Plush white carpet. Armoires and oil paintings. Valerie Jane was standing in front of the bed, along with a young actress named Kiki Wales, who'd been popping up fairly steadily of late in supporting roles. Kiki was costumed in a long, clingy and totally see-through slip, beneath which she wore flesh-colored pasties and a G-string. Valerie, on the other hand, was dressed conservatively (at least for Valerie): charcoal pants suit, which looked to be Armani, but which she had no doubt knocked off on her own sewing machine; Reinstein/Ross earrings; comfy-looking flats. She was fiddling with a string of pearls around Kiki's neck, coercing them into a perfect ellipse over the actress's collarbone.

The director came bounding onto the set. It was Arne Bonner, whose specialty was steamy thrillers—a little agitated-looking guy with a scraggly red beard. His eyeballs made a quick run of Kiki's torso, stopping dead at her groin. "What the hell is that?" he croaked.

"That is a G-string," Valerie replied matter-of-factly.

"I know *what* it is. I mean, what the hell's it doing there?"

"It's there so we can get the appearance of nudity beneath the slip, without actually showing nipples and pubic hair."

Bonner wheezed out an extended why-am-I-so-afflicted sigh. "Ladies. This is supposed to be an erotic scene, not a fucking lingerie ad. We want to see nipples, we want to see a bit of snatch. Take those goddamned things off her!"

"I'm not showing my pubic hair to the whole world," pouted Kiki.

"Sweetheart, you signed a contract. And if you remember, in this particular contract, it specified a nude scene. A full *frontal* nude scene. I can make you do it without even the fucking slip!"

"The hell you can. I'm calling my agent. Somebody bring me a robe!" Kiki hollered into the darkness. A slender young man scrambled up with a terry-cloth robe and a pair of scuffs. Several minions simultaneously rushed to Bonner, whose complexion had mottled into an interesting shade of maroon.

Valerie gazed coolly on the entire scene. "When you two figure it out, let me know," she said, and strode long-legged off the set.

"Valerie Jane!" I called, stumbling my way toward her.

"Lucy!" She bent to press her cheek against mine. I caught a waft of her distinctive scent—roses, soap and licorice. "How long have you been here?"

"Long enough to have a good laugh. Who do you think is going to win?"

"My money's on Kiki. Her agent's a kid at CAA who eats guys like Bonner for breakfast." I giggled. She crooked her arm through mine. "C'mon, let's go back to the truck."

We hit the midday glare. Once again reduced to blinking blindly, I followed Valerie's lead to the wardrobe truck, an enormous white hulk squatting across the road. Inside, a long space lined with double-hung racks of riotously colored clothes. Yet another etiolated young man threw garments into a dryer.

Valerie collapsed wearily in a canvas chair, motioning me into another. "I've been dying to talk to you. Tell! Tell all!"

I treated her to an encapsulated history of my past week, omitting a few details. Like Julia's striptease for Kit's edification. And my whatever-it-was with Justin. Valerie listened raptly, eyes half-closed. "You really think the cops suspect you and Kit?" she murmured when I had finished.

"They certainly haven't ruled us out. One of them, a woman detective, is practically wetting her pants to get something on us. It's been absolute hell."

"Kit should be shot for leaving you alone right now."

"He had no choice. The movie . . ."

"Screw the movie! What about you?"

The very refrain that had been playing over and over in my head the past week. I shrugged wanly. "I'll be okay."

She studied me dubiously. Then she leaned back, crossing her amazing legs. "You know, I worked with Julia once."

My attention perked up. "When was that?"

"Eight or nine years ago, just before I met you. It was a film called *The Delano Reunion*. Remember it?"

"Yeah, it came out while I was pregnant with Chloe. I seem to associate the title with tossing my cookies in the john."

"The critics had the same reaction. It died a tragic death at the box office."

"I forget what it was about."

"A family of kooky daughters in the fifties who all return home for their papa's sixty-fifth birthday. An ensemble cast, all women except for Jack Lemmon, who played the kooky dad."

"Who did Julia play?"

"The eldest daughter—the one who'd gone to New York and let everyone think she was a big-time success in the theater. It turns out she's really an usherette at Radio City." Valerie laughed her reedy laugh. "We were shooting in one of those little towns out in the Antelope Valley, it must have been over a hundred every day. Poor old Julia in her fifties wardrobe, all those scratchy crinolines and girdles and a fox stole! It had to have been sheer torture."

"She must have bitched like crazy."

"Actually not. As I remember, she did exactly what she had to do without even a whimper. That was one very determined lady. God knows how far she might've gone with just a little bit of talent." Valerie smiled. "And speaking of talent, you know who else was in that movie? Mattie Ballard! It was one of her first parts. She played the slut of the family—on and off camera."

I raised a brow. "*The* Mattie Ballard? The one who's now practically a walking ad for Mommy and Me classes?"

"The very same. I seem to recall that Mattie and Julia had the same manager. An extremely hyper lady named Frances, Francine something."

"Francine Latch?"

"That sounds right. She drove everyone nuts, blowing every little thing into a major crisis. You know her?"

"Her son's in Chloe's class. She's remarried now to Sandy Palumbo, who runs Newgate." I mused for a moment on the Julia-Francine-Mattie connection: for the first time, I regretted not having been chummier with that clique of Hollywood Moms.

"Well, Mattie didn't stay with her very long. In the middle of the movie, she got signed by David Rossner, who was moving up fast at ITA, and she immediately gave Francine the kiss-off."

"So David Rossner was in the mix as well," I said excitedly.

"Yeah, I remember seeing him on the set once or twice. Checking out his new client." Valerie got to her feet. "They're going to drag me back onto the set any second, so let's get you fixed up. What exactly do you need?"

I rose as well. "An outfit that says money's no object. A lady-who-lunches type of thing."

"Rich bitch with taste," Valerie muttered. Her anthracite eyes began sweeping the variegated racks. "You're a six, right?"

"A perfect six," I said smugly. One small benefit of hell week had been losing my usual hearty appetite and whittling off a becoming seven pounds.

"I think I've got just the thing." Valerie Jane scurried up a little ladder and began furiously raking through clumps of hangers. She removed a cellophane-wrapped garment and skipped back down. "Normally I couldn't let you have anything from principal wardrobe, just extras. But this . . ." She pulled off the cellophane. It was a Richard Tyler suit, silk the color of sea foam, double-breasted, with a fluid, slim skirt. "Wales was supposed to wear it, but frankly, she's become a tad too fat in the can to get the skirt closed. Try it on."

"Right here?" I glanced at the young guy in back, who was now unloading the washer. "I'm not wearing a bra," I whispered.

Valerie grinned. "Believe me, James won't even notice."

Self-consciously, I took off my blouse (crepe forties sailor style), shimmied out of my clam diggers and slipped on the suit. The heavy silk felt cool and fluid as water against my skin.

"Nice," pronounced Valerie. "But the skirt's too long. James!" she called. "Can you do me a quick hem?"

Picking up a tape measure and a box of pins, James ambled over and appraised my lower half. "Two inches?"

"Two and a half."

He shrugged, knelt and began deftly measuring, folding the skirt under and pinning. While he worked, Valerie arranged a scarf of filmy ivory chiffon at my neck. "A little added softness," she murmured. "As for your hair, I think a chignon. Simple, but elegant." She gathered my wavy shoulder-length hair and twirled it into a knot, securing it with a gold clasp that she seemed to pull from thin air.

James completed his circle around my legs. He sprang up, went to a counter and selected a roll of masking tape, then sank back down at my feet. Plucking out the pins, he fastened the new hem with the tape. "Is that going to hold?" I asked nervously.

"Unless you're planning on doing calisthenics in it," he said tartly.

"Don't worry, we do hems like this all the time," Valerie

assured me. She turned from a table, holding a small black velvet box. "If you really want to look the part, you'll need some jewels." She flipped the box open. Nestled inside were a pair of diamond and emerald earrings, so dazzlingly brilliant they almost seemed on fire.

"God, I couldn't!" I gasped. "What if I lost them?"

"Oh, they're paste. Though rather good paste. I don't think anyone who wasn't a real expert could tell." She clipped them onto my earlobes and nodded. "Perfect. Take a look." She rotated me toward a full-length mirror.

I drew in a breath. The suit both delineated and flattered the contours of my body. The color of the silk lent a subtle glow to my skin and kindled new lights in my hair. The earrings blazed like little stars.

I looked . . . rich. The kind of rich that stops counting its income after the first seven figures. The kind that sends Rolls-Royce limos to pick up the kids at school.

The kind of rich worth killing for.

With a sudden shudder of revulsion, I began to pull it all off—jacket, skirt, earrings—and scrambled back into my familiar clothes. "This will do fine," I told Valerie. "Do I have to sign something?"

"Lord, no. This transaction is strictly *entre nosotros*. Just try not to get anything on the suit, gravy stains or bodily fluids or whatever." Valerie Jane folded the suit tenderly and tucked it, with the earrings and scarf, into a Fred Segal shopping bag. Then, wishing me good luck, she pressed her cool, brown cheek once more against mine.

THERE'S GENERALLY A SIGN POSTED at the exit of studios that says something to the effect that if the powers that be so choose, they have the right to stop and search your car. In the past, I'd never paid much attention to it, but now the words seemed to be flashing in hot-pink neon. Beads of sweat popped out on my forehead as I returned my pass to the guard—I was certain it would tip him off to the contraband stashed in my trunk. For the second time that day, I pictured myself being hauled into custody—this time to studio jail, which I fuzzily pictured as the hoosegow on the Western set.

But the guard absently plucked the slip from my hand and swiveled back to continue arguing with a teenager in a Geo who insisted Christian Slater's "people" had left his name on the list. I floored it, nearly clipping a dog walker crossing Hollywood Way, and high-tailed it for the freeway.

Given such an exquisitely tuned sense of paranoia, it was remarkable how long I took to realize I was being followed.

8

MY NEXT STOP WAS VIDEOCOPIA, a video rental store
in Westwood Village famous for its all-inclusive inventory
of titles: "If it got made, we got it" was its slogan. As I
was parking in the mini-mall parking area, a metallic
blue Taurus thickly covered in dust swung into the last
space—a handicapped space, I noticed—with a splutter
of Good Citizen indignation, though there was no little
wheelchair symbol on either windshield or license plate.
I could barely make out the driver through the dusty
windows, a woman in a brimmed hat and oversized dark
glasses; I shot her what I hoped was an eloquent look
before I headed into the shop.

The register clerk was built like a Popsicle stick, long
skinny frame topped with straw-colored Rasta braids and
a straw stubble of beard; he was staring, mouth agape, at
a Three Stooges episode blaring on an overhead monitor.

"Excuse me," I said loudly.

He yanked his eyes reluctantly from Curly and Moe.

"I'm looking for a movie called *The Delano Reunion*."

"We've got that." The kid loped from behind the
counter to a section of the stacks marked CLASSIC, dou-
bling up his sticklike torso to select a cassette from the
bottom. He carried it back, holding it with the tips of his

fingers as reverently as if it were the original celluloid of *Casablanca*.

"A real underrated flick," he pronounced. "You know, it's the first appearance by Mattie Ballard in a feature film. She's outstanding. Plus, it's the last-known acting role of Tora Merrick, if you remember her."

"Sure, I remember her," I said. In the late sixties, Tora Merrick was an ascending starlet, being groomed (in the last of those days when actors *were* groomed) to inherit the sex-kitten mantle of Ann-Margret and the "Barbarella" Jane Fonda. But the sex-kitten thing—big boobs, pouty lips, little-girl voice—went out in the seventies, and with it went Tora Merrick's career; the last time I'd heard her name was in a game of Trivial Pursuit.

"But, hey, I guess you know this already," the clerk said, scanning my account on his computer screen. "You guys rented it just three weeks ago."

This was news to me. Which meant it had been Kit—and it might mean nothing, I reflected, signing the receipt. Movie junkie that he was, on any Friday night he'd sweep up armfuls of videos: classics, horror, soft-core, anything that caught his eye—as long as it flickered, he was happy.

I sauntered back to my car, vaguely registering the fact that the blue Taurus was still hogging the handicapped space. I thought no more of it until, some minutes later, while waiting for a herd of moviegoers to migrate across the street to the Broxton Avenue theaters, I noticed the same car behind me—same make, same color, the same desperate need for a car wash. It had a sizable dent in the right headlight; with a crawling sensation, I suddenly recalled that as I had pulled onto the freeway ramp after leaving the studio, a car with a dented headlight had been tailgating me.

Experimentally, I swung a sharp right onto Gayley. Thirty seconds later, the Taurus sailed into view. I made a few zigzags, ending up on Hilgard, and for an exhilarating moment I thought I was free—but no, there was the Taurus two cars behind. In a panic, I veered into the entrance to the UCLA campus; the student guard inside her kiosk goggled bug-eyed as I whipped past and sped onto the narrow lane, scattering bicyclists and book-bagged strollers. The entrance to one of the school's stadium-sized parking structures yawned ahead; I shot up the ramp and spiraled down to the lowest rung, where I jammed into a space between two Hondas. Shutting off the motor, I crouched low in the seat.

What was so scary? I asked myself. A lady in an unwashed Ford was on my tail—what's the big deal? Nothing . . . except for the alarming fact that I had no idea who it could possibly be. Any self-respecting Hollywood Mom would no more be caught driving a mid-priced American sedan as she would be lunching at El Pollo Loco in a synthetic-fiber leisure suit.

Okay, so who *did* I know who owned a Taurus? The only suspect I could dredge up was a personal trainer I'd hired at one point back when we were rich, a muscle-bound girl whose peppiness at seven-thirty in the morning promptly drove me nuts. Hers was even the same color—"moonlight blue," she'd called it. But why would I be followed by Wendy Give-Me-Ten-More-Tummy-Crunches Shastremski?

I huddled in my Honda-sandwiched space for fifteen minutes before my Parking Structure Phobia overtook me—which was that this was the precise moment the 8.2 quake would hit, crushing both me and my Grand Cherokee under thirty-ton chunks of concrete and steel. Cautiously, I inched out of the space, crept back up and out the exit. Edging out onto Hilgard, I peered at the traffic. A white Miata, a beat-up minivan, a taxi . . .

Not a dusty Taurus in sight.

BACK HOME, EVEN WITH THE electric gates clinked firmly shut and all doors latched, I was jittery as hell. I sat in the kitchen, sipping Mint Magic tea, doing deep-breathing exercises left over from my Lamaze training, and tried to relax; but when the phone rang, I gave such a start, I whacked my elbow on the toaster oven.

"Hi, it's Justin."

"Oh, hi." The pain in my elbow ebbed away, replaced by a tingling in my fingertips. "How are you?"

"Dead tired, actually. I was out till one last night carousing with a couple of L.A.'s finest. Christ, can these boys suck back the Bud! But they did cough up some interesting information that I think you'll want to hear. Should I come over?"

I caught a reflection of my frazzled face in the black panel of the microwave. "Make it in an hour?"

"I'll be there."

I raced upstairs to take my second shower of the day, shampooed, rinsed with chamomile, blow-dried. Meticulously reapplied makeup, needing two tries with the eye-liner pencil because of a trembling hand. Threw on a swirly Mexican-flavored dress with bandana top and a pair of open-toed mules. Decided I looked like Carmen Miranda and furiously changed back to clam diggers with a fresh blouse. Took two minutes to compose a casual expression, just in time for the buzzer at the gate to sound.

Justin slouched in looking Byronically fatigued, and draped himself rather glamorously on the living-room couch.

"Something to drink?" I offered. "Snapple, or an herb tea . . ."

"You know what I really need? Hair of the dog that bit me. Tequila, no ice. Salt and lime, if you've got it."

I made a quick trip to the wet bar, grabbed a bottle of Cuervo gold and two of the thumb-shaped blue tequila glasses, souvenirs of a vacation in Oaxaca. Whacked a lime in two, put it all on a tray with a salt shaker and carried it back. Justin filled our glasses, handed one to me. He sprinkled salt on the back of his hand, licked it, tossed back the shot of tequila and finished by sucking the lime.

"I think you just saved my life," he murmured.

I sat where I could comfortably admire the way his shoulders worked under his denim shirt without being totally obvious about it and took a dainty sip of my own drink. "I just had something of an adventure," I told him.

"Yeah? What?"

"I had to shake a car that was following me." Gratified by his immediate interest, I launched into the tale of the dented blue Taurus, my peregrinations through Westwood Village and ultimate refuge in the UCLA garage. "I've been racking my brain trying to figure out who it could be," I finished. "But I'm totally stumped."

"It's obvious," Justin declared.

"It is?"

I hung in suspense while he refilled his glass, repeated the salt-shot-lime routine. "What you described," he said finally, "fits perfectly the description of an unmarked police car."

I flushed furiously. Of course! With a woman driver: who else could it be but Detective Shoe? "The bitch!" I muttered.

"Who?"

"This god-awful detective by the name of Teresa Shoe. I know exactly what she wants—to catch me in the act of throwing the still-bloody murder weapon into some Dumpster or vacant lot."

"Now that you know she's watching," he said, "you'll just have to keep it locked up in the trunk."

I glanced at him sharply. "Do you really think I could have killed Julia?"

"Do I really think so? No. Do I think you *could* have?" He bared his teeth in his most lupine smile. "I haven't quite decided."

I took a more fortifying gulp of tequila. "Let me assure you, I'm not the murdering type. If I needed to get revenge, I'd take a more subtle approach."

"I'll bet," he grinned.

"Your turn," I said. "What did you find out from the cops? I'm dying to know."

"Okay." He swung his feet up on the couch, locked his arms

behind his head. "Number one: Julia's last lover was what's known as a secretor, meaning that the antigens that determine blood type also appear in the semen and other body fluids. From which forensics can determine the guy's blood type—in this case, B negative, which didn't match any of the immediate suspects."

"Kit's A positive," I remarked.

"Husband Woody was also eliminated. Wrong blood type. Also, it seems, good old Uncle Roy shoots blanks."

I nodded. "He had a vasectomy."

"Then that explains that. Number two: witnesses in the general neighborhood reported seeing several cars at roughly that time of day, particularly a dark late-model Mercedes."

"The Prentices own two dark Mercedeses. S-six-hundreds, one black, one dark gray. Both pretty new."

"Yeah, but so do seventy-five percent of the people in this neighb. Anyway, this one was apparently driven by a 'suspicious character'—some kind of long-haired, bearded hippie."

A hippie in a new Mercedes—it didn't summon anything to mind. "Anything else?"

"Yeah. A partial fingerprint was lifted from the body—from the left inner-thigh area, to be exact. Again, it didn't match any fingerprints of any suspects."

"So Kit and I should be in the clear."

"Not necessarily. One thing the cops know is that before her marriage to the venerable Woody Prentice, Julia was into kinky sex. At one time, she was a star customer of the Pleasure Trove, that sex shop over in Hollywood. Made some very specialized purchases."

"Specialized how?"

"From what I gather, of the whips-and-chains variety."

I raised a brow. PROMINENT HOLLYWOOD MOM INTO BONDAGE: it would have made a catchy *Enquirer* story. "But how does that implicate Kit and me?"

"The way the cops see it, *kinky* could also mean more than

two people were involved. There might have been a third, even a fourth. A regular group grope." He laughed. "Look at it from the cops' point of view. They've got a bunch of rich, bored Hollywood types, they figure this might be how you get your kicks."

"Well, it's not!" I snapped fiercely.

Justin turned amused eyes to me. I had the uneasy feeling I'd given away something of my uncertainty about Kit. But all he said was, "Does it bother you to be here all alone?"

"You mean, with a crazed killer on the loose?"

He shrugged. "Even without."

"I don't know. I guess I'm used to it. I spent a lot of time alone while I was growing up."

"Yeah? Why was that?"

"Oh . . ." I settled uneasily back in my chair. "My mother died when I was ten. Traffic accident. She and my father were coming out of a market, both of them carrying sacks of groceries, and a cow trailer pulled suddenly out of a side road. It skidded on the ice and hit them straight on. Mom died instantly. Dad broke about sixty bones and had to have a foot amputated. When he could hobble around well enough without crutches on his new metal foot, he married his physical therapist, a woman named Anna-Linda. She had two daughters of her own a few years older than me."

"Aha. Enter the wicked stepmother and stepsisters."

"Except they weren't wicked. They're actually very kind-hearted people. Just kind of . . . well, brassy. And Dad, who'd been a tax accountant, ran for alderman, and what with election-eering all the time and stumping around town on his metal foot, he became something of the town character. So, I just took to spending a lot of time alone in my room with my paints and crayons, pretending I had a normal life."

Justin gave a snort. "A normal life. What in god's hell is that?"

Good question. A normal life was what I thought I'd finally managed to achieve, and what I'd been scrambling like mad these last few weeks to get back to. But so far, all I'd found was that nothing was really what I'd thought it was, including—maybe even particularly—my so-called normal life and marriage.

In confusion, I picked up the Videocopia bag I'd left on the coffee table and made a fussy show of removing the cassette.

"The Delano Reunion," Justin observed. "Julia's in that, isn't she?"

"That's why I rented it. It seems to connect her with this clique of high-powered women I know from my daughter's school. Of course, it could be nothing, just a coincidence."

"Put it on. It's exactly what I'm in the mood for."

I snapped the cassette into the VCR. Justin sat up to make room for me on the couch; I squinched down at the end, leaving a discreetly wide space between us.

The film faded in on one of those dusty little California towns that would be cooked back to the Mojave Desert in about two weeks if Colorado ever cut off the water. The titles began to roll. Jack Lemmon had top billing, followed alphabetically by the ensemble of actresses. I watched with little attention until the credit for associate producer appeared—one Sander D. Palumbo.

Well, well, I thought, the gang's all here.

"Palumbo!" Justin snarled. "That goddamn bastard!"

"Sandy?" I'd never heard anyone speak badly of Sandy Palumbo. If Hollywood were a beauty pageant, he'd be a shoe-in for Miss Congeniality.

"He stiffed me on a script," Justin said. "I sweated for months on the sucker, even flew to Santa Fe on my own dime to research it, and now all my agents get from Newgate is the old check's-in-the-mail runaround. And I'll tell you something else—I'm not the only one this is happening to."

Sandy Palumbo's company was stiffing writers—I tucked this away as an interesting fact.

But now Julia had appeared on the screen, wearing a Mamie Eisenhowerish toque, a long, fanny-hugging skirt and the kind of fox stole made from whole dead animals, each nipping the tail of the other. I took another sip of tequila and settled back to enjoy the show. Julia turned in her usual lip-grimacing, eyes-popping performance, but the Videocopia clerk was right—Mattie Ballard was outstanding, one minute all dewy innocence, the next, a red-hot baby temptress.

But where was Tora Merrick? She wasn't one of the five Delano daughters fussing over Jack Lemmon between cat fights. Finally, more than an hour into the film, a new character appeared, a neighboring divorcée with eyes for Papa Delano. The actress was blowsy in the manner of *The Poseidon Adventure* Shelley Winters, but with a harder, more used-up face framed by a sort of post–shock treatment frizzy-blond coiffure.

"Is that Tora Merrick?" I gasped.

"It sure is," Justin sniggered.

"She looks about sixty years old! Was she sick or something?"

"Yeah, a disease called cocaine. Also uppers, downers, booze and, for all I know, airplane glue." He added in a hard voice, "The lady never met an addictive substance she didn't like."

Her part was little more than a cameo; she quickly vanished from the screen. The Delano daughters continued to squabble, until Mattie Ballard's character took off on a reckless joyride in Daddy's cherished Buick, crashed and died. A predictably touching graveside family reunion, and fade-out.

The movie seemed to have put Justin to sleep. I couldn't blame him—it was pretty much a snore. But when I got up to eject the tape, his hand grabbed my wrist, and he pulled me back down. His eyelids lazed open. He smiled and began to bring his mouth to mine.

I pulled away. "I can't," I said.

"Why not?"

"For starters, we're both married."

He gave a little laugh. "Well, I'm in the process of getting a divorce. And don't tell me I've only imagined what I've been picking up from you."

"Like what?" I said stiffly.

"Like some heavy sexual sparks between us."

"Even if I happened to be a little physically attracted to you, it doesn't mean I really want to do anything about it." Lucy the Chaste. I should have been wearing white and cradling a sheaf of lilies. I added, "*I*'m not getting a divorce. I'm perfectly happy being married."

"Speaking for myself, when I'm happily involved with someone, I don't go around sending out signals that I'm hot to trot."

I opened my mouth to protest. But what, exactly? That my marriage really was hunky-dory? That I wasn't really drooling at the prospect of ravishing Justin's body?

And I suddenly flashed on Kit with the ace reporter of *Vanity Fair,* whom I now pictured as looking like a younger and bespectacled Diane Sawyer. I imagined them going at it hot and heavy in a heart-shaped bathtub, while I was eating mystery-meat goulash and trying futilely to keep my toes from freezing in Merrie Olde Budapest.

As if sensing my thoughts, Justin pulled me close again. This time, I shut my eyes, let his lips meet mine. I tasted mint and tobacco and melted into a luxurious, deep kiss.

The phone rang.

We sprang apart and stared at it, shrilling on its pine sideboard across the room. Chloe, I thought, with a rough stab of guilt. On the fourth ring, I bounded up and grabbed the receiver.

"It's me," said Kit. "You sound out of breath."

"I was just doing some exercises. A, uh, video workout."

"You sure you're okay? I mean, I've been kind of worried."

There was real concern in his voice. The curtain between us seemed to open a crack. Now would be the time to really talk— except for the fact that right behind me was a man who three minutes ago had his tongue in my mouth.

"I'm managing fine," I said.

"You always do," he said crisply.

Down came the curtain. There was a moment of strained air between us. "How's the location hunting going," I asked.

Kit launched into a story about finding the perfect Victorian for their haunted house, but how the owner was giving them a hard time about ripping up the floorboards and putting a few really insignificant holes in the walls even though Kit had assured him everything would be restored and all the cobwebbing would wipe right off.

I politely commiserated. And when we had said our polite good-byes and I had hung up, I turned to find that Justin was gone. Damn! I thought. Damn, damn. Though I wasn't exactly sure why.

TWO

9

AT FIRST I THOUGHT I had stumbled into the wrong office.

The Rodeo Drive address I'd been given for Dr. Stewart Goodrow, cosmetic surgeon, proved to be located roughly midpoint between the boutiques Chanel and Azzedine Alaia, but the modest brass plaque fastened to the façade was simply marked SUITE B; I pressed the buzzer, heard the almost inaudible click of a lock released and let myself inside the anonymous, black-painted door. A doll-sized lift whisked me to the second floor and opened onto a reception room of hushed pastels, roseate lights and floral arrangements lavish enough for a funeral of state. There was nothing remotely medical about it, nothing suggesting a surgeon's antechamber—unless you counted the framed Herb Ritts photos of nude torsos so godlike in perfection, they made eloquent ads for liposuction.

Several patients were waiting. A sleek-haired young man who, except for the heavy black stitches pinning his ears to his scalp, was of such male-model beauty, I nearly expected to see copywriting across his knees. Across from him sat, incongruously, a poor-looking Hispanic woman with a boy of about eight who was busy morphing a Mighty Morphin Power Ranger. What possible cosmetic procedure could they be signed up for? I wondered. The little boy swiveled his head to stare up at me. I drew a sharp breath: where his nose and upper lip should have been was just a gaping, mangled cavity.

"Good afternoon, Ms. Spielberg."

A young woman ascended from behind a Queen Anne desk. Cleopatra hair. Collagen-puffed lips. Her rustling voice I recognized as the one on the phone. "Welcome to the Goodrow Clinic. I'm Bethany." There was at least six feet of Bethany, augmented by a pair of four-inch platform pumps that gave a kind of tilt to her walk as she circumnavigated the desk. "Please have a seat," she gestured. "Could I bring you something to drink?"

"Water would be fine," I said.

"Flat or sparkling? Lemon, lime or peach slice?"

"Sparkling, lemon."

I sank onto a sofa covered in soft leather the color of a breath mint and smoothed my silk skirt over my thighs. Bethany teetered back, a tumbler of spritely fizzing water in one hand, a clipboard in the other. "If you could fill this out . . . Just some background for our records."

I settled back with my water and clipboard and spent a lively five minutes composing a health profile for the fictional Laura Spielberg: she turned out to be a strict vegetarian with a wheat allergy, a social smoker, prone to insomnia and occasional fainting spells. Interestingly, she'd had a bout of the clap when she was seventeen. Sadly, there were sporadic incidents of schizophrenia on her maternal side. I submitted this fantasy to the Amazonian Bethany, then picked up a copy of *Vogue*, thumbing through several spreads before realizing it was in Japanese. There was also a Japanese *Mirabella*, several fat, glossy numbers in Farsi and a Brazilian travel mag.

"So, what are you having done?" It was the male model speaking.

"I'm just here for a consultation," I told him.

He nodded knowingly. "I had my ears pinned. You should've

seen them before. They were, like, flapping in the breeze, little
Dumbos."

"Clark Gable's ears stuck out and nobody minded," I said.

He shot me a fishy look: I might as well have pointed out that
Moses had a flowing beard or Robin Hood wore green tights, for
all it seemed relevant to him.

"Come this way, Ms. Spielberg." Bethany ushered me into an
inner chamber tricked out in the same antiques and fresh-flower
opulence as the reception, with the high-tech addition of a computer, a monitor and VCR, and a video camera mounted on
a tripod.

I examined the diplomas on the wall—Duke, Stanford—and
reviewed what tidbits I'd gleaned about the excellent doctor from
my *People–Vanity Fair* perusing. I knew he specialized in aging
male actors, tightening up faces and bodies so they could continue to play roles that had them somersaulting out of airplanes
and romancing twenty-five-year-olds, without looking like they
needed a cardiologist standing by. I'd also read that Goodrow
piloted his own helicopter; once, while choppering over the
Painted Desert, he'd put down to take a pee on a particularly
sacred stretch of the Navajo Reservation, nearly setting off a
contemporary Indian war.

I'd also heard he would do anything—any procedure, no matter
how unorthodox—if the price was right.

The door blew open, and the eminent doctor himself bounded
in, a trim, middle-sized guy with one of those spookily preserved
boyish faces, in the manner of Dick Clark or George Hamilton—
thirty going on sixty-five. He paused for a moment while his eyes
swept me head to foot, appraising not my body but my outfit: his
pupils turned into little cash registers, ringing up—*cha-ching!*—
the price of each sartorial item. Diamond and emerald earrings
in gold Cartier setting: *cha-ching!* fifteen grand. Richard Tyler
peau de soie suit: *cha-ching!* twenty-two hundred. Christian La-
croix scarf: *cha-ching!* four-fifty, easy.

The resulting tally seemed more than satisfactory; he smiled broadly and thrust out a rather meaty hand. "Stew Goodrow," he boomed. "It's a great pleasure to meet you. I'm a very big fan of your, uh . . ."

"My cousin?" I suggested.

"Exactly. Love his work. *Schindler,* a masterpiece! *Jurassic Park,* brilliant! You know, I ran into Laura Dern last year at the U.S. Open and suggested we could do something about that chin."

I could find no suitable rejoinder to this, so I said, "There's a little boy out in the reception . . ."

"Tiko, yes, fascinating case. He was found in the slums of Caracas by Doctors Without Borders. I'm going to reconstruct his lower face. Our progress will be featured week-to-week on *Dateline.* But now, more to the point . . ." He rubbed his hands together, like a dinner guest preparing to dig into a feast. "What is it we can do for you?"

"I'm not exactly sure. You see, my husband and I are having some, well, difficulties. Things just aren't the way they used to be between us." Here, at least, I was touching on some semblance of truth. I made my voice go a little weepy. "I feel I need something . . . Oh, I don't know . . ."

"I understand completely. You want to win back your husband's affection—make yourself as attractive as possible, so he remembers why he fell in love with you in the first place."

"Exactly."

"So, then." He subjected me, face and figure, to another long, hard, presumably professional, stare, producing little grunts of appraisal. "Tell you what. Let's do some computer imaging. Ever have it done before?"

I shook my head.

"You'll really enjoy this. If you'll just stand in front of the camera, we'll get a picture of your face." He positioned me. "Just look natural."

I immediately assumed the expression of glazed delight that appeared on my face whenever I had to pose for a photo.

"Superb! Now, have a seat and let's get to work."

I took a seat in front of the video monitor. A split-screen image appeared, both showing a close-up of my face. Goodrow sat beside me and picked up the mouse.

"What I'm going to do," he explained, "is paint a picture of your ideal face. We'll work with what you already have, simply bringing out the best of what it can be." He began to manipulate the mouse. Little circles and crosses appeared on the left-hand image of me. "Let's start at the top. Your eyebrows are uncommonly low. We could do a forehead lift, a very easy procedure. It would raise them like so."

Clickety-click went the mouse. On the right-hand me, the eyebrows rose like little elevators, becoming miraculously pruned and lightened in the process.

"You see, that also elongates the upper eyelid," Goodrow crowed, "gets rid of that tired look. Now, your nose—the bridge is fine, but let's contour the tip just a fraction, like so. I'd also like to redefine that upper lip, give it more fullness." I watched with stark fascination as my mouth swelled to the size of the wax-candy lips I used to suck on at Halloween. "And now those cheekbones. What say we give them more emphasis? What we can do is siphon a little fat from the buttocks and inject it here. . . ." My cheekbones on the monitor began to puff, chipmunklike. "Whoops, too much." They deflated back to being merely prominent. The doctor leaned back to admire his handiwork. "You have a broad jawline," he declared, "but it's not unattractive."

Thank god, I thought, I'm not a total Quasimodo.

"So, what do you think?" he pursued.

I gazed at the right-hand face in the monitor. It was no longer me. Who it *was* was Geena Davis, specifically as she appeared in *Thelma and Louise* right after she blew away the guy in the parking lot who was trying to molest Susan Sarandon. All that was missing was the hot-pink lipstick.

"I don't know," I said. "It seems a little extreme."

"Not at all! These are very subtle changes. Your friends won't even know you've had surgery, they'll just think you've spent a month at Canyon Ranch getting thoroughly rested. But naturally, these are just options."

"Naturally," I echoed, adding, "There's one other thing . . ."

He swiveled to face me, a slick sheen of greed suffusing his features. "Yes?"

"This is a little embarrassing. It's about my breasts. I've noticed in bed . . . during sex, my husband doesn't find them quite satisfying enough."

"Then let me reassure you." Goodrow reached out and laid an avuncular hand on mine. "If your husband's pleasure and ultimately your own would be enhanced by us giving you larger breasts, then I say let's go for it!" He rotated back to the computer controls. "What say we get a full-body picture of you and try out some different profiles?"

I was intrigued by the idea of seeing myself equipped with Dolly Parton bazooms, but I needed to get to the point. "The only thing is," I said in a wispy voice, "I'm kind of afraid of having something go wrong. You see, one of my best friends was Julia Prentice."

"Ah, yes, poor, poor Julia. What a terrible tragedy." He sighed and stared piteously into the middle distance. I almost felt sorry for him. After all, if Julia had survived, she'd have been good for an unending series of lifts, tucks and adipose-fat-cell redistribution procedures.

I went on, "I'm just afraid that what happened to her after her first operation would happen to me."

Goodrow's face darkened. "What do you mean?"

"How she had to have it done over."

"Have *what* done over?"

"Her implants . . . The bubbles in the silicone, how it had to be replaced. . . ."

"Just wait one holy second. I don't know where you're getting your information from, but it's a slander, a total slander. Julia Prentice underwent one breast enlargement from this office, and she was entirely satisfied with the result. In fact, six months afterward, she sent a case of '67 Petrus as an added thanks!"

"God, you're absolutely right, it's my mistake," I said quickly. "I'm confusing her with someone else. Julia was thrilled with everything you did for her." I took a gamble: "Particularly getting rid of those terrible scars. It made her so happy she could finally wear a thong-bikini again."

Goodrow gave a mollified grunt. I pressed on: "How did you do it? With lasers?"

"Pah! Lasers, in my opinion, are highly overrated. *Star Wars* gimmickry, nothing more."

I fixed a rapt gaze on him, letting him know that *I* knew I was in the presence of a genius. "How *did* you do it?" I asked breathlessly.

"Classic surgical technique." He shrugged with becoming modesty. "First I cut away the wide outer part of the scars near the skin's surface and reclosed them for a finer suture. Then I used some of the scar tissue itself to build up the depressed area. Excellent result! The line that was left was so shallow and thin, it could hardly be noticed."

"I didn't notice anything at all," I said.

A mistake. Goodrow stared intently at me. The association with Julia had finally jogged his memory—all that less than flattering footage of me on *News at Four* and *Current Affair*.

I jumped to my feet. "Tell you what. Why don't I think all this over, consider the options, and then let you know how I'd like to proceed."

His eyes suddenly swung down to the vicinity of my knees. I glanced down and gave a silent *"aaak"*: part of the masking tape holding up the hem of my suit skirt had given way, causing three inches of hem and tape to droop, bag-lady fashion, at my knee.

We both gaped at the dangling hem open-mouthed for an

instant; then I made an ungraceful plunge for the door and bolted back into the reception area, nearly body-slamming the giant Bethany.

"We'll bill, of course, Ms. Spielberg?" she said placidly.

"Of course," I squeaked, and scuttled sideways, like a stone crab, into the safety of the tiny lift. As the doors closed, I caught a final glimpse of the Hispanic woman still sitting where I'd left her, Aztec features staring straight ahead, at everything and nothing.

I had the feeling she was very used to waiting.

I INVESTED $12.95 IN MASKING tape at The World's Most Expensive Five-and-Dime, also called the Beverly Rodeo Pharmacy, and patched up my drooping hem. By now I was late for my lunch date with Sandy Palumbo. I retrieved my car—actually, Kit's posh new Beemer, which had seemed more suitable than climbing into my sports utility vehicle in my grande dame duds. I hit the road, mulling over what I had just learned from the eminent Dr. Goodrow.

First, that the nanny, Audrey Huff, had been right about the nasty scars on Julia's otherwise alabaster butt.

Second, that Justin was right in suspecting that Julia had had them surgically removed.

Third, that Julia *had* lied to Marsha Moss-Golson about her scar-removal surgery, claiming instead that she was going in to have her breasts repadded—which could only mean she had been desperate to conceal her kinky past from the world at large.

But why, I pondered, reapplying Chanel's *Soleil Nuance* to my nonenhanced upper lip, would any of this lead to a death warrant?

*   *   *

THE GOLDEN-HAIRED VALET HOVERING at the entrance to
Morton's leaped to attention as I pulled up. He sank with an
almost sexual sigh into the parchment-colored leather seat,
cocked an eye at the sixty-two miles on the odometer. "This
baby's hardly been on the road!" he exulted, and peeled off with
an excruciating squeal of tires.

I was late, but Sandy was later: I was ushered over to a well-
placed table for two and nursed a Pellegrino for another ten
minutes before he appeared. He was wearing one of his trademark outfits: muted gray Turnbull & Asser shirt and jazzy-
patterned mauve silk Zegna tie, faded jeans, black and silver
cowboy boots. I admired the way he fluidly worked the room,
pausing at almost every table to pump a hand, squeeze a shoulder, lingering just the correct fraction of a second longer at a
group that included Billy Crystal.

"I'm sorry," he said, slipping into the chair opposite me.
"Things are wild down at the shop. I practically needed a gun
to get away."

"You don't have to explain," I said. "I'm married to a
workaholic."

Sandy gave a tired smile. Deep grooves forged into his forehead and from his nostrils to the corners of his mouth; for a
moment he looked almost repulsively ugly. Then, as if some
inner switch were thrown, his features became reanimated, and
he gazed directly into my eyes with utter absorption, as if I were
the only other person in the room and that was exactly the way
he wanted it. Once again, I felt the pull of the famous Sandy
Palumbo magnetism.

"You look ravishing," he murmured. "I always appreciate it
when a woman makes the effort to dress. It's far too rare these
days."

No wonder he went for Francine, I thought, a woman who
practically bathed in coordinated Chanel ensembles. Still, the
compliment gave me a bit of a glow as I picked up the menu.

Sandy called for a bottle of Bâtard-Montrachet. The waiter filled our glasses with the velvety wine; I took a deep sip and met Sandy's smile with a rather sultry one of my own.

"Let me apologize again for Francie's tantrum," he said. "You know how high strung she is, especially when it comes to Ollie. I've seen her go ballistic if someone even gives him a dirty look."

If so, it seemed to me that Francine must spend a fair amount of her time going ballistic. I said, "I have to apologize for Chloe as well. I don't know where she got these slugger tendencies—Kit and I have always considered ourselves essentially nonviolent. I hope Ollie's nose is okay."

"Yeah, it's fine, but he's got a stunning shiner. It's only just starting to fade."

He grinned, relishing the thought. For a moment we basked in comradely enjoyment of young Oliver's black eye.

"Sandy, kid, how are ya!"

We'd been interrupted by a guy doing the work-the-room boogie. Dulce & Gabbannaed, bad hair transplants—I recognized him as a producer who churned out soft-core porn that masqueraded as art. He launched into a motor-mouth hype of his latest project, while I started on my second glass of wine, feeling shamelessly thrilled to be in the orbit of Sandy's power. And Sandy did have real power: a "yes" from him could actually get a movie made—actors were cast, directors hired, cameras started to roll. Plus, he was sexy—as sexy as Justin in his own way. Plus, he was so damned nice. My mind drifted for a moment to how, back in high school, my best friend, Carrie Hoenneker, and I would huddle for hours in her room gorging ourselves on Screamin' Yellow Zonkers! while sorting the boys in our class into three categories: Nerds, Studs and GHMs, which stood for Good Husband Material. Until recently, I'd always thought of Kit as prime GHM—it was what had attracted me to him in the first place. Sandy Palumbo was definitely GHM. I began to spin a little fantasy: he'd leave Francine and I'd leave Kit, and we'd get married and have another three or four kids of our own and live on a working ranch that was somehow, magically, just ten minutes away from Sunset Boulevard. The idea made me giggle.

The porn producer shot me an affronted look, then sailed off to accost his next victim.

"What was so funny?" Sandy smiled.

I blushed. "Nothing, really. This is a lovely wine." The waiter set our food down and I took a quick bite of my pasta, angel hair with wilted radicchio. "I saw one of your old movies yesterday," I said.

"Oh, yeah? Which one?"

"*The Delano Reunion.*"

A shadow skittered across his face, so briefly, I might have imagined it. Then he laughed deeply. "I wouldn't call it one of 'my' movies. I was just a lowly associate producer on it."

"Is that where you met Francine?"

"Met, yeah, but that was as far as it went. She had absolutely no use for me at the time. I was just another Joe Schmo, schlepping around town with a few scripts under my arm, and licking boots to get any piece of crap at all off the ground. It wasn't till four years later, when I pulled off the funding for Newgate, that she bothered to look my way. And then it was a whirlwind romance. We were married in a month." I must have shown a disapproving expression, for he added, "Look, I don't mind that Francine needs money. She came from dirt, and when Patrick Latch ditched her, she found herself scrambling in dirt again. It's totally understandable that she'd want something better."

I remembered how eagerly he had justified Francine's gold digging at The School's commencement. A little too eagerly, I decided.

"So, how is it that you happened to catch *Delano*?" he asked.

"I rented it from Videocopia. I wanted to see if I could find out anything new about Julia. I don't know what I was hoping to learn." My voice fell dejectedly. "I guess I'm so desperate to get this murder cleared up, I'm grasping at straws. I'm beginning to think it's going to hang over our heads forever."

"Hey," he said softly. "If you need a shoulder to cry on, I'm available."

For a moment I did have the urge to burst into tears, to press my head against his English shirting and sob that I didn't know what to believe anymore about anyone or anything, including my own husband. But I contented myself with another swallow of the seductive wine.

"How well did you get to know Julia during the movie?" I asked.

"Professionally, I guess you'd say I got to know her pretty well. But, like Francie, she had far bigger fish to fry. Off the set, we had almost nothing to do with each other." He forked a delicate slice of poached chicken and chewed it meditatively. "I did go to bed with Mattie Ballard once."

I tilted my head. "Really?"

"No big deal. So did the key grip, the second AD and half the electricians. With Mattie, at least back then, it was wham, bam, thank you, man. You had your turn, and then she moved on."

At Windermere's last Parents' Day, Mattie Ballard, movie star, had brought in six dozen banana cupcakes, which she had whipped up herself from scratch from purely organic ingredients—practically implying she had churned her own butter, milled the whole wheat flour and sortied out to the plantations to pick her own bananas. Not just a Hollywood Mom—a Hollywood Uber-mom. "Here's an idea," I said. "What if Julia was threatening to talk about Mattie's sleep-around past and ruin her reputation? Wouldn't that give Mattie a good reason to have Julia permanently shut up?"

Sandy gave a low chuckle. "I don't think so. There could be videotapes of Mattie going down on the entire Seventh Marine Corps Division, but to her fans she'd still be pure as the driven snow. She's like that Greek goddess—the one who screwed every male in sight, but at the full moon was always restored to perfect virginity." He refilled my glass. "Nice try, though. Got any other theories? Anything the cops have said that sounds promising?"

The wine had begun to swim deliciously to my brain. "Julia tried to seduce Kit," I blurted. "And when he backed out, she told him she was going to call someone else. Except she *couldn't* have. The cops checked all the phone records, both ours and the Prentices'. Car phones, even the fax lines. There was nothing."

Sandy considered this with a thoughtful frown. "Maybe she was *plan*ning to go call somebody, but then someone else just happened to come by first."

"Yeah, a neighbor borrowing a cup of sugar," I said caustically. An image of Justin popped into my mind. I quickly banished it.

The waiter took our order for coffee and futilely tried to tempt us with an array of decadent desserts. "By the way," I said to Sandy as a steaming, oversized cup of *caffè latte* was set before me, "whatever happened to Tora Merrick?"

"Why?" he asked sharply.

His tone took me by surprise. "No particular reason. Just that seeing her in *The Delano Reunion* made me wonder whatever became of her."

"Christ, who knows. At the rate she was going, it wouldn't surprise me if she was dead. I never met anyone more self-destructive in my life. You know, she originally had a much bigger part in *Delano*. She was supposed to have this big romantic scene with Jack Lemmon. But she was such a loose cannon on the set, they had to do a quick rewrite and cut her down to almost nothing." He stirred his mud-thick double espresso rapidly and said, "So, what do you think about Windermere lately? Francine's very concerned that it might be going downhill."

We spent the next fifteen minutes pleasantly dissecting The School's theories of progressive education. Then Sandy, with a surreptitious peek at his Rolex, signaled for the check; he paid it and we rose to go.

"Just let me say hi to David," he said.

I turned my head. In a table catty-corner to us, David Rossner was lunching with two bald and elegantly suited young black men. He seemed uncannily able to keep up a running conversation while simultaneously stoking his mouth with shoestring potatoes, one after the other, in a pistonlike motion.

Sandy strode up to the table. "David, great to see you," he said heartily and put out his hand.

David Rossner didn't even glance at it. Just continued talking and piston-popping French fries, eyes fixed on his lunch guests, who fidgeted uncomfortably. For what seemed like an eternity, Sandy's hand dangled like a deadfish in midair.

Then abruptly, he snapped it back and began walking to the exit with a fixed smile and jaunty gait, as if he had not just been viciously cut by the *capo di tutti capi* of Hollywood—as if, indeed, David Rossner had kissed him on the lips and called him "Friend!" I scrambled along behind. It seemed to me that every face in the room was turned our way, grinning with sickly Schadenfreude.

Outside, we surrendered our chits to the valet and waited several moments in grim silence. "Thank you for lunch," I piped up finally. "I really enjoyed it."

Sandy turned and stared at me. An aqua '57 T-bird squealed to a stop, and the valet leaped out and tossed Sandy the keys. Without a word, he slid in and drove away.

So much for my gauzy fantasies of Sandy Palumbo, I told myself scathingly. For what I had seen in his eyes was the same look of loathing he had directed at Oliver at the Windermere commencement. But this time I had no doubt it was meant purely for me.

10

I SHOULDN'T BE DRIVING, I realized, as I cruised unsteadily in the Beemer up Wilshire Boulevard. I'd had too much wine, my reflexes were fuzzy and, given this unfamiliar, ultraresponsive car, I might easily miscalculate, hit the gas instead of the brake and plow into some innocent pedestrians. I could already picture the headline: MURDER SUSPECT CONTINUES ON DEATH RAMPAGE; given my current streak of luck, the victims would be a toddler, Janet Reno and a nun.

I steered toward one of the Beverly Hills municipal lots, figuring I'd ditch the car, then walk off my tipsiness in the designer aisles of Neiman Marcus—perhaps running into Francine Palumbo, who, from all accounts, haunted the place like Banquo's ghost. But at the intersection of El Camino, I formulated a new plan: I was very near the offices of the Schwartzman Pemmel Publicity Agency. Why not pay a visit to my old friend and fellow film-school graduate, Pamela Pemmel? She might be able to shed a little light on the whereabouts of Tora Merrick.

* * *

PAMELA, OR "MELLY," AS SHE was called back in NYU
days, had been a chunky, self-important, serious-minded girl,
with long, lank, dun-colored hair and incipient frown lines groov-
ing her forehead, whose greatest fame was for having eyes of
different colors—one hazel-brown, the other aquamarine; magnified by a pair of thick-lensed spectacles, they gave you a strange,
almost seasick feeling of displacement. Her serious turn of mind
revealed itself in the form of a succession of passionate crusades:
she was, in turn, antisugar ("the white death"), anti-depilatories
("carcinogens in a tube"), antinukes ("no nukes is good nukes")
and—after being raped late one night during her final year by a
teenager with a Saturday night special in the graffitied and urine-
reeking stairwell of her Avenue A walk-up—antimale (her thesis
film was a poignant plea for legalizing castration). It was during
her antimale phase that I first started going with Kit; he'd referred
to her ever since as "that ball-snipping pal of yours."

I would see her from time to time in the first few years after
we'd both migrated to L.A. By then, she'd dropped twenty
pounds, taken up chain-smoking, streaked her hair green and
was busy writing unsalable screenplays about homeless people
in love, supporting herself, like many an aspiring writer, actor
or director, with temp jobs. After being sent for a two-week gig
at the newly formed Schwartzman Publicity Group, she wrangled
a permanent job as Kirk Schwartzman's executive assistant. A
year later, she married him. A scant year after that, she became
his partner.

By now, Schwartzman Pemmel was one of the top boutique
agencies in the business. Pamela's superstar clients hired her as
much to shield them from publicity as to drum it up—which
meant that, like most people with power in Hollywood, Pamela
spent the majority of her time saying no.

Which also meant that, old buddy or not, I wasn't certain
she'd see me. But the snooty male receptionist, after calling in
my name, became almost respectful. "Ms. Pemmel's in conference, but asks if you could wait several minutes . . . ?"

I gave a boozy nod. "Ladies' room?" I inquired.

"Down the corridor, first on the right."

I followed his directions to a gleaming little lounge with gilt mirrors and a petit point love seat. Beside the bisque-colored porcelain toilet hung a bisque-colored phone, so that Barbra or Goldie or Meryl would never have to miss a call while answering the more urgent one of nature. I peed, splashed cold water on my face, slapped my cheeks to revive the circulation; feeling sufficiently pulled together, I headed back to the reception area.

Pamela was walking out a client. It was the heavy-metal rocker Jackel Welch, leader of a group called Wax, whose particularly loathsome CD I had recently confiscated from Chloe. He had clotted waist-length hair. He had tattoos of death heads, rattlesnakes, daggers, dirks, and black widows webbing both his skinny arms. The bulge of his penis was clearly visible at the crotch of his filthy jeans, and a little pink plastic fetus dangled from his left ear. "If I do the cover of *People* in October," he was whining, "then *Rolling Stone*'s gonna bounce me off their November issue."

"Jackel. Jackel, love." Pamela had a voice like a foghorn, deep, monotonal and persistent. "Trust me on this. *Rolling Stone* needs you a hell of a lot more than you need them. Who else are they going to run, some geriatric fart like Paul McCartney? Puh-leese! Leave these logistics to me."

"I want negative approval this time. That shot of me in *Newsweek* last month made me look *fat*."

"Anything you want, my darling. Just consider it done."

The rock star dragged himself to the door. I could swear I heard chains clinking in his wake.

Pamela turned to me. "Lucy, my dearest, what a splendid surprise!" The foghorn voice faltered as she got a really good look at my getup. "This is something of a new look for you."

"I just came from lunch with Sandy Palumbo at Morton's," I said breezily.

Nothing stirred Pamela's blood like the dropping of power

names, especially when paired with power restaurants. "Really?"
she cooed. "*Dar*ling Sandy, I must give him a ring. But to be
frank, Lucy, I'm not positive this is the right image for you. You
have your own creative style and it's very charming. This is just
too . . . well, chic."

She herself looked almost terrifyingly chic. Black, tubular,
pleated Issey Miyake jacket over gray leggings. Auburn-rinsed
hair sculpted in an angular bob. Her formerly two-toned eyes
were now tinted (presumably by contacts) to a uniform, and rather
startling, amethyst.

And this was a woman whose hairy legs, even by NYU standards, had been a campus phenomenon!

A multijeweled hand fluttered onto my shoulder blade. "Come
on back. I've got a three-thirty, but we can yak till then."

I followed her to a vast corner office with views of the rooftops
of Beverly Hills and the hazy residential hills beyond. The walls
were collaged with photos, mostly black and white, all of them
featuring Pamela in the company of celebrities. Pamela being
smooched on the mouth by Madonna. Pam inserting herself between Paul Newman and Joanne Woodward. Pam matching
scowls with Oliver Stone, dippy faces with Macauley Culkin.

She motioned me onto one of the four couches, plumped herself down on the other end and kicked off her pumps. "You
didn't return my call," she said reproachfully.

"What call?"

"You didn't get my message? I rang you the second I heard
the news. I mean, my god, Lucy, you're one of my oldest and
dearest friends. I had to let you know I was *there* for you." She
began to massage her leggings-covered ankles. "I talked to some
sort of policeman who promised he'd give you the message, but
I should know you can't rely on those kind of people."

A soft, disembodied voice suddenly floated in the air: "Kathy
Bates's office on two."

"I don't have the dates yet," Pamela announced to the atmosphere. "Call back." Then she leaned forward to me, purple eyes

glittering. "I mean it, Lucy, you really are very special to me. And just between us two, what's the *real* story? There's got to be a lot to this that the press hasn't been told. Of course, anything you tell me will be strictly confidential."

Yeah, confidential to Liz Smith. I suddenly realized why I'd been granted an immediate audience: I had potential information to share. And information, in Pamela's biz, was currency. For a moment I was tempted to feed her some juicy fabrication, picturing Detective Shoe reading it tomorrow over the breakfast table, smoke coming out of her ears. But I wasn't nearly drunk enough for that. "Believe me, Pamela," I said, "whatever the cops don't tell the press, they certainly don't tell me. Don't forget, I'm still on the top-ten list of suspects."

She blinked rapidly. "Lucy, did you . . . you know . . . ?"

"Did I bump Julia off? No, I didn't. But thanks for thinking me capable of cold-blooded murder."

"Oh, but that's not . . . I mean, I didn't . . . Of all the people I know in this insane business, you are just about the most stable. Remember how in the eighties we used to talk about having it all? You've actually pulled it off. A career, a great kid, a husband who adores you . . . You're the envy of us all."

I hesitated. Maybe it was true. Maybe I *did* pretty much have it made and was just overreacting to whatever little bumps there were. Maybe I was crazy to even think of jeopardizing such an enviable situation. But wait a minute, I reminded myself—this was Pamela, the queen of the PR spin. She could make the Menendez family sound functional, if she put her mind to it. "The Prentices were also a very close family," I said dolorously. "Isn't Woody a client of yours?"

Her face darkened. "*Was* a client. He sacked us a month ago."

"Oh, yeah? How come?"

"He wanted to renegotiate our fees—in his favor, of course. I explained to him for about the hundredth time that he was getting a bargain for a star of his caliber, especially since half our efforts went to getting Julia coverage. Every time that woman ate lobster soufflé at some Democrat fund-raiser or smacked a tennis ball for cerebral palsy, she expected to see it in George Christy. I pulled in favors all over town to keep her name in print. And still every billing turned into a battle royal, down to the last nickel. The man is *cheap!*" Pamela's toes wriggled furiously in indignation at Woody's penny-pinching ways. "I heard he buried Julia in Boise. I'll bet you anything it was just to save himself the cost of a plot in Forest Lawn."

"Kirk on line one," susurrated the ghost voice. "Needs to speak to you ASAP."

"Five minutes!" Pamela snapped.

"Listen, Pamela," I said, "I need to ask you a favor." She turned a wary eye to me. "I'm trying to track down Tora Merrick and thought you might be able to help."

"Tora Merrick. There's a blast from the past." The well-greased wheels of her mind started spinning. "She and Julia were in something together once, weren't they? Does this have anything to do with the murder?"

"Probably not. I'm just trying to stick some pieces of Julia's past together to see if I can scrape up anything the cops might have missed. Of course, if I do ..." I let a tantalizing beat go by. "You'd be the first to know."

The bait was irresistible. She tapped a button on the red multiline phone beside her. "Cynthia, my love, check Celebrity Finder and get me a contact for Tora T-O-R-A Merrick." To me, she said, "Cynthia's only twenty-three. Tora's a little before her time. She's a bit before *our* time too, if you get right down to it."

Almost immediately, the disembodied Cynthia piped up, "No manager or agent listed for a Tora Merrick. The last confirmed address was the Betty Ford Clinic, September of 1993."

Pamela arched a brow. "Do some calling around, would you, sweets? Try Jack Gamby at Rogers and Cowan; he always seems to keep tabs on the has-beens. You know, frankly," she added to me, "I thought she was dead."

"That seems to be the popular opinion," I said.

"Well, if she's not, we'll find her. Our network is very comprehensive."

Here was a creepy concept: the Schwartzman-Pemmel network that nobody could evade, like the secret police of some pre-glasnost Iron Curtain country.

"Demi Moore on one."

Pamela snatched up the receiver and slammed it to her gold-studded ear. "Demi, my darling, this is ESP. I was just this moment thinking about you! What? Oh, yes, I'll hold for her."

I rose to my feet. "You're busy. I'll get out of your hair."

"I'll call when I've got something on Merrick. Kiss kiss."

I mouthed a sociable kiss kiss back.

THE ALCOHOLIC COBWEBS IN MY brain had dissipated sufficiently to let me trust myself back on the road. As I sped home, another idea popped into my mind: I hadn't heard from Justin since he'd left me on the phone to Kit, but now I had the perfect excuse to call *him*—to report to him the fruits of my day's investigative labor. I just wanted his perspective on it all, I assured myself. Nothing more. I switched on the radio. Kit, whose taste in pop music was as limited as his taste in movies was broad, had tuned it to a jingly oldies station. I found myself singing loudly along to Herman's Hermits, "I'm in for so-omethin' good," even bouncing to the beat as I turned into our cul-de-sac.

When the car behind me turned as well, I felt a brief spurt of panic. But it was not the filthy blue Taurus; it was a convertible, a silver Mercedes SEL, driven by the kind of honey-streaked blonde that seems to come as standard equipment with that kind of car. As I waited for my gates to chug open, she swept past me and into the driveway next door.

Justin had company.

I nosed the Beemer into the garage, then went on up to my room. Through the open windows drifted the faint strains of music—Al Green, that smooth-as-a-caress voice—coming from the pool house next door. This wasn't two-pals-hanging-out-together music. It definitely wasn't business-meeting music. It was, plainly and simply, fuck-me music. I felt a curious lurching in my stomach.

Morosely, I started to peel off my finery, thinking of how I'd started the day convinced that both Sandy and Justin were lusting after my body. Lucy Kellenborg Freers, femme fatale . . . it was really quite a laugh. I couldn't even keep my own husband interested. I tugged on some old gym wear, sweat pants that bagged in the seat and a shapeless T-shirt the color of prune juice, then yanked the clasp from my chignon and let my hair drop witchily around my face. The face that, according to Dr. Goodrow, cried out for a complete surgical overhaul. Pamela was right, I had no business trucking in glamour.

My Self-Pity Fest was cut short by someone ringing at the gate. I peered out to see a ratty white truck, the logo POOL PERFECT emblazoned in a watery blue script on its side. I'd totally forgotten—the police had granted permission to drain the scene of the crime, and I'd arranged for Conrad Kominsky, our pool-maintenance man, to do it this afternoon.

The pump motor was already churning by the time I reached the top terrace, and Conrad was scrubbing a slick greenish film from the top tiles. He was shirtless, as usual, the better to show off the bulgy pecs, delts and latissimus dorsi that had scored him the All Southern California body-building crown, light heavyweight division. His hair, chrome yellow and mowed in a bristling brush cut, looked Crayolaed on his head.

"Hi, Con!" I called. "Thanks for coming today."

"Hey, no problem. Guess you'll be glad to get back to normal, huh?"

Normal . . . At the moment, I seemed to have a better chance of attaining nirvana. I stepped closer, catching a nose-wrinkling whiff of Hawaiian Tropic coconut oil, Conrad's tanning aid of choice. "How've you been doing in competition lately? Won anything?"

He pulled a face. "A crappy fifth in Fresno last week. It's my pissing skinny thighs. Always been my weak point." He sighed. Then he stared moodily at the murky, leaf-clotted water gurgling steadily lower. "This kind of gives me the creeps. It's kind of like digging up somebody's grave."

"They removed the body," I said quickly. "It's not as if it's still down there."

We both gazed uncertainly for a moment at the roiling water, as if expecting Julia's blackened corpse to come shooting up at us, à la Sissy Spacek at the end of *Carrie.*

Next door, the whipped-cream music turned up a notch, accompanied by laughter—the kind of throaty, have-a-martini laughter that seems to go naturally with streaked-blond hair and silver convertibles.

"Hey, you know that dude living in Doc Pennislaw's pool house?" Conrad spoke up.

"Justin Caffrey," I said hollowly.

"Right. Well, it was with him that was the one time I met . . . you know . . ." He cast his eyes back down at the water.

"Julia Prentice? You met her with Justin?" He nodded gloomily. "When was that?"

"Shit, I don't know. Three, four weeks ago. I do the Pennislaws right after you. I was in the middle of skimming, which always takes me longer over there, 'cause they've got those avocado trees hanging right over the deep end. And Natalie, you know, the doc's wife, comes out of the main house with the two of them."

"Julia and Justin?"

"Right. Julia had fixed it up with Natalie that he could rent out the pool house. So, while Natalie's showing the dude around his new place, I went ahead and laid a business card on Julia. I happened to know she used Canyon Pools and they do a for-shit job. Overchlorinate, which is cool if you happen to like swimming in a tub of Clorox bleach." Conrad gave himself a little shake, like a terrier frisking off water. "When I heard she was killed in a pool, I'm like, 'Oh, shit, they'll find my card, and I'll be, like, a suspect.'"

I was only half listening. The majority of my brain was busy processing the fact that Justin had lied about how well he'd known Julia Prentice.

"You know, if I was you," Conrad continued, "I wouldn't leave this out in the sun. It's the kind of stuff that fades real quick." He nudged with his foot a green-and-pink-striped canvas cushion. It usually rested atop the built-in bench inside the Casita, but it now lay, as if it had been hurriedly tossed, just outside the casita door.

I stared at it, feeling now-familiar prickles rising at the back of my neck. Yesterday evening, I'd finally summoned the nerve to go into the casita and straighten things up; and in my muddled state, I might have taken the cushion off the bench and tossed it outside. But there'd have been no reason for me to do it.

And I was almost positive I hadn't.

11

I RETURNED THE CUSHION TO its place on the bench and took a careful look around the casita. Everything else seemed just as I'd left it. My imagination was running wild, I decided, conjuring up boogie men in every shadow.

I left Conrad to his ministrations and went back into the house, shutting myself up in Kit's den, the one room in which I couldn't hear the music from next door. Forget Justin, I told myself. A slick pretty boy who evidently couldn't be trusted to tell the truth. Concentrate on Julia. Think of the next step.

And the next step seemed obvious: I needed to exchange a few words with Mattie Ballard, former slut, present maternal paragon.

Her phone number proved to be listed in the Windermere School Directory. Actually, the ménage of Ballard and her action-film superstar husband, Tommy Farmer, merited an entire page of numbers. There was the Brentwood house (four numbers plus fax); the Malibu beach house (ditto); the compound in Bozeman, Montana; the condo in St. Barts; plus assorted car phones, cellular phones and pagers. Using eeny-meeny-miny-mo, I tried Malibu first and gave a spiel to a harried-sounding house-keeper: I was a Concerned Windermere Parent, worried that The School was Going Downhill. I wanted to meet with other Concerned Parents and plot a course of action.

Afterward, I picked up a designer pizza at Delucca's—fontina cheese, prosciutto and wilted arugula; as I sat nibbling at it and staring at *Wild Kingdom* with the sound off, Mattie herself called back. Of *course* she knew who I was, I had that *sweet* little girl in the fourth form, Cathy . . . Right, Chloe . . . Anyway, she (Mattie) just started a new film for TriStar, had *sworn* she wasn't going to take another job until she got pregnant again, but couldn't pass up a chance to costar with Sir Anthony Hopkins, he was *so* brilliant, which meant she had a five-thirty call, but she went jogging an hour before, and if I wanted to come run with her, we could talk then.

Jogging at four-thirty in the morning? I'd rather die.

"I'd love to," I said.

I'VE NEVER BEEN A MORNING person. When the clock radio clicks on at its customary seven A.M., burbling twenty-five-year-old rock and roll, my instinct is to hurl a pillow at it and burrow back for another couple of hours in the toasty hollow of sleep.

Nevertheless, at four-fifteen the following A.M., I was zipping north on the eerily deserted Pacific Coast Highway, blinking fat sleep grains from my eyes, the Pacific Ocean a faint silvery gleam on my left, the Malibu hills lumps of dark menace on my right. What the hell am I doing here, I groggily asked myself, at an hour when any sane person would be deep into rapid eye movements?

The private guard at the Malibu Colony seemed to wonder the same thing: he eyed me with as much squinting suspicion as if I'd had a stocking pulled over my face. He carefully jotted down the license number, make and model of my Cherokee, then revealed the way to Mattie Ballard's beach house, in a tone that implied: "I'm wise to you, lady. One slipup and it's curtains."

The Ballard-Farmer residence was one of those Colony houses

that look modestly shacklike on the outside, but inside open up to a couple of million dollars' worth of Pacific Ocean view. As I pulled up, all was silent, all was dark. Maybe I'd gotten the time wrong, I thought hopefully, opening my door.

A snapping, snarling German shepherd came hurtling toward me. I reshut the door fast and cowered in my seat. The dog pressed its drooling snout to the window, no doubt sizing me up for breakfast.

"*Nein,* Tulli! *Platz!*" Mattie Ballard materialized from the night. She grabbed the beast's collar and yanked him back. "*Platz!*"

The dog *platzed*—or at least settled back on its haunches with a few token snarls in my direction. Mattie tapped on my window. "It's okay, you can get out."

I timorously cracked open the door. "Are you sure?"

"Oh, absolutely. Tulli's a Schutzhund; it means attack dog in German. They're specially trained for personal protection. I had to get training too and learn the German commands. *Bleib!*" she snapped at Tulli, who was straining under her hold. "You're a little late." This reproach was to me, not the dog.

"It took a while to get past the gestapo checkpoint," I said. "I didn't know the right German commands."

Mattie smiled fleetingly. "Let's get started, okay? This is Lindy, my trainer."

Another shadow emerged from the dark, a small woman in running shorts, with ropy limbs and no discernible breasts. A cyclops beam of light seemed to emanate from the center of her forehead. I blinked, thinking that sleep deprivation was making me hallucinate: then I realized she was wearing a coal miner's headlamp.

Mattie, I now noticed, was carrying two more of these devices. She handed one to me, positioned hers on her head and switched on the little lamp. "So we can see where we're going," she explained. "I always run on the road, 'cause Lindy says running on the beach is a sure way to get tendinitis."

"The sand's got too much drag," declared the trainer.

"I'm not really much of a jogger," I confessed, donning my headlamp.

"Don't worry, I set a very slow pace. Ready?"

"Set, go," I mumbled.

Mattie took off with strong, even strides. Lindy, the trainer, kept smooth pace beside her, hollering on alternate beats, "Breathe, breathe!" Tulli, the attack dog, leaped and bounded ecstatically around them, like a frisky little lamb. I brought up the rear.

After five minutes, I was panting heavily, swearing to myself I'd get back in touch with my Wendy Shastremski and really stick with her this time, no matter how obnoxiously peppy she was in the morning.

After ten minutes, knives of agony were carving up my side. I began to fixate on the idea of a fatally burst appendix.

After twelve minutes, I sank in a quivering heap by the side of the road and dropped my gasping head between my knees, wondering again what the hell I was doing there. A has-been, third-rate actress got herself dispatched to the great shooting stage in the sky, and because she chose to do it in my swimming pool, my life seemed suddenly to have gone through the looking glass. I sat pondering this for twenty minutes until, with the first pale glimmer of dawn in the sky, Mattie, trainer and Schutzhund reappeared down the road. I leaped up and began to jog sprightly in the homeward direction.

Mattie effortlessly sprinted up beside me. "How far did you get?"

"About two miles," I lied.

She flashed me a pitying look: *Wimp!* then pumped on ahead. Gritting my teeth, I forced the rubberbands that had once been my legs to stay in motion the distance back. Wheezing, doubled over, I staggered up to the house.

A white stretch limousine, ghostlike in the dim gray light, sat idling in front, no doubt waiting to take Mattie to the set. Mattie, ignoring it, was fussing with Tulli's collar. Nice to be a star, I thought. You could keep a limo and driver cooling for as long as you like.

Then I gasped.

A man was stumbling toward us from the vicinity of the house. A dangerous-looking derelict. Unshaven. Balding. Bleary-eyed. Wearing what looked like prison-issue garb. I glanced at Tulli— now was the time for the attack hound to attack—but the dog began nuzzling the derelict as affectionately as if he were a human Milk-Bone. The limo driver bolted from the car; but instead of drawing a firearm, he smartly snapped open the door to the backseat.

"Morning, Mr. Farmer," he said, touching his cap.

The derelict grunted and lurched closer, metamorphosing into Tommy Farmer, action star, whose current price per picture was fifteen million bucks, plus gross-point participation. Tommy Farmer, sans hairpiece and shave. The San Quentin—escapee uniform was actually cotton pajamas, blue with white piping.

My feeling of having wandered through a looking glass was getting stronger by the minute.

"Bernice crapped on the bed again," Tommy announced.

Mattie stepped belligerently forward. Her tank top sagged, her light hair dripped in wet strings around her flushed, shiny face: she looked about as glamorous as a fishwife. "What do you want me to do about it? Tell Guadalupe to change the sheets."

"She's your fucking dog, *you* let her sleep on the bed, and I wake up with my feet in shit."

There followed a thirty-second ping-pong of "Do not," "Do too," topped with a round of "Fuck yous." With a final but pithy "Eat me," Tommy lumbered to the limo and crashed facedown onto the backseat.

"He gets so cranky when he's got a five-thirty call," Mattie said placidly. "Come on in."

We handed our miner's caps to the taciturn Lindy. I followed Mattie into the house, Tulli at our heels. Compared to the hushed streets, inside was pandemonium, voices laughing and talking in loud, rapid Spanish, footsteps pounding on stairs. A child shrieked, a dog barked, dishes clattered from some distant kitchen. A frail-looking East Indian houseman met us with huge fluffy white Pratesi towels. A Welsh corgi, presumably the defecating Bernice, padded up and sniffed appreciatively at Tulli's private parts.

Mattie led me into a family room. The decor scheme was Rummage-sale Baroque, every inch crammed with stuff, most of it expensive, none of it part of any overall design. Mattie cleared a space for herself on a Chippendale-ish couch, blotting her streaming face with the towel. The East Indian reappeared with lacquered tray and set it ceremoniously on a low table before her. On the tray was a heaping plate of steamed broccoli and a glass of something orangy-brown—a breakfast that made my own virtuous bran cereals and fresh OJ suddenly seem like Twinkies and Kool-Aid.

"For you, lady?" inquired the houseman.

"Coffee," I croaked.

Mattie's lips curled in a superior smile. "Sorry, there's no caffeine in this house."

"Rose hip tea," declared the houseman.

"Fine." I moved some French ormolu knickknacks off a Deco-ish love seat and, while Mattie dug into her broccoli, gazed out at the expanse of dawn-lit Pacific.

"Look, I know you don't really want to talk about The School." Mattie's voice came out muffled through a mouthful of green mash. "You want to talk about Julia, right?"

I sheepishly nodded. "Do you mind?"

"Me? Lordy, no. But Francine Palumbo called yesterday in a real snit. She practically ordered me not to say anything about Julia to anybody."

"So, why did you let me come?"

Mattie gave a chiming little laugh. "In the first place, you know Francine, right? She always makes a mountain out of a molehill. Mount *Ev*erest. And in the second place, if I'd ever done *any*thing Francine told me to do, I'd still be waiting tables on Melrose right now." She affected a waitressy voice. "We have some specials today, and I really recommend the mahimahi."

I grinned. "So, I take it you weren't thrilled with Francine as a manager."

"Sweet lord god! Look what she did with Julia's career—managed it right into nowhere."

"But was that all Francine's fault? I mean, let's face it. Julia wasn't exactly brimming with talent."

"She was the worst!" Mattie chortled. "Except for one thing. I think she could've made it in sitcoms. She did a guest shot on *Cheers* playing this nympho cousin of Kirstie Alley's, and she had this kind of cute sex scene with Ted Danson, and she wasn't too bad. You know those muggy faces she made?"

"Yeah," I nodded. "I do."

"Well, they kind of work in a sitcom. If she'd gone up for a series, who knows, she might've become another Murphy Brown. But her brilliant manager, Francine, kept pushing her for dramatic feature parts. Like she was really going to be heavy competition for Meryl Streep." Mattie gave a rather bitchy snicker.

The Indian man shuffled in with my rose hip tea. The cloying floral scent rising from the cup made my stomach turn. I managed a polite sip, then put it down.

"Julia ended up marrying a sitcom star," I said. "There's a kind of irony there."

Mattie took a glug of the orangy-brown drink and unceremoniously wiped the orangy-brown mustache off her lip with the back of her hand. "You want to hear the real irony? Even after Francine obliterated her career, Julia never stopped relying on her. I mean, if Julia's lipstick smeared, she'd call Francine for how to fix it. It was like Francine had some kind of mysterioso hold on her."

I mused on that a moment. "I wonder if Francine was the brains behind Julia's new social career."

"I don't get you."

"From what I've heard, Julia was angling hard to become the head of the Magic Wand Foundation. Francine could've been helping her strategize how to overthrow Summer Rossner."

"I wouldn't bet on it," Mattie snorted. "Francine Palumbo's got a few ambitions of her own. She'd never in a million years have crossed the Rossners just for Julia's sake. In fact, I don't even think she'd do it for her husband's sake." Mattie expelled a breathy little sigh. "Poor old Sandy. Francine's gonna stick with him for about eight seconds after he goes bust."

"Is Sandy going bust?"

Mattie's eyes, those celebrated green half-moons, regarded me coolly. "All indies go bust sooner or later."

There was a pattering of footsteps behind me. I turned to see a boy of about two and a half come scampering in, a strapping kid with Mattie's half-moon eyes and pale hair. A fat Mexican woman waddled quickly after him, catching him by the hand.

"There's my princy-pie!" Mattie cooed. "There's my precious lovey bunny!"

The boy threw off his nurse's hand and ran to her, scrambling up on her lap. Mattie yanked down one strap of her tank top. Out bobbled a pale breast. The boy took it in two hands and greedily clamped his mouth to the nipple.

Mattie smiled beatifically at me over her son's fair head. "You know, if you really want to see Francine kiss Summer's butt, you ought to come to the Magic Wand benefit. It's Saturday night. Or maybe Sunday. Tommy can't stand that kind of thing, but we'll have to show our faces."

AFTER LEAVING THE COLONY, I drove straight to the nearest open diner and poured two cups of black coffee down my throat while massaging my still-vibrating hamstrings. A couple of sun-kissed boogie boarders sat in the booth behind me discussing the morning's surf condition. Their consensus was it sucked.

The caffeine jump-started my brain. I replayed my conversation with Mattie, particularly the part about Julia's relationship with Francine. Maybe the hold Francine had on her wasn't really that mysterioso. Maybe it was something downright tangible. Like the knowledge of how Julia had acquired those interesting stripes on her derriere.

"Another refill, hon?" The waitress, whose name tag identified her as BENNY, stood poised with a glass pot. I shook my head, paid the check, adding a hefty tip, and wobbled out.

Attending the Magic Wand benefit wouldn't be a bad idea, I decided, climbing into my Jeep. I could ask Justin to come with me. A strictly platonic invitation, naturally. It would give me an opportunity to pump him for the truth about his past relationship with Julia.

So, assuring myself of the purity of my motivations, I pulled out onto the PCH, checking the rearview mirror.

It reflected back a dented headlight.

I glanced behind me. Definitely the blue Taurus, looking, if possible, even filthier than before, as if it had somehow found some rain to be left out in. So damned typical of Detective Teresa Shoe! Couldn't be bothered with such mundane matters as washing the car. Hell, no—she was far too busy divining the evil in the hearts of men.

And so smugly sure of herself, she didn't even suspect I was on to her: just puttered along two car lengths behind, brazenly changing lanes when I did.

Let her follow me, I decided, flooring the pedal. I intended to spend the rest of the day at my studio, working on my flying hedgehog. Let Madame Shoe sit parked in the asphalt lot, sweltering in the Culver City sun for a good nine or ten hours.

The idea of it, in fact, even cheered me up.

*   *   *

INSIDE MY STUDIO, I ADJUSTED the blinds to half-mast, neatly stacked my completed drawings, snapped Fleetwood Mac into the tape deck and, when I could find no other excuse to procrastinate, settled at my desk.

I'd reached a tricky part in the drawings. Amerinda, having crash-landed in the pig heaven of Happy Days Farm, dances a tango with a rakish sheepdog; but getting a dance to come out right in animation is always a problem. Each step has to be held for a certain pause: too long, and it looks like the characters' feet are landing in glue; not long enough, and they seem to be just walking around at weird and spastic angles.

After an hour of wrestling with it, I had two cartoon animals doing a kind of goose-step. Adolf Hedgehog and Heinrich Dog. "Damn!" I hissed and swept it all aside.

Then I took a fresh new sheet of drawing bond, and began to doodle. Barnyard animals—except, I began to realize, each was turning into a portrait of someone connected to Julia. The gabbling white goose was, unmistakably, Marsha Moss-Golson. An adorable, nibbly-toothed bunny could only be Mattie. The Palumbos emerged as equine: Sandy, a protuberant-eyed quarter horse; Francine, a sleek Shetland pony. The affable wolf lounging on the roof of a hen house was, of course, Justin. I finished the nanny, Audrey, as a gaunt moo-cow and Woody Prentice as a benevolently smiling old billy goat. But I'd left out Kit. I hesitated, charcoal pencil poised at paper. Puppy dog? Chicken? Snake?

Did he even belong in this picture?

My eyelids suddenly felt as heavy as cement. I let them fall shut, sank my head on my arms, and was fast asleep.

12

"SHE'S ALIVE AND KICKING AND making the world safe for dolphins!"

"Wha . . . ?" I mumbled. It took me several seconds to realize I was not still in the middle of my dream about inventing licorice ice cream, but sitting upright with a phone receiver at my ear. And I'd cricked my neck; it was sharply sore from my shoulder blade to my ear.

Pamela Pemmel's foghorn voice boomed on. "Tora Merrick, babycakes! It seems that reports of her demise were premature. She did not kick the bucket, as is widely assumed, but survives to this day under her real name, which is . . ." A pause, as Pamela checked her sources. "Janice Kovalarsky. Huh! No surprise she changed that! Anyway, it seems she got herself cleaned up and is now working with some animal-rights organization. Friends of Animals. Short and to the point."

"So where do I find her?" I asked eagerly.

"In the darkest wilds of the Hollywood Hills, at 1132 ½ Columbine Terrace—that's the address of their headquarters. Phone number 555–1112, area code 213. Hold a sec, will you, love?" Sudden dead air: Pamela Pemmel had the fastest hold button in the west. Then, presto, back again. "Now, remember our deal, Lucy. I show you mine, you show me yours. If you turn up anything juicy, I get to know."

"A deal," I agreed, "is a deal." I just didn't promise *when* she'd get to know.

NO MOONLIGHT BLUE TAURUS WAS in the asphalt court when I left my studio. No moonlight blue Taurus appeared behind me as I headed east. Maybe the indefatigable Detective Shoe had been called away to investigate another tasty murder. Maybe she'd slipped off on a doughnut run. Or maybe she'd received a flash of divine revelation that I really had nothing to do with the whole sordid mess, and had decided to leave me alone—though from what I recalled of her solid waistline, the doughnuts were the most likely explanation. Still, to find myself Taurus-free gave me a heady sense of relief, like being sprung from a particularly claustrophobic locked closet.

I bolted a chicken salad sandwich at a coffee shop that catered mostly to development types from the nearby Sony studios, then headed out on the trek to Hollywood.

In the maze of tortuous little streets and cul-de-sacs above Franklin in the Hollywood Hills, there was a Columbine Road, a Columbine Heights, a tiny Columbine Lane. A teensy, scarcely paved passage off the lane, scarcely wide enough for my Cherokee, proved to be Columbine Terrace. Number 1132½ was a wee English cottage, a yellow-painted Dutch door, the yard a riot of English garden flowers—hollyhocks, primroses and daisies. I followed the little crooked stone pathway to the door, wondering if Snow White or Rapunzel or, perhaps, the Wicked Witch of the West would answer my knock.

The door was partially open, which I considered an invitation to let myself in. The front room had been converted to an open-space office suggesting the type of organization that thrives on conviction rather than cash flow. Teetering stacks of metal filing cabinets. Wire baskets overflowing with paper. Metal desks occupied by people who were not exactly slaves to fashion. The walls were papered with heartrending posters of man's inhumanity to the animal kingdom: a wolf caught in a spring trap; the rotting carcass of an elephant slaughtered by ivory poachers. With my leather bag and suede sandals, and the chicken salad still digesting in my stomach, I felt creepily like a serial killer.

At the desk nearest me, a young guy in a dingy white shirt was engrossed on the phone, speaking in low, urgent tones about the condition of highland gorillas in the L.A. Zoo. I presented myself instead to his neighbor, a plumpish, middle-aged lady with silver-threaded dark hair.

"Excuse me," I said. "I'm looking for Janice Kovalarsky."

"You've found her." I gaped rudely at her. Her brown eyes twinkled from behind plastic-framed bifocals. "Not what you were expecting, am I? Don't worry, a lot of people have the same reaction. But even starlets grow old. We don't stay sex symbols forever."

"But you look so much better than I expected," I blurted. "I mean, since the last movie I saw you in . . ." She continued to twinkle at me, and I flushed. "I'm sorry, I'm being incredibly rude. My name's Lucy Freers. Julia Prentice was murdered in my backyard, and I wanted to talk to you because I'm trying to find out as much as I can about her."

"Yes, I know who you are. Naturally, I've followed Julia's murder closely. For the first couple of days, I was glued to the TV. And anyway, Francine Palumbo called to say you were asking Sandy about me, and that I'd probably be hearing from you."

"Francine!" This was so startling, I nearly shouted the name. "You mean she knew where you were?"

"Well, obviously."

"Does Sandy know too?"

"I suppose so," she shrugged.

Yet wanted me to think you were dead or disappeared. "By any chance," I inquired, "did Francine ask you not to speak to me?"

Tora, or Janice, as I'd have to think of her now, gave a forthright laugh. "Francine *ordered* me to keep my trap shut. But one thing I've learned in life is there's never any reason to be afraid of the truth." Her phone jangled. "Christmas! It never stops. Sonia," she called to a woman at an adjoining desk, "cover my calls a sec? I'm going to take a break." To me, she said, "We can talk in the kitchen. I could use a munchie. I've been at it straight since eight A.M. So much to do, it's overwhelming."

She rose, a very well-padded figure in a nondescript blouse and skirt. It was hard to believe that this was the body that had, back in 1967, inspired a million wet dreams.

I followed her into a Hansel and Gretel kitchen, with doll-sized appliances; there was an old enameled stove that looked as if it might well have crisped a few wayward children.

"Had lunch yet?" Janice asked, rummaging in the minifridge. From its tiny recesses she managed to scavenge an astonishing quantity of food: bagels and cream cheese, a carton of buttermilk, bags of fresh fruit and raw vegetable sticks, jars of olives and pickles and half a frozen Sara Lee cheesecake. The entire feast she set on a table already occupied by a puddle of tortoiseshell fur. "Dig in," she cheerfully exhorted, and began smearing a bagel liberally with cream cheese.

To atone for my carnivorous ways, I selected a nectarine. "I had a tough time finding you," I said. "After *The Delano Reunion*, you seemed to disappear."

She swallowed a mouthful of bagel and reached for a dill pickle. "Your problem was you were looking for Tora Merrick. Most people think she's dead. And Tora Merrick *is* dead. It's only by a gift of god that I'm not as well. I was sure doing my blessed best to kill myself."

"With drugs," I said bluntly.

"Yes, indeed, with drugs. Do you have any idea how much

cocaine I was once stuffing up my nose?" I shook my head. "At my peak, which was during the good old *Delano* days, I had a thousand-dollar-a-day habit."

I choked on a bite of nectarine. "How did you get that kind of money?"

"I took calls," she said flatly.

"Calls?" I had the baffling image of her done up like Lily Tomlin as Josephine the phone operator: "Number, puh-leeze." Then it dawned on me: "You mean like in *call girl*."

"Sounds almost glamorous, doesn't it? You think of a girl in a black mink coat calling on some suave gentleman in a penthouse. Champagne on ice. Tony Bennett on the stereo. Satin sheets. Let me tell you, it wasn't glamorous. It wasn't glamorous at all. It was . . ." She paused, picked out a blue-black plum and took a bite; a tiny rivulet of black juice ran like blood from the corner of her mouth. "You know why I work here, for the animals? It's because I know what it's like to be treated like a piece of meat. At least what I was doing to myself, I *chose* to do. These poor creatures have no choice."

"Could you actually make a thousand dollars a day?" I pursued.

"More than that. You get some sweaty little man from Denver or Tel Aviv who's raked in millions in real estate or plumbing widgets or whatever, and you give him a chance to go home and brag to his buddies he slept with Tora Merrick. *The* Tora Merrick. What do you think he'll pay for that? The problem was, by the time of *Delano*, I'd started to let myself go." She chuckled lightly. "That's the understatement of the year. I looked like fright night. The fellows suddenly became very reluctant to part with the big bucks. Some of them didn't even believe I was who I said."

"So you could no longer pay for your addiction."

"Oh, I wasn't through yet. If I couldn't do straight calls, I could do specialties."

"Specialties?"

"You know. Fantasy stuff. Johns who wanted to act like puppy dogs, roll naked at my feet, get their faces pushed in dog food. Or the ones that got off on being worms—they'd squirm around on the floor while I'd tell them what filthy vermin they were and pretend to squash them under my heel."

I leaned a little forward. This was fascinating in an appalling sort of way.

Janice finished off the plum, sucking the last morsel of flesh from the pit, then started on a stalk of celery. "My biggest thing was age play. Mommy-baby. I'd put the john in a diaper, stick a bottle in his mouth and lay his head in my lap while I talked baby talk to him. Or I'd make him do little dances, or sit in a corner in a kiddie chair. And when he wet his diaper, he'd have to be spanked. I used a hairbrush." She smiled again. "A Mason-Pearson. I found it gave me the best grip."

"You mean there are really a lot of men who want to do this stuff?" I marveled.

"More than you can imagine. These Hollywood moguls, they spend all day long giving orders. Power, power, power. But deep inside, they feel like bawling little infants."

An idea was taking form in my mind: a connection with the woman who'd lately been boosting the price of Pacific Bell shares with all her frantic phoning around. "By any chance," I said, "did Francine have anything to do with this?"

"Francine Latch was my manager," Janice said evenly, "in *both* my careers."

I drew a sharp breath. "So she arranged all these . . . dates for you."

"Not all of them. There was always word-of-mouth. Some of the johns would call me directly, which was fine and dandy with me—I didn't have to give Francine her cut. But many of them came through her. When it comes to money, Francie is extremely enterprising. She'll do almost anything to get it."

My mind was racing. "And was Julia into this too?"

"Not as a general practice."

"You mean she was kind of a pinch hitter?"

"Funny way to put it, but I guess that describes it. Listen," Janice said with sudden sharpness. "Here's my advice. Don't get involved in any of this. I don't know much about your life, but from what I could see of it, it looks like a pretty nice one. The sort of stuff we were into, Julia and Francine and me, it was like a rotting disease. My advice to you is don't come anywhere near it."

"Thanks," I said, "but for one thing, my life isn't as storybook as it might look. And even if it was, it got pretty much rearranged the minute Julia Prentice got knocked off on my property." I gave a wry smile. "So you don't have to worry about contaminating me or anything. I'm already up to my neck in it."

Janice twisted open a jar of Laura Scudder's all-natural peanut butter, smooth-style, and began to spoon heaping tablespoons of it into her mouth. "Okay, then," she said. "There was one thing that happened during the *Delano* shoot. About ten days into it, out there in that broiling little town. Francine came to me, all excited. She'd been contacted by a man—she called him Mr. Pete. He was willing to pay five thousand dollars for a single night. But he had a special request. He was into pain."

"Needed a good whacking with the hairbrush?"

"Not *receiving* pain. He was into inflicting it. Real S and M, and he was the *S*."

A sadist. Things must have been *really* hot out there in that desert. "So you turned it down."

"I did not. Hey, I was desperate. I owed money all over town—every dealer I knew was threatening to cut me off or, worse, hurt me if I didn't pay up. This was five grand, and the john, this Mr. Pete, promised there'd be no permanent mutilation."

"My god!" I breathed.

"Disgusting, isn't it? It seems like a terrible dream to me now."

"So what happened?"

"The night before this lovely date was supposed to happen, one of the grips turned me on to a new type of cocaine. It was called crack; you smoked it rather than snorted it. It was heaven—and then it was hell. I guess I got violent, went out of control. All I remember is Sandy Palumbo and the first AD dragging me into a trailer and locking me in. I was totally out of commission the next day."

"So Francine had to round up a new playmate for Mr. Pete."

Janice nodded. "She tried Mattie Ballard and Mattie spat in her face. Even then, Mattie knew what she had, how far she was going. She knew damned well she didn't have to make it by that route."

"At which point Francine recruited Julia?"

"Exactly. Julia realized her career was fizzling, and, having a very practical head on her shoulders, she was looking to accumulate a nest egg."

The tortoiseshell puddle stirred, then morphed into the shape of a crouching obese cat. It sniffed the cream cheese, then began greedily lapping. "Bad Milady," Janice said in an indulgent voice.

"You were lucky you didn't keep that date," I said. "It seems that Mr. Pete went back on his word."

"What do you mean?"

"About no permanent mutilation. I've got reason to believe he left Julia with some nasty scars."

"Oh, that." Janice gestured airily. "That was Julia's own doing. You see, she liked it."

"Liked what?"

"The pain. She had a taste for being hurt."

I recoiled.

Janice began attacking the Sara Lee. "She was what's known in the trade as a greedy sub—a submissive who keeps wanting to step up the pain factor, going beyond what's safe. She kept on seeing this Mr. Pete, even after she married Woody, and she let what they did get out of hand."

"How do you know?" I asked.

"I saw Julia about two and a half years ago. I'd hit rock bottom. Been on a binge that was impressive even for me. I ended up falling, or maybe being pushed, down three flights of stairs in some West Hollywood dive, and breaking my arm. Somebody dumped me at the Cedars emergency room. I sat waiting for hours while dying people were wheeled by. There was a kid with a knife in his eye. A woman shot with an assault gun, screaming and screaming. And then, around one in the morning, who should show up but Julia. She looked like she'd been in a prize fight, she was so beaten up."

"Mr. Pete?"

"Exactly. She had bruises on her face and arms. And blood on the seat of her pants. She swore it was the last time she was going to let it happen. But you know, what scared her was not so much the possibility of getting really hurt, but of it being found out and ruining all her future plans."

I could understand this. It would be hard to keep up the image of the Holy Family of Hollywood if it became known that the Madonna had a penchant for being slapped and whipped. "Where was Woody?"

"I asked her that. She gave me a truly terrified look and said, 'Aspen.' He was at their ski place in Aspen."

"So then she had to hide the scars from him till she could get them surgically removed," I said. "Luckily for Julia, they kept separate bedrooms."

"I don't know how she managed to hide it from Woody. If she even did."

"Did you ever talk about any of this to her again?"

"I never had the chance. I tried getting in touch once or twice, but Mrs. Woody Prentice would have none of that. A coked-out has-been like me had no place in her social schemes." Janice scarfed down the last of the cheesecake, scraping the residue off the sides of the tin with her fork. "So that's the whole sordid little story. And now poor Julia's in her grave."

"And you're here," I said. Then added tentatively, "How did you finally manage to get clean?"

For a moment I thought I'd overstepped my bounds. Her face closed up, her shoulders hunched, as if she were trying to absent herself from the very room. But then she reached out and gently stroked the cat's electric fur. "My third time in rehab was the charm. And then I found my little niche with this group, working for the poor animals. Frankly," she said, "it gave me a reason to go on living."

IT HAD BEEN A DISQUIETING meeting—that comfy-looking woman chatting on so matter-of-factly about drug debauches and kinky sex for hire, all the while stuffing herself with strictly vegetarian snacks.

I drove at random after leaving her, getting thoroughly tangled in the twisty, winding streets beneath the Hollywood sign. Stumbled at last onto Cahuenga, where, just north of the intersection with Vine, squatted a lurid purple bunker of a building—which, as I happened to know, was the renowned sex emporium called the Pleasure Trove, where Julia Prentice had, once upon a time, been a highly valued customer.

The *reason* I happened to know it was that for Kit's thirty-sixth birthday, I had presented him with the following items: a laser-disc copy of *Singin' in the Rain*, Laker's tickets four rows directly above Jack Nicholson's, and a pair of ruby-red fringed crotchless panties—the last of which I'd purchased at the Pleasure Trove.

They had been an enormous success, those crotchless panties, I recalled, turning into the building's parking lot. As soon as Kit opened the black foil-wrapped package, he suggested I slip them on, and we'd had wild teenager sex right there and then on the living-room rug; after which we popped a bottle of Veuve Clicquot, and then Kit, hoisting me over his shoulder, caveman-style, carried me up to the bedroom, where we went at it for another long and inventive round, and never made it to our dinner reservation at Röckenwagner.

That was the last time our sex life came anywhere near to

inspiring angelic hallelujahs. Now and then, I still came across the panties in the back of my lingerie drawer. But I had never gotten around to giving them another outing.

Big mistake.

INSIDE THE GARISHLY PINK-LIT shop, I was struck, just as I had been three years ago, by how wholesome the clientele appeared. Maybe at three in the morning the place filled up with slavering degenerates in suspiciously stained raincoats; but at the moment, the handful of shoppers could've passed for an offshoot of the Davenport, Iowa, PTA—with the possible exception of the two clean-cut guys in flannel shirts who were sporadically tongue-kissing.

I went up to the nearest register, manned by a plump Asian boy engrossed in a computer-science textbook.

"Excuse me," I said in my most ladylike tones. "Could you tell me where I could find the S and M section?"

"All the way back, behind the lubricants." His eyes never shifted from the textbook page.

I wound my way back through racks of rubber and leather goods, Naughty Nanette outfits, dildos crowded on shelves like stalagmites in a cave. In the farthest recesses of the shop, where even the lighting was dimmer, was a wall lined with locked glass cases. Another lower display case ran perpendicular to it.

"Are you looking for anything in particular?" Behind the lower counter, a Bambi-eyed, bald-headed young man surged toward me. He had a pierced tongue, multipierced ears and nostrils and, through some enigma of engineering, an ebony stud fastened to his forehead.

"I'm just browsing," I said.

"Certainly." If my own appearance surprised him, he gave no indication. I suppose he figured I was one of those straight-looking people with a rich inner fantasy life.

I turned to the wall cabinets, not really sure *what* I was looking for. But since Julia was into this stuff and I wanted to learn all I could about Julia, it seemed worth checking out.

I began my survey with the display of whips: birch, bullwhip, cat-o'-nine-tails, with a shopper's choice of silk or rubber tails. Which, I wondered briefly, had Julia favored? Directly beneath the lashes, a nice selection of leather gags and blindfolds. There was a leather hood, medieval executioner–style, little zipper at the mouth. Handcuffs and ankle cuffs for every body size. The adjoining case featured harnesses, both full body and genital, three rings or five. As I was examining these, trying to determine exactly what you *did*, anatomically speaking, with the rings, the Pierced Kid popped up behind me. "If you're into restraint," he advised, "we do carry a straitjacket. But it's pretty expensive, and to tell you the honest truth, Saran Wrap works just as well."

"Oh, really?" I said. "That's handy to know."

"Our hospital restraints are reasonably priced, though, and they can be used in many combinations—wrist-to-ankle, ankle-to-ankle, wrist-to-thighs."

"Interesting," I murmured.

I moved on to the next tier of shelves. Collars, in leather and steel, some spiked, some studded. Paddles—a cute little leather one called The Devil's Hand. A pair of surgical forceps for $39.95. "What's this for?" I asked, pointing to a contraption called a spreader bar.

"That? It forces your legs to stay separated. Very useful. We sell a lot of them."

"Ah." I was beginning to feel a tad squeamish. Quickly, I turned to the low case, which featured an assortment of clamps and clips. They came in pairs connected with lightweight chains and sported catchy little names like Baby and The Dominator and Sheer Delight. "Quite a variety," I remarked.

"Yes, I think we carry the largest selection of nipple clamps around. The Boss is very popular." He removed a largish pair that featured tiny screws through the clamps. "Custom quality. And you see, with the screws you can adjust the tension."

I took it and experimentally pinched the skin of my forearm. "Ow!" I squealed. It hurt.

It was sup*pos*ed to hurt, I reminded myself, shoving the device back across the counter.

That was exactly the point.

13

"IT CAME AS A TOTAL surprise. Kiki's agent talked her into going with the pubic hair." Valerie Jane selected a cold asparagus from her paper plate, picking it up in the Continental manner, with her fingers, and crisply bit off the tiny Christmas tree head. "He figured," she went on, "that if it could work for Sharon Stone, why not Kiki Wales? There was only one condition: Kiki's snatch had to be dyed to match the color of the hair on her head. I mean, god forbid the world should suspect she wasn't a natural redhead." Valerie let out a deep peal of laughter. "I think a henna rinse was the eventual product of choice."

We were lunching *en plein air* at the Brentwood Country Mart, a medley of roasted vegetables for Valerie, a plate of rather soggy tabouli and Moroccan chicken for me. I had returned my borrowed finery to Valerie with more than a little relief, and was back in more familiar clothes, white duck pants and a vintage Hawaiian shirt.

"So, now tell me," she said, working on a charred red pepper, "how did the outfit go over?"

"Like a charm. The excellent Dr. Goodrow was very impressed. That is, until my skirt hem came tumbling down."

Valerie Jane paused in mid-bite. "It didn't!"

"It did. His jaw nearly fell to his knees. I had to beat it fast, before he sicced his security on me."

"Lord, I'm sorry, Luce. I'll have to tell James to change our brand of masking tape."

"Lucky I already got the information I was after. He *did* remove some scars from Julia's butt—or at least smoothed them out so they were almost invisible." I squooshed the tabouli around on my plate, a useless attempt to make it more appetizing. "By the way, guess who I talked to yesterday?" Valerie looked up expectantly. "Tora Merrick. Or, I should say, Janice Kovalarsky."

"No shit? Tora! Someone told me she picked herself up from death's door and rejoined the ranks of the living. What did she have to say?"

"Some pretty juicy stuff, actually. Do you have any idea just what was going on behind the scenes of the *Delano* shoot?" I filled Valerie in on the Francine-Tora-Julia shenanigans, the shadowy Mr. Pete and Julia's evident fondness for pain, the more the merrier. It was impossible to shock Valerie Jane, but she did look gratifyingly impressed.

"*¡Dios mío!*" she whistled. "All that carrying on and I never suspected a thing. I was such a naïve little creature back then. Though, to tell you the truth, it was so hideously hot in that ghastly little town, it was impossible to imagine anyone ever wanting to have sex anywhere in the world."

"If you call that sex." I felt again the sharp bite of the nipple clamp on the skin of my arm and shuddered.

"So you think it might have been this Mr. Pete who did in Julia?"

"I don't know. It's a theory. Let's say that after Julia decides she's had enough of the S and M thing, she calls it quits, but Mr. Pete won't let go. Say he becomes obsessed, starts following her, watching her house. That might explain how he could've shown up in my backyard without having been phoned. And then, finding Julia alone, he rapes her and then kills her."

"Except," Valerie said, "didn't the police rule out rape? No evidence of forced entry, if I remember right."

"Well, okay, maybe she gave him a freebie for old time's sake—but then, when she tries to make him leave, he becomes enraged, bashes her head with the nearest handy blunt object and dumps her in the pool."

"Mmm . . . but this guy's a sadist, remember? So even if they'd had consensual sex, wouldn't he have left a few trademarks, a few good bruises or welts or teeth marks?"

I gave an exasperated sigh. My theory was rapidly being shredded to bits.

"I'm worried about you, Lucy." Valerie's black eyes fixed intently on me; her tone was suddenly no-nonsense. "There's some asshole running around out there who's definitely dangerous and maybe even deranged. He's already killed once. If you keep poking around in things, he might damned well decide to do it again."

"Who's to say it's a *he*? The actual killer could be a she. My good pal Detective Shoe seems to think Julia was holding a regular orgy in my backyard. Taking on all comers."

"Be serious!" Valerie snapped. "You could get yourself in real trouble."

I became serious. "If it's any reassurance to you, I've come to a dead end. The only person left for me to talk to is Francine, and she not only won't take my calls, she's tried to put a gag on everybody else."

"Good, then. You're calling it quits."

"At least until Sunday night."

Valerie narrowed her eyes warily at me. "What's Sunday night?" she asked.

"There's a benefit for the Magic Wand Foundation," I explained. "A lot of the featured players in this thing will be there. The Palumbos, the Rossners, Mattie and Tom Farmer . . . I thought it might be interesting to watch them all in action. Summer Rossner's assistant is holding a pair of tickets for me."

"Mmph," Valerie said. She removed a cigar from an embossed red leather case, lit it with a silver lighter and drew on it langorously—the only woman I knew who could get away with this without looking like David Letterman in drag. "I guess nothing much can happen at one of those shindigs," she mused, blowing out a fragrant stream of smoke. "Too many photographers."

"So I've got your permission to go?" I asked caustically.

"Mmm. But I still don't like the idea of you all alone in that house. Stay at my place—you'll have it all to yourself. Jackie's coming to town tonight. She takes a suite at the Beverly Wilshire and naturally I'll be with her."

"Jackie?"

"Jacqueline DePres is my lover," Valerie said simply. "I thought you knew."

So the rumors had been true. "I had heard some talk," I admitted. "How long have you been together?"

She smiled in a voluptuously pleased way. "Almost five years. But it's only recently we've come out."

"Are you faithful to each other?" I suddenly blurted. Then added awkwardly, "That's a personal question, I know."

"Absolutely, we're faithful to each other," she said. "In all the ways that count."

"I mean physically. After all, you spend long periods of time away from each other."

"Just like you and Kit." She leaned merrily closer to me. "Lucy, are you having an affair? Is that what you're getting at?"

I shook my head. "No, I'm not. But I've considered it. I just found out that Kit had an affair once. Or at least once that he admits to."

"So you figure what's good for the goose is good for the gander? Or is it something you've really wanted to do, and knowing about Kit now gives you permission?"

I squirmed a bit at this idea. "It doesn't matter anyway. I had a little flirtation, but it turned out the guy wasn't particularly interested in me."

"Thereby saving you from yourself. How convenient." I glared at her. Valerie coolly stubbed out the cigar, then tilted her head in a contemplative posture. "To answer your question, I don't know if Jackie sleeps with other women or not. Or other men— she's perfectly capable of that. I don't ask and she doesn't tell. But yes, I'm completely faithful to her. You have to remember," she added matter-of-factly, "she's the only family I've got."

AFTER PARTING FROM VALERIE JANE, I wandered into the indoor market and cruised the displays of fancy produce. A great wave of loneliness sloshed through me. I thought of the way Valerie had glowed when merely pronouncing her lover's name and envied her her romantic tryst, while my evening plans consisted of dinner for one. What had happened to all those people who, when I was fresh tabloid sensation, had been insisting we *must* get together? Why hadn't I made some firm dates?

Morosely, I gravitated to a pyramid of fat, red tomatoes and began to fill a plastic bag. From the corner of my eye, I spied Oliver Latch-Palumbo come sidling around a bin of avocados. I scrunched down, hoping the tomatoes would screen me. But it was too late, he'd already fixed me in his sights. He made his customary beeline to me.

"Are you gonna eat those?" he asked scornfully.

"Evidently," I said. With deliberate motion, I continued to fill up my bag.

"If you do, you're gonna get diarrhea. They come from Mexico and they don't give a crap about germs down there." Ollie's look *du jour* was South-Central gangsta: baggy pants, like an old-time vaudeville comedian's, basketball sneakers, Raiders cap turned back-to-front. The residue of Chloe's shiner was concealed by yet another pair of three-hundred-dollar shades. Too bad I thought—I'd have loved to have seen it.

As if divining my last thought, he said, "If my nose had been broken, I could've sued you guys and taken your house and cars and everything."

"Lucky, then, it wasn't broken," I lied.

He reached for a tomato from the display, jammed his thumb Jack Horner-like into it, then placed it back on the pyramid.

"Don't do that, Oliver," I said.

"*I* wanted to sue you anyway, but Sandy said no. Sandy's got no balls." Oliver selected another tomato and stuck in his thumb.

"I said cut it out!" I yanked his spindly arm so hard he went "*woof!*" and plucked the mutilated tomato off his finger.

"Leave my son alone!" boomed a female voice.

Francine Palumbo was barreling toward me. At first I thought it was maternal fury that accounted for her frazzled appearance; but as she came closer, I caught a sharp waft of Scotch, and realized she was drunk. Reeling, staggering drunk. Her yellow hair, usually a sleek, perfect bell, was ratted into a kind of peak on her head, making her look like Tweety Bird. Her lipstick was smeared, and a largish raspberry-colored stain, roughly in the shape of New Jersey, defiled the lapel of her ecru linen jacket.

She clutched Oliver to her body, protecting him, no doubt, from further violence at the hands of one of the bloodthirsty Freers. "Don' you dare touch him!" she slurred.

"Are you okay, Francine?" I asked stupidly.

"M'I okay? That's a sick joke, right? You go sneaking around behind my back, snooping into my affairs and, la-di-da, you wanna know if I'm okay. Well, screw you, Lucy. Go screw yourself good!" Francine usually spoke in a genteelly modulated contralto, but the booze had given her voice carrying power—people as far back as the fresh-baked-pie counter were craning their heads to observe us.

I lowered my own tone to a whisper. "Believe me, Francine, I wasn't intending to snoop into your affairs."

"Like hell. Like friggin' hell! Doncha think Sandy told me what you're up to? Just happen to be looking for Tora Merrick. Huh, that's a good one! Well, lemme tell you, Tora's cracked.

Totally 'round the bend. You can't believe a goddamn thing she says."

"I've already seen Tora. I thought she was extremely lucid."

Oliver tried to wriggle out of his mother's grasp; she restrained him in a sort of standing half nelson. Remarkably, her voice ascended to an even louder pitch. "What gives you the right to judge me?" she bellowed. "You dunno what I went through. You have no idea what my life was like back then. It was hell, sheer fucking hell! My first husband, the fucking bastard, he battered me. I was a battered wife! He threw me against a wall and shattered my collarbone. One time he punched me in the neck. Bruises! You shoulda seen the bruises. I hadda wear scarves for *weeks*."

People were starting to edge interestedly closer. An old lady set down her selection of Japanese eggplants to give us her full attention. Several teenage boys in jammers grinned and nudged each other. A clerk paused while stacking tangelos to listen.

Oblivious to her swelling audience, Francine ranted on, "When I got pregnant, that man, that Patrick Latch, he dumped me cold. This child . . ." She gave Oliver a Heimlich-maneuver hug. He went *"woof!"* again. "It's a *mira*cle he was even born. I almost lost him. The doctors said for sure I was gonna lose him. They had to *sew* my cervix closed. I hadda lie flat on my back in bed for seven entire months. No one even came to *visi*t!"

The Miracle Child sharply elbowed his mother in the ribs and broke free; but Francine was now far too wrapped up in her tirade to notice. "That bastard Patrick Latch left me with thousands of dollars in debt. Thousands! The bills kept coming and coming, he had twelve credit cards all in my name, and he spent them all to the limit. The IRS was *per*secuting me, like I was a master criminal, they said they could take my child away, they could put me in *pri*son! They were gonna confiscate everything I owned. I was gonna end up beggin' out on the street like some friggin' homeless bag lady!"

"Let's get some coffee, Francine," I pleaded. "Come on outside, we'll sit down."

To my astonishment, Francine did just that—stepping forward, she wobbled a bit on her Bruno Magli stiletto heels; then, as if the bones in her legs had suddenly liquefied, she oozed slowly down against the produce stall into an inelegant sitting position. The tangelo clerk rushed forward, grabbed one of her arms. I took the other, and together we hauled her back to her feet. Our assistance seemed to set her in a fighting mood; she belligerently smacked us away. "Get 'way from me, I'm go'n home," she hollered. "Ollie! C'mon, Ollie, go'n home."

"You can't drive," I said firmly.

"Yeah, I can. Betcha I can." She began to ransack her enormous straw bag in search of her keys.

"You're not going to drive like this, you're coming with me. I'll take you home. Oliver!" I said sharply. "Let's go."

I must have sounded like I meant business: mother and son filed obediently behind me. I marched them double-time to the parking lot. Francine clambered into the front seat of my Cherokee, Oliver sullenly insinuated himself into the back. I got in, started the motor.

"It smells like puke back here," declared Ollie.

I swiveled violently in my seat. "One more word out of you, you rotten little shit, and you'll be out of this car and walking so fast you'll think you're dreaming! You got that, buster?"

Oliver's plummy little mouth opened and closed several times. He glanced at his mother for reinforcement, but Francine had lapsed into a semistupor, staring with glazed eyes out the windshield. Finding himself friendless, he settled into stunned silence.

"Excellent," I declared and hit the gas.

THE ADDITION OF A NEW country kitchen to the Palumbos' already sprawling Holmby Hills mansion had been chronicled

half a year ago in *House Beautiful.* It was a vasty space on which
Francine had spared no expense, from the Tuscan limestone tiles
to the Gaggenau restaurant-quality stove; nor, according to the
copy, had she skimped on her time—two months alone devoted
to searching out the perfect French Empire–period chopping
block. "The kitchen is the family room of the nineties," Francine
had been gushingly quoted. "We do most of our living and entertaining in our kitchen, because it just naturally fits our relaxed
and informal lifestyle." This *mot* was accompanied by a hilarious
photo of Francine, her Donna Karan handkerchief-linen sleeves
rolled to the elbow, kneading bread dough on a marble slab.
Martha Stewart Palumbo. Another shot featured all three—Francine, Sandy and Oliver—lounging around the reclaimed brick
fireplace, looking almost loonily relaxed, as if someone had
slipped Prozac into their cocoa.

Just your typical *Leave It to Beaver* family, the layout seemed
to imply.

One that just happened to live on a million bucks a year.

It was with some difficulty that I managed to steer Francine
out of my car and into this wondrous Family Room of the Nineties, pouring her onto a ladderback chair at her nineteenth-cen-
tury Portuguese refectory table. An elderly Latina woman
materialized from nowhere and began wordlessly grinding coffee
beans—evidently this wasn't the first time Francine had come
home plastered. Oliver slunk out the back door, presumably to
hunt up some small creatures to torture.

I took a chair beside Francine, waited till she had taken a sip
of black coffee. "Francine," I said, "I need to ask you
something."

Her bleary face turned to me.

"Do you know if Julia was having an affair with someone?"

"Julia?" she muttered, as if the name rang a bell, but a rather
distant one. Her eyes darted around the room, then came to rest
on a package of Stoned Wheat Thins lying open on a far counter.

"Yeah, Julia. Remember," I prompted, "she's dead, someone

killed her. I think it might have been someone she was having an affair with."

"She had lots of 'em."

"Affairs?"

"Hadda be young. Old guys' bodies gave her the creeps."

"Old guys like Woody, you mean?"

Francine tried to laugh, but it came out a hiccup. Then she began to hiccup uncontrollably, a stuttering cascade that, to my alarm, threatened to go on indefinitely. After a full minute, it stopped as suddenly as it had begun. She gave herself a little shake and, as if for ballast, reattached her sights on the wheat thins box.

"Listen, Francine," I said gently. "I don't blame you for anything you've done, I swear."

"Like hell," she muttered. "You, Miss Goody Two-shoes."

Me, Miss Goody Two-shoes? "What do you mean?"

"Bet you never done anything wrong your entire life. Too much a goody-goody."

"I am not."

"Are too!"

It occurred to me that arguing with someone as sublimely shit-faced as Francine was bound to be futile. "Believe me, Francine," I said evenly, "I've done plenty of things I'm not proud of."

"Huh! Like what?"

Like, for starters, entertaining the notion of running off with your husband just to avoid the problems with my own.

I thought it best to keep away from the whole messy present. She had spilled her past to me. I might as well return the favor. "Okay," I began, "there was the time right after I got out of film school. I went completely nuts. I had no idea what I wanted to do or where I was going. I broke up with Kit and started sleeping with every guy in sight. . . . They could be drooling, they could have bad breath, they could be homicidal maniacs, I wasn't picky. I was your basic pin cushion. I got crabs. I got a fungus."

Francine was gazing at me with what I could interpret only as new respect. Encouraged, I went on, "Once I slept with this fat German guy I picked up outside Bendel's on Fifty-seventh Street just because he said he was a friend of Wim Wenders and could get me an introduction. He was the one who gave me crabs. It turned out he was really a salesman for some kind of industrial refrigerant. He didn't even *know* Wim Wenders."

Francine's body jerked in a hiccup-laugh.

"So, you see, I've got no right to judge you or anybody," I summed up piously. "And believe me, I don't." I let that sink in a moment. "But there's one more thing I need to ask you. The man, Mr. Pete, you once fixed Julia up with—did you know who he was?"

"Mr. Pete." Francine drew her eyes away from me. She reached for her cup, hand shaking: coffee sloshed over the edge.

"I'm sure you remember," I coaxed. "He was a guy who was into inflicting pain. A sadist. First you tried to send Tora, then Mattie, then you finally got Julia. Look, I don't care about that, or anything else you've done. But who that man was could be important."

I assumed what I hoped was my Jungian shrink's I-have-all-the-time-in-the-world-to-listen expression, also effectively employed by the detectives Downsey and Shoe. Francine peered at me like a trapped animal through bloodshot eyes. It's going to work! I thought with a thrill. She's going to tell me!

Then, suddenly, her shoulders sagged; she sort of collapsed into herself, shifting her eyes away from me. "I dunno," she whispered. "Dunno who he was. Never knew." She placed both hands flat on the table and hoisted herself to a standing position, swaying a little, like a folkie at a Peter, Paul and Mary concert. "Don't feel too well," she croaked.

"Francine, listen . . ."

"Need to go lie down." And down she went again, into a sort of sloppy yoga lotus. The housekeeper trundled over. For a woman well into her sixties, she was amazingly strong—gripping

Francine under the armpits, she hoisted her in one swift yank back to her feet. Glassy-eyed, Francine tottered off into the hall.

I let myself out and headed home. Suddenly I felt almost sick with repulsion from everything I'd seen and heard in the last few days. What I wanted now was a vanilla milkshake. Flannel pajamas, *Ozzie and Harriet* on TV. I wanted to talk to my daughter about kittens and picnics and circuses, and I desperately wanted somehow to rewind the last out-of-control reel of my life.

One thing was certain, I swore to myself—I was through spying on the sordid little twists in other people's psyches.

A resolve I instantly forgot as I turned onto my block and discovered that Woody Prentice had come home.

14

A BLACK STRETCH LIMOUSINE HOGGED most of the Prentices' drive, so its accompanying litter of Beemers, Benzes and the odd Lexus was stacked along both sides of the street—a sight so reminiscent of one of Julia's parties that for a moment I expected to hear salsa music gaily pulsing from the house. But the place was actually shrouded in an almost preternatural silence; even the breeze ruffling the silver-tipped leaves of neighboring sycamores seemed to die an abrupt death as it hit the Prentice grounds.

This was the nearest I'd been to Woody since I'd stumbled upon the water-logged corpse of his wife—not counting, of course, his brief and minatory telephone communiqué the day of the Windermere commencement festivities. And it was high time, I decided, that I paid him my condolences.

When you visit the bereaved, it's customary to bring flowers. I grabbed a pair of shears and a wire basket and tripped out to my rose garden—or, more accurately, rose thicket; the thorny bushes were planted so close together, it was impossible to cut blooms without looking like you'd just had a run-in with a gang of particularly feisty cats. I filled my basket with a riotous assortment, heavy on the splashier numbers—Lucille Balls, Candy Apples, orange juice--colored Caribbeans. Inside, I arranged them into a passably artistic bouquet, twirling a silver ribbon around the stems; then throwing on a long-sleeved shirt to cover my scratched arms, I headed across the street.

Marsha Moss-Golson answered the door. At the sight of me, her plucked-to-parabola eyebrows shot to her hairline. "Whadda *you* want?"

"To pay my respects to Woody," I replied haughtily. "We *are* neighbors, don't forget. We *do* know each other. I want to offer my sympathy for his terrible loss."

"I hate to say this, but you're kinda like poison around here."

"I didn't kill her, Marsha," I said. "I merely found the body."

"Yeah, but it's the association, if ya see what I mean. It's like rubbing salt into the wound. The poor man's already suffered so much."

"Just tell him I'm here," I snapped. "Let him decide for himself if he wants to see me."

Marsha grudgingly widened the portal, allowing me to step into the inner sanctum. With a prod of her acrylic nails, she herded me into the family room overlooking the pool and gardens, where, three weeks and an eternity ago, Julia had thrown a bash for little Quanxi's anniversary. A motley group of people sat, stood or sprawled about the room in an atmosphere of glum patience, like courtiers awaiting the pleasure of royalty. It appeared to be the usual star's entourage: an agent type, a manager type, a personal nutritionist-astrologer type, several all-purpose gofer/yes-men types.

Marsha directed herself to a thick-set man in a Planet Hollywood jacket who was pacing restlessly in front of the window. He was the only one of the retinue who was not immediately categorizable: he didn't have the ready-to-suck-shoe-leather look of a gofer, or the squinty I'm-a-mean-mutha-who-can-lick-any-one-in-this-room mug of a bodyguard. He and Marsha conferred in muffled tones while I hovered awkwardly, clutching my home-

grown roses like a stood-up bride. Then Planet Hollywood shuffled out of the room, and Marsha returned to my side.

"Griff's gonna tell Woody," she said. "But he thinks you got
a lotta nerve."

"Who's Griff?" I asked.

"He's Woody's older brother's son-in-law from back in Okla-
homa. Woody depends on him a lot to get things done. Personal
kind of stuff. Like, for instance, he arranged the whole funeral
up in Boise." Marsha's eyes, beneath their awnings of false eye-
lashes, went all misty with emotion. "Griff says it was a lovely
affair. At the end, Woody released a whole flock of white doves
into the air. I tell you, I started to bawl like a baby just hearing
about it."

I summoned a sympathetic smile. "So, is Woody back home
to stay?"

"Home here? You're kidding, right? Ya think he could stand
to go on living here with all the memories in this place? He
never even wanted to see it again. But, ya know, he's doing this
miniseries, up in Will Rogers Park, and Woody, he's a true
professional, he carries on even though his heart's breaking. Except today the strain finally caught up with him, and he had
some kinda little fit or something. Griff thought since this house
was only fifteen minutes away from the set, it'd be best to just
bring him here. Didn't even wait for him to change his costume."
Marsha waggled her huge, sticky head of hair. "Minute he walked
in, he broke down completely, poor suffering man."

"How did you get here so fast?" I asked.

"Me? I was here already. I pop in every day to make sure
everything's okay, and the maid's been keeping up and all."

The Poor Suffering Man came doddering into the room. A
dozen bodies bobbed to attention. From their collected midst
there arose a mantra consisting of the word *Woody*—"Woody!";
"Hey, Woody!"; "Woody, man, you okay?"; "Woody, Woody, you
need something, Woody?"

The cynosure of their concern stared around the room with

blank bewilderment. His face was lined and pinched with grief; his saintly silver locks were plastered, homeless-style, against his skull; there were bits of something yellowish and crusty on his chin; even the vivid blue of his eyes seemed to have deadened into the color of clay. He no longer looked like Everybody's Grampa; he looked like a guy about to cadge some spare change for a pint of Thunderbird. Or at least he did from the neck up. From the neck down, he looked like a lieutenant colonel of the United States Army, cavalry division, circa 1870: long blue coat with brass buttons, polished high black boots, service revolver strapped to his hip.

Griff propelled him toward me. I clumsily proffered my rose bouquet. "I brought these," I mumbled. "I just wanted to tell you how deeply sorry I am. Julia was an extraordinary woman, and . . . well, I know nothing can truly console you for her loss, but if there's anything I can do . . ." My voice trailed off awkwardly.

Woody's muddy gaze fixed on the flowers, which might as well have been a bouquet of newts and frogs. A dreadful moment passed in total silence; then Marsha whisked the bouquet out of my hands.

"I'll put these in some water. They're from that garden of yours, aren't they?" *Cheapskate*—she didn't actually say the word, but the message was clear.

Griff stepped assertively forward. "Thanks for coming by. It means a lot to Woody to have the support of his fans. And friends," he amended. He squinted at me dubiously, as if suspecting I was neither.

"Don't go yet," croaked Woody. The sound of his voice was so unexpected that both Griff and I gave a start. "I want to talk to you a minute," he said to me. "In the living room. Griff, you stay here."

"Sure, Wood, no problem. Holler if you need me." Like a sulky dog, Griff slinked back into the bosom of the entourage.

I trailed Woody across the hall into the formal living room.

Marsha, had once confided to me the information that Julia had sacked three decorators before she achieved just the right look of hand-me-down gentility: the pouchy down furniture, the throw pillows covered in faded cabbage rose brocades, the tacky bridge lamps—all suggesting it had been looted from the attic of some spinster great-aunt in, say, Pensequott, Rhode Island. Woody stumbled toward a sofa and collapsed dejectedly onto it. I chose what my own great-aunt Verna would have called a settee.

"I feel I owe you an apology," Woody said. "That phone call I made to you, it was inexcusable. I was not in my right mind. I hope you understand."

I made a dismissive anyone-in-those-circumstances-would-have-made-death-threats gesture.

"From what the police have told me, your husband is no longer a suspect."

"Oh?" I said.

"At this point, I've got to go along with their thinking—that it was just a random act of violence. Some low-life bastard, maybe trying to break into your house, came across my poor darling . . ." His voice cracked. "I realize it's taken a terrible toll on your family as well. I hope for all our sake it's over now."

This was all news to me. But if random violence was the pet theory of the police, I thought, then why was the redoubtable Detective Shoe still on my tail?

Woody bravely met my eye. "Did she . . . When you found her, did it look like she had suffered much?"

"I think it all happened quickly," I said softly.

His head jerked in a nod. With a shaky hand, he reached for something on the coffee table—a small speckled rock, which he cradled in his palm tenderly, as if incubating an egg. "Julia found this on the beach at Positano. It's just a rock, nothing special about it. But my darling girl, she could always find the unique beauty in things, ordinary things. You probably thought she was a frivolous person. But you didn't know her. No one really knew her. She loved to read, you know, and not junk either, good stuff like Proust and Hemingway and Jane Austen."

I tried to picture Julia Prentice curled up of an evening with *Swann's Way*. The image wouldn't gel.

Woody absently turned the stone in his hands. "And the way she really cared about people. . . . All she wanted was to make a little difference in the world. If she could help out at all, do anything to make things better, she would."

"Like rescuing your daughter," I prompted.

The silver head bobbed up and down. "She desperately wanted a child, you know. She could've had her pick, any blond, blue-eyed kid, but it was so exactly like her to want one that nobody else did. A child who'd be dead by now, if my darling hadn't saved her." The pink-rimmed eyes swam with tears. "And now my poor baby girl's going to have to grow up without her mama. But she's going to *know* her," he added forcefully. "I'll make sure of that. I intend to talk to her every day about Julia."

"You mean you want Quanxi back?" I said with surprise.

"Back? What're you talking about? Jesus, she's my daughter, of course I want her back. At the moment, she's being taken care of by . . . by a relative, but as soon as I find a new place to live, I'm bringing her home." Tears were coming fast now, streaming down the craggy face. "I'm sorry," he sniffled. "Please understand."

I tactfully looked away. It was genuine grief, that much I was sure of. To my surprise, I'd discovered that Woody Prentice had loved his wife. Even more than that—he must have worshiped her. He'd blinded himself to her lash-and-leather past—not to mention her more recent sexual predations. Idealized her into a cross between Eleanor Roosevelt and a small-town librarian. Put up with separate bedrooms, the intimacy of Francine Palumbo and shabby chic decor.

Greater love hath no man.

Great love made me think of Audrey Huff—that stern face

mushing into dough as she gazed at tiny Quanxi. Audrey was convinced that Woody didn't want the child back; when she found out he did, how far would she go to prevent him? I remembered the fierce determination in her eyes, and didn't doubt she'd kill to get what she wanted.

If she hadn't already.

The thought gave me cold chills. I turned my eyes back to Woody. My attention was caught again by the odd crusty yellow bits clinging to his chin and upper lip. Remnants of an eggy breakfast?

But before I could study this further, Griff crept into the room on the tiptoes of his Italian loafers. "Wood? I hate to disturb you, kid, but the costume's gotta go back to be cleaned. Sandra's waiting to run it over to the studio."

Woody gazed down at his torso, as if astonished to find himself dressed to lead a charge at Little Bighorn.

Griff let out at nervous giggle. "Hey, look, kid, if it's a problem, I'll tell wardrobe to go to hell."

Woody hauled himself to his feet, mouth clamped tight with show-must-go-on resignation. "No, no, I'll go change," he muttered. Slowly, and with various joints creaking, he made his way out of the room.

"DADDY WAS UP IN A helicopter," said Chloe. She was eating as she talked, a grating crackle in my ear.

"It's not polite to eat when you're on the phone."

"Sorry. And guess what else. He's going to have breakfast with the governor of Washington!"

Bully for Daddy. May he choke on a croissant. "That's nice," I said. "Listen, I miss you lots. Do you miss me?"

"Yeah," she said perfunctorily. "Listen, Grammy says I can't wear my Nirvana *In Utero* T-shirt. She says it's not *seem*ly, so tell her I can, okay?"

"As long as you're at Grammy and Grampy's, sweetie, you've got to do what *they* say."

"Yeah, but . . ."

"How are Lily and Evie," I cut her off.

"They're okay. Except they never heard of Jane's Addiction or Hole, and they don't even have a Discman. Plus, they wear these lame kind of shorts, and you know what time they have to go to bed? Nine-thirty, if it's a school night!"

Evie and Lily sounded enviably wholesome compared to my prematurely teenaged daughter. When had Chloe started getting her values from MTV? When she came home, I resolved, some changes were going to be made.

I told her to sleep tight, don't let the bedbugs bite, which got a snorting "Oh, Mom!" in response; then I hung up, had my dinner for one and indulged myself by running some classic cartoons on Kit's sixteen-millimeter projector—Goofy on skis, Felix the Cat dancing on a candyland moon.

A LOUD *THWACK!* MADE ME sit bolt upright. The luminous numerals of the Braun clock read 12:17 A.M.; I hadn't been asleep for more than half an hour. The sound came again, *thwack!* Someone was trying to break into the house from the backyard. Some crazed maniac, desperate enough to not even give a shit about being stealthy! I sat, heart thumping wildly, listening for the sound again, too paralyzed by fear and grogginess to reach for the phone.

Then there was an enormous whooshing sound and another *thwack!* and I exhaled with relief. It was just a Santa Ana, the powerful hot wind that gusted in from the desert, tossing a piece of patio furniture against the house. A weird time of year for it—autumn was Santa Ana season—but the weather this spring had been consistently nutty.

"Like my life," I muttered to myself as I rolled out of bed.

I padded downstairs barefoot, wearing only the extra-large "I [heart made from chile peppers] Taos" T-shirt that was my less-than-alluring bed wear when I slept alone. Another welling gust of wind, another twackety-*thwack!* I followed the sound to the kitchen, flicked on the outdoor lights and stepped out the door.

It was a stunning night; ragged clouds shirred the moon, and the air was scented with jasmine and eucalyptus. I looked around to see what had woken me up. I was right: one of the wicker chaises had been upended by the wind and was being slapped by the sudden gusts against the kitchen side of the house. I dragged it to a sheltered corner of the patio, then stepped a little farther into the yard.

Most people find the Santa Anas disturbing. It makes them irritable, jumpy, depressed. When the hot winds blow, the suicide rate soars, pals from childhood suddenly pull forty-fives on each other, straight-A students rob 7-Elevens. But I've always found them exhilarating—I feel the same quickening of expectation that, back East, I get from the first snap of frost in October.

I spread my arms, laughing as the wind went *whoosh!* It billowed my T-shirt. It fanned my hair.

And it gave a nice rippling effect to the man's shadow stretched out on the lawn beside me.

With a gasp, I started to whirl around. Hands shoved me hard from behind and I went toppling, catching sight only of a pair of feet as I fell. For some puzzling reason, the thought of Gordon, Chloe's pet gecko, flashed through my mind.

Then my head cracked against a hard surface and everything went black.

THREE

15

I CAME TO WITH ROSE petals and sand blowing in my face and my T-shirt hiked immodestly above my crotch. I pulled myself to my feet and teetered for a wobbly-kneed second until I hit on the foggy realization that I was still in my own backyard; then I sprinted back into the house, slammed the door, latched the latch and dialed 911, something that was beginning to feel uncomfortably like a habit. For good measure, I also hit the alarm to our private security.

I huddled in a corner of the kitchen, clutching a Wusthof carving knife, until the *whoop whoop whoop* of a police car reverberated through the canyon. It disgorged two cops, one tall and burly, with a jutting Dudley Do-Right chin, the other medium-sized and mustachioed. Hard on their heels, the security guy from Fast Alert, white-haired and beer-bellied; the two policemen eyed him with the appropriate contempt of duly sworn officers of the law for a rent-a-cop.

"Situation's under control," sneered the mustachioed cop. His badge ID'ed him as Officer Gutierrez.

"No problem, officers," said the man from Fast Alert. "I was responding to an alarm, but I can see you've got it well under control." He shuffled away with undisguised relief.

The two cops trudged into the house. "Wanna tell us what happened?" said Dudley Do-Right, aka Officer Sulley.

"There was a prowler in my backyard," I said, rather shakily. "He hit me, and I fell and blacked out. And when I came to, I ran back in the house and called nine-one-one."

"So you went outside when you heard this prowler?"

"No, I went out to move a piece of furniture. A chaise longue. The wind was knocking it against the house and woke me up."

"About what time was this?" inquired Gutierrez.

"I know exactly. It was seventeen after twelve when I woke up."

"So you were blacked out for wha'? Ten, fifteen minutes?"

Could that be all? I glanced at the digital clock on the microwave, amazed to find it was now only 12:51—I thought I'd been unconscious for hours. "The guy could still be on the grounds!" I cried.

"We'll check it out," said Gutierrez smoothly. "Didju request EMS? The paramedics?"

He was looking meaningfully at the crest of my forehead. I touched it, felt a stickiness; when I saw the blood on my fingers, my knees went rubbery again. Officer Sulley steadied me. "We'll get 'em here. In the meantime, you oughta put on a robe and something on your feet. You could be in shock, so it's important you gotta stay warm."

Not to mention decent—I suddenly realized my skimpy T-shirt was giving Sulley and Gutierrez a rousing eyeful. I slunk upstairs and wrapped myself in my primmest Lands' End flannel robe and a pair of fleecy slippers. Then I examined my wound, which was now beginning to throb and sting. There was a matting of blood at my hairline the size of a baby's fist, but after I dabbed at it with a damp towel, it didn't look too bad at all.

Then I perched on the edge of the bed and called Kit's Seattle hotel. "No answer in that room," the operator burbled after six rings.

It was nearly one A.M. Where was he? More interesting, who was he with? Kit was not the type to do the town alone. And I was sure he wasn't with Jon Sugerman, who, as every *People* magazine subscriber knew, hit the hay religiously at ten o'clock in order to be up and chirping at a quarter to five. Of course, Seattle must be teeming with women willing to show Well-known Movie Producer Kit Freers a whopping good time. "No message!" I snarled and slammed down the phone.

I sat for a moment, trying to sort out my thoughts. Of all the times Kit had been away on location over the past years, I'd never before had these kinds of suspicions. Of course, I hadn't known about Ms. *Vanity Fair* before. Nor had I ever come so close to having a fling of my own.

More sirens were screaming down the street, reawakening whichever of my neighbors had managed to get back to sleep. Wearily, I padded back downstairs.

Gutierrez was ushering a paramedic into the kitchen, a stocky black woman wearing the sort of aviator glasses once beloved by women's libbers. And just to make my night totally complete, they were shadowed by Detective Teresa Shoe. She returned my baleful gaze with a narrow-eyed frown, then went into a huddle with Gutierrez by the Amana No-Frost fridge, conferring with him in an ominously low voice.

The paramedic peered at my bruise through her bra burner's spectacles. "This looks very superficial," she pronounced with disgust.

"It was enough to knock me out," I said huffily.

This perked her up. "Oh, yeah? You'll want to get it X-rayed in the morning. You never know with head injuries, you could have a concussion." She began briskly swabbing, blotting, bandaging. "Don't forget that X ray," she said, packing up her stuff. "If it is a concussion, you could find yourself suddenly blacking out again." With this comforting caveat, she departed.

Detective Shoe took her place. She was wearing the same medley in taupe she'd had on the day of Julia's murder, now accessorized by deep mauve circles under her eyes. It made her look older, but by no means mellower.

"How did you get here so fast?" I asked.

"I picked up the four-fifty-nine on the radio. Luckily, I happened to be in the neighborhood. Vehicular homicide over on Amalfi."

"Somebody shot a Chevrolet?"

"Huh? Oh, hee, hee, that's cute. No, a guy found out his wife was cheating on him, ran her down with his Acura." She shot me a penetrating glance, as if there might be a moral lesson in this for me. "So, let's see if I've got this straight," she went on. "You went out in your backyard at approximately twelve-seventeen in order to move around some furniture, and someone, a prowler, came at you from behind and knocked you out."

"Basically."

"Uh-huh. So, if you were hit from behind, how come there's this abrasion on your forehead?"

"It was more like he *shoved* me from behind. You see, I saw his shadow, and when I started to turn around, he pushed me down. When I fell, I must have knocked my head against something."

"You say 'he.' You're sure it was a man?"

"It seemed like a man's shadow. I guess I'm not a hundred percent sure."

"So you started to turn around, but you got no look at the assailant? No identifying features?"

I shook my head. The motion seemed to dislodge a hazy recollection. "Wait, there was something," I said. "Gordon the gecko!"

"Who?"

"Not a who. A what. It's my daughter's pet gecko lizard named Gordon. I remember thinking about him just before I went unconscious."

The detective was eyeing me testily, as if at any moment she'd have to call for the boys with the straitjacket.

"It was an association," I added hurriedly. "It's coming back to me now. I *did* catch a glimpse of the guy's feet—and it was

the shoes that reminded me of Gordon. Some kind of green lizard shoes."

"The assailant was wearing a pair of green lizard shoes?" Her
call-for-the-straitjacket tone was stronger than ever.

"Look," I said wearily, "it was dark, I could only see by
moonlight, and I was pretty damned startled. I can't be totally
sure of any of this."

The detective gave a noncommittal grunt. My head was beginning to feel like one of those ancient Anacin commercials, a
little hammer and anvil and drill all slamming away inside.

"Those gates you got out in front," Shoe continued. "Were
they locked?"

"I think so. I mean, I'm sure they were. But it wouldn't be
impossible for somebody to climb over them."

"You've got a security system, right? Armed response and
all that?"

I nodded. "Fast Alert."

"The system's got a beam outside?"

"An electric eye at the gates."

"So if somebody hopped the gates, he'd set off the security
alarm."

This stumped me a moment. Then, rather triumphantly, I said,
"When I got up to check out the noise, I shut off the security
system. He could've got in then."

"So what you're saying is, some guy, by sheer chance, happens
to leap over a pair of six-foot-high gates with spiky tops in the
exact few minutes the security's off. Then he makes it all the
way around to the back of the house just in the nick of time to
surprise you and then knock you out."

I suppressed a frustrated shriek. "Look, there are other ways
to get back there. A few days ago, a neighbor's dog dug under
the hedges. Scared the hell out of me."

"Quite a lot of activity in your backyard."

"I wouldn't say that exactly."

"A stray dog, a midnight intruder, a dead body, all in the space of a coupla weeks. It's better than Disneyland. You ought to sell tickets."

My loathing for the woman had reached a purity I had hitherto thought reserved for the more exalted emotions, such as love and desire.

"According to Officer Gutierrez," she continued in a syrupy voice, "you didn't have a whole lot on when they arrived. Just a flimsy kind of shirt."

"I was wearing a long T-shirt. It was what I was sleeping in." I added huffily, "Maybe someone else would've had the presence of mind to pop upstairs and slip into something more appropriate. But I'm afraid that after having been attacked and knocked out cold, I was just a little too distracted."

A grunt from Detective Shoe. Her eye wandered to some point over my shoulder, in the vicinity of the Krups espresso machine on the counter; for a moment I had the distinct feeling she was going to demand a cup of coffee. Her eyes shifted to my collection of old cookie jars—shameless pieces of kitsch shaped like clown heads, Aunt Jemimas, grinning babies.

"Who are you trying to protect, Mrs. Freers?" she said abruptly.

I glanced up, startled. "What do you mean?"

"Why don't we get down to what really happened tonight? Who are you covering up for?"

"That is outrageous!" I croaked. "I'm not covering up for anyone!"

"You got a lover? Some hotheaded fellow who gets a little carried away from time to time?"

"Absolutely not!"

"Someone who might've come looking for you and happened on Mrs. Prentice instead?"

I rose to my feet, shaking with indignation. "How dare you! I'm not covering up for anyone! I am not a liar, I am certainly not a murderer and I am by no means cheating on my husband!"

This last declaration must have sparked my guilty conscience, since I suddenly had a vision of Justin Caffrey slouched in the doorway behind Detective Shoe. I gave a start as the apparition took a few steps closer and said, "Is everything okay here?"

Detective Shoe whipped her head around. Both our eyes slid to Justin's footwear: slightly scuffed brown loafers.

"It's Mr. Caffrey, isn't it?" Shoe remarked.

He nodded. "I saw the black-and-white outside and I was worried about Lucy."

"Just happened to be taking a stroll at one in the morning?"

He gave a strained chuckle. "No, I've just come back from a wrap party for the new Jim Carrey movie at Fox. It was at the House of Blues over in West Hollywood. A buddy of mine did sound on the film and invited me along. I would've stayed even longer, but I'm catching an early plane to Montana—going up to do some fly-fishing on the Yellowstone."

He was volunteering a lot of information. This seemed suspicious, until I remembered how that yellow-eyed stare of Detective Shoe could provoke a Trappist monk to start babbling.

Officer Sulley materialized at the back door. In that peculiar divide-and-multiply way of policemen, he had now acquired four or five confederates, all of whom trooped in. It was just like old times, my kitchen filling up with cops. The squawk of their walkie-talkies, the clinking of their cuffs—it was beginning to feel nostalgic.

Sulley shook his head in the direction of Detective Shoe. "No one on the grounds. It's about all we can do till morning."

Shoe swiveled back to me. "If you should happen to remember anything more about this 'assailant' "—she definitely pronounced the word in quotation marks—"give me a call, or talk to one of the officers." She rose, directed a last penetrating stare at Justin and, with a snap of her head, commandeered her troops out through the front of the house.

"Wow," Justin muttered, straddling a chair facing me. He

looked, I was not too distraught to notice, sexy as hell. Beat-up bomber jacket. Well-worn jeans. Little lick of brown hair flopping into his eyes. "So what happened?"

"Nothing much. I was taking a midnight breather in my back-yard and I got mugged."

"What?"

I smiled grimly. "There was a prowler. He came at me from behind and shoved me and I hit my head. Good night Gracie for about fifteen minutes. By the time I came to, he was gone. I never got a look at him."

"Jesus, you're lucky you're alive," he said. "I mean, considering Julia and all. You sure whoever it was didn't . . . touch you?"

"He might've copped a feel or two while I was out cold."

"Seriously."

I gave a sober shake of my head. "I wasn't raped, if that's what you mean."

"Thank god."

"Speaking of Julia," I said gingerly, "why did you tell me you hardly knew her when she was the one who got you the Pen-nislaws' pool house?"

He blinked. "So you know about that."

"My pool-maintenance man happened to be working there when you were looking at it."

"Okay," he said. "The truth is, I had a brief thing with her a few months ago. We met at a dinner party—she practically jumped me right at the table. We spent a couple of hot afternoons together in a room at the Shangri-La. When I mentioned I was looking for a quiet place to write, she hustled me over to the Pennislaws'. I guess she was looking forward to having me right across the street, so she could pop over whenever it was convenient."

"Too bad she didn't know she'd be dead before she could exercise those privileges," I said crisply.

"Hey, I know this makes me look like a cold-hearted son of a bitch. But the thing is, by the time she was killed, she'd already dropped me. As soon as she found out I was getting a divorce—that I didn't just want the pool house to work in, but I was actually going to shack up there for a while—she dumped me cold."

"That sounds right," I allowed. "From what I know, Julia liked her lovers to be happily married, so they'd have as much to lose as she did. She probably thought that since your wife was also your writing partner, you'd be doubly safe."

"To tell you the truth, I was relieved when she dumped me. She was good-looking, I guess, but I prefer women who are more—well, complex." He treated me to one of those Big Bad Wolf smiles that made my toes tingle. "Anyway, the reason I kept all this quiet is because of this goddamned divorce. If my wife got one whiff of the fact I'd ever been mixed up with Julia, her lawyer would be painting a nice picture of me as a sex-crazed homicidal maniac."

"She couldn't be that bad."

"You don't know her. The ultimate bitch goddess. I had her come over yesterday, thinking we could have a civilized evening, a little Merlot, some pleasant music, and maybe we could talk everything over in a reasonable manner. My darling wife doesn't know the meaning of the word. She wants everything we've got, plus my balls thrown in for good measure."

So the drop-dead blonde in the silver convertible turned out to be merely his wife. "Sorry she's giving you such a rough time," I said, not feeling very sorry at all.

"Yeah, well, breaking up is hard to do. Look," he said in a softer tone, "I don't want you to be alone tonight."

I caught my breath. Was I really ready for this?"

"I'm going to bring Lola over to you," he added.

Lola? Who the hell was Lola? Then I remembered—the Saint Bernard puppy.

Justin got up. "I was going to leave her at the vet while I'm away, but this'll be perfect. She's a great little watchdog—if anyone gets within fifty feet of the house, you'll know about it. I'll go get her, be right back."

It struck me after he'd gone that since he'd be away for the weekend, there went my chance to invite him to the Magic Wand benefit and dazzle him with the more glamorous side of my persona. Instead, he'd be left with the image of how I looked now—Mother Hubbard with a bandaged-up forehead.

I treated myself to three Nuprins and a glass of apricot nectar to ease the throbbing in my brow. Five minutes later, man and puppy reappeared at the door. Lola bounded in, sniffing everything in sight, yapping and gyrating in ecstatic circles.

"Okay?" Justin said.

I nodded bravely.

"See you Monday, then." He ruffled the puppy's thick fur, then disappeared again.

I trudged upstairs, Lola cavorting behind me, and crawled back into bed. The puppy snuggled up lovingly at my hip. "Nice pup," I muttered. Yeah, I was really quite a femme fatale. For all my would-be seductions since Kit left town, the only warm body I'd managed to lure into my bed turned out to be a Saint Bernard.

16

THE DOUBLE FRONT DOOR OF the Rossner mansion was a massive black walnut affair carved in elaborately looped and entwined Spanish Baroque detail. It was opened by a butler, whose name, which I happened to know from Chloe's breathless reports, was Deltoro. It was the first genuine butler I'd actually come nose-to-nose with, and as such, he was something of a dud: I was expecting a cross between William Powell in *My Man Godfrey* and Anthony Hopkins in *The Remains of the Day;* this Deltoro looked more like a shorter, squatter version of Edward James Olmos. But the deadpan demeanor that accompanied his "Yes, madam, Miss Winifred is expecting you, come this way" was straight out of central casting.

I had come to pick up my tickets for the Magic Wand benefit, but I was also curious for a peek at the renowned Rossner spread. In Hollywood, it's more often the moguls who live like movie stars, they being the ones who haul in the kind of eight- and nine-figure-a-year incomes that can finance Babylonianly opulent lifestyles. The Rossners were a case in point. Their pied-à-terre was an unassuming thirty thousand square feet of Italianate palazzo sprawled on an ocean-view summit off Mulholland. Five years in construction. Enough imported marble to have kept Michelangelo chiseling away his entire lifetime. Art collection worthy of a provincial museum, and more working fountains than the average upscale neighborhood in Rome. And since the site had originally been nine acres of fire-scorched chaparral, it had taken an additional year of nothing but landscaping to make the grounds bloom like Capri. There was, in fact, still a lawsuit pending after Rossner helicopters hauling in full-grown acacias had blown a neighbor's outdoor bar mitzvah party to bits.

But my real lowdown on the place had come from Chloe's almost daily bulletins: Alwyn Rossner had her own playroom that was *twice* as big as our living room, with an entire make-believe jungle and an electric train you could actually ride in; at Alwyn's house there was a *real* bowling alley and a soda fountain where you could make your own sundaes, any kind of ice cream you wanted—Häagen-Dazs, or Ben & Jerry's, or McConnell's of Santa Barbara; Alwyn didn't have a dinky outdoor playhouse, she had an entire *village,* with a church and school and everything; and Alwyn's mom had a closet with eighteen windows in it, and when you pressed a button, the clothes whirred round and round, like at the dry cleaner's.

Now, as I trotted along behind Deltoro down an antique-crammed corridor, I could vividly recall the envy in Chloe's voice. Compared to Alwyn's, her life was shabby and mean. Other kids think it's not fair if they don't get a Super Nintendo. My daughter thought it wasn't fair that she didn't have her own bowling alley.

Kit, it struck me now, had also been wallowing in envy for the past couple of years. "It's not *fair!* All the *other* producers get to drive brand-new top-of-the-line BMWs, while I'm stuck with a lousy four-year-old Saab."

And I wasn't exempt either, I realized as we passed through a hall wallpapered with Impressionist paintings. I cast a yearning glance at a glowing little Degas. When you're rubbing elbows with people who have this kind of loot, who wouldn't give in to a wallow of acquisitiveness now and then?

AFTER WE HAD HIKED FOR what seemed a quarter of a mile, Deltoro steered me into an office aggressively furnished with period chinoiserie. "Mrs. Freers," he announced in an orotund tone and melted away.

Winifred, Summer Rossner's social secretary, hailed me from a dragon-legged writing desk snowed under with paper; she was a ruddy Australian with an eager, buck-toothed smile and a beer can–crushing handshake. "Right, Mrs. Freers," she chirped after mangling my hand. "I've got your tickets just here." She frowned, tapped her temple, then rummaged furiously through the snow, sending up a small blizzard of pasteboard, and when it settled, she plucked a small beige envelope from the top. "Right in front of my nose, always the last place you look. Now, if I could just collect a check, we're all square."

I fished out my checkbook. Winifred proffered a Mont Blanc fountain pen. "And the amount?" I asked, rather heartily.

"They're fifteen hundred apiece. So, that would make us three thousand even, wouldn't it?"

My fingers cramped around the Mont Blanc. Three thousand bucks! The usual bite for a charity affair was $250 a ticket, including valet parking. I groped for a face-saving excuse to back out. . . . My dog ate my last check. . . . I just remembered I'm leaving tomorrow for Buenos Aires. . . .

Then, out of the corner of my eye, I caught a shimmer of pink and ivory and pale gold. Summer Rossner had graced us with her presence.

She was murmuring into a tiny cellular phone held at her ear—an elegant device, slim as a Hershey bar and pale pink, as if to match her sheer handkerchief-linen shirt. At the sight of me, she raised a perfectly feathered brow, mumbled something hastily into the phone and flipped it closed.

"Hello, it's Lucy, isn't it?" she said, floating toward me. "What a nice surprise. Someone should have told me you were here. But gracious, whatever happened to your forehead?"

I touched the bandage on my hairline—a fresh one applied by a nurse at St. John's that morning, where I'd dutifully reported for an X ray. "Nothing," I said. "I was reaching for a book on a top shelf and got bonked. It's nothing."

"I didn't think I had to call you," Winifred pouted defensively. "She's just come 'round to collect tickets for Saturday night."

"Tickets? But I thought we were totally subscribed."

"We are, but there was such a last-minute demand, I squeezed in four more tables. We're going to catch bloody hell from the fire marshal, but I can deal with that."

Summer gave out a laugh like a wind chime made out of icicles. "You're such a wonder, Winifred. Whatever would I do without you?"

Several phone lines jangled at once and Winifred the Wonder began to jockey them. Summer's arctic eyes traveled back to me and made a swift appraisal of my clothes—black capris, maroon peplum-skirted rayon jacket, silver Scotty dog pin circa 1940, covering a tiny moth hole in the lapel. "Sweet outfit," she cooed. "You always manage to look so perfectly original. I don't know how you do it."

"Thanks," I said. Compared to her costly-but-simple ensemble, I was dressed like the Little Match Girl.

"I'm immensely grateful for your support, Lucy," Summer went on. "This cause means the world to me. And I have to say I'm very gratified by the response. The governor's coming, and I can't tell you how many *top* stars."

I was still clutching my checkbook. There was no way I could wriggle out now—not without terminally disgracing myself in front of the Queen of the Hollywood Moms. I made the check out, scribbling the amount *three thousand* in a rather wavery hand. "I can't help thinking how tragic it is that Julia Prentice won't be there," I said, signing my name.

At the mention of Julia, there appeared on Summer's face something I had never seen before—a genuine emotion. But it appeared so fleetingly and vanished so completely, I couldn't really read it. "Very sad," she said evenly.

"The foundation was a real passion of hers," I pursued. "She talked about it constantly. I think she even dreamed of being chairman one day."

"Ah, well, poor Julia, she always reached a little too high. I loved her dearly, of course, but she had no organizational skills."

"But she did know how to cultivate people. And of course Woody is so extremely popular."

"It takes more than popularity to run a charity like this." A hint of an edge had sneaked into Summer's voice. Catching herself, she added placidly, "It's been lovely visiting with you, Lucy. But as you can imagine, I'm simply swamped."

"How is Alwyn liking camp?" I blurted. (Another petulant bulletin from Chloe: "Alwyn's going to this circus camp in Bolinas, and she'll get to swing on trapezes and do clown makeup and ride ponies bareback.")

"Oh, she adores it! She's made a marvelous new friend, one of the Costner kids. From what she says, they've become inseparable."

"Chloe misses her."

"And she misses Chloe, I'm sure. But I'm afraid we're not sending Alwyn back to Windermere in September. We feel The School's heading in a seriously destructive direction. Letting in too much of the wrong element. *Persians*." She hissed the word under her breath—exactly as my uncle Anders, who lived in Bad Axe, Michigan, used to pronounce the word *Communists*.

The tiny cellular phone went *brrr-up, brr-up*. Summer flipped it open, melodiously burbled "Hel-lo?" and floated back to her connecting office.

"Cute phone," I remarked to Winifred, handing her the check.

"Isn't it the sweetest? It's the latest thing, got a tiny solar battery that can hold a charge for up to three or four weeks. And it can store three hundred numbers. Of course," she added reverently, "that's hardly enough for Summer." She squinted at my signature as if possibly suspecting a forgery. "Right, Ms. Freers, we're all set. Here are your tickets. Enjoy!"

THERE WERE AT LEAST AS many cop cars littering the street in front of my house when I returned as there had been when I'd left several hours before. Inside, I found the kitchen strewn with Styrofoam coffee cups, Egg McMuffin cartons, bags of Dunkin' Donuts and remnants of other artery-clogging delights. Teresa Shoe, to my vast annoyance, was stationed at her usual place at the table, lighting into a sugared bun.

"There you are," she said, popping to her feet.

"Did you think I skipped the country?" I asked sourly.

"No, no, nothing like that. Here, sit down. How's that head of yours?"

"It's fine. I had an X ray. There's no concussion."

"Glad to hear it. Hey, I brought you this, it's a real cappuccino." She shoved a large Starbucks cup in my direction, then began to peer into various take-out bags. "And I picked up some of those cranberry muffins you like. . . . Yeah, here they are. I tried one, got a taste kind of medicinal, like maybe Robitussin. But they're healthy, right?" The little brown bag she handed me was from the Heart's Ease natural-foods bakery on Main, where I bought my low-fat, high-bran-content muffins. This motherly solicitousness on the part of Detective Shoe put me instantly on my guard.

"I'm not hungry," I said, petulantly pushing away the bag. "Where's the puppy?"

"Downsey's got her outside with him. He's a real animal nut, anything—hamsters, snakes, you name it. It's a nice little dog, though, I gotta say. Belongs to Mr. Caffrey next door, right?"

Here it comes, I thought—she's moving in for the kill.

"Justin had to leave town," I said, "and he thought it would be good to leave Lola here. For my protection."

"He was right, it was a good idea." The detective sat back down and regarded me, head atilt, with a serious squint. "We found some evidence out in back that appears to corroborate your story."

"You did? What kind of evidence?"

"Footprints, male, back up on top of your hill. And some broken branches in the bushes. From the look of it, the guy got into your backyard by climbing up the cliff."

"That's impossible. It's a sheer drop of fifty feet, at least."

"Puh, anybody's done any kind of mountain climbing, that's a piece of cake. What do they call it, free-climbing—you don't need ropes or pitons or any of that."

"Yeah, but wearing lizard-skin shoes?"

"You could've been mistaken about that. You know, some of this athletic footwear comes in wild colors."

I considered this. I was almost positive I'd seen lizard-skin shoes. But at least the rest of my story had been corroborated. "What do you think he wanted?"

"My guess? He thinks he's left something behind."

"You mean something that could link him to Julia's murder?"

She shrugged.

"But the cops went over the entire grounds. They found nothing."

"It's a good-sized piece of property you got here. And the mud slide made everything a lot more complicated. Add to that, what-ever it is could be pretty small—a key, a ring, a cap from a tooth, a scrap of paper. Or nothing at all. This theory could be all wet. He could've been after something else."

"Like what?"

"Like possibly you."

"Me?"

She shrugged. "The way you've been snooping around, it's possible he wanted to shut you up."

Suddenly, I could hardly breathe. I tried a sip of the cappuccino and sputtered as it lodged in my throat. "Why, then," I said, "why didn't he . . . ?"

"Finish you off? I don't know. Could be he got scared off. Like you said, the wind was banging things around. Maybe something blew over, startled him. Maybe when you blacked out, he thought you were dead."

My hands felt numb. I could still hardly breathe, and there was a constriction in my chest that was getting worse. I'm having a heart attack, I thought wildly, which prompted the room to start spinning like an out-of-control carousel.

Teresa Shoe suddenly dumped the cranberry muffins onto the table and slapped the Heart's Ease bag over my nose and mouth. "You're hyperventilating," she snapped. "Just keep breathing into the bag."

Now I was not only having a heart attack but suffocating as well—I was going to die with the smell of all-natural but slightly medicinal cranberry muffins as the last thing I'd ever know! In sheer panic, I tried to thrash the bag away, but Detective Shoe, no doubt well trained in the art of subduing pissed-off perpetrators, managed to keep it firmly clamped at my face. "You'll be okay, just keep breathing," she commanded. "I'm going to count to twenty. One, two, three . . ." She continued to count slowly and steadily. The carousel slowed and came to a halt. "Okay?" the detective asked. I nodded, and she withdrew the bag. "I didn't mean to panic you. It was just one theory and not even the most likely one. Just relax a couple of minutes. Eat some muffin."

"God, no." I gagged at the thought; my taste for cranberry muffins was forever gone.

Lola was yapping at the back door, and Armand Downsey

appeared, looking very natty in a tan linen-blend suit. Shoe brusquely waved him away. He gave a thumbs-up and retreated.

The gleam of the gold band on the detective's ring finger caught my attention. "That's a pretty ring," I said. "Is it a Korean wedding band?"

"Not really. Koreans don't have what you'd call traditional wedding rings. Frank and I sort of designed this ourselves when we got married." She removed the band, handed it to me. "You see these ideographs? They're actually Chinese. For some reason, don't ask me why, Koreans like to use Chinese ideographs for decoration. The top one is *pok*, which means bliss or well-being. The bottom is *su*, meaning long life. The traditional Korean way would be to have them reversed—first long life, then well-being. They're very practical folks. But the way I see it, what's the use of living to ninety if you're not having a good time? I mean, better short and sweet than long and lousy, right?"

I managed a wan smile. "I guess cops have to be prepared for short and sweet."

A disparaging snort. "What, you think it's like in the movies, every ten minutes you're dodging bullets? Maybe twice I've been under serious fire, and both times it was easy to get out of the way. As long as you watch your back, you've got a pretty good chance of making it to retirement." She slipped the ring back on her finger, wedging it with some difficulty past a thick knuckle. "So, how are you feeling? Breathing okay, no dizziness?"

I ran a quick hospital check on myself. "I'm fine."

"Then I think it's about time you tell me just what the hell you think you've been doing for the past week."

"What I've been doing," I said frostily, "is trying to clear myself and my husband from the suspicion of having bumped off our neighbor. It might sound peculiar, but I don't happen to want to spend the rest of my life feeling like my face has just been featured on *America's Most Wanted*."

She cracked a grin. "So in other words, you've been doing my job?"

"If that's the way you see it."

"And with all this brilliant detective work, did you come up with anything worth risking your neck for?"

"It wasn't exactly my intention to risk my neck. All I did was talk to a few people. And," I added, "I do think I've come up with some interesting leads."

"So shoot." She folded her arms on the table. The expression in her amber eyes was now all maternal concern, a wary doe regarding her fawn in hunting season.

I didn't trust her. I still resented every one of her loathsome insinuations. Yet suddenly I heard myself telling her everything with what sounded like relief in my voice. I could hardly get the words out fast enough, from my first chat with Audrey Huff to my predawn jog with Mattie Ballard. I breathlessly described hunting up Tora Merrick and then browsing through the S and M wares at the Pleasure Trove. By the time I spilled out my theories about the mysterious Mr. Pete, it was almost gibberish.

Teresa Shoe continued gazing at me like Bambi's mother.

"Doesn't any of this sound like it could be relevant?" I asked plaintively.

"In an investigation like this, everything is relevant."

"So, am I still a suspect?"

I expected something along the lines of "I suspect everyone and no one." Instead, she said simply, "No."

All of a sudden I felt bone-tired, as if I'd just finished a stint at some calisthenics-before-dawn, eight-hundred-calories-a-day health spa. I flopped in my chair.

"Look," she said, "all this has actually been good for me. It puts me back on the case."

"You were kicked off?"

She gave an impatient shrug. "Always happens in a big high-profile case, the hotshots from RHD take over. Downtown robbery-homicide division. Anyway, for *your* own good, I suggest you stay the hell out of this from now on. You're just gonna screw things up for us as well as endanger yourself. Think of that daughter of yours—you've got a responsibility to her to keep yourself safe, instead of ending up on a slab in the morgue."

"Okay," I said meekly. "No more snooping around. But what if the prowler, whoever he was, comes back?"

"I don't think he will—not after he's attracted all this attention. But you might think of getting out of here for a while. Go join your daughter. Catch a plane to Atlanta and chill out for a while."

"I can't go before Sunday night," I said.

"Why not?"

"I just anted up three thousand bucks for tickets to the Magic Wand Foundation benefit, and I don't intend to just toss them away."

"Three thousand dollars?"

"Correct." I was happy to see there was something that could actually impress her. "There are hundreds of people in this town who'd die to go to this party," I said lightly. "Why should I be an exception?"

If Detective Shoe caught the humor in this, she didn't let it show. Her lips remained compressed.

"Besides," I babbled on, "a lot of the people I've just told you about will be there. I might be able to learn something."

"There you go, still playing the detective."

"If you're so worried," I snapped, "maybe you should come too. I've got an extra ticket."

"Me?"

"Yeah. You can be my bodyguard."

"I've never been to anything like that before. There'll be a lot of movie stars, right? My kids'll flip when I tell them." She was the one who looked excited. "Yeah, I'd like to go, thanks."

"Great," I said. But what I'd just done was beginning to sink in: I'd invited Detective Teresa Shoe, who walked like a duck and dressed à la Wal-Mart's finest, to be my date for the most glamorous Hollywood event of the year.

17

IT WAS A RELIEF TO go a couple of days without thinking of murder or deviant sex or actually anything more exciting than battling the white-fly infestation of our tangerine trees.

In a burst of manic creativity, I whipped out the rest of the "Amerinda Discovers Gravity" drawings and started to plot out the next episode. (Inertia: Amerinda, despite much coaxing and prodding from her barnyard pals, simply can't drag herself out of bed, thereby illustrating the principle that a flying blue hedgehog at rest tends to stay at rest.)

Saturday night, I attended a dinner party given by Jeff and Casey Blumlak, who were a husband-and-wife agent team at William Morris. The over-the-table gossip was all about the daytime talk-show hostess who'd just caught her husband in flagrante with the baby nurse, and the movie-star-of-the-minute, who, for her novelist boyfriend's birthday, had his name tattooed on her ankle, and no one mentioned poor stone-dead Julia at all.

It almost felt like I had my old life back—that everything had gone back to normal.

Everything—except for the blank, silent façade of the Prentice house, which seemed to stare balefully at me from across the road, like a stillborn ghost.

*   *   *

BY SUNDAY EVENING, MY STOMACH was in butterflies. I was primped and ready several hours in advance. For the occasion, I had selected my most gala dress, an authentic Balenciaga gown, vintage circa 1955, which I'd plucked from the back of a dusty rack in a Hollywood thrift shop called Pioneer Women New and Used. Marked $29.95, it had been a genuine find, with just a few easily mended rips at the seams. It was peacock-blue taffeta, with a gathered waist and full Cinderella skirt—in fact, very much something Julia Prentice's character in *The Delano Reunion* would have worn, twirling a bit Loretta Youngishly as she made her entrance into a crowded salon. The only problem was that the color clashed with the bruise on my forehead, which had taken on an interesting, if rather lurid, palette of green, purple and brown; but this I solved by parting my hair on the side and sweeping it over my brow, anchoring it at the temple with a sparkling marcasite barrette.

As I fastened my earrings (pavé diamond clips, a tenth-anniversary present from Kit), a flurry of yipping, growling and arfing arose from the hall. This, I had by now learned, meant that Lola was enthusiastically destroying some particularly cherished piece of our personal property. This time it was one of Kit's favorite leather belts.

"Bad, bad puppy," I scolded. After a brief tug of war, I managed to yank the belt away and rehung it, teeth marks and all, in Kit's closet.

There were his clothes: the jumble of rejected running shoes; the platoon of identical oxford collared shirts. The spiffy new Ralph Lauren dinner jacket that he'd now be climbing into, grumbling every other second about how it made him feel like a head waiter. And beside it, the fourteen-year-old tux he was married in, frayed and unmodish now, with it's post–Dance Fever sharp lapels. Looking at this, I felt a sudden wave of missing my husband.

Except who was it I missed, exactly? Not the hotshot who was currently tossing millions of movie bucks around Puget Sound. No, I missed the boy in that silly old tux, the one who dreamed of making a movie as good as *Raging Bull*, even if he never got paid a dime.

GHM. Good Husband Material.

I was getting misty-eyed. Get a grip, Lucy, I scolded myself, or the twenty-five minutes you spent blending eye shadow will end up as twin little Jackson Pollocks.

I marched downstairs and poured a stiffish shot of Cuervo. Which promptly reminded me of Justin. *He* probably looked sensational in black tie. It was his body Giorgio Armani had in mind when designing men's formal wear.

"Salute," I forlornly toasted myself, and put the glass to my lips. The phone rang.

"Lucy? Francine Palumbo here." Her voice was no longer liquor-slurred, but had reacquired its usual gracious-lady lilt. "I've been working up the courage to call you for some time. I can't begin to apologize for the state I was in the other day."

Apologetic phone calls from Palumbos were becoming another constant in my daily life. "I'm just glad I was there to help, Francine," I said demurringly.

"No, really, I know I made an absolute spectacle of myself. It was totally inexcusable. I admit I have a drinking problem, I've been in AA for years, and mostly I do have it under control. But every now and then I fall off the wagon. Not often, but it happens." She heaved a ponderous sigh. "The worst thing is that *this* time it happened just before I picked up Ollie from his drama coach."

"Is Ollie taking acting lessons?"

"Mmmm. He's booked a few commercials, but what he really wants is to get on a series."

"Like *In the Same Boat*?" I couldn't resist.

"Well, yes, except without so many co-stars. But my point is that seeing me like that, well, it was just devastating to him. You know how sensitive he is."

I let that go by. Vlad the Impaler's mom probably thought he was sensitive as well.

"I hope I didn't leave you with a wrong impression," she went on.

The tequila was rapidly mellowing me. "It's okay, Francine. I'm sure you do have your problem under control."

"No, no, about Julia, I mean."

"What about Julia?" I said quickly.

"I don't want you to think I'm hiding something. I can truly understand how anxious you are to clear all that up. I mean, my god, I'm sure you've been through living hell! And it's not that I don't want to help you. It's just that I really don't think dredging up the past is going to be of any use." She lowered her voice. "You see, that person you were asking about . . ."

"Mr. Pete," I said bluntly.

"Mmm. Well, he's dead."

"Oh?"

"His name was Gardiner, Lawrence Hanningay Gardiner. A retired banker, lived up in Montecito. He passed away last year, of a cerebral aneurysm, I believe."

She was lying. I was absolutely certain of it. I suspected that what she had done was fluttered over to the Santa Monica library, scanned the obits in last year's *Times* and pounced on a suitable candidate. "Why didn't you tell me this the other day?" I asked.

"He had a family, wife, kids, grandchildren—I suppose I had some idea of protecting them. Why drag his name through the dirt after all this time, when it couldn't possibly do anybody any good? But I know that I can count on you, Lucy, to be discreet."

"Oh, sure. Mr. Gardiner's secret is safe with me."

"Great, I knew you'd understand. I'd love to chat longer, but I've really got to run. We're attending that Magic Wand thingy tonight, and I've got to dig up something to wear that won't be a total disgrace."

"Then I'll see you there," I said.

A pause. *"You're* going?"

"I'm afraid so. Summer reserved a few tables for the hoi polloi."

"Really, Lucy, that's not at all what I meant. But of course I know how outrageous you always like to be." Breezy laugh. "I'll see you later then, it'll be such fun."

She hung up. I put down the phone and outrageously tossed back the Cuervo.

AN HOUR AND A HALF later, a car cruised into the driveway. The front bell chimed. I opened the door to Teresa Shoe.

"Here I am," she announced. "How do I look, okay?"

She looked, in fact, extraordinary—packed into a shiny tube of sweetheart pink, with a kind of Carmen Miranda ruffle on the hem that rumbaed up one stocky calf to the knee. The ribbon-banded top revealed an inch and a half of cleavage. Detective Shoe had cleavage! This was so disconcerting that for a moment I couldn't speak.

"You look very nice," I finally managed.

"Good. I borrowed the dress from my neighbor's kid, Sonia. It was supposed to be her prom dress, but turns out she's three and a half months knocked up and can't get it zipped. So I'm doing the honors." She hooked two thumbs into the top of the dress and yanked it higher, reducing the décolletage a quarter of an inch. "Should we hit the road? I might as well drive, my car's already out."

Was I going to tool up to this shindig in a bashed-up Taurus caked with road dust? Not a chance. I picked up the keys to Kit's Beemer and moved purposefully toward the garage door. "I think we'd be more comfortable if we took Kit's."

"Suit yourself."

We got into the Beemer, and I backed it out, past the car parked in the driveway. Not the Taurus. A newish white Jetta. "Is that your car?" I inquired.

"Actually, it's my husband, Frank's. Mine's in the shop. The brakes sound like a cat in heat."

Translation: she didn't want me to recognize the car she'd been tailing me in. I pulled out into the street. We both flicked a tropistic glance at the Prentice house. The atmosphere inside the Beemer was suddenly so thick it might have been squeezed from a tube.

"What does your husband do?" I asked conversationally.

"Frank? He's a minister."

"You mean like in a church?"

"No, like in a Seven-Eleven. Of *course* a church. Methodist. For some reason, don't ask me why, there's a whole mob of Methodist Koreans."

"A homicide detective and a minister. Unusual combination."

"I don't know. When you think about it, we both deal in what they used to call sin. Nowadays you've got to say social pathology."

I grinned. "By the way," I said, "it's probably not a great idea for me to keep calling you 'Detective.' "

"Probably not."

"So, what do I call you—Teresa?"

"Terry, if you don't mind. Teresa's got too saintly a smell to it. Mother Teresa. Saint Teresa, the Little Flower. It never really fit me."

I agreed with that. We inched onto the Santa Monica Freeway, clogged at this hour with homeward-bound beachgoers. The setting sun behind us edged the windshield with refracted fire. "I've been meaning to ask," I said airily. "Have you made any progress in tracking down the hippie in the Mercedes?"

Terry shot me a sidelong glance. "What?"

"You know—the hippie-looking bearded guy driving a Mercedes. The one witnesses reported seeing about the time of Julia's murder."

"Where did you hear that?"

"And what about the fingerprint on Julia's inner thigh? Any leads on it?"

"None of this information was released. I'd like to know where you acquired it."

I gave an enigmatic little shrug. "I have my sources."

"You want to be more specific?"

"Not really."

"You know it's a crime to interfere with an investigation, don't you?"

"I wouldn't dream of interfering with it. I just want to know if you're making any headway in the case. I mean, I've heard that if a homicide isn't solved in the first forty-eight hours, it's usually never solved at all."

"Yeah, I've heard that too," she said. "Listen, I've cleared eighty-two percent of my cases."

"So you get a B minus."

"Huh, that's a goddamn A plus." She rather smugly shifted her oversized beaded evening bag from her lap to the floor. We drove for several minutes in silence. "So, fill me in on this Magic Wand thing," she said. "Where's your three thousand dollars gonna go?"

"To terminally ill kids. The money the foundation raises is used to grant them a special wish."

"What's that supposed to mean?"

"Well, for instance, if a kid really loved Batman movies, Magic Wand might arrange for Val Kilmer to spend a day with him."

A peculiar sound issued from the detective's mouth, something between a honk and a hoot. "There's real Hollywood thinking for you. A kid gets to pal around with Val Kilmer for a day and suddenly his life's complete, it's okay for him to drop dead."

"I think you're missing the point," I said icily. "And maybe that was a bad example. There are plenty of more meaningful things . . ."

She cut me off. "If I was a kid about to check out, you know what I'd wish for? I'd wish for a goddamn cure."

"Well, naturally," I flashed back, "but if a cure wasn't possible, wouldn't the next best thing be to have some dream come true? If it was one of your kids, wouldn't you want that?"

"Look," she said, "if it was one of my kids, and god please forbid it should ever be, but if it was, and some do-gooding charity wanted to blow a wad of money on him, you know what I'd say? I'd say spend every last dime doing whatever to keep my kid alive for another year, another month, another day if that's all that's possible! Because I'll tell you something. I've seen a hell of a lot of death, in just about every shape it comes in. And maybe it's not the end. Frank doesn't think so. My mother, who's practically the main support of Our Lady of Mercy up in Modesto, *she* certainly doesn't think so. But you can't prove it by me."

There was nothing I could reply to this. I merged onto the downtown exit pondering the odd thought that I might have to start liking Detective Teresa Shoe.

IT SAID A LOT ABOUT Summer Rossner that she had chosen the restored old Biltmore for this affair—not only that she had the taste to select the most splendidly opulent venue in L.A., but also the power to make hundreds of the town's major players schlep to the wilds of downtown on a Sunday night.

The limos began five blocks away, black and white stretches and superstretches, all with darkened ogle-me-not passenger windows. I cruised into line, feeling like a puppy in a school of barracudas. We were still two blocks away when a red-liveried valet tapped on Terry's window.

"We get out here?" Terry asked me.

"Apparently we do."

On any ordinary Sunday night, the sidewalks of downtown would have been as lifeless as if a neutron bomb had been detonated in the vicinity just minutes before; but now Olive Street and the bordering Pershing Square were mobbed ten deep with gawkers, cordoned off from the red-carpeted sidewalk by velvet ropes. As Terry and I trudged past their ranks, a hundred faces lit with the question "Somebody . . . or nobody?" "Nobody" was the swift conclusion, and a hundred faces switched back off.

We veered into the motor arcade at the hotel's entrance and the carpet became thickly strewn with flower petals. Flanking the doors were eight harpists dressed as angels and strumming Vivaldi. The other side of the drive was jammed with photographers and on-camera reporters.

"I hope I don't get on TV," Terry muttered, patting down her wind-blown bangs. "Downsey would never let me hear the end of it."

I chuckled mirthlessly at the thought that anybody was going to take our picture. The arrival of nobodies like us was generally a cue for the media to grab a few moments' R and R. But suddenly the pack sprang alive, cameras and mikes brandished like weapons of assault. They've recognized us! I thought in a panic. It's going to be the post-Julia frenzy all over again!

Then I realized that the lenses were focused behind us. I turned to see Mattie Ballard and Tom Farmer emerge from a white Mercedes limo. Mattie breathtaking in a gown of silvery chiffon, Tommy svelte in a bespoke black dinner jacket. Waving graciously to the cheering throngs in the manner of Charles and Di in Happier Days.

"Maybe there really is a magic wand," I said to Terry. "The last time I saw those two, they looked like a couple of derelicts."

Terry stared, mouth agape. "They sure look like movie stars to me."

*   *   *

WE CONTINUED ON INSIDE. HEAVEN was the theme of the benefit, and for one dazzling moment it seemed we'd actually wandered through the pearly gates. The Grand Ballroom, lit in dusky violet, was permeated with spangles of light that fell gently and continuously, like a shower of stars in an evening sky. The tables, covered in gently billowing white gauze, appeared to float in this spangled sky like puffs of clouds. And all around the clouds swirled eddies of gorgeous people.

"Wow!" Terry gasped.

I agreed: wow! Every so often Hollywood really could produce magic. "I guess we should get ourselves a drink," I suggested.

We moved a little farther into the hereafter. Waiters circulated with trays of hors d'oeuvres, some decked out as angels in white robes and golden halos, others as monks in brown, rope-belted sackcloth—the itchy-looking sackclothed ones cast looks of dolorous envy at the flowy-robed ones. A small orchestra tucked into a corner played heaven-themed songs.

As "Pretty Little Angel Eyes" segued into "Pennies from Heaven," the figure of Pamela Pemmel emerged from the star-spangled gloaming. "Lu-cy!" she shrieked and lip-smacked the air beside both my cheeks. She wore a one-shouldered mini-sheath in a tiger print, with tusk-shaped earrings and a dozen clattering bangles. Sheena of Rodeo Drive. "Isn't this spectacular?" she bubbled on. "Isn't it to die for! No pun intended, of course. You've got to hand it to Summer. Frigid as an Eskimo Pie, but what style!"

Terry Shoe let out a dry laugh. Pamela realized I had a companion. She took in Terry's Carmen Miranda getup and her brows rocketed to the top of her hairline.

"Terry Shoe, Pamela Pemmel," I said.

"Pleasure," Pamela said faintly. "Where are you sitting?" she asked me.

I glanced at my seating ticket. "Table one-sixty-four."

"Siberia. We're forty-two. Between the Newgate table and one of TriStar's."

"Newgate Cinema has an entire table?" I asked.

"One has to at this event, doesn't one? *We* do. In the eighties, what counted was how much you made and what you paid for your house, but in the nineties, it's how much money you give away. I'm forever twisting my clients' arms to get them signed on to the right causes. When it comes to charity these days, it just doesn't pay to be cheap. Though, speaking of cheap . . ." Her voice dropped to signal she had a scoop. "Guess who's here? Your bereaved neighbor."

"Woody?"

"The very same."

"That's strange," I said. "I saw him just a few days ago—he seemed almost shattered with grief. It's a miraculous recovery."

"Yeah, but Julia had already sprung for six tickets, and Woody Prentice would rise from his *own* grave rather than let nine grand piss down the drain."

"Who's using the other tickets?" Terry spoke up.

"Nobody. Entourage. Two Morris agents, one with a wife. That creepy bodyguard of Woody's, Griff whosis. And some trash princess that Griff says is his niece, wink wink." The entire time Pamela had been talking to us, her eyes, now tinted jungle green, had been darting constantly around the room—it was, after all, a Happy Hunting Ground of new clients. Now they suddenly lit on prey. "There's Daryl!" she squealed. "The grapevine says she's shopping for a new publicist. Ciao, Lucy. Nice to meet you, uh . . ." She scurried off.

I turned to Terry. "So, what do you think?"

"That can't be her real eye color."

I made an exasperated sound. "I mean about what she told us. Aren't you surprised that Woody's here?"

She shrugged. "Life goes on. It's my experience that after the first shock, people handle their grief in different ways. Some seem to bounce back fast. It doesn't always tell you anything about what's going on underneath."

"Okay, then, how about the fact that Sandy Palumbo's company, Newgate Cinema, which has been bouncing checks all over town, has bought an entire table. Fifteen thousand bucks. Not bad for a company that's supposed to be going belly-up."

"Palumbo—he's the one with the gold-digger wife, right?"

I nodded. "Francine. Come on, I'll find them for you."

Terry seemed more interested in gawking at Michelle Pfeiffer, who'd just made an entrance, but she followed me farther into the eddies of star-spangled meeters and greeters. At the far end of the ballroom was a dais, also covered in cloudlike billows, and, through another feat of Hollywood magic, a shimmering rainbow arced above it. As we approached the tables directly in front, I nudged Terry. "There are the Palumbos," I said. "Just to the right of Tom Arnold."

"They look like they're running the whole show," she observed.

It was true: Sandy and Francine stood haunch-to-haunch, hundred-watt grins blazed across their faces, and pumping a continuous succession of outstretched hands. Francine, I noted, had managed to scrape up something not totally disgraceful to wear— a stunning little Isaac Mizrahi number made of silk organza roses I'd just happened to see while flipping through the pages of *Mirabella* in my dermatologist's office.

"That dress Francine's wearing . . ." I whispered to Terry. "It cost over six grand."

She sucked in her cheeks. "The lady sure knows how to spend. But *he* doesn't dress so hot. He's wearing cowboy boots with his tux."

"Sandy always wears cowboy boots. It's his trademark. He probably even wears them in bed."

Before we could move farther, another party surged up on an intercept path. It was Woody Prentice, combed, dapper, trailing his entourage. At the sight of him, both Palumbos froze like elk caught in headlights of a Chevy four-by-four. Woody also stopped dead in his tracks. For a moment, it was a standoff: they regarded each other with unmistakable loathing.

Then Francine pronounced Woody's name and held out her arms.

Woody produced a crooked smile and tottered forward.

Woody hugged Francine. Sandy hugged Woody. The pony-tailed Griff strode up and squeezed Sandy's hand. The two Morris agents and the one wife bopped up for handshakes and social kisses.

The only member of the entourage not included in this one-big-happy-family was a girl of about twenty-two. She hung back, looking as if she'd just stumbled in by mistake from the Viper Club—her sleazy black slip dress was straight out of Frederick's of Hollywood.

"That must be Griff's niece, wink wink," I said to Terry.

But I was talking to myself. Terry had suddenly disappeared.

18

OUR TABLE REALLY WAS SIBERIA, within elbow-smacking distance of the emergency exit. When I finally navigated my way to it, I found Terry, to my great annoyance, ensconced in her seat, absorbed in examining the lavish centerpiece.

"These are real," she declared, fondling the petal of a tiger orchid.

"Of course they're real," I snapped. "Summer Rossner would hemorrhage at the mere thought of an artificial flower." I settled in my seat, my knees tangling in the voluminous gauze of the tablecloth. "What made you disappear like that?"

"I didn't want to take the chance of Woody recognizing me. And he probably would've—Downsey and I spent a lot of time talking to him, you know."

I hadn't thought of that. "Were you the ones who broke the news to Woody about Julia?" I asked.

"Yeah. Downsey's good at that kind of thing. He'd've made a hell of an undertaker."

"How did Woody react?"

"You still think he's faking it?"

I shrugged.

"Well, if you wanna know, he took it pretty bad. He

kind of crumpled up on himself. Got ten years older right as we were watching him. Then he just kept saying, 'How did it happen? How did it happen?' over and over again." She plucked a pale yellow lily from the centerpiece and studied it, as if still not convinced it wasn't plastic. "Of course," she added, "he is an actor. We've taken that into consideration."

"A sitcom actor. Not exactly in a league with Olivier."

"That's a point. That girl who was with him—the one wearing her underwear? Did you catch a look at her?"

I nodded. "If she was Griff's niece, he didn't seem too anxious to introduce her to the Palumbos. But the rest of them sure got kissy-face. Except, did you notice their reaction when they first saw each other?"

"Yeah. Like wet dogs on a hot night."

"And yet Francine Palumbo was supposed to have been Julia's best friend."

Terry Shoe's response to this statement was to turn her wine-glass upside down—then I noticed one of the haloed waiters hovering behind us, bottle in hand. "You don't drink?" I asked Terry.

"Jeez, yeah, I drink. But I promised Frank I'd stick to soda tonight."

Fortunately, I hadn't made any such promises. I didn't protest as my own glass was filled with an amusing little Rheinhessen.

A gilt shopping bag decorated with Raphael putti sat on each plate. Terry began to explore the contents of hers—favors from all the major studios, videos, CDs, T-shirts embossed with the titles of upcoming movies, a Fox paperweight, an MGM key ring, Disney wind-up toys. "So this is what your fifteen hundred dollars buys," she said with some disdain.

"No, all that money goes to the charity. These are gifts."

"Yeah, I've noticed that the richer people are, the more they love getting freebies."

"Isn't there some cop rule against accepting gifts on the job?" I asked.

"I'm not on the job. I'm your guest." She tucked the bag proprietorially under her chair.

The orchestra had launched into "Stairway to Heaven," in what seemed to be a cha-cha beat. The rest of our table began to fill up. Each new arrival made a quick scan of the table, ascertained it was celebrity-less and mogul-less, and assumed an air of "I'm only at this seat because I left my *real* ticket in a suit sent to the dry cleaner's."

The waiters began to serve the entrée, a task made difficult by their flowing celestial sleeves, which tended to get entangled in the contents of the plates. The current culinary vogue was Tall Food—all the ingredients of a dish stacked artistically on top of one another; ours was a tower of salmon, blue-corn waffles and zucchini curls, topped by two waving stalks of scallion, like the antennae of some extraterrestrial insect.

"How do you eat this?" Terry hissed to me.

"I don't think there's a protocol. Just dig in."

She dubiously prodded the salmon layer with her fork, and the entire tower toppled in ruins. With a laugh, I laid siege to my own.

I'd nearly finished when a man plopped into the vacant seat beside me. He was so tiny, the table came almost to his chin, giving me the urge to go hunt up a phone book for him to perch on. His head was a miniature pink dome sparsely populated with wiry black hairs. "I've just had the most hectic drive from LAX," he announced in a piping voice. "My driver hadn't the first clue where he was going—we *near*ly ended up in Pasadena! Can you believe this table? Any further back, they'd've had to provide us with oxygen masks!" He'd been speaking as chummily as if we were already old buddies, so it was almost a surprise when he put out his hand. "Buster Wallace."

I knew the name—columnist for *Movietown* magazine. Known for always digging up the freshest and muddiest dirt. "*You* look familiar," he prompted.

"Lucy Freers."

His brow furrowed, then cleared. "Ah, yes, you're the one who fished Julia Prentice out of your swimming pool."

I made a little moue of acknowledgment.

"Now, doesn't it strike you as pe*cu*liar," he said intimately, "how fast the story simply evaporated from the media? Here we are, not even a month gone by, and it's as dead as Marilyn."

"There've been no new leads. Nothing for the media to milk."

A waiter tried to set down a plate, but my tiny neighbor waved it away. "I couldn't eat a thing. I've just spent three days on an Oliver Stone set, and my stomach's in absolute turmoil." He turned back to me. "I think the story's been squelched!"

"Really?" I set down my fork. "By who?"

"How about by Mr. Woody Prentice? That man's an eight-hundred-pound gorilla in the business. If he said *squelch*, squelched it would be."

"What are you saying?" I asked breathlessly. "You think it was Woody who killed his wife?"

"Nothing of the sort. I'm saying he's exercising damage control. Since Mrs. Prentice *is* dead, and under somewhat risqué circumstances, *Mr.* Prentice is anxious to keep that gravy train he's been riding on from coming to a halt. Sweetheart, wouldn't you, if you were pulling down three or four million smackers a year?"

"Does Woody Prentice earn that much?"

"Easy." Ticking off on his doll's fingers, he recited, "First of all, he's got the series. Then the syndication of the series. Parts in other movies. Personal appearances. And those commercials, all those big, fat commercials, with their big, fat, juicy residuals. Honey, I'd say conservatively four million a year."

This was a surprise. The Prentices lived well, but not *that* well. Though, of course, if Woody were as tight-fisted as Pamela Pemmel claimed, it figured he'd be hoarding his fortune rather than spending it.

"So, who *do* you think killed Julia?" I pursued.

"*Cherchez l'homme.* Look for lover-boy. Though, from what I know about the late Madame Prentice, that would mean having to check out practically every hetero male under forty in the three-one-zero area code."

Dessert was being served, a decadent slab of chocolate with a raspberry-perfumed crème fraîche. Buster Wallace did allow himself one of these. "Chocolate's my weakness," he confided, shoveling it in. "I crave the endorphin high."

Mouth full, I nodded dreamily, one chocoholic to another.

The babble of the crowd began to die down as Morgan Freeman, the night's master of ceremonies, appeared under the rainbow arch at the podium.

"Impeccable choice," pronounced Buster. He shook his head admiringly. "How does Summer do it? Every detail perfect!"

I was getting a bit fed up with hearing paeans to Summer Rossner's benefit-throwing perfection. I was beginning to understand why Julia had itched to knock her off her pedestal.

A projection screen whirred down and a short film was shown depicting the foundation's many good works—heart-wringing scenes of wasting kids being feted by Mickey and Donald or clinging to pony manes on Wyoming ranches. Even Terry Shoe's eyes looked damp by the end. Then awards. To Richard Dreyfuss for service above and beyond. To various studio honchos who'd been particularly generous with their studio's money. To a fat, motherly looking soul whose name and organizational function nobody really did catch or care about.

And now Morgan Freeman was calling for "the person who made this all possible." Summer Rossner bobbed up from her seat. She was wrapped in cloth of gold—so tightly wrapped, in fact, she was forced to move in mincing little steps like a geisha. The crowd held its collective breath as she hit the steps to the dais—would this be the time the preternaturally cool Mrs. Rossner did something as unprecedented as literally fall on her ass?

But she managed to make it intact to the podium, rewarded Morgan Freeman with an elegant peck on the cheek and presented a glowing face to us. There was applause. Which swelled to tumultuous applause, punctuated by scattered cheering. A few people rose to their feet; then, suddenly, the whole room was standing—studio heads, movers and shakers, bona fide legends of the silver screen—all on their feet clapping and whistling and cheering for Summer Rossner, Hollywood Mom *über alles*!

It was, without question, a moment of sheer glory. One that Julia Prentice had been threatening to steal.

Was that enough to kill for?

Buster Wallace's piping voice carried even over the din of applause. "We all know how David Rossner gets his jollies, don't we? Bondage, my dear! Tie me up, tie me down. Ms. Summerpie knows more knots than an Eagle Scout."

"How do you know?" I shouted.

"Sweetheart, I have sources everywhere. Ms. Summer goes through maids like most ladies go through Tampax. And when the poor darlings are fired, they're always willing to *habla* to me."

David Rossner into bondage . . . This was definitely interesting. As everyone began to settle back into their seats, I turned to share this tidbit with Terry. But she was not sitting down—she was heading at a brisk pace toward the exit. Damn her now-you-see-me-now-you-don't routine! I got up and started after her.

"Terry, wait!" I called, catching sight of her in the corridor. I followed her as she turned into the ladies' lounge. As I pushed open the door, I had what, if this had been in movie, would have been a flashback.

It was to when I was twelve years old. It was December 13, the Swedish festival of Santa Lucia, which my stepmother, Anna-Linda, though actually three-quarters Polish, always celebrated with traditional gusto. The highlight of the festivities was when the girl chosen to be St. Lucy appears in the darkened dining room, dressed in white and sporting a wreath of blazing candles on her head. That year, my stepsister Jilly was to have played the role; but several days before, she'd been caught in semi-dishabille with her pothead boyfriend, and since the saint portrayer had to be a virgin, Anna Linda, taking no chances, tapped me instead. For some reason, I now vividly remembered the sensation of hovering in the gloom while everyone sang endless choruses of "Santa Lucia," terrified that at any moment my hair was about to burst into flames.

That was also the year I got the almond. The Santa Lucia dinner featured a rice dish containing one almond, and whoever received it got a special prize. When I found I had it, I'd kept it, as the custom required, hidden under my tongue until the meal was over, the almond taste aromatically flavoring everything else I ate. And now I suddenly realized why these memories were flooding into my brain: an odor of bitter almond hung in the otherwise antiseptic air of the Biltmore's ladies' lounge.

The room was deserted, except for Terry Shoe. She was leaning into a mirror, applying a heavy coat of lipstick in a party-on! shade of tangerine.

"What . . . ?" I began.

She held a silencing finger to her lips.

A toilet flushed and two young women came stumbling out from one of the stalls. One was the trampy-looking babe from Woody's entourage. The other was an undernourished brunette in hot pants, fetchingly tattooed with a daisy on the shank of one skinny thigh. They advanced in a wobbly fashion, as if, with each step, they weren't a hundred percent certain there'd still be a solid floor beneath their feet.

"Well, ladies," Terry said into the mirror.

Two pairs of kohl-rimmed eyes swung in her direction.

Terry flicked open a Cover Girl compact and began to cake powder on her nose. "If I were you, I'd keep a low profile. Rumor has it there's some cops around. I'd hate to see anything spoil this nice time we're all having, if you see what I mean."

The girls' eyes began to dart helplessly to various points in the room, as if they were trapped. It finally dawned on them that the door was still available, and they propelled themselves unsteadily out.

"What was that all about?" I demanded, dropping onto the bench beside Terry.

"About smoking in the john," she said. She peered closely at her nose, dabbing an extra powder layer on a freckle.

"Since when is that such a crime?"

"Since when what you're smoking is heroin. Can't you smell it?"

My eyes widened. "That almondy smell?"

"Yep. Smack's made a big comeback with the under-thirties. 'Downtown,' they call it now. It's the latest thing on the club circuit."

"Terrific." I had a sudden vision of Chloe some five or six years hence, whining: "It's so unfair! I'm the only kid in my class who's not allowed to do heroin. Alwyn Rossner's even got her own pusher!" "Poor Woody," I said.

"Why 'poor Woody'?"

"A guy who's supposed to be Everybody's Grampa, just about the patron saint of family values . . . And meanwhile, everybody around him seems to be into sex and sin."

"That's show business." Terry snapped her compact shut and stowed it back in her knapsack-sized evening bag.

"Speaking of sex and sin," I said, "I just heard something I thought you should know."

"Yeah? Like what?"

"The guy sitting next to me is a gossip columnist, the kind that knows everything about everyone. And according to him, David Rossner is heavily into bondage."

"So?"

"So, don't you think that could be significant? I mean, it's possible he could be Julia's Mr. Pete. Don't forget, he became Mattie Ballard's agent during the filming of *The Delano Reunion*, which means he was hanging around at the right time."

"If I suspected everyone in this town with a kinky sex life," Terry said, "I'd be investigating this case till the end of my natural life." She lifted herself up and trundled off into one of the stalls.

*　　　*　　　*

WHEN WE GOT BACK TO the ballroom, Summer was wrapping up a lengthy list of thank-yous, in itself an illuminating survey of Who Was In and Who Was Out in show biz. More tumultuous applause, and then that was it. Nobody lingers over coffee at these events; the end of the speeches is the cue for a mass charge for the exit. Buster Wallace had already gone, vanishing as precipitously as he'd appeared.

It seemed to take about a week for the valet to summon up our car; we stood in the arcade clutching our gift bags, while all around us the more privileged hustled into already-hovering limos. Finally, Kit's Beemer inched into sight. I stuffed a ten-dollar bill into the valet's hand, scarcely waiting for Terry to close her door before I peeled out.

"Maybe you shouldn't be driving," Terry said. "I noticed you had a few glasses of wine, not to mention that champagne with dessert."

"I'm fine," I snapped and whipped into the jam of cars heading for the freeway. I braked. The car behind me was following so closely, it braked with a sharp squeal. I glanced into the rearview mirror. "Oh, my god!" I cried.

"What?" said Terry.

"That car right behind us . . . Look and see if the left head-light's dented."

Terry swiveled to look. "Yeah, it is. So?"

"And is it, by any chance, a blue Taurus?"

"It's too dark to tell for sure. But it's definitely an American make. Could be a Taurus. Looks like it hasn't been washed in a while."

The light changed. I swung a right, away from the main flow of traffic, onto the semideserted Hill Street.

"You're going the wrong way," said Terry. "The freeway's straight."

"Is the car with the dented headlight still behind us?"

She glanced back again. "Yeah. Somebody you know?"

"It's supposed to be *you*," I said.

"I don't get you."

I speeded up a bit. The headlights behind me kept pace. "I've noticed that car following me at least twice since Julia was killed. It's a woman driver, so I figured it was you tailing me in an unmarked car."

Terry giggled. I glared at her. "What's so funny?"

"Believe me, if I did tail you, you'd never know it."

"I'm really thrilled to know you're such a pro at surveillance," I said tartly. "The question is, what do I do now?"

"Signal you're pulling over. We'll let them make the move."

I flipped on the directional and began slowing down. I jumped at the sound of a loud bang. Shit, I thought, I've blown a tire. Kit's going to kill me.

"Jesus Rodriguez!" Terry exclaimed. "They're firing on us!"

I goggled at her. "You mean with a gun?"

Another retort and the side mirror beside me exploded. "Yeah, like with a gun," Terry said.

I stamped on the gas pedal. The Beemer shot forward; I breathed a silent prayer of gratitude to those Teutonic engineers who came up with a machine that could do zero to sixty in 6.8 seconds.

Terry snatched up the car-phone receiver. "It's not activated yet," I said, accelerating another ten miles per hour. "Kit decided to wait till he came back from location." The one time in his life Kit had ever practiced economy, and it had to be now.

Terry slammed the phone down, then delved into her bag. I had the odd sensation that she was going to take out her compact again; but instead she fished out a revolver.

"What's that?" I squeaked.

"What the hell do you think it is?"

"I mean, what are you going to do with it? Shoot out their tires?"

She issued one of her give-me-a-goddam-break snorts. "You movie people, you've got no sense of reality. In the first place,

the wheel would probably deflect the bullet, injuring some innocent party . . ."

I cut her off. "You call this reality? I thought you said you
were never really under fire."

"I didn't say never. I said *hardly* ever."

This sounded disturbingly like a nursery rhyme I had once
animated for *Sesame Street*. It had something to do with a lesson
in temporal relations. But this was clearly not the time to dwell
on the coincidence: I shot a yellow light and hung a two-wheeler
to the left, then began taking turns at random. The speedometer
edged over eighty. "Slow down!" I heard Terry shout, but her
voice seemed to be coming from over an intercom, scratchy and
far away.

Then suddenly we were the only car on the road. We were in
a desolate part of the old Los Angeles port area—the only sign
of life was the odd malt-liquor can rattling against a curb.

"I think we lost them," Terry said, looking back.

"Thank god," I breathed. There was a loud thumping noise in
my ear, which I vaguely identified as my heart pumping furiously.

"Uh-oh," Terry said.

"What?" I checked the rearview mirror. Several blocks behind
us gleamed a pair of headlights—it might not have been the
Taurus, but then again, it might *have* been. I swung the nearest
sharp right and careened into a narrow alley.

"Oh, jeez, it's barricaded!" Terry gasped.

This was true—we were hurtling at seventy-five miles per hour
toward a line of low wooden barricades blocking off the alley's
exit. I slammed on the brakes; we went crashing through, strew-
ing sawhorses in all directions. Then we fishtailed to a stop in
the middle of the adjoining street.

Without thinking, I bolted from the car. "Hey, you!" someone
yelled. Figures were running toward me from out of the dark.
Fingers clamped tightly around my arm.

Then two more gunshots rang out. I wrenched myself free and, with a burst of speed that would have made Jackie Joyner-Kersee stare, sprinted into the haven of a brightly lit sidewalk.

The thought had just begun to register in my brain that perhaps it was *too* brightly lit when a man's body crashed *splat!* on the pavement beside me.

19

"CUT!" BELLOWED A MEGAPHONED VOICE. "God friggin' damn it, cut!"

I was still staring transfixed at the body sprawled at my feet. It appeared to be dressed in a suit made of jonquil-yellow Reynolds Wrap, with a color-coordinated helmet on its head. And its arms and legs seemed to flop in weirdly rag-dollish angles, as if the fall had not just broken the bones but totally disintegrated them.

Yet even in my state of muddled panic, the word *cut* meant something. I dragged my eyes up from the ground, and suddenly everything came into focus. Arc lights. Camera cranes. Cables.

Congratulations, Lucy, I told myself. You've just insinuated yourself smack into the middle of a film shoot. Specifically, into a no doubt wildly expensive special-effects shot. The body was a dummy. It had come plummeting from the top of an adjacent skyscraper.

I jumped as something swooped down behind me. It was the camera crane, the operator slicking back his hair with perplexed agitation. In fact, everyone around seemed to be making the same sort of whatta-we-do-now? gesture.

Two youngish guys were converging on me. One, a second assistant director, laden down with pouches, fanny packs, clipboards, eyes bulging with I'm-never-gonna-work-in-this-business-again terror and shouting frantically into a headset: "What the fuck happened? Talk to me. How did this happen?"

The other guy, an aristocratically unencumbered first assistant director, came up, eyes shooting daggers at the second. "Jesus, Ronny, you tell me the sets are locked up, I assume they're secure!"

"I *had* the sets locked up," the second whimpered.

The first stuck a thumb at me. "Does this look locked-fucking-up? You're in deep shit."

A small woman burst out from behind a bank of monitors. Brandeis University sweatshirt, Reebok air soles, blue corduroy baseball cap mashing down a strawberry-blond frizz of hair—all standard-issue director's garb. She came charging across the set, fire streaming from her nostrils, yelling bloody murder.

Both ADs began to resemble quaking aspens in a high wind. In an instant, the director was on them. "Who the hell's responsible for this?" she screamed.

"That's what I'm finding out," the first said promptly. "Don't worry, I'll get to the bottom of this." Covering your ass—a time-honored Hollywood tradition.

The director pivoted on an air-cushioned heel and began on me. "You, lady, you've just ruined my fucking seventy-five-thousand-dollar shot!"

"Helene?" I said.

She paused, mid-rant. "Lucy?"

It was Helene Kaplan, one of the first female directors to make the big time. Also big-time Hollywood Mom, with a daughter, Tara Melisande, in the first form at Windermere. At one point, we'd been fairly friendly. I'd even attended her baby shower—a bona fide "power shower," my recent Oscar nomination having qualified me for the guest list. I recalled that Helene had opened my gift right after Barbra Streisand's. Barbra's had been a museum-quality Art Nouveau bed lamp signed by Louis Comfort Tiffany. Mine had been a denim jacket from Baby Gap. My friendship with Helene had rather petered out after that.

I also recalled reading in *Variety* that she was shooting something futuristic, starring Keanu Reeves as an android private eye—which would explain why I now saw Keanu Reeves pacing by the monitors in a platinum wig and another of those pastel aluminum-foil suits.

Helene was eyeing me in a way that suggested that this sudden renewal of our acquaintance was not about to make her burst into a warm chorus of "Auld Lang Syne." I could see her point— here she'd worked long and hard to create a realistic vision of L.A. in the year 2020, and up pops a woman in a Mamie Eisenhower— era gown. What could I say? That some maniac in a Taurus was taking potshots at me, and the only way I could save my life was by making a sudden cameo appearance in her movie?

"Would somebody please tell me what's going on?" she finally spluttered.

Another second AD, a chunky young woman with pens hanging like dog tags from a cord around her neck and bulging many-pocketed pants, came running up. "Keanu's gone back to his trailer," she announced. "He says this has all made him fall out of character, and he's gonna need at least an hour to get his concentration back."

"Piss on a stick! We're already three hours behind schedule." Helene executed another pivot and charged off toward the trailers.

The remaining ADs seemed at a loss for what to do now; we stared edgily at each other, none of us daring to make the first move. A beer-bellied prop man ambled up, hoisted the "body" over his shoulder and trudged off with it.

Two leather-jacketed cops who'd been lounging against their motorcycles evidently enjoying the festivities now began to head toward me; they walked in a bowlegged gait like old cowboys. Terry Shoe materialized from some indeterminate point behind me. "It's okay, officers, she's with me," she announced. "Shoe, West L.A. Homicide."

Both pairs of cop eyes glommed immediately onto her cleavage. With an exasperated snort, Terry riffled in her bottomless bag and fished out her ID. The unit cops, who were probably retired beat officers, instantly looked impressed. The three went into one of those huddles cops seem to delight in, while I took the opportunity to melt out of the limelight. I cowered in a murky spot near the honey wagons, watching as they exchanged a hearty laugh, no doubt at my expense. They broke formation, and I ventured out of hiding.

Terry gave a thumbs-up. "We're out of here."

"So what did you tell them? That I was an escaped lunatic you were escorting back to the asylum?"

"Something like that. We better make it snappy, before that director decides she wants your scalp."

I began a brisk, if wobbly, trot to the car. "I'm driving," Terry declared. "No arguments. Your hands are shaking."

I looked down at my hands. It seemed vaguely interesting to me that they were, indeed, shaking uncontrollably. I handed her the keys.

"Also, I suggest you come home and stay the night with me," she added. "Just to be on the safe side."

"Okay," I said meekly.

THE FIRST THING I WAS aware of when I awoke in the morning was that my feet felt gritty, as if I'd spent the better part of the night at the beach. The second was that Simba, the Lion King, was hovering in soft focus just beyond my nose.

I blinked, and Simba, along with the rest of his jungle pals, consolidated into a pattern on a pillowcase. "This is my room, you know," piped a soprano voice.

I rolled onto my other side. A little boy with black eyes stood beside the bed, staring solemnly at me. It all came back to me: I was in Terry Shoe's house, a cedar-shingled ranch in Canoga Park. Bedded down in her youngest son's sandy bed. Wearing a borrowed nighty, pink polyester with rosettes.

"I had to sleep with Joey, and he kept sticking me in my leg with his gross toenails."

"Gee, I'm sorry," I said. I clutched the sheet to my neck and sat up. I was definitely in a kid's room. Every inch of surface space was covered by something either repulsive, silly or of questionable sanitation.

"It's okay. Mom said some bad guys were after you, so you gotta stay here." He sounded so nonchalant, I wondered if Terry frequently brought her work home.

Terry herself appeared in the doorway. "Patrick Suk, you move your butt out of this room, pronto. Mrs. Freers needs privacy."

"I just wanna get my soccer ball."

"Then get it and scram."

The boy fished a ball out from a clutter of stuff under a dresser and scooted out of the room. "Did you sleep okay?" Terry inquired. "This room's a real hellhole. I'd've put you in Sunny's, but her gerbils tend to get out of their cage, and I figured you had enough excitement for one night." She set down a pair of navy sweatpants and a white T-shirt. "These are Frank's, so they should sort of fit. I'm guessing you don't want to get back into that ball gown."

"You're guessing right. What time is it, anyway?"

"Quarter to eleven."

"God!" I'd had trouble getting to sleep. Every time I dozed off, I heard a gunshot and jerked back awake. "Don't you have to get down to the station house or whatever?"

"I'm on call today, but I'll go in later. I've got paperwork up the kazoo. Frank wanted to say hi, but he had budget meetings and had to get up to the church hall."

Guiltily, I remembered, "His car's still at my house."

"He rode his bike. Wasn't thrilled about it, but so it goes. I

put a new toothbrush on the sink in the john across the hall.
When you're ready, there's some breakfast in the kitchen. Oh,
and don't say anything to the kids about the shooter last night.
I don't want them to get worried."

THE SMELL OF FRYING BACON, at once enticing and sick-
ening, greeted me as I slouched into the kitchen.

Terry handed me a steaming mug of coffee. "I don't have
those gourmet beans of yours, but it's Yuban. How do you like
your eggs?"

"Anything. Scrambled is fine."

I grasped the mug tightly and sat down at a speckled Formica
table of a type which, should it suddenly materialize in Francine
Palumbo's Family Room of the Nineties, would send her into
convulsions. In fact, just about everything in the Shoe establish-
ment would offend the aesthetic sensibilities of most of my Hollywood acquaintances. For several moments, I entertained myself
by redistributing Terry's furnishings among them. To Summer
Rossner's palazzo, I bequeathed thirty thousand square feet of
baby-blue wall-to-wall carpeting. For Marsha Moss-Golson's
white-on-white contempo: the harvest-gold fridge with magnets
in the shape of broccoli, cauliflower, and a squatting dachshund.
To the Prentices' Down Maine abode, any of the Hummel
figurines.

Terry removed a carton of Tropicana HomeStyle orange juice
from the magnet-adorned fridge and began shaking it like an
oversized martini. "We ran a make on the license plate of the
Taurus," she said.

"You got the license number?" Brilliant detective that I was,
it had never even occurred to me to jot it down.

"Yeah, there was enough light on Hope for me to read it. It's
registered to an Ida Soniez. Filipina, legal resident. Mean anything to you?"

I ran a quick mental-directory search of all the Filipinos I knew. Our former gardener. Kit's chiropractor. The wife of one of the producers of Amerinda. The name Ida didn't attach itself anywhere. "Nothing," I said. "Did you get an address?"

"An apartment in Northridge. Downsey's already checked it out. The landlord said Soniez left in January, no forwarding."

This was unsettling. I took a gulp of the slightly bitter coffee. "Do you suppose she could be some kind of hired killer? You know—like a hit woman?"

"Hee, hee," giggled Terry.

I glared at her. "What's so funny about that?"

"She's sixty-four years old."

A Filipina granny racing around in a Taurus trying to blow my brains out—just about everything was wrong with this picture. "Okay, then, what's your theory?" I asked.

"I don't want to speculate until I have more facts."

She set the Tropicana carton on the table, then a plastic glass and a set of turquoise glass salt and pepper shakers. I perked up at the sight of the shakers. Authentic Depression glass. I picked up the salt, all too happy to focus on something other than my possible demise. "Did you know these shakers are collectors' items?" I said.

"Those things? They've been kicking around my family for years."

"They were made by a company called Saturn in the late thirties. This color, called zircon, is the most valuable. You could get about three hundred dollars for the set."

"It's hard to figure how some people like to throw away their money." She shot me a particularly meaningful look. Me! The haunter of flea markets, the one who'd insisted on listing our house! Kit was the impulse buyer, the one who never glanced at a price tag. Before I could protest this injustice, Terry went on, "You remember that movie set last night?"

"I do," I said coolly. "I don't think I'll ever forget that movie set last night."

"You know that actor, whatchamacall? He was wearing that shiny robot costume?"

"Keanu Reeves. He was an android, not a robot."

"Same difference. Anyhow, there was another guy hanging around the food table who looked just like him. Same exact costume, same height, same silver wig."

"It was probably his stand-in. Or else, it could have been his stunt double."

"Wait a minute. If you're an actor in a picture, there could be two other guys running around who look just like you?"

"There could be, yeah."

"It must get pretty confusing."

I shrugged. "If you're the poor AD who's supposed to keep track of the star between takes, it can be a real headache. Speaking of headaches, do you mind if we change the subject? The thought of my performance last night is starting to give me a doozy."

"You'll feel better if you eat something." She cracked two eggs into a bowl and began to beat them with a fork.

"I still don't see why you dismissed my tip about David Rossner," I said petulantly. "He certainly had the means, and now maybe a motive."

"So what did you want me to do, march right over and read him his rights? Anyway, you said he was into bondage. This Mr. Pete's thing was sadism, right? The one doesn't necessarily follow the other." She dribbled the beaten eggs into a pan of butter, then set strips of steaky bacon into a frying pan. "I worked vice before moving to homicide. I got a real good look at all the different games people like to play."

"Yeah? Like what else? Just out of curiosity."

"Jeez, where do I start? Okay, well, first off, you've got your fetishes. Shoe fetishists. Panty sniffers. Latex and rubber freaks. They've got whole magazines devoted to this kind of stuff. Then you got your water sports—golden showers, brown showers, if you know what they are."

"I do," I said queasily.

"Enemas are really big, don't ask my why. Water enemas mostly, but sometimes, for variety, they go for coffee or Dr. Bronner's peppermint soap. For some reason, enemas and latex seem to go together. For instance, there was one case, a guy who wanted to experience childbirth, right? So, he straps himself into a tight latex ladies' corset and does a three-hour enema session. Stomach swelled up like a beach ball. Killed him, of course."

"Yeah, of course."

"Sicko, huh? What else?" She stared dreamily down at the bacon sizzling in the pan. "Oh, yeah, branding. Folks that love the smell of frying flesh. And then you've got your minor specialties, like scarification, mummification. . . . You get the picture."

I definitely got the picture. And no longer wanted to tune it in. What I suddenly did want was to stay right here, in Terry's home, where the furniture was Scotchgarded and the calendar on the wall gave a daily reason to be happy ("rocky road ice cream with chocolate jimmies!"), and where husbands rode bikes instead of BMWs to work, even if they weren't so thrilled about it.

Terry put a plate in front of me. Scrambled eggs oozing butter. English muffins oozing butter. Four glistening strips of bacon. The news about saturated fat had apparently not yet reached the Shoe household. I nibbled a strip of bacon, discovered I was ravenous and began to wolf the food down.

A girl shuffled into the kitchen. Aside from shoulder-length black hair and the almondine shape of her eyes, she looked strongly like Terry. "Mom?"

"Say good morning to Mrs. Freers, Sunny," Terry instructed.

"Hi," she said shyly. Then, in almost the same breath, "Mom, Kelsey's mom is taking us to the mall 'cause Kelsey's only seen *Clueless* once, so I need five dollars."

"You got your allowance on Friday."

"Yeah, but I'm saving that for eight-eyelet Doc Martens, which *all* my friends got except me." This in a whining tone that was remarkably familiar. A compromise was reached—advance granted in exchange for yard chores—and Sunny pocketed her cash and tripped happily out.

"That sounded exactly like Chloe," I said.

Terry theatrically rolled her eyes. "It's that stage where everything's a negotiation, right? It drives Frank's folks crazy. It kills them that their grandkids are little Americans. They smile too much, they don't do enough homework, they got mouths. My oldest, Joey, the little snot, once asked Frank's mom if she ate dogs back in Seoul. I thought she was gonna skin him alive."

"Dogs!" I dropped my fork and jumped to my feet. "I forgot all about Lola!"

THIRTY MINUTES LATER I PULLED into my driveway, stopping next to Frank Shoe's Jetta.

"You got my card, right?" Terry said, getting out. "My pager number's on it. You got any problems, give a call."

I glanced nervously around. "Do you think I could get some protection? Like a squad car out front?"

"Yeah, like in the movies, right? You think this city can afford police protection to everybody who's ever threatened, then you're completely out of your mind. I still think your best bet is to get out of town." She hopped into the Jetta and backed it away.

I maneuvered the Beemer back into the garage. It no longer looked like a brand-new car. It looked more like a low-placing contender in a demolition derby. The trunk was nearly destroyed (Terry had blithely told me that a "firearms guy" had come to dig out the bullet while I was still asleep). One entire side had been battered by our run-in with the barricades, and, of course, that shot-out side mirror . . . Kit was going to faint.

Screw Kit! *I* was the one who'd almost become a permanent resident of Forest Lawn. Angrily, I stomped into the house.

No Lola came bounding up to greet me when I called her name.

I dashed from room to empty room, whistling and shouting for her, but no puppy yipped excitedly in response. I've killed her! I thought. She dropped dead of fright and starvation! What was I going to tell Justin? How could I, as a murderer of puppies, ever face my daughter again?

Behind the kitchen was a room scarcely bigger than a closet. It had been a maid's room back in the days when stifling cubbyholes had been considered suitable living space for "the help." Now we used it mainly to store the hundreds of screenplays Kit carted home—Kit had dubbed it "the old script graveyard." In here, behind a toppled stack of dog-eared scripts, I discovered a screen dislodged from a window, low enough for Lola to have easily escaped outside.

I raced out back, shouting her name. To my relief, there was an explosion of Saint Bernard from the thick of the rose garden. "Good puppy!" I crooned as she leaped and pranced around me. "Bad, bad me for forgetting about you."

Then I turned to survey the roses. They were in ruins. Bushes uprooted, blooms decapitated. My Myrna Loys that the butterflies loved . . . my Hula Girls that had nearly succumbed to rust . . . my showy Taj Mahals and Candy Apples and Cary Grants—all lay mangled together.

Lola barked proudly at her handiwork. "Yeah, I know, it serves me right," I said. I led her inside and settled her before an enormous bowl of Sci Di for puppies. Then I rang Justin's number.

"Yeah?" he answered.

"Hi, you're back," I said brightly.

A grunt.

"It's me, Lucy," I pushed on. "Since you're home, why don't I bring Lola on over?"

"I'm working. Hold on to her till later, okay?"

"Look," I exploded, "I've just had one bitch of a night. I've been chased and shot at and nearly killed. I made a total ass of myself in front of an entire feature-film crew, and had to sleep in a trundle bed with Lion King sheets and sand in my toes. So, if you think I'm in the mood to take any more crap, you can damned well think again!"

I slammed down the phone. It rang immediately. "What?" I shouted into it.

"You were shot at?"

"Twice. The second time was a goddamned close call. You wouldn't happen to know the price, offhand, of a new BMW side mirror, would you?"

"Jesus, this sounds wild!"

"It would be nice," I said frostily, "if you could sound a little less entertained and just a little more concerned."

"Hey, I am concerned, really. Look, I apologize for sounding like such a shit when you called. I get kind of wound up when I'm working."

I maintained an aggrieved silence.

"Why don't you come over for dinner?" he went on. "You obviously need some pampering and I'm a terrific cook, swear. It'll be more relaxed, we can really talk." He lowered his voice to a sexy bass-baritone. "I really do want to see you."

My last shred of resistance crumbled. "What time?"

"Eightish. Do you eat red meat?"

"I eat everything," I admitted.

I hung up, and sat for several moments, swept by a confusing array of emotions. On the plus side, I was about to have a tête-à-tête dinner with a man with whom I was decidedly in lust.

On the minus side, somebody out there wanted me dead.

I wandered to a front window and peered out at the ghostly residence across the street. Then I recoiled violently.

I had the distinct and eerie feeling that I was being watched.

20

THE PENNISLAWS' POOL HOUSE, UNLIKE my own spartan little casita, was truly a house—cathedral-ceilinged, with capacious loft bedroom, Mexican-tiled kitchenette and a massive, mirrored wet bar stocked with everything from Absolut vodka to zinfandel. It presided over a pool constructed in classic kidney shape—though, given Dr. P's medical specialty, I couldn't help thinking of it as a huge, shimmering aquamarine ear.

One wall inside the pool house was covered with a mosaic of gold- and platinum-plated CDs and albums, a clue to how Dr. Pennislaw had raked in his millions. He was no ordinary ear, nose and throat man—he was the rock and roll ENT. Whenever a top-of-the-charts rocker developed throat polyps from screaming "Baby, baby" into a mike, or suffered a touch of hearing loss from the constant decibel assault, or blew a hole through his septum with one snort of cocaine too many, it was Dr. Benes Pennislaw who was called to the rescue; and the next time the grateful patient had a record that went gold or platinum, he was likely to bestow the award on the good doctor as an extra token of thanks.

This gilded mosaic twinkled charmingly in the candle-light as Justin served dinner. He had not exaggerated his skills as a chef: there was marinated filet mignon grilled over mesquite, with a juniper, green peppercorn and cabernet sauce; grilled new potatoes in their jackets; a salad of wild greens filmed lightly with walnut oil and lemon.

"Superb," I said, savoring a tender bite of the filet.

"I'm thrilled that you eat meat," he grinned. "Half the women I meet in this town are on some kind of designer diet. No dairy, no wheat, no nonorganic. Julia, you know, passed herself off as a vegan—she claimed no animal protein ever passed her luscious lips."

"It wasn't true?"

"Hell, no. I caught her once scarfing down a cheeseburger on the sly."

"It's funny," I said with a little smile, "but I suddenly feel a lot more sympathy for her. All those pretensions and strivings of hers—they seem kind of endearing to me now. Maybe it's because of my recent brush with death—it's made me identify with her. I mean, we both nearly ended up as attractively young corpses."

Justin poured me some more Médoc. "I want to hear the whole story of this recent brush with death."

As we ate, I related my saga of the night before. It now suddenly seemed brave and daring and rather humorously adventurous. When I reached the part where I made my sudden debut under the bright lights, Justin laughed loudly. "I did a project with Helene Kaplan once," he said. "She takes herself just a little more seriously than the pope. I'd've given anything to see her reaction when you materialized."

"It was one of the most excruciating moments of my life," I said gaily. "A few minutes before, I'd been terrified I was going to die, and now I was beginning to regret that I hadn't."

Justin laughed again. "How did you escape?"

"Helene ran off to pacify her star. Then Terry Shoe patched things up with the unit cops, and we slunk off into the night."

"Wild." Justin raised his glass to his lips and sipped. "I'm still not sure I've got all this straight."

"What part?"

"The Who Killed Julia Prentice part. We're pretty sure she was clocked by a man, right? A guy who had sex with her just before doing her in, and who may or may not have had something to do with her fun-and-games past. Perhaps even her former whipping pal, this mysterioso Mr. Pete."

"Right . . ."

"And you're also pretty sure it was a guy who knocked you out in your backyard. Except that whoever's been following you and tried to blow your head off was a woman. Possibly a little old lady from the Philippines."

"So it appears."

"Then we're talking teamwork. Mother-son, husband-wife . . ."

"Employer-employee." Terry Shoe notwithstanding, I still wasn't willing to relinquish my hit-woman theory. Visions of Kathleen Turner in *Prizzi's Honor* danced in my head.

"Let's look at it from another angle," Justin went on. "Who knew you were going to that benefit?"

"The Rossners, of course. And Summer Rossner's assistant. And Mattie Ballard—she was the one who suggested I go. Oh, and the Palumbos— I'd talked to Francine just a couple of hours before. Also, one or two of my friends who've got nothing to do with any of this." I tapped my fork on my plate in an anxious tattoo. "It doesn't have to be someone who knew I was there. The Taurus could've followed me from home."

"Our pal, the nanny," he suggested. "The Filipina could be one of her friends on the nanny network."

Something about this pricked at my memory. Didn't I know someone with a Filipina nanny? If I did, I couldn't place it now. I slapped my palms on the table in frustration. "After all this, it should be getting clearer. Instead, everything just keeps getting murkier."

"This detective woman, she really has no leads?"

"That's what she claims. Except every so often she gets this smug cat-who-ate-the-canary look, as if she knew more than she was letting on."

"Maybe she just wants you to think that, instead of 'Duh, I don't know nothin'—which wouldn't reflect so hot on her detecting skills."

I grinned. He grinned back, eyes fixed on mine. Those blue, blue eyes. I felt a quick tightening in the pit of my stomach.

"How did Kit react?" he asked.

At Kit's name, I gave a guilty start. "About what?"

"Your getting shot at. He must be pretty freaked."

I glanced down. I hadn't called Kit. He'd left a message on the machine, something about heading up into the Canadian Rockies for a few days; but he'd been on a car phone and kept fading in and out of audibility, as if he really couldn't give a damn whether I could make out what he was saying. "I couldn't get hold of him," I lied. "They're out in the bush somewhere. You know how it is with location hunting."

The dark blue eyes looked searchingly at me. "So that explains why he hasn't come rushing back to protect you."

"Yeah," I said. But would he come rushing back? Ditch Sugerman and his precious movie, just because his wife had a harrowing escapade? Maybe I didn't want to put it to the test.

We sat silently a moment. The candle flames wiggled provocatively in a passing current of air, and Sting crooned in soft falsetto from hidden speakers. Then Justin sprang to his feet. "Dessert," he announced, picking up our plates. "You, stay where you are. You're being pampered, remember?"

He moved to the kitchenette, Lola at his heels, begging for scraps. This gave me a fine opportunity to ogle his body. He was wearing faded button-fly Levi's, an item of men's clothing I happen to have a thing for. I'd bought a pair for Kit once, but there was something peculiar about the fit—they bunched in a funny way in the seat, and he never wore them. Justin's, I couldn't help noticing, scooped his buns perfectly.

He brought back a plate heaped with cookies—madeleines and chocolate-dipped *biscotti*. "Not very inspired, but I've got something definitely more exciting to go with it." He crossed to the massive wet bar, removed two flutes off a shelf of glassware and a bottle of champagne from the minifridge. "Moët et Chandon eight-five," he pronounced, stripping off the foil. "I was saving it to celebrate my liberation from the bitch goddess, but this is a more fitting occasion." He popped the cork and poured. Frothy geysers of pale golden wine rose in the flutes.

We raised them, hesitating at a toast. "To neighbors," Justin proposed, "both dead and alive."

This was startling. I glanced at Justin, but he was already sipping his champagne, not waiting for a response. He really hadn't meant to be callous, I decided, and tasted my own. It was delicious, simultaneously crisp and creamy.

"So, what is this screenplay you're working on?" I asked. "Or is it top secret?"

He shrugged. "It's a thriller. Kind of noir, but with edgy humor, like Tarentino. I'm banking on it to resuscitate my career."

"What do you mean? You've got a hit movie to your credit."

"Yeah, but it was a collaboration, and now it seems I've got to prove to the studios I can do it on my own. *Irresistible* was considered a chick flick, so they all think it was mostly Nancy. But the fact is, *I* did most of the writing. I carried the bitch, and she waltzes off with the credit."

"Totally unfair," I agreed. I was all too prepared to hate the soigné blonde in the convertible.

"Forget that. I'd much rather hear more about you. Tell me— why animation?"

"What do you mean?"

"You're an outstanding artist. You could've gone in a lot of different directions. How did it happen to be animation?"

"I don't know . . ." I bit into a madeleine, the fabled food of memory. "I guess it was just the natural thing for me. I always loved to draw. I'd use anything—crayons, watercolors, lipstick, you name it. And I'd draw *on* anything—paper bags if that's what was there. The thing is, I'd be drawing a tree, but the branches would start to turn into arms and hands, and the trunk would sprout tiny eyes, and it would end up looking like my Aunt Bettina. But if I started *out* drawing my Aunt Bettina, she'd end up being a goose or a hat rack or something."

Justin chuckled appreciatively.

"Then in college I had an art professor, Mr. Steincreutz—he loved the way all my people turned into things and my things into people. He was the one who said I had the natural instincts of an animator. He suggested I go to film school and helped me get financial aid for NYU."

"And the rest is history."

"So to speak." Either the madeleine or the Moët was acting on me like a truth serum. "But I think there's another reason. Maybe the real reason . . ."

"Yeah?"

"Well . . . it's that in animation, there's no consequences. I mean, Wile E. Coyote gets flattened by a steamroller and then *boing!* he's three-dimensional again. Roger Rabbit can smash a whole stack of plates over his head and not even get a lump. Nobody stays dead. Nobody gets crippled. You just bounce back to what you were before." My voice faltered. Embarrassed, I reached for my glass.

Justin intercepted my hand. "Hey," he said softly.

I shrugged. "It's no big deal. I've been through the Jungian therapy bit. I worked this out a long time ago."

"Yeah, right." His fingers closed over mine, gently kneading. I tried to draw my hand away, but he held it firmly. "Relax," he murmured.

I tensed.

He smiled, lips parted, white teeth bared. Big Bad Wolf.

"Look, we both know there's this heavy thing between us. If we let it happen, I can promise you this—no consequences. No pressure. No jeopardy to your marriage. And I also practice safe sex."

I was suddenly finding it difficult to catch my breath.

Over the unseen speakers, a new CD began. Silky old Al Green. Justin turned my hand over and with a forefinger traced a shivery path up my palm, wrist and underarm. Again I felt the tight grip in the bottom of my stomach, and at the same time, something else—a peculiar feeling of displacement. This wasn't really me this was happening to. It was someone else, some other woman who just happened to be wearing the same bias-cut peach silk dress from the mid-thirties. And as long as this wasn't the real me, there seemed no harm in letting him pull me into his arms. Or in responding to his deeply probing kiss. Or in allowing his hands to slide langorously down my silk-clad back and buttocks.

"Let's do this right," he whispered after a moment. Grabbing the Moët bottle, he led me to the small spiral staircase that climbed to the loft bedroom. My knees felt rubbery, though whether from passion or nervousness I couldn't quite tell.

"Stay!" Justin suddenly said. For a startled moment, I thought he meant me. But then I realized it was directed at Lola, who was trotting behind us. She gave a cringing little whine, traced a tight circle, then lay down. "Good baby," Justin praised. He took my hand, and we continued upstairs.

A year or so ago, while Dr. Pennislaw was on tour with Snoop Doggy Dogg in Australia, his wife, Natalie, had checked into The Ashram for a couple of weeks of yoga, meditation and brown rice, and, having dropped eleven pounds, returned with a temporary mania for all things stripped down and Zen. The bedroom decor was obviously a spillover from that time: the only furnishings were a low platform bed with a tea-green cotton spread, a plain cherry-wood dresser and a basic desk with a straight-backed chair.

But the stripped-down Zen-ness was substantially challenged by Justin's bachelor messiness. Wrinkled clothes, Nikes, boxer shorts, issues of *Wired* and *Spin*, stray script pages, were strewn everywhere. "Shit, I meant to straighten this up," he muttered. He scooped up the detritus from the bed in one armful and deposited it in a pile on the dresser. Satisfied with this effort at homemaking, he turned back to me. "More champagne?"

"Please." I thrust out my glass rather desperately. He refilled it, and I chugged it back as if it were Bud Light.

He pulled me close again, and we exchanged another Moët-flavored kiss. Somewhat tentatively, I stroked his chest, surprised to feel the architecture of ribs and muscles rather than the little layer of insulation I was used to with Kit. The taut play of those muscles under my touch was admittedly thrilling. I allowed myself to melt langorously into the kiss.

Justin drew away. "Make yourself comfortable. I'll be right out," he murmured.

He disappeared into the connecting bathroom. Through the closed door, I could hear him taking a splashy pee. Listening seemed hardly conducive to romance, so I focused instead on making myself comfortable. I perched on the edge of the bed, but this was too prim a pose. I leaned back and draped myself in a come-hitherish pose against the pillow. Too slutty. I sat up, crossed my legs, Indian fashion; but this made me feel about six years old. Finally, I stood back up, pacing a little.

For god's sake, relax, I told myself. It's not like you really were the sainted virgin Lucia before you were married. You did have a bit of experience sleeping with strangers. And it's not like something that, if you don't use, you lose, like French, or a killer backhand, or solving quadratic equations.

The toilet flushed, and Justin began to bustle about. If he was getting undressed, then I should too. Eliminate that first-date awkwardness of fumbling for zippers and bra straps. Now I began to obsess about the state of my thirty-something body. Would he be grossed out by a touch of cellulite? I decided on a compromise. I'd be naked under a robe or a dressing gown, if I could find something suitable to put on.

I swung open the folding doors to one of the two closets. The racks were groaning with shirts and jackets, which was interesting—I hadn't figured Justin for such a clothes horse. And geeky clothes, at that. Here was a blazer, for instance, a supper-at-the-golf-club number with ersatz gold crest buttons—not quite something I could visualize Justin the Hip slipping into for a night at the Roxbury. It must be stuff his wife had made him wear. No wonder he was getting a divorce, I laughed to myself.

I rummaged through the racks, parting a set of button-down bleeding-madras shirts to get a better look. Then my heart skipped several beats. Tucked into the very back corner of the closet floor was a pair of Gucci loafers.

Green lizard-skin Gucci loafers.

Scarcely breathing, I bent to pick them up. Suddenly I was swept with a powerful sense of déjà vu. Then I realized where I had déjà vued this: in a movie, *The Jagged Edge*, the scene where Glenn Close goes poking through Jeff Bridges's closet looking for fresh sheets and stumbles on the typewriter with the out-of-whack letter *E,* thereby proving he was the cold-blooded murderer.

It's Justin, I silently gasped. He killed Julia! It all added up. After finding out I was snooping into the murder, he obviously wanted me followed, no doubt enlisting a female accomplice—someone with access to her mother's or aunt's or elderly neighbor's Taurus. Everything clicked into place. I must have been blind not to see it before: how he'd thrown me off track by planting the suggestion that the Taurus was an unmarked cop car; how he'd just "happened" to show up shortly after I was knocked out; how he was conveniently "out of town" last night while I was dodging bullets.

How without warning his voice could turn so chillingly hard and cold.

"What are you doing?" said the chillingly hard and cold voice.

I whirled, dropping one of the Guccis. Justin stood behind me, wearing nothing but a white towel wrapped sarong-style at his hips.

"Nothing," I said hoarsely.

"Looking for something?"

"Not really." I moved in a nonchalant manner in the direction of the staircase, hiding the other shoe behind my back. Justin sidestepped to block my path. As he did, his towel parted open, revealing a flash of pink. A lurid, bubblegum pink. I froze, transfixed. The fact that his penis appeared to have been "done" by Marsha Moss-Golson's decorator, Lois, struck me as singularly horrifying.

Justin abruptly readjusted the towel. "I told you," he said. "Safe sex."

"It's a condom," I blurted.

"Yeah. What'd you think I was doing in there?"

"Nothing." I added quickly, "I was just looking to see if there was a robe in the closet. You know, something to slip into to make myself comfortable." I attempted a breezy little laugh, but it came out a cackle.

He shot me a fishy look. "I've got a bathrobe in the john," he said and padded back into the bathroom.

On tiptoes, I made for the staircase and crept down it as quietly as I could, clutching the telltale Gucci. I hit the ground floor running.

But I had forgotten about Lola. She leaped up, barking ecstatically at our reunion.

Justin's face appeared at the top of the staircase. "For Chrissake, Lucy!" he exclaimed. He began to clamber down after me. Lola, now beside herself with delight, made a loving charge at him; while he disentangled himself, I beat it out the door.

Fog had settled in, the moss-dense gray fog that local weathermen insisted on referring to as "the marine layer"; it rolls in from the ocean, making everything clammy to the touch and nothing visible more than three yards away. I groped my way to the Pennislaws' front gate, certain that Justin was several paces behind; as I fumbled at the gate's bar latch, I imagined that at any second a blunt instrument would come bashing down on my skull. Then the latch gave way, and I burst out onto the street.

There was the most beautiful sight in the world—a Fast Alert security car cruising down the road on its appointed neighborhood rounds. "Stop!" I yelled and stepped off the curb, madly flapping my arms. The car rolled up beside me, and the officer at the wheel peered suspiciously out. Not the same guy who'd shown up after my run-in with the prowler—this one was small and wiry, with caterpillar eyebrows and a significant Adam's apple.

"Let me in!" I yelled.

"Wha'sa matter?" His voice was muffled by the glass.

"I need protection! That's what you're here for, isn't it, to give me protection?"

He scratched his Adam's apple while he weighed the merit of this logic. I pummeled the window. "I pay seventy-three fifty a month for your goddamned service! Open this door." Rather grudgingly, he released the door locks. I threw myself into the backseat. It reeked of fast food—ketchup, burger grease and powdered sugar providing the dominant theme, with a counterpoint of pickle, coffee and French fries.

The rent-a-cop clearly thought it unwise to keep his back turned to me; he shifted his buttocks, allowing a semirotation of his upper body. "So, what's going down?" he said. Obviously he picked up his cop jargon from *NYPD Blue.*

"Radio the police," I directed. "Ask for Detective Teresa Shoe in homicide. Tell her I've discovered the murderer, and I've got evidence to prove it."

"Evidence?" he repeated.

"Yeah, evidence." I brandished the Gucci loafer. His brows knit together in one thick, furry line. "Just call her," I insisted. "She'll understand."

Through the mist, I could make out Justin emerging from the Pennislaw gates. He had redonned his jeans and shirt and sneakers with the laces trailing.

The security man whirred down his window. "Hey, you!" he hollered.

"Don't call him!" I hissed, scrunching down in my seat. "He's the one."

Justin trotted across the street and peered bewilderedly at me in the backseat.

"Did you threaten this woman?" the cop demanded.

"Not to my knowledge. I thought what we were doing was consensual. What the hell's going on, Lucy?"

I peeked over the seat to make sure the officer had a gun. Fast Alert advertised "Armed Response," but you never know. Assured, I met Justin's eye with a steely glance of my own. "I found the shoes in the closet."

"What shoes?"

I displayed the loafer at the window with a triumphant flourish.

"Pennislaw's Guccis? So what?"

"Dr. Pennislaw's?" My voice cracked.

"Yeah. You don't think it's mine, do you? Christ, look at the size of the fucking thing."

I looked. It was enormous, at least a size 13. And Dr. Pennislaw was a bear of a man, six feet four or five. "Oh," I said.

"And anyway, you think I'd be caught dead in Guccis? Or in any of that shit in that closet? It all belongs to the doc."

I bit my lip hard. "Officer," I said, "I think I've made a mistake."

"So, you want me to call the detective or what?"

"No, that won't be necessary." He squinted at me again. I was becoming adept at interpreting law-enforcement body language, and what I now read suggested I cut short our interview. I quickly opened the door. "I'm really sorry to have bothered you. Have a nice evening," I added and slid out of the car.

The security man, with a last hard look in my direction, rolled his window back up.

I walked sheepishly with Justin back across the road. The dense, swirling fog lent a weirdly *Casablanca*-ish feeling to the scene, as if we were about to part romantically and go our separate ways to save the world. "Well . . . here," I said, awkwardly thrusting the Gucci at him. "I don't know what I was thinking. Sorry about all this." I took a few steps toward my own gate.

"Wait a second," Justin said, keeping up with me. "Do I have this straight? Were you actually going to finger me for killing Julia?"

"Look, the guy who attacked me in my backyard was wearing green lizard shoes. I find a pair of green lizard shoes in your closet. What was I supposed to think?"

"Well, hey, you missed the obvious. Pennislaw's your man. The doc's the murderer! Ear, nose and throat specialist brains ex-starlet! He never went to the Balkans, that was just a smoke screen. And now we've got him by the Guccis!"

"Go to hell," I snapped.

"Hey, I'm the one who should be pissed off. Having just been accused of cold-blooded murder."

"Can you honestly tell me that you never, even for an instant, suspected *I* might be guilty?"

His eyes briefly sidled sideways. "Okay, score one for you. So, now we're even, why don't we just go on back to my place and finish what we started."

"I think the mood's been broken," I said with astonishment.

"Then we'll just have to get it back." He reached out and slid a finger seductively down my upper arm. "The night, as they say, is still young. There's some Moët left. And now the fog's in, I could get us a fire going."

I pulled away, shaking my head. "It's not going to work. You were right, those clothes in the closet were obviously not yours. I think I was just looking for something to grab on to to stop myself from making a mistake. I'm just not cut out for casual sex."

"It didn't seem so casual fifteen minutes ago." He stepped purposefully toward me. I skipped several steps back.

"I'm not saying I'm not physically attracted to you," I said quickly. "But if I did go to bed with you, it would probably have more to do with some screwed-up idea of getting back at Kit."

"I told you," he said truculently, "it's not going to interfere with your comfy little marriage."

I stiffened. "My marriage is neither little nor, at the moment, particularly comfy. But that's still not enough for me to jump into bed with you." I decisively pushed open the gate. He started to follow me in; I slammed it shut and latched it. "Good night," I said, "and thanks for dinner."

He pushed his face against the bars of the gate, snarling like a caged animal. "You mean you're just gonna blue-ball me?"

"I wouldn't put it quite like that."

"You wouldn't, huh?" He gave a nasty laugh. "You fucking bitches are all alike. You think you're all such goddamn ball-breakers. Well, let me tell you something, you're just another uptight, frustrated broad who could use a good screwing. If you want to know the truth, I was doing you a fucking favor."

He jerked himself around as if yanked by a string and swaggered off into the marine layer.

I hugged myself tightly. Tears began to drizzle down my face, mingling with the heavy droplets of fog. Terry Shoe had a point. It was high time for me to get out of town.

21

"SO YOU'RE JUST GOING TO blow town and leave everything unsolved?"

Valerie Jane sat on the edge of my bed watching me pack. It was the first time she'd ever been in my house; it still seemed odd, almost unreal, to see her here, as if a fictional character who had lived vividly but firmly in my imagination had suddenly popped up in the flesh. She had telephoned the night before to see how I was getting along; and with Justin's vitriolic little tirade still stinging in my ears, I'd sobbed piteously about feeling all alone and blue, until Valerie had promised to come over in the morning.

"You bet I'm leaving," I declared, wadding several pairs of white anklets into balls. "Eight-thirty A.M., Delta Airlines nonstop to Atlanta. Business class." I stuffed the sock balls into a pair of straw-soled wedgies; then I fitted the wedgies *farcies* into a suitcase that yawned open on the rug. "I no longer care who killed Julia Prentice—Mr. Pete, or the FedEx man, or Felix the Cat. My main concern at the moment happens to be staying alive. If I leave, I'm hoping it'll send a very eloquent message that I'm off the case. You should be happy about this," I added. "You were the one who was so anxious for me to keep out of it in the first place."

Valerie kicked off her ballet flats and planted her size 10 stockinged feet on the quilt. "I talked this all over with Jacqueline before she left. She thinks it's important that you see this through. Otherwise, she says, you'll never have closure."

"You mean like in having a coffin lid closed over my face? Tell Jacqueline thanks a heap."

"Well, if you really think you're in danger . . . I mean, if you don't feel you're not just running away . . ."

"I feel exactly like I'm running away. That's the entire point!" I glanced with exasperation at Valerie; her recent tryst seemed to have made huevos rancheros of her thinking processes. "Anyway," I went on, "the only thing I've proved by all my detecting is that I'm a rotten detective. I've gone running up a lot of blind alleys and leaping to a lot of utterly wrong conclusions. Last night being the topper."

"The guy was a total prick."

"Maybe. But a lot of guys are total pricks. Which doesn't necessarily make them all killers."

Valerie looked rather dubious at this. Giving up, I turned my attention back to the more pressing problem at hand, namely, wardrobe selection. "Hot, hot, hot and humid," Stacey Freers had said when I called that morning to ask about the weather. "We've been just about *liv*ing in our swimsuits." With sauna weather in mind, I picked out a marigold-print cotton sundress with rickracked halter top, very Ann Sothern. Short-sleeved Hawaiian shirt. Pineapple-yellow clam diggers. To fill in, a stack of basic shorts and T-shirts in assorted sherbet colors.

"You probably didn't look at the trades this morning," Valerie said idly.

"No. Why?"

"Newgate Cinema's gone bankrupt."

I turned, clutching a half-folded pocket tee. "No shit?"

"No shit. Front page of both *Variety* and the *Reporter*. Sandy Palumbo's in a bucket of hot water. There's going to be an investigation into what they're calling financial irregularities. Bad checks, fancy accounting . . . The article in *Variety* made some crack about how the money financed the Palumbos' jet-set life-style. Did you know they owned a manor in Ireland?"

"No, but it doesn't surprise me." I thought of Francine pranc-ing about in her lavish finery at the Magic Wand benefit: Marie Antoinette before the deluge. "I have to admit I feel sorry for Sandy," I said. "Francine's probably already changed the locks on the doors. And if you ask me, she's the one who got him into the whole mess. She's the climber, the one who's got to keep up with the Rossners."

"I just remembered something I once heard about Sandy," Valerie said. "I've got a friend who was working in development last year at Newgate. She told me a story about how once she was in a meeting in Sandy's office, going over readers' reports or something, and he started pacing around the room, not lis-tening to what she was saying. She said he started muttering, 'I used to think if I made a million a year, it would be enough. But it's not, it's not enough. I've got to have more.' "

I turned back to my packing with a shudder. Suddenly I couldn't wait to get out of a town where a million bucks a year was considered chump change.

I crammed the rest of my things into the valise, and struggled to zip it closed. Chloe had supplied me with an inventory of items she simply, positively, couldn't live another day without— her fourteen-carat-gold horse necklace, her entire feather collec-tion, Spouty, her stuffed humpback whale—and in a moment of weakness, I'd agreed to bring it all. Plus Kit had appropriated all the good luggage, leaving me with just a smallish bag that had been ripped in one corner by an overzealous baggage handler at Orly and was now patched inelegantly with a slab of electrical tape. With a renewed spurt of resentment of my husband, I furiously yanked the zipper shut.

Valerie Jane picked up a spiral of sixteen-millimeter film from my bed table. She pulled down a strip of it and examined the frames. "What's this?"

"That? Something I did ages ago—an experiment with painting directly on film with Magic Marker. For some reason, it was in this old suitcase."

She got up, loped over to the window and held the strip up to the light. "It looks like a lot of dots and squiggles."

"It's supposed to be an abstract animation. Shapes and colors moving rhythmically, like a musical piece." I went over to join her at the window. Standing there, I gave a sudden start.

Valerie glanced at me. "What's the matter?"

"I don't know. I keep getting the creepiest feeling that I'm being watched."

"By who? Somebody over there?" She gestured to the top of the Prentice house across the street. It was barely visible through a dense calico of eucalyptus leaves. "I thought the house was empty."

"As far as I know, it is." I gave a deprecating shrug. "It's probably just me and my overactive imagination. Which is another reason for me to get my ass out of town."

Valerie shaded her eyes with her hands and peered at the opposite roof. "God, Lucy, it's catching," she said. "I'm starting to get the willies too."

AFTER A HURRIED LUNCH, VALERIE returned to the Burbank lot. I set off for a three o'clock meeting at Curious Animation to deliver my new Amerinda storyboard.

The producer, Warren Schotte, was a twitchy twenty-eight-year-old with Anglo dreadlocks and a galloping case of Hollywood grandiosity—he seemed to believe he was producing the animated equivalent of *Lawrence of Arabia*. "What's Ramos the Rooster's moti*v*ation for rounding up the goat and the crows?" he demanded, scrutinizing the panels on the storyboard with an intensely furrowed brow.

"To go get Amerinda out of bed," I patiently explained.

"But we've seen nothing in the arc of his character to suggest this kind of leadership."

I nodded, as if struck by his insight. "Yeah, I see what you mean." I'd discovered by now that if I simply agreed with everything he said, I wouldn't have to actually address any of it. The strategy prevailed: by the end of the meeting, Warren had signed off on the board, leaving it virtually intact. I beat a hasty retreat.

A CAR FROM FAST ALERT SECURITY was cruising on its appointed rounds as I returned home. The current officer had apparently been tipped off by Adam's Apple that I was a sandwich or two short of a picnic—he flashed me an exaggerated okay sign, nodding, the way you'd assure a particularly simple child that everything was hunky-dory. I grinned and okayed back, signaling my relief that he was on the case.

Now what? I thought as I went inside. My packing was done, and since I was leaving at the crack of dawn, I'd made no plans for the night. But maybe I could make myself useful. I decided I'd try to repair at least some of the devastation Lola had wreaked on the rose garden.

I put on a pair of heavy jeans, a denim jacket of Kit's and thick gardening gloves. Taking a trowel, a ball of twine and a bunch of tall wooden stakes, I waded into the thorns.

For some time I worked happily. The sky was blue. The sun was golden. The air was soft and fragrant with the mingled scents of honeysuckle, roses and acacia. Was I really going to quit such a paradise to swat mosquitoes in a semitropical heat wave? Chloe would be back in six days. Security was on the job. Why should I be chased out of town?

A gust of breeze carried Lola's yapping from next door and a girl's voice: "Justin, I can't find my . . ." Then the wind shifted and the rest of her words were lost. Couldn't find her what? Her drink? Her panties? Her diaphragm? Any minute now, old Al

Green would begin crooning. Whatever regret I'd had about leaving quickly vanished.

Squatting, I stabbed my trowel into the earth around a particularly mutilated Cary Grant. I had moved deep into the patch now, almost to the property line; and there was, I noticed, something different about the soil. It was less dry and crumbling, more viscous. And lighter in color, more a milky gray than the dusty, almost colorless brown I'd been digging in so far.

Gray . . . as in dried mud.

I straightened up with a jerk.

In my mind's eye, I ran a replay of myself the day of Julia's murder. Celebrating Kit's movie with my little Apache victory dance. Suddenly having trouble yanking my feet from the sucking gray mud. Mud that had come streaming from the top of the back hill, cascading over Julia's bobbing corpse and down the terraced levels, sweeping everything in its path. One tributary of that relentless stream must have branched off to the perimeter of the property, trickling into the rose thicket.

The police, when they were conducting their search, hadn't noticed the divergence. Which is why they hadn't attempted to challenge the thorns.

But suppose, I told myself excitedly, the mud had carried something from the murder scene into these bushes. Like, oh, just for an example . . . the murder weapon.

My pulse racing, I moved farther into the thicket, following the mud trail. The bushes were now grown so densely together that not even Lola had been able to do her dirty work. Thorns tore at my jeans as I edged between the branches, slashing them back with a wooden stake. At the far edge of the thicket, the mud had eddied in a pool against the Pennislaws' border hedge. Within this caked pool, something gleamed in the late-day sun. A rosy glint of light, like a metallic petal . . .

I pushed quickly toward it, bent down and picked up Summer Rossner's little cellular phone.

"It's impossible!" I said aloud. I wiped it against my jacket, removing the carapace of dried mud. No doubt about it. It was the same slender, pale pink little device, with the state-of-the-art solar battery that could hold a charge for up to weeks and store hundreds of numbers, which still wasn't hardly enough for Summer.

But of course it wasn't Summer's.

It was Julia's.

If it hadn't been for the thorn bushes, I'd have sat down. I could imagine Julia getting an eyeful of Summer's cunning new toy and nearly wetting her pants. She probably leaped right into her Mercedes and caromed to the nearest Sharper Image, AmEx at the fore. And if she'd bought it just a day or so before she died, she would not yet have been billed for the service. Which is why the police hadn't known to check those records.

I stared at it in my hand. *This* is how Julia had summoned her last, fatal lover. The same lover who, one windy moonlit night, came back searching for it and was surprised by me in my "I [chile pepper heart] Taos" T-shirt.

I thrashed my way out of the rose thicket and back to the house, where, under the shaded eaves of the porch, I noticed a light flickering slightly on the base of the phone. The solar battery still had a charge. I flipped the phone open, held it to my ear. A dial tone, weak, but nevertheless there.

There was also, I noticed, a redial button. Which could still hold in memory the last number called!

Tampering with evidence! Terry Shoe's voice rang in my brain. *Maybe you heard somewhere that's a crime?*

Yeah, but the battery could fail at any second, erasing any possibility of retrieving the number. That was a good enough rationale for me. I pressed the redial, my heart skipping with excitement as I heard a distant, barely audible ringing. Someone picked up. A tinny, faraway voice said, "Start talkin' and make it snappy."

"Hello?" I shouted.

The battery gave up the ghost.

"Damn it," I muttered. I went inside and set the little phone on the kitchen table, scene of so many recent doughnut-and-coffee cop pig-outs. Could I identify that voice? It had been high-pitched, but not a woman's, more like a boy's. Yes, definitely a kid's voice. Sneering and nasty in tone. And there was only one kid I knew of whose nasty quotient was high enough to answer a phone that way.

Oliver Latch-Palumbo.

The invisible Terry Shoe piped up again: *Still trying to play the detective?* No guessing. I had to be absolutely sure.

I scrambled upstairs to my bedroom, nearly breaking my neck on the suitcase still lying on the floor. I dug out the Windermere School directory from my bed table, flipped to the Palumbos' number and dialed it from the bedside phone.

"Hay-lo?" A different voice. This one definitely a woman's. Not young. Pronounced accent.

"Who is this?" I asked breathlessly.

"This is the Pay-lumbo raysidence. Who is calling, please?"

I hung up. I'd gotten the housekeeper, proving nothing. Probably the same elderly Latina who'd helped me pour the sloshed Francine onto a kitchen chair the afternoon I'd hauled her home from the Brentwood Mart.

What if she hadn't been a Latina? What if she'd been Filipino? The hot-rodding, trigger-happy Filipina granny. What was her name? Ida. Ida Soniez.

I desperately tried to remember what she looked like. Small, stocky, stony-faced. With features that could well have been Filipino. I'd just leaped to the typically Anglo assumption that any dusky-skinned domestic must be from south of the border. Lucy Freers, white supremacist.

Later for the guilt fest. I had to think this through.

Okay, then. Assuming that she was the redoubtable Mrs. So-niez and that it made no sense for her to be racing around taking potshots at me, then what *did* make sense? The answer, I realized with a frisson, was obvious. Substitute Francine Palumbo's name for Ida's.

I needed to run this by someone who didn't carry a badge. I picked up the phone again and called Valerie, praying she'd be available. After a few long moments on hold, I breathed relief when she picked up.

"What's up?" She sounded harried and distracted.

I babbled a quick fill-in, ending with calling back the Palumbo number.

"I'm not following. Julia called this Filipino lady?"

"No, no, Julia called Fran*cine*. It was who she always called when she needed anything. Which means Francine must know who Julia's last lover was. In fact, Francine probably set it up."

"Still procuring after all these years?"

"That's how it looks. And I think it's Francine who's been following me, trying to make sure I didn't stumble on any of this. She used her housekeeper's car so I wouldn't recognize her while she was on my tail."

"Which means she's the one who shot at you!"

"Francine does tend to get carried away," I said.

"She sounds seriously off her rocker. And dangerous."

"What do you think I should do?"

"You even have to ask? Call that detective and have her check it out."

"But what if I'm wrong? Like I was with Justin."

"So what if you're wrong? I thought this Terry's become a great pal of yours."

"She's hard to figure," I said. "I know that when she hears I pressed that redial button she's going to hit the roof. If I send her on a wild-goose chase on top of that, god knows what she'll do."

"I don't see that you've got any alternative," Valerie said firmly.

"No," I agreed, "I guess not."

There was an eruption in the background of Valerie's line.

Old Arne Bonner in full voice: "What's this schmatte she's got on? It's the color of dog shit! This is *not* what I approved. Valerie! Where the fuck is Valerie?"

"I've got to go," Valerie said. "Little Hitler's having one of his grand mal seizures. Thank god we wrap in two days! Promise me, Lucy, you'll call the detective and not get creative on your own."

"Promise."

I hung up, then decided a drink would help me steel myself for fessing up to Terry Shoe. I went downstairs and, to procrastinate further, fixed myself a martini, carefully measuring out the Tanqueray and vermouth, cracking ice, shaking it all up in my Russell Wright cocktail shaker. It occurred to me that lately I was quite often deciding that a drink or two would be just the ticket; if I didn't watch out, I'd be holding hands with Francine Palumbo at the next Brentwood chapter meeting of AA, affirming my belief in a higher power.

With a *boing!* a light bulb suddenly popped over my head. What if I just casually dropped in on Francine? Bringing something of Chloe's, a toy or a book . . . "I found this on the backseat of my Cherokee," I could say, "and I was wondering if Ollie had left it there." If the housekeeper answered the door, I could interrogate her right there; if not, I could ask for a glass of water and possibly waylay her in the kitchen.

Even Francine the Hysterical wouldn't be crazy enough to start shooting at me in her own home.

At the moment, I was covered with enough dirt to play an extra in *The Grapes of Wrath*. I shucked off my gardening ensemble, applied first aid to my scratched-up legs, quickly showered and changed. Then I grabbed a book at random from Chloe's shelves and jumped into my car.

Into the teeth of rush hour. It was a twenty-five-minute horn-blaring slog to Holmby Hills.

The Palumbo property was enclosed by a high hand-laid stone wall. Since the gates were open, I didn't bother to announce myself, but drove directly in. The house featured a deep veranda punctuated by slender Doric columns, My Old Kentucky Home—style. A crushed-stone drive extended the length of the façade and swept around the left to a detached six-car garage. I pulled up in front of the veranda and reached for the book I'd snatched from Chloe's room. "Shit!" I muttered. I'd picked up a Baby-Sitters Club book, *Stacey's Big Crush.* Not even I would have the temerity to pretend to think this was Oliver's.

Hee, hee, the invisible Terry Shoe giggled. *Still trying to do my job?*

I chucked the book onto the backseat. I'd just have to wing it. Leaving the motor running, I climbed out of the car and headed for the door. Buzzed the buzzer. Waited. Buzzed twice more, then rapped loudly with the brass knocker.

No response.

I stepped down from the veranda and peered at the upper-story windows. No sign of life. Shit and double shit. In the hour it had taken me to get here, the entire household had flown the coop.

The front gates wide open, the house left unattended . . . I walked nervously toward the garage. One of its three doors hung open as well. All this neighborly come-on-in-ness . . . it just didn't say "Francine." If Chloe were here with me now, I thought, she'd be humming creepy Attack of the Killer Creatures music: "ooo-ee-oo."

What the hell . . . As long as I was snooping, I might as well go the distance. I headed into the garage.

There was Francine's mulberry-colored Jag.

And beside it, as soap-and-water–challenged as ever, was my old friend, the moonlight blue Taurus.

Someone sat behind the wheel. "Ida!" I called, skipping toward it. "Mrs. Soniez! Wait, don't go yet!"

But it wasn't Ida. As I came up toward it, I realized it was Francine, her sleek blond head slightly atilt against the headrest, as if she were asleep. "Francine?" I began, approaching her window. Then I gave a startled laugh. She was making a funny face at me, popping her eyes and sticking her tongue out of one corner of her half-opened mouth. And that man's tie dangling at her collarbone, mauve and navy zigzags with the Zegna label turned outward—that looked pretty silly too.

Then my laugh choked in my throat as other details asserted themselves: the blood-red splotches in the whites of her popping eyes . . . the purple ring around her neck like a lurid necklace . . . the rigidity of those lips, parted as if straining to say something immensely urgent . . .

But what message she'd been so desperate to convey would never be known. Francine Palumbo had been strangled with an Ermenegildo Zegna tie.

And I'd discovered my second Hollywood Mom corpse.

I let out a rattling shriek. For several seconds, my feet did a kind of frantic scramble in place, like the Road Runner warming up; and then suddenly I was propelling myself in a backward scuttle, making pretty good time, until I stumbled over a pair of green lizard shoes.

22

EXCEPT THEY WEREN'T LIZARD SHOES.

What they *were* was a pair of green alligator cowboy boots. To be exact, Rios of Mercedes handmade hornback alligator boots; they sold for thirty-two hundred dollars a pair, something I happened to know because a year or so ago Kit had tried on a pair of them on sale at Thieves Market—had them, in fact, at the counter ready to be wrapped up, his Discovery card whipped out and presented to the clerk, when I'd come up and thrown a fit, pointing out that Windermere tuition was due and the roof over the spare bedroom needed patching and at the moment we had no actual means of income. Kit had called me a penny pincher who wouldn't take the long view; didn't I know how much appearances counted in this business? And I had spat back that his values were in the toilet, and it escalated in the car on the way home into a drag-out fight. And that was the beginning of the Big Chill our marriage still seemed to be frozen in.

But none of this crossed my mind at the moment. I was far too distracted by the fact that this particular pair of Rios of Mercedes boots happened to be attached to the feet of Sandy Palumbo.

He was sitting with his back against the garage wall,

face ashen and stubble-chinned, exophthalmic eyes half-closed. The booted feet were sprawled out in front of him. His hands dangled between his legs, like a schoolboy who'd just been scolded for losing his homework.

He glanced up at me with a brief smile, as if he wasn't surprised to see me. As if he'd even been expecting me and had just been marking time against the wall till my arrival. "Hello, Lucy," he said.

"Where's Oliver?" I croaked.

"I sent him off to the movies with Ida. I let her take one of my cars so they wouldn't have to see"—he made a vague gesture—"this. Poor kid, he's gonna have it rough."

The invisible Terry Shoe spoke up again: *There's typical Hollywood thinking for you. Treat a kid to a movie so he doesn't have to watch you snuff his mother.*

Sandy fumbled with something in his lap. With a horrible squeeze of terror, I realized he was cradling a gun. An ugly flat little pistol, the color of drawing-pencil lead.

"What are you going to do, Sandy?" I asked hoarsely.

He gave an almost winsome little shrug. "She was leaving," he said.

"Francine?"

"She was going to Nantucket, taking Ollie. For three weeks, she said. She wanted me out of here when she got back."

"Because you went bankrupt?" The words came automatically.

He smiled vacantly. "You saw the trades, huh? 'I read the news today, oh boy.' Belly-up. One dead fish." He fidgeted with the gun. "Ah, Christ, if I could just've kept a lid on things a couple more months. I've got two films set for release, the test scores on *Jack Rabbit* are through the roof . . . I could've recouped everything. . . ."

The perpetual Hollywood *if* . . . Even now it had Sandy in its thrall.

He shifted the gun so that the barrel was now pointing roughly at my appendix. Keep him talking—that's what they do in the movies when some desperate character is waving a gun. Just keep him chattering on. "It was you with Julia, wasn't it?" I blurted. "It was you with Julia at my pool."

"Me and Julia and sex by the pool. Sounds like a drink, doesn't it? Bartender, I'll have a Sex by the Pool." He reached behind his hip with his non-gun-gripping left hand and drew out a bottle. Glenlivet single malt Scotch whiskey. Sandy always did have class. He raised it to his lips and took a swill.

Now would be the time to make a dash for my car—I could still hear the motor chugging away—but my feet felt Krazy-Glued to the floor. "Julia had called Francine that morning, hadn't she?" I babbled on.

Sandy set the bottle down delicately, as if it were something immensely fragile. "Francie was out. Shopping. She was always shopping. It was the only time she ever really felt secure."

I nodded. It came as no startling revelation that Francine Palumbo regarded her platinum American Express card the way Linus did his blanket. "When Julia called, you answered the phone instead," I said.

"Yeah. I happened to be home." A puzzled crease appeared in Sandy's forehead. "How come? Avoiding, I guess. Everything was starting to fall apart. Agents, lawyers, studio suits, all screaming for my ass. So I was hiding out at home. And I picked up Francie's phone, and it was Julia."

"And she wasn't screaming, right."

"No, she wasn't. She was friendly as fucking peach pie. Surprised, sure, she didn't expect to get *me*. But she was friendly as hell. Said she was hanging at a friend's pool and there was nobody home, and as long as I was playing hooky, why didn't I just mosey on over and keep her company? I had no idea it was *your* house, Lucy," he added. "Not till I heard it on the news. You never had us over for dinner." This last he delivered in a rather reproachful tone.

This didn't seem to be the optimum time to point out that Kit and I didn't quite measure up to Francine's social agenda. "And, of course, it was you in my backyard that night," I went on. "You came back to look for Julia's little phone."

He nodded. "At The School's commencement you told me you didn't know how Julia could have called anyone, the cops had checked all her phone records. So I guessed they didn't know about the cell phone. I thought maybe I could keep them from ever knowing about it. I'd just gotten my bill from L.A. Cell that morning. So, after the party, I cruised by her mailbox. It was taking a chance I wouldn't be seen. But you know this town, nobody's ever out on the street."

"The bill was in the mailbox?"

"I was in luck." He gave a sharp laugh. "No one had picked up the mail for a couple of days. I paid it and canceled the account." He paused for another quick hit of Glenlivet.

"But then you still needed to find the phone," I said. "So, you climbed up the back of our cliff in the middle of the night."

"That was no big deal. I'd been doing a lot of free-climbing lately. Up in the Sierra, sheer faces at ten thousand feet. Your little hill was a piece of cake."

"Even in cowboy boots?"

He glanced briefly at his pointed toe tips. "Yeah, that did make it a little tricky. But it was a spur-of-the-moment decision. I never planned on becoming a prowler, you know. And I certainly didn't mean to hurt you, Lucy." He gazed at my forehead with a rueful little smile. "You've still got a bruise. I feel like a first-class shit."

"It's nothing much," I said, almost flirtatiously. It was remarkable: a gun pointed at my groin and Francine a stiffening gargoyle scarcely two yards behind me, but I still wasn't immune to Sandy's charm.

"You scared the shit out of me when you appeared like that," he went on. "The way you were standing in the shadows with your arms stretched out, and the light kind of flickering . . . I had this insane idea you were a ghost. Julia's ghost." He tilted his head against the wall and banged it softly. "Christ, I've been so fucked up!"

"You've been under a lot of pressure," I said soothingly. "Anyone would break under the circumstances." I edged an experimental step back. His fingers tightened on the grip of the gun. Was it loaded? I wondered. Was the safety catch off? How come, if I'd seen so goddamned many movies, I didn't even know where the safety catch was?

The thin wail of a siren became audible in the distance, causing both of us to glance outside. I willed it closer, police, fire, ambulance, I didn't care which. But whichever it was rounded a hill and the siren died away. Sandy sighed and gazed blearily back up at me.

"Is that why Francine was following me?" I asked. "To make sure I didn't find out about you?"

The puzzled look scrunched his face again. "Francie didn't know about any of this. She had no idea I fucked Julia. She was following you to make sure you didn't figure out about *her*."

"But I already had. What she was doing back in the *Delano* days, a lot of people knew . . ."

"Not about her past," he cut in irritably. "What she was doing now."

Something jolted in my mind. Sandy was going broke. Francine needed to have money. And Julia, as Mrs. Woody Prentice, was rolling in loot. "It was blackmail, wasn't it?" I whispered. "Francine was blackmailing Julia."

"Yeah." Sandy gave his head another, firmer, thwack against the garage wall. "And that marvelous morning I'd just found out about it. By accident, I found a financial statement. Francie had a secret account with Morgan in New York. Nearly two million bucks."

I raised my brows. That was some blackmailing! "But how do you know it was coming from Julia? Maybe it was money Francine saved up." This sounded idiotic even before I finished saying it.

Francine, the thrifty housewife. Squirreling away millions by switching to generic mouthwash, frequenting the sales at Yves St. Laurent.

Sandy hoisted the Glenlivet, but this time set it down without sampling. "It was from Julia. My brother's a senior VP at Shearson. I had him pull some strings to get access to the account. It had been opened almost two years ago. The last deposit was from a company called Jewelwood. A private corporation owned by Julia and Woody Prentice." Another bitter laugh. "That fun couple."

So Julia *was* paying out. Which stood to reason. If Francine had gone public with Julia's S and M hooker history, it would've put a sudden and total stop on Julia's Hollywood Mom ascendancy. Good-bye cover of *People;* hello center spread in the *National Enquirer.*

"I suppose Francie was afraid that with all my snooping around, I'd stumble on the truth," I continued. "So she trailed me around, using Ida's car, so I wouldn't recognize her. And when I wouldn't give up, she decided to blow my head off."

"You mean after the Magic Wand party? No, that was a mistake. She just wanted to scare you. She didn't mean to come that close."

"Well, it worked," I said. "I decided to give up."

"Then how come you're here?"

There seemed nothing I could reply to that. Sandy's gaze shifted to the Taurus hulking behind me. "I really loved her, you know." He continued, "When I found out she was planning to cut out on me, I lost it. Went completely nuts. I hated her, and I hated Julia even more for giving her the money. Then, all of a sudden, there's Julia on the phone, giving me a come-on. It seemed like good revenge to go fuck her brains out."

"But you got carried away," I whispered, "and bashed her brains out instead. And then, when Francine said she was leaving, you killed her, too."

Sandy's hooded eyes turned back to me, cast with a look of

intense disappointment—the way a teacher might look at a once-promising pupil who just declared that two and two make five. When he spoke, it was in a voice so low I had to strain to listen.

"I haven't killed anyone yet," he said.

The siren suddenly emerged from whatever hill it had vanished behind, sounding now as if it were only a block or two away. Sandy raised the gun. Aimed it dead between my eyes. A hard fist of terror slammed into my stomach. There was one thing I'd forgotten about all those scenes in the movies: the reason the desperate guy with the gun was happy to keep blabbing on about his crimes was because he was about to wipe out the person he was telling it all to.

My mouth was so dry I could hardly form the words. "You don't want to do this, Sandy."

"There's no other choice," he murmured.

"That siren's just down the street. If you shoot, they'll probably hear it. They'll head right here and find you."

He smiled rather tenderly, as if the recalcitrant pupil had finally gotten it right.

Then he put the gun to his temple and pulled the trigger.

FOUR

23

MY MOTHER-IN-LAW BUSTLED into my room carrying a rattan tray groaning with a smorgasbord of breakfast foods. Stacey had brought me all my meals in bed since I'd arrived in a state of collapse four days before. It was Stacey, too, who'd removed the extension phone from my room and allowed no one in to see me except Chloe.

She set the tray on the bed table, gave a token smooth to my coverlet and pushed back the blue mesh curtains to let the Georgia daylight seep into the room. "Land, it's hot!" she exclaimed cheerfully. "One more day of this and I do believe we're all just going to melt away. But they're predicting thunderstorms, so let's hope that'll clear the air." She chattered on about her morning golf game, how the *sweet*est little old Baltimore oriole had lit itself on the seventh hole, causing her to muff a putt that the merest *child* should've been able to sink, and other bulletins of the same nature; then she bustled on out again.

I picked desultorily at a fruit salad. Then I slipped back into another fitful doze, permeated as usual with images of the horror in the Palumbo garage.

The black-and-white had come screaming up to the house seconds after Sandy shot himself. Two uniformed cops scrambled into the garage, weapons drawn, eyes bulging at the tableau that greeted them. Body number one slumped on the floor, the top of its head splashed in a gory fresco on the wall behind it. Body number two positioned almost perkily behind the wheel of a filthy blue Taurus. Myself, ostensibly alive and kicking, but frozen, still as a corpse, in shock.

Barely minutes after the squad car, the paramedics barreled up and plied me with blankets and oxygen, at which point I seemed to slide into a state of uncanny control. With a sangfroid worthy of a secret agent, I recounted the details of the last hour, and no, thank you, I did *not* need any further medical treatment. Lucy "Nerves of Steel" Freers. Somehow, amid the babble of cop talk and the squawk of walkie-talkies and the shriek of other arriving sirens, I picked up the fact that it had been Sandy himself who had called 911—this too I accepted in stride.

When Terry Shoe arrived, I maintained my cool. Went over my grisly story again, beginning with my hunting up Julia's cell phone among the trashed roses. I declared firmly that I was leaving for Atlanta in the morning, no ifs, ands or buts; I'd be available for further statements only when I returned. Had Terry and Downsey accompany me home, where I handed over the pink phone and collected my suitcase and plane tickets; then, one scant step ahead of the media hordes, I slinked off to stay the night incognito at the airport Sheridan, managing to board the plane undetected in the morning.

But at the sight of Chloe at the arrival gate, jiggling up and down in a pair of brand-new canary-yellow Keds, I came apart. Stacey and Walter Freers had half carried me home and hustled me straight to bed.

I AWOKE AN HOUR LATER from my fitful doze, feeling, for the first time, tentatively ready to face the world again. I ran a tepid bath, put on my Hawaiian shirt and shorts and tottered out to the backyard.

Chloe and two identical freckled-faced girls lay sprawled on beach towels, slurping melting Popsicles in seemingly inedible colors, fuchsia and electric blue. Stacey was reclining in a sling-back canvas chair; she glanced up with surprise from her J. Peterman catalog. "Lovey, you're up! Land, you look thin as a rail."

"Yeah, Mom, you look terrible," declared my unsentimental daughter. No kidding. The four of them boasted tans of rich glowing copper; by contrast, I was the color of old soap.

Neither the heat nor the humidity had lifted since my arrival. I felt like I was moving through hot glue. Stacey steered me into an umbrella-shaded chaise. "You just sit yourself and relax. I mixed up some lemonade and I'm going to bring you a big ol' glass, and some of my maple shortbread, and you're gonna eat every bite."

"Could you also bring me the newspaper?" I asked. "The back ones too, if you still have them."

Stacey gazed at me a moment, absently twirling a lock of her hair. She had only recently surrendered her Southern society bouffant for a more up-to-date bob and still seemed to miss that glorious teased-up height. "Are you really sure you're ready for that?"

"I think so. I can't keep my head stuck in the sand forever."

"All right, then," she said dubiously. "But if it makes you upset, I'm taking them right away."

She headed into the house. There was a low grumble from the nukelike thunderheads erupting in the distance. I sat back, listening to Chloe and her friends. They were playing a game in which they came up with new and possibly improved names for themselves.

"Dulci Dawn Ramira Freers," proposed Chloe.

"Amber Tiffany Cloud Loomis," countered one of the twins.

Stacey reappeared with one of her overladen trays and four days' accumulation of *The Constitution* and *USA Today*. I started to get cold feet. "What do they say about me?" I asked nervously.

"Really not that much, thank god. I guess since we wouldn't

let them talk to you, they lost interest. And the police said right off you're not suspected of any involvement."

"I just have a knack for popping up wherever there happens to be a corpse of my acquaintance."

"You have bad timing, that's all," my mother-in-law said firmly. "It's not your fault." She stacked the papers on the grass at my feet. "If I see this is making you upset, I'm taking them right away, you hear me?"

I began with the Atlanta paper dated the day I arrived. The story had made the front page, of course. Everyone loves a Tinsel Town sensation.

I raced through the coverage. Sandy Palumbo emerged as the uncontested villain. He was the would-be mogul who had cavalierly run his company into the ground. The crook who'd scattered bum checks like birdseed over two coasts, cooked his books and, presumably, cheated on his taxes.

The depraved killer of Hollywood Moms.

It appeared to be gospel that Sandy had murdered both Julia and Francine. Forensics had confirmed that he had indeed been Julia's last fling; it was logical to assume that postcoitally, in lieu of the traditional cigarette, he had brained her with some still-unidentified blunt object, then rolled her body into the swimming pool—my swimming pool. Possibly to keep her mouth shut about their affair. Or (as one of the more salacious reports hinted) because she had mocked his "performance."

And with one murder under his belt, naturally it was a snap for him to dispatch his wife when he discovered she was going to leave him. He had a handy murder weapon in the form of one of his numerous Italian silk ties. But then, overcome by remorse and the inevitability of being caught, he stuck a Ruger Bearcat twenty-two revolver to his head and fired.

"Are you okay, lovey?" Stacey called over.

I nodded weakly and pushed on. Stacey was right—I got very little play. "Unavailable for comment," inevitably followed any mention of my name.

Julia, however, did not fare as well. She suddenly seemed open game for attack. Much mention of her "wild" past as a struggling starlet, as well as her more recent "affairs"—though not of her fondness for the lash. My face burned when I read a quote from "neighbor and former lover" Justin Caffrey: "Julia Prentice was just one of a common type of aging Hollywood woman—they desperately try to hang on to their fading youth by having sex with younger men."

And Woody . . . Everybody's Grampa somehow bobbed above it all. Through "a spokesman" he declared that he was "devastated, but anxious to put it all behind him." He expressed his deep gratitude for the many wonderful letters of support and love he had received from fans and hastened to assure them that he wouldn't desert them. Uncle Roy would still be on the boat.

What a trouper! I thought. The show must go on. Those millions must keep rolling in.

"That's enough for now." Stacey pried the paper out of my clenching fingers. "Are you sure you're doing okay?"

"Yeah. Or no, it still gives me the horrors. But I'll be fine."

"The important thing is it's over and done with."

"I suppose so," I murmured. I drained my glass of lemonade, the ice cubes clinking against my teeth. There was also a thought clinking in my mind: was it really over? There were still too many things that didn't add up. Like those "management fees" Julia anted up to Francine. How had she gotten Woody to agree to paying them—Woody, who, from all accounts, could squeeze a nickel so tight the buffalo bellowed? But if she didn't have Woody's consent, how had she managed to siphon two million dollars out of their account without his knowing?

And then there were Sandy's last words: "I haven't killed anyone yet." That hopeless half-whisper that haunted all my dreams. If he was on the brink of blowing himself to kingdom come, why would he lie?

The phone rang. "I'll get it!" yelled Chloe. She padded into the house.

"She loves talking to reporters," Stacey said. "She tells them very ladylike, 'I'm sorry, but my mother is incommunicado.' It always makes me chuckle."

Chloe reemerged with a Siamese kitten squirming on her shoulder. "Mom, it's Daddy. He's been calling every day and says will you please get on the phone."

Here was the other part of my life I'd been blissfully avoiding.

"I don't know why he's on that telephone," Stacey said crossly. "He ought to be right here with his family."

"So what should I say?" Chloe asked.

"I'm coming." I dragged myself to my feet and shuffled in to the phone.

"Lucy?" Kit's voice competed with heavy static. I was beginning to forget what he sounded like when not being processed through a Waring blender. "What the hell's been going on?"

"I'm sure you get the news, even up there in the hinterlands."

"Of course we get the news. Why do you think I'm going ape-shit? It's mind-boggling. The Palumbos, jeez! But how the hell did you get mixed up in it?"

Because you started it, I wanted to say. With your famous lunge for Julia's boobs—you set the whole garish nightmare into action. "Bad timing," was all I said. "Just like your mother says, I was in the wrong place at the wrong time."

Snap, crackle, brrr-k, went the phone. Kit's voice crackled back in. ". . . worried out of my skull. Mom says you're on the verge of a breakdown."

"I'm pretty shaken up. I mean, god, I've got a reason to be. But I'm not about to crack up, if that's what you're worried about. Where are you, anyway?"

"This little mining town in the Canadian Rockies. We can't get out, there's been this freak blizzard, in June for Chrissake! The airport's shut down."

"You're all trapped?"

"Not all of us. Sugerman and most of the crew have already

gone back to Seattle. It's just me and the head of the location team, Paula."

Snowbound with a babe. How convenient. "What?" I said, having missed his last sentence.

"I said, maybe you should stay on with my folks for a while. It would be the best thing."

"It's not the best thing. It's not the best thing at all." My voice began its up-the-scale ascent to Amarinda-ville. "In the first place, your parents are taking that Aegean cruise next week; they've had it booked for ages. Secondly, I've got my own work to get to, in case you forgot, and Chloe starts her tennis program on Monday. None of which I'm sure has any significance compared to producing a Jon *Sug*erman movie, but it happens to be important to *us*!"

"Mom was right, you do sound pretty damned shaky," he said. I exuded a long sigh.

"Shit, it's snowing again. We're never gonna get out of here."

"You and Paula will just have to rough it," I said caustically.

"What?"

"Nothing." The air had become almost unbearably sultry as the thunderstorm rumbled closer. We had come to a point in our conversation that we always seemed to come to—an awkward pause. I could have said, "I love you," or, "I miss you," or, "I really need you with me now." What came out of my mouth was, "It's hideously hot."

Krr-kk, bruck, snrrk, went the phone. The Waring blender on the line escalated from "mince" to "liquefy" to "frappé," and then the connection went dead.

24

THE SIX DAYS I'D BEEN away felt more like six months. For one thing, the weather had changed: it was now bona fide "June Gloom"; the dense marine layer no longer rolled in and out, but sat permanently, day and night, on silent haunches all along the beach, brightening only for several hours in the afternoon. Some people find this romantic in a Dickensian hansom-cab-and-gaslight way, but to me it just feels claustrophobic, as if I'm trapped in a humongous pill jar sealed up with thick cotton wool.

Another difference: the phones were silent. I'd had our numbers changed from Atlanta, and no one had as yet sniffed out the new ones. But the absence of jangling phones was more than made up for by Megadeath howling from Chloe's room. My monitoring of her listening fare was getting lax—me, who used to be the sine qua non of CD confiscation. But Chloe was somewhat spooked about being back, and if screaming heavy metal could ease the transition, then so be it.

TERRY SHOE HAD ARRANGED TO come by at noon. Ever punctual, she popped up on the dot with her partner-in-crime-stopping, Armand Downsey.

"What a happy dress," Downsey greeted me. I smiled in acknowledgment. To counteract the gloom of both the atmosphere and my mood, I'd tossed on one of my most garishly printed forties frocks, a pattern of mango-red and banana-yellow parrots perched on Day-Glo green trapezes.

The two detectives shuffled in. "I brought you this," Terry said, thrusting a crumpled brown bag at me. Please don't let it be Heart's Ease organic cranberry muffins, I prayed, peeking gingerly into it. To my great relief, it was the pair of Saturn zircon-blue salt and pepper shakers.

"They go with all your old stuff, right?" Terry said.

"Yeah, but I can't take them. You said they've been in your family for years."

"Only because no one's ever got around to shipping them off to the Salvation Army. Tell you what, I'll trade you for one of your pictures of the buildings with the little faces. My kids'll get a charge out of it."

"Deal," I said. We all awkwardly filed into the kitchen, where I had the requisite coffee brewing. I poured, automatically serving Terry black, Downsey milk and Sweet'n Low. "I suppose you want me to give a complete statement now," I said.

"It can wait a day," Downsey said. "Get yourself settled, then come in to the station." He mugged sympathetically at me. "You must be glad this is all over."

"Does that mean the case is being closed?" I asked.

"Any reason it shouldn't be?" Terry said blandly.

"I don't know. I just feel there's something still missing."

"You want to be more specific?"

"All the evidence fits," Downsey put in. "Palumbo's fingerprints match the print lifted from Mrs. Prentice's body and his blood type corresponds with the sperm sample. Ditto with his footprints—they're a match with the prints made the night you were attacked in your backyard."

"Yes, yes, he admitted all that to me," I said impatiently. "But he also told me he didn't kill anyone yet."

"Are you sure that's what he said?" Downsey asked gently. "You had a gun pointed at your heart. You must've been pretty scared. You might have just *wanted* to hear something reassuring like that."

"It wasn't reassuring. When he said 'yet,' I thought he meant I'd be his first."

"Then maybe you misunderstood," Terry chimed in. "Maybe he said something like 'I didn't kill *everyone* yet.' Meaning he still had himself to go."

I hesitated. It was possible. Sandy hadn't exactly been speaking with network-news-anchor diction. A half-sloshed mumble was more like it. And scared didn't begin to describe what I was feeling; rather, stark wet-your-pants-and-nearly-pass-out terrified. The more I thought about it, the less convinced I was that I really knew what I'd heard him say.

A rap number blasted down from Chloe's room, volume upped to the max. We all levitated about an inch from our seats.

"Naughty by Nature," Downsey said, and grinned at my flustered expression. "That's the name of the group. I don't mean Chloe."

"I don't know where she gets this stuff," I said primly. "Ordinarily I'd never let her listen to it."

He nodded. "When does Kit get back?"

"They've got another week in Seattle. Except he's snowbound up in this little town in the Rockies. At least that's the last place I heard from him." Snowbound with a babe. The two detectives were looking at me, I thought, rather pityingly. Poor Lucy, with the schmuck of a husband who couldn't give a rat's ass if she lived or died.

Then, as if by telepathic signal, they both rose. "We'll leave you in peace," Downsey said.

"By the way," Terry added, "did you notice the Prentice place is up for sale?"

"No," I said, with interest. "It was dark when we got home

last night. But I'm not hugely surprised that Woody wants to move on."

"There's some kind of real estate open house going on. Getting quite a turnout."

"It's a regular traffic jam out there," Downsey chuckled.

After they left, I hustled myself to the window and peered out. The overcast had brightened just enough for me to see the Anglophile CHAS WHITE REALTY sign fastened to the Prentice gate, a bright red OPEN hung above it. The case was closed, Woody was decamping. In a few weeks Justin would no doubt be gone as well. I should be popping corks to celebrate that the nightmare was finally over.

Yet I still had this intense feeling of uneasiness. Either a piece of the puzzle was missing or it had been jammed into a space it didn't fit. I'd never feel really safe until it was put where it belonged.

"Mom?" Chloe came tripping into the kitchen, cuddling the very vocal Siamese kitten I'd allowed her to bring home. It seemed a reasonable alternative to the seven or eight years of therapy she'd need to work through the trauma of having to leave it behind. "Miri Pleischman had to come back from riding camp 'cause she fell off her horse and sprained her wrist, and she wants me to come over, so can I?"

"Sure. Just let me run across the street for a few minutes, then I'll drive you." Out the window, I spied a white van threading its way down the crowded street, the logo POOL PERFECT on its side. "Conrad's here."

"Cool, I can show him Furball!" Chloe ran to buzz him through the gates.

IT'S A LITTLE KNOWN BUT accurate fact that there are more real estate agents in Los Angeles than there are actors; and a

fair sampling of this multitude had turned up for the Prentice
open house. It was heading to closing time when I arrived, so
most were just leaving, but a couple of dozen still roamed the
first floor. The men were mostly gay, spruce and smiling. The
under-forty women wore tasteful designer earth tones; the over-
forties veered, for some reason, to the sartorially eccentric—as
if years of trooping strangers in and out of other strangers' homes
led inexorably to harlequin glasses, purple felt jackets with cat
appliqués and miniature Temple of Isis earrings.

The mid-week open houses were technically only for other
agents, so I was afraid Marsha might unceremoniously boot me
out. I slunk into the kitchen, which was happily Moss-Golson—
free. Picked-over trays of refreshments languished on the count-
ers—curling charcuterie and dissolving-to-crumbs Pepperidge
Farm cookies—as well as mussed-up stacks of full-color brochures. I helped myself to one of these and silently whistled at
the asking price: 2.25 million. Celebrity death apparently had a
salubrious effect on property values.

I looked up to see Marsha striding in as if leading a charge,
an effect heightened by the martial-looking jacket she had on,
the shoulders broad enough to land navy jets on. She double-
timed it over to me. "So, when are we gonna relist your home?
Right now, it's a sellers' market for this neighborhood. You
oughta take advantage."

"I'm not really sure we want to move," I said quickly.

"You're kidding, right? You're saying you could ever stick a
big toe into that pool again, after everything? I don't know about
you, but it would give me the heebies."

The heebie-jeebies: that was as good a way as any to describe
what I'd been feeling since I'd been home. I said airily, "We're
thinking of bringing in an exorcist. Have him drive out any ghosts
that might still be hanging around."

She pursed her lips, actually considering this as a possible
course of action: sometimes I forgot I lived in Southern California. "If it was me, I'd unload the place," she concluded.

"Where's Woody going?" I asked, to change the subject. "Back East?"

"Yeah, if you count Beverly Hills as east. We got a bid accepted yesterday, an estate used to belong to William Holden. Prime location, right above the hotel. Six bedrooms nine bathrooms two maids gym projection room north-south tennis court fifty-foot diving pool with waterfall. Asking seven-point-eight, they took seven even."

"Million?"

Marsha shot me a that's-too-moronic-a-question-to-answer look. Seven million smackers for a home within spitting distance of the Polo Lounge—Woody was finally living up to his reputed income. Once again I felt a tug of pity for poor, defunct Julia. It sounded like the kind of spread she'd always aspired to. I could just see her queening it over that fifty-foot diving pool with waterfall. "What about Quanxi?" I asked.

Marsha looked as blank as if I'd asked, "What about Howard the Duck?"

"His daughter," I prompted. "Does he have her back?"

"Oh, the kid. I haven't seen her. I think she's still up with the family."

A blond young man with a Halloween tan—out-of-the-bottle orange—barged in on us, or rather on Marsha. Had a new listing Marsha might be interested in. Eight approved lots in upper Bel-Air. Owner willing to trade for a plane. "Turbo prop or jet?" countered Moss-Golson.

It was my opportunity to slip away. I headed to the second floor, which I had never seen.

The entire floor had been converted to two enormous suites. The famous Julia and Woody separate bedrooms! The west suite, though now stripped of personal effects, had clearly been Julia's, all chintz and gingham and braided rugs. I paused at the foot of the canopy bed: this could have been the very spot where Julia, caught in her birthday suit, had lobbed the vase at nanny Audrey's head!

I crossed the landing to check out Woody's domain. Straight out of a Ralph Lauren catalog—tweedy fabrics, rough-hewn dark woods. Even the accessories seemed plucked from a layout: pipe rack, repro butler's friend, a telescope pointed out the back window to the distant ocean. All that was missing was a roaring fire in the hearth and a brace of Irish water spaniels curled up beside it.

A pair of women agents cruised into the room. Identical noses and lantern jaws proclaimed them a mother-and-daughter team, daughter in sand-colored Anne Klein II, Mom in a patchwork pullover and go-go boots. "I smell fresh paint," sniffed the daughter.

"The ceiling," Mom observed. "Methinks there's a leak and they're covering up the evidence."

"But wouldn't they have to disclose that?"

"Huh, Marsha Moss-Golson? She wouldn't disclose it if the house had burned down to the ground. She'd march us through the foundation and point out all the fabulous views."

The two continued into the cavernous bathroom. For lack of anything else of interest to look at, I wandered to the street-side window and gazed out through the bright haze toward my own house. It was almost completely screened by foliage, eucalyptus and the denser-leafed black acacia.

"This boy kept following us around, but he was, like, a serious dork" came a sudden high voice.

I gave a start: It was Chloe! I couldn't see her, but by some trick of the haze and the hill acoustics, I could hear her as clearly as if she were four feet away.

Suddenly I whirled and stared at the telescope pointed out at the opposite view. What if it were focused instead at this window?

The two women agents sailed out of the bathroom, exchanging snotty comments about the gold-plated fixtures. I waited till they had strolled back out to the hall, at which point I legged it across the room, hoisted the telescope and hauled it back to the street-side window.

At first I could see nothing through the lens but a blurry camouflage of leaf patterns. I twirled the lens ring. The blur consolidated to blobs, and then suddenly my own bedroom window popped into sharp focus.

So sharp, I could make out details halfway into the room—the quilt on my bed, my white goose pull toy. My skin crawled. Those times I'd felt like I was being watched—maybe it wasn't just paranoia after all.

I tilted the scope up, above my roofline, to the top terrace of the hill behind the roof. Now Chloe loomed in the lens, hopping on one bare foot at the edge of the pool. "What's that?" I heard her say, pointing to the water. Conrad moved into focus, skimming hibiscus and dead hornets from the pool's surface. He mumbled something inaudible. "Gross!" Chloe squealed and hopped out of my view.

"Up here we got two luxury master suites, each with fireplace, Jacuzzi tub, walk-in closets . . ." Now it was Marsha's clarion tones assaulting my ears from the landing. I quickly straightened up and lugged the telescope back across the room, frantically trying to adjust it back into position before Marsha appeared. One of the tripod feet caught on the edge of the rug. I tugged it. It snagged further.

"Hey, watch it!" Marsha was hovering behind me. "You're pulling the rug." She squatted and freed the snagged leg. Then she pulled out something lodged under the rug against the baseboard, a long metallic object. "What the hell's this?" she said, dangling it.

I gave a short laugh. "It's The Boss."

"The who?"

I took it from her hand. "It's a nipple clamp. A gadget used in S and M sex. See, it's got these little screws so you can adjust the tension."

"Jesus, you've gotta be kidding." Marsha stood up and glanced nervously at the other agents who'd come in with her and were now scattered about the room. "What's it doing here?"

"Julia was into that kind of thing."

"This wasn't her room. It was Woody's."

"Yeah. Funny, isn't it?" I slipped The Boss into my shoulder bag.

"You can't just take that!" Marsha barked. Several of her colleagues glanced our way with interest. Guessing Marsha wouldn't care to make a scene, I turned and ambled out of the room and continued on downstairs.

There was something of a commotion in the foyer: agents were jam-packing it as if someone had shouted "Twenty percent commissions!" I edged through the mob to see what was going on.

It was the venerable owner of the house himself, Woody Prentice, in his Uncle Roy guise, the famous faded plaid shirt and crumpled Tilly hat. He was signing brochures. He was squeezin' hands. He was dispensing folksy charm to all and sundry. In short, he was working the room.

Cuckoldry, murder, suicide . . . nothing was going to prevent Woody Prentice from getting top dollar for his home.

Marsha came flying down the stairs, her celebrity radar blipping full tilt. "Gang, isn't this a great surprise!"

With everyone raptly attuned to Woody, I slipped out the front door unnoticed and went back home.

"Mom, can we *go* now!" Chloe whined, waylaying me as I came through the door.

"*Okay,*" I said. I dropped The Boss into one of my kitschy cookie jars, and tried to squelch down those old heebie-jeebies that had gripped me even tighter than before.

25

NEXT TO ALWYN ROSSNER, MIRI Pleischman was the girl at Windermere whom Chloe envied the most. First off, the Pleischmans lived in a real, actual log cabin. It had been built on the MGM lot as a set for a 1950 Clark Gable Western, then trucked to an acre pad in the Palisades by a developer who slapped on an extra wing and five tiled baths, but it still looked exactly like the maple-syrup bottle, at least from the front.

Second, Miri and her sister Sophie's live-in nanny was a *guy*, just like *Charles in Charge*, a USC dropout named Renny who could belly-board and was superexpert at Mortal Kombat; and all of this was so totally cool, Chloe could just about die!

I deposited Chloe with Miri and the totally cool Renny, who did look like a stumpier version of Scott Baio, figuring the Pleischmans, who were both criminal attorneys, would have made reasonably sure they hadn't employed a twenty-three-year-old pederast. Then I continued on to my studio—plunging back into work seemed the best antidote to the heebies.

A week's worth of *Variety*s and assorted junk mail had accumulated outside the door; otherwise, everything was exactly as I'd left it. This I found comforting. Good old tea-stained Donald Duck mug. Nice faded poster of *The Fantastic Planet.* Wonderful, marvelous Chloe preschool finger paintings.

There too was my last acetate drawing of Amerinda. The little blue hedgehog was curled up fast asleep in bed. I now planned to work on the nightmare sequence that was going to propel her out of her stay-in-bed inertia. My inspiration was the spooky old Max Fleischer cartoons of the thirties, the ones in which Betty Boop and Ko-Ko the Clown are chased through haunted houses by weird and terrifying objects. For Amerinda's nightmare, it would be the barnyard: I saw a white picket fence turning into a line of Rockette-dancing skeletons, haystacks becoming Cousin Itt–like monsters, a milking machine morphing into a grinning octopus.

Before plunging in, I opened a diet peach Snapple and flipped through the latest *Variety,* my usual procrastinating routine. There was a double truck ad for the upcoming miniseries *Firesticks:* cavalry officers, saloon ladies and Indians picturesquely grouped before a backdrop of purple mountains majesty. An all-star, multicultural cast: Tom Berringer, Graham Greene, Cybill Shepherd as "Gretchen," Eriq LaSalle as "the Preacher" . . .

And Woody Prentice as "Colonel Lawrence T. Rawlins."

I almost couldn't recognize him. He wore a long, Custer-like yellow wig and matching goatee; only the twinkling blue eyes gave him away as Madison Avenue's favorite pitchman. "Of course," I muttered to myself—those yellowish flecks I'd noticed on his chin the day I'd gone to pay my condolences . . . what I'd attributed to the remains of a breakfast omelet . . . they were actually what was left of the glue that had attached his fake goatee. How dense I was not to have figured that out!

The more I stared at the picture, the more he reminded me of someone else. A name tickled at the edge of my consciousness. . . . Yes, Ronald Gruenloft. A custodian at NYU when Kit and I were there, a pot-puffing longhair celebrated on campus as an authentic throwback to hippie days.

Suddenly I sat back so hard in my chair that it shot on its

little wheels three feet into the room. Then I leaped up, grabbed my handbag and overturned the contents onto my worktable, and fished through them for Terry Shoe's card. Punched up her beeper number. When the phone rang five minutes later, I snatched it up.

"Teresa Shoe."

"Terry, it's Lucy," I shouted. "I've got it all figured out! Francine Palumbo wasn't blackmailing Julia. She was blackmailing *Woody!*"

If I was expecting a gasp of astonishment or an excited "Eureka!" I still didn't know my Terry Shoe. "Oh, yeah?" she deadpanned.

"Woody was Julia's Mr. Pete, the guy Francine originally fixed her up with. *He's* the one into sadistic sex. Sandy Palumbo wasn't lying—he didn't kill either Francine or Julia. Woody did!"

"You got any proof of this?"

"Look, witnesses said they saw someone who looked like a hippie driving a Mercedes around the time Julia was killed. If Woody had taken a quick break from the set of his miniseries, he'd still be in full costume, including a long wig and goatee. He'd look exactly like a hippie if you saw him driving by."

"That's the extent of your evidence?"

"No. I was over at his open house just after you left, and I found a nipple clamp, this thing that's used in S and M sex. It was in Woody's bedroom, not Julia's." No immediate response. I babbled on, "Look, I think I can explain how everything fits together. I'm at my studio right now, but I can be home in fifteen minutes. Why don't you meet me there?"

"Okay, we'll swing by," she said. Not sounding wildly enthusiastic about the prospect.

I hung up and scooped all my odds and ends back into my bag. One of those colossal species of insects that breed in L.A., this one a cross between a horsefly and a cargo carrier, was batting itself against the window. It seemed a bad omen to let it continue its impotent thrashing. I raised the pane and it curlicued out into the gloom. Then I reshut and locked the sash and hurried out to my car.

I drove my usual shortcut through a residential section of tiny stucco bungalows. Raymond Chandler country—I imagined that behind every screen door sat a peroxide blonde in curlers and frowsy negligee. The bungalows gave way to warehouses—long, flimsy edifices that housed marginal companies with names like Dotti's China Closet and Wejetit Carpet Cleaning. A semi was lumbering from a loading bay, taking up most of the road. I shot daringly through the remaining strip. The truck driver protested my recklessness with a deep blare of his horn.

I tooled on to the outskirts of the district, the buildings now only sporadically occupied and separated by wide, vacant lots. There was always so little traffic in this area, it came as a jolting surprise when a car hit me from behind.

Getting rear-ended is a fact of life in L.A. I'd had the honor twice before, once by a pickup crammed with nine Nicaraguans, all of whom fled before I could get out of my car, and the other time by a dazed and confused eighty-year-old guy in a Grand Torino. This was one for the records, I thought—I'd been hit by a stretch limousine. At least this time they'll probably have insurance, I consoled myself as I pulled over.

The limo nosed up behind me. The chauffeur hopped out. Yellow baseball cap, wrap shades, black muscle shirt and jeans. Music biz, was my guess. Who else but a rock star would employ a driver who looked like he spent his leisure time dealing crack to schoolkids?

I got out and approached him, adopting a firm but friendly stance, the way they advise in traffic school. "Hi," I began. "I'll need to see your license and registration."

The driver's response to this request was startling. Rather than producing the requested documents, he made a sudden lunge at me, pinned my arms and, yanking open the back door of the limo, thrust me inside.

"Hello there, Lucy Freers," said Woody Prentice.

I gaped at him. He was straddling the jump seat, still decked out as Uncle Roy, crumpled Tilly hat and all. "Woody?" I said stupidly.

The driver hopped back into the front seat. A rubberbanded little ponytail poking from beneath his cap identified him as Creepy Bodyguard-cum-Cousin Griff. The door locks clicked shut and we began to roll.

"What's this all about?" I asked, keeping my tone light.

"You and I need to have a little chat," Woody said.

"If you wanted to talk to me, you're always welcome to come over to the house," I said. "Or I'd be glad to drop over to you."

Woody responded with a folksy chuckle.

"Okay, then, what do you want to chat about?" I went on.

"I'm told you took something you shouldn't have from my house."

Marsha Moss-Golson, blabbermouth extraordinaire. She probably lost no more than 6.4 seconds before blabbing to Woody that I'd pocketed The Boss. "That thing from the bedroom?" I said breezily. "I didn't know what it was, so I gave it to the police."

"Well, no, you haven't had time to do that. And I'm pretty darn sure you do know what it is. You've done a swell job finding out about all sorts of things." That just-us-folks voice with its throaty little catch—so familiar I half expected the Allstate Insurance jingle to cue up in the background.

"You're giving me far too much credit," I said dismissively.

"Well, no, the problem is I didn't give you enough credit. And that's the problem we've got to contend with now." He scrunched his face in one of his trademark Uncle Roy humorous grimaces. I could almost swear I heard a laugh track.

It vaguely occurred to me that I should be more scared. I'd been afraid of Justin, who was a rat and a shit but not a murderer. With Sandy Palumbo, who, when it came down to it, couldn't harm anyone but himself, I'd been so terrified I thought my bones would melt; yet here I was, trapped in a limousine with a man who'd already done in two women—who was running a regular dead Hollywood Moms Society—and I'd hardly broken a sweat. It just seemed almost impossible to be afraid of the irascible but kindly-underneath-it-all Uncle Roy Self.

"You know, you really are an excellent actor," I marveled.

He bowed his head in modest acknowledgment. "I started out in legit, you know. Not many people realize that. I did *Salesman, Streetcar, Henry IV* and *V.*"

"I had no idea."

Griff glanced back through the partition. "So, what do we do, head out the ten?"

This gave me a jolt of alarm. Route 10, if I remembered correctly, led eventually out to the Mojave Desert, where, deep among the vast, deserted tracts of Joshua trees, you could do just about anything short of nuclear detonation undetected.

"Look," I said to Woody, "the cops and everybody else think Sandy was guilty. I can't prove otherwise. Why don't we just let this go? It'll stop right here."

"I wish it were that easy." He sounded genuinely regretful.

"If I turn up dead as well, it'll just kick off a whole new investigation."

"You're not gonna turn up," sniggered Griff from the front.

"They'll find my car."

"With a nail in the tire," Woody said. "You had a flat, you went to get help, unfortunately in the wrong kind of neighborhood."

"I'd have called AAA on my car phone."

Griff, with another snigger, brandished my car antenna like a sorceror's wand. "Not if you'd lost your antenna."

"I see," I said glumly.

We were cruising the most desolate part of the district. Keep calm, I ordered myself. Think. An idea struck me. . . . It's a limousine, not a paddy wagon; the driver can automatically lock all locks, but can't prevent the passengers from *un*locking them. . . . The car snaked around a corner. As it slowed to approach a light, I lunged forward, snapped the lock and leaned down with all my weight on the door handle. The door flew open.

"Hey!" Woody yelled indignantly and grabbed the hem of my dress. For a moment I was caught half-suspended over the road; then there was a long ripping sound. Bless this fifty-year-old dress with its fifty-year-old seams! The back skirt panel of my dress tore away and I tumbled free.

I leaped to my feet and scooted to the curb, my buttocks and the backs of my thighs now ingloriously exposed to the breeze— why did I have to choose today to wear my skimpiest bikini panties? I scrambled up a sandy gradation, slipping and sliding in my cork-soled sandals. "Sensible shoes, sensible under- wear"—that, I promised myself, would be my future mantra. Pre- suming, of course, that I *had* a future.

This thought propelled me to the top of the rise. Here there was one of those weird only-in-L.A.–type places. Two working oil pumps, prehistoric grasshoppers, their heads dipping in perfect syncopation. On the clearing around them, the Culver City fathers had seen fit to install several anemic shrubs, a few splintery wooden benches and a rusting jungle gym, making it a kind of petroleum theme park—inviting only to the odd transient looking for a place to sleep off a drunk. In a less preoccupied moment, i.e., when not being pursued by the Hollywood Strangler, I might have stopped to wonder at the sheer nuttiness of it all. Now I streaked through with hardly a glance.

I had rounded the first pump and was just pulling abreast of the second when Griff tackled me. "Help!" I screamed. His damp hand clamped over my mouth.

Woody came lumbering up the slope, panting either from exer- tion or in anticipation of his kind of fun. A festively colored scarf fluttered from his hand, like the colors of some knight of yore. "Hold her!" he barked to Griff, puffing up closer to us. He quickly cased the clearing. "Behind the pump," he directed.

"*Mmpff!*" I protested, kicking and struggling as Griff dragged me behind the bobbing machinery. We were now, I realized, totally screened from sight of the road. Everything seemed eerily intensified: the complaining creak and groan of the pumps, the

homey Chevron station reek of oil, the *"eep eep eep"* of newly
hatched mockingbirds in some nearby nest—nature produced by
Imax. My eyes bulged with fright as Woody loomed in front of
me, wringing his scarf into a ropy length. It had parrots on it, I
noticed, festive red and yellow parrots perched on lime-green
trapezes—it wasn't a scarf, it was the ripped-away back piece of
my dress.

No! I thought frantically. It can't be happening like this! Not
in Culver City, a nice family place whose motto was "The Heart
of Screenland"! Not by America's most beloved sitcom star! And
absolutely, definitely not with my own goddamned parrot-festooned
vintage dress!

I began squirming with every ounce of my strength, kicking
out blindly, landing a solid hit on a shinbone. "Fucking bitch!"
Griff snarled. He wrenched my pinned arms so hard I gasped.

His other hand uncapped my mouth and I let out another
scream. "Shut up!" he said. He grabbed a fistful of my hair and
yanked my head back. Something slipped around my neck. For
a split second, it felt fluid and cool. Then there was a sharp burn;
I made a *"grrawk!"* sound as my breath was cut off abruptly from
my windpipe. Pain seared through my entire body, red and orange in intensity, obliterating everything but its own reality. I
stopped kicking. And then I stopped struggling at all.

When death is imminent, your entire life is supposed to roll
before your eyes; but what now suddenly flashed before my optic
nerve was a hedgehog. A flying blue hedgehog. It was Amerinda,
of course. Even with exploding lungs I could recognize her: she
was soaring through a vividly sunlit sky, doing loop-the-loops
and fancy barrel rolls, like some hot-dogging air force ace. Then,
whipping herself into a little whirlwind, she plunged straight
down into a nose dive, snout first, wormy tail pointing directly
at the sun. A feeling of elation flooded through me, even through
the searing pain. I was being saved! Amerinda, brave, marvelous
Amerinda, was coming to my rescue!

Except why did she seem to have yellow eyes?

And why was she yelling something about police officers?

Then, all at once, the pain stopped, and I was on my knees in the dirt, retching in great dry heaves at the foot of one of the Jurassic grasshoppers.

And Terry Shoe, in the most beautiful-awful powder-blue suit, was bending solicitously over me.

26

"I TOLD YOU IF I tailed you you'd never know it," Terry said with a smug little chortle.

We were in a sort of conference room at the station, luxurious by police-precinct standards. I imagined this was where they broke the bad news to the loved ones of murder and rape victims: it was a jukebox of bad vibes. My hands were clenched in involuntary fists; listening to Terry, I had to restrain myself from slugging her.

Instead, I sat up a little straighter in my uncomfortable chair and placed my fists on the blond wood table. "So, have you been tailing me ever since I've been back?" I asked.

She giggled. "You gotta be kidding. We don't have the budget for that kind of surveillance."

"So, when did you start?"

"Just this afternoon. I figured that after we pointed out that Prentice open house, you'd get your ass over there pronto—you being the original Nosy Parker. Then, as we were leaving the area, we noticed the limo heading there too. Had to be Woody, right? So we also figured that, knowing you, when you ran into him, you wouldn't be able to keep your mouth shut. You'd spout off your theories about things not adding up and the killer still at large. At which point, he might decide he had to get rid of you."

"You were wrong, we never exchanged a word. Marsha was the blabbermouth. She told him about my finding his little sex toy, and that's what set him off."

"So we got lucky."

I clenched my fists tighter. She certainly had a singular notion of what constituted luck. "Why tail me?" I asked. "Why didn't you tail Woody?"

"Because we weren't a hundred percent sure he did the dirty himself."

"You mean he might have called the job in to a strangler-for-hire?"

Terry shrugged airily. I glared at her, sitting there so smug and aren't-I-brilliant. "You used me as bait," I said bitterly. "I could have been killed. But I suppose that didn't matter so long as you got to close your case and keep up your goddamned record."

"We certainly did not use you as bait. On the contrary, we were trying to protect you. Which, I might point out, we did."

"If you were so damned anxious to protect me, then why didn't you just warn me about Woody? A little hint that he had murdering tendencies."

Her face puckered with disgust. "We couldn't do that. We accuse a prominent citizen of murder and can't prove it, we can end up with a whopper of a lawsuit. That's the times we live in. I don't like it, but what can I do?"

"Okay then, why didn't you move in as soon as Griff pushed me into the limo?"

She looked momentarily sheepish. "We got held up a couple blocks back by a semi backing out of a dock. Then we came across your abandoned vehicle and presumed you'd been abducted. We played a hunch they'd headed in the direction of the freeway."

"That's all that saved me? A goddamned hunch?"

"Hey, you're upset, and I don't blame you. You want to go to the ladies'?"

I shook my head. I had the urgent need to keep talking, the only way to assure myself that this was real, I was safe, it was over. "I want to know if I was right," I said. "About the way everything happened."

"You tell me, and I'll let you know if it sounds correct."

"All right. First of all, Woody has long been into S and M, specifically the *S*. He was Mr. Pete, the john Francine set Julia up with during the *Delano* shooting."

"It seems like a reasonable assumption." Terry leaned back and crossed her hands behind her neck.

"At that time he was a has-been, just living off whatever he had left from his old *Bryer* series. Then, a few years later, he makes it back into the big time with *In the Same Boat*. When he goes shopping for his dream house, he runs into Julia again, who's now a real estate agent. It occurs to Julia that if she can't be a star herself, the next best thing would be to become a star's significant other. It would certainly beat scrounging for six percent commissions the rest of her life. So she gives Woody a free demonstration that she can still cater to his needs—no doubt something far kinkier than the straightforward blow job she'd later report to Marsha Moss-Golson."

My teeth started to chatter. Terry sympathetically pushed a can of Dr Pepper my way; I pressed the cool, humid metal against my cheek until my teeth stopped their flamenco. "Julia's demo is a success," I continued. "Woody buys in to both house and marriage."

"The American dream," Terry snorted. "They had it all—house, pool and cat-o'-nine-tails."

I managed a grim smile. "So then, after a few years of fun and games, the sex play starts to get out of hand. Julia ends up with a bloody butt and freaks out. Moves into her own bedroom and tells Woody he'll have to get his kicks somewhere else. What she really wants now is social power, to run with Summer Rossner and her set. So she trendily adopts a Chinese baby, and signs up for every high-profile charity in town, and starts climbing the Hollywood Mom ladder."

Terry nodded. "And by the way, starts getting her own rocks off with cute young guys."

The thought of Justin still made me wince. I went on hurriedly, "In the meantime, Julia confides everything to her bosom buddy Francine, just like she's always done. And Francine, who's always planning ahead, probably makes tapes of some of their juicier conversations. When Woody starts hauling in millions as the spokesman for family and apple pie, Francine's ready to pounce." I let out a harsh laugh. "I can just picture it. She invites him to lunch at The Ivy, so she can get points for being seen with the famous Uncle Roy at the same time she's blackmailing him. Probably wears her best pink Chanel, orders the Cobb salad, no dressing. And while picking at her chopped avocado, she murmurs to her dear old friend that she's got Julia on cassette spilling the beans about his secret hobby. Here's her deal: Woody will make hefty payments to her, under the guise of management fees for Julia, and, in return, Francine will *not* treat Geraldo Rivera to a private listen." I paused and drew a deep breath. "Am I on the right track?"

"So far, I'd say yes. It's pretty certain Woody was paying out to Francine."

"Which, given how cheap he is, must've driven him nuts." I let out another semimanic laugh. "Right off the charts."

"People have killed for a lot less than what Francine was squeezing him for," Terry said. "A hell of a lot less."

"Yeah, I guess so," I said in a more sober voice. "Anyway, this brings us to a month ago and my swimming pool. The day of Julia's murder, Woody is on the set of *Firesticks*. He decides to drop home for whatever reason."

"Maybe a change of underwear."

"Could be. That would certainly have given him a reason to be up in his bedroom. Which is where he discovers the hanky-

panky going on at the side of my pool. A magnified view through
the lens of his telescope."

"That's something I have trouble with," Terry said. "What
tipped him off to look through it?"

"A funny thing happens when you stand at the front window
of Woody's bedroom. Some trick in the way sound bounces off
the hills—you can hear people talking at my pool as clearly as
if they were just a few yards away."

"Huh," Terry grunted. "Woody must've got a real earful."

"Julia and Sandy going at it hot and heavy. *That's* when he
drags the telescope over, and gets a visual to go along with
the audio."

"It must've raised his blood pressure a tad."

"Yeah, just a tad," I agreed wryly. "Here he's stuck with a
wife who's not only no longer satisfying his own needs, but who's
also becoming increasingly reckless with her own partying. Plus,
it was her loose lips that caused him to be blackmailed. Not to
mention the millions a year he's got at stake by keeping up a
squeaky-clean image. So when Sandy leaves, Woody heads across
the street." I paused, considering the scene a moment. "I think
it's possible he wasn't actually intending to kill Julia. It could
have just happened in a spurt of fury."

"But it did happen," Terry put in bluntly.

"Yeah, it did. After which he rolls the body into the pool and
beats it back to the set. It's been hardly an hour, and he quickly
makes sure no one's really noticed he's been gone."

"With all those stand-ins and stunt doubles hanging around."
Terry smirked, pleased at her own insider's knowledge.

I nodded. "They've probably also seen his driver hanging
around while he was gone. Union rules require all principals to
use a union driver. But actors sometimes take their own cars
and let the drivers and the hired cars sit around unused. Which
is what Woody had done that day. So now all these production
assistants swear he's been on the set the whole time, and he's

got his alibi. Except," I added, "there's still the big problem of Francine."

Terry issued an eloquent sound.

"I think that last week, when Sandy's company went bust, Francine probably got desperate. She calls Woody, announces she's leaving town, says she'll give him the tapes in return for some huge lump sum. Knowing Francine, it had to be a couple million at least."

"Just to tide her over until she hooked her next meal ticket." Terry's lips tightened sourly.

"Right. And, of course, Woody agrees to come by with the payment. But shows up instead with a Zegna tie, which everyone knows is one of Sandy's trademarks. He strangles Francine, pretty sure all the evidence will point to Sandy. And almost gets clean away."

The door opened, and a couple of cops poked their heads in. Forget muggers, wife beaters, pimps and burglars: I was definitely the star attraction of the day. "Out!" Terry snapped, and the cop heads retracted like twin box turtles.

"So what do you think?" I said. "Does that jibe with the way you've got it figured?"

"Give or take a few details."

I felt an absurd little flush of satisfaction, as if I'd just been awarded an A+ on a term paper. "When did you start suspecting Woody?" I asked.

She waved a dismissive hand. "Right from the start. Old husband, young wife who runs around—there's a possible motive right off. The S and M angle clicked in later, when you and I were at that party."

"The Magic Wand benefit?"

"Yeah. You remember that gal who was smoking H in the john?"

"The one who was supposed to be Griff's niece."

"Some niece! I ID'd her as a hooker I picked up four years

back when I was working vice. That's why I followed her into the john, to get a close-up look. It was the same gal, all right. She used to work for a madam in Venice who catered to a specialized clientele."

"Let me guess," I said. "The S and M crowd."

"Bingo. This kid was only about nineteen at the time. Her thing was taking pain—cigarette burns, hot wax, paddlings."

I shuddered, remembering Janice Kovalarsky's vivid descriptions of the profession. "So you figured if she was with Woody, Woody had to be the sadistic Mr. Pete."

"I entertained it as a possibility," Terry corrected, with a haughty lift of her brows. I got the message: I was the amateur who leaped to reckless conclusions; she was the pro who moved only on conclusive evidence.

"Okay, so you weren't ready to send Woody to the chair yet," I said. "But at that point, he did become a stronger suspect."

"Yeah. Except there was still the problem of those production assistants vouching for him. Then, luckily, you went barging into that movie shoot."

"Oh, yeah, that was my lucky night."

"What I *mean* is I got to see how easy it would be on a movie set to think you saw the star, when actually it was the stand-in or the stunt double. But that still didn't give me any hard evidence."

"Until I conveniently offered myself as the worm on the hook."

"I wouldn't put it that way." Terry wrinkled her nose, with a fastidiousness that was rare for her.

"By the way," I said, "what do you think Woody used to kill Julia?"

"My guess? His prop revolver. A nice heavy old chunk of Smith & Wesson—just the thing to bash your wife's gorgeous skull in. The lab's got it now. He probably cleaned it pretty thoroughly, but maybe they can pick up some trace evidence. If they do, then we can charge him with the murder of his wife."

I stared at her. "What do you mean?"

"The only thing we can make stick right now is on your case.

Abduction, assault with a deadly . . . If we're lucky, maybe the DA will go for attempted murder."

"But everything I just said . . ."

"Circumstantial or speculation. It won't fly before a judge."

I suddenly felt like I was going to throw up.

Armand Downsey breezed into the room. He came over to me and pressed a pill into my hand. "Valium. You didn't get it from me."

"Thanks," I murmured. It was the blue ten milligram—just what the doctor ordered.

"I just heard some news," Downsey said. "Woody Prentice has had a heart attack. Sounds like a massive coronary. He's been rushed to UCLA, but the word is he'll be pronounced on arrival."

I gasped. "You mean he's dead?"

"Save the city the expense of a trial," Terry muttered.

Downsey tightened his lips, nodded solemnly. "If Woody buys it, Griff will no doubt cop a plea, and that'll be that. The big losers are the tabloids—they won't be able to milk the story for more than another week. Lucy, you're the winner." He smiled at me.

"Me?" I said bleakly.

"Sure. You and your family will finally be left in peace. You can start to get back to normal."

Yeah, right. Back to that normal film-biz family lifestyle, the one that takes just a couple of million a year to support. And if you can't keep it up, hey, no problem, just go ahead and shoot yourself. "It's funny," I said, after a moment.

"What's funny?" Downsey asked.

"This whole family thing that Hollywood's into. Kids and causes, that's what it's supposed to be all about now. What Julia and Woody and the Palumbos were supposed to be all about."

"So it surprises you that underneath there's still as much sex and greed and cutthroat ambition as there always was?" Terry said caustically.

"I don't know. Maybe not. But I just think it's kind of funny that after all this parading around of family values, there's two kids who are now orphans."

A gloomy silence descended on the room. Then Downsey cleared his throat, a stertorous let's-get-back-to-business. "The captain's ready to talk to us," he said to Terry.

She nodded. "Hang tight," she told me. "I'll be back in a while."

She got up and started out with Downsey. Mutt and Jeff. I remembered how I once thought of them as a comedy duo working the Laugh Factory. "One more thing," I said. They turned. "Is it really over? Or is another homicidal maniac going to come popping out at me some dark night?"

"It's really over," Downsey said firmly. *"Finito."* He raised his hand in an "I swear," then filed out with Terry.

I still had the Valium clutched in my palm. I popped it down with a long draft of Dr Pepper, upending the can the way they do in commercials, though without the TV actors' gleeful relish. From the corner of my eye I saw another plainclothes cop sidle into the room. Come on in and check out the sideshow.

"Sweetie?" the cop said. "Are you okay?"

I lowered the soda can. "Kit?" I whispered.

He looked ridiculous: baggy camp pants, dirty sweatshirt with a leaping trout and the logo "Life's a Fish & Then You Fry." Chin sprouting several days' worth of white-blond stubble. This was reassuring—if I were just imagining him, it would probably be in a spiffier format. "How did you get here?" I said awkwardly, rising from my chair.

"They finally opened the goddamned airport. We charted a Piper Cub to Vancouver, then I grabbed the first flight down."

"You left the movie?"

"For the time being."

"You actually left Jon Sugerman and the rest of them?"

"Christ, what did you think, I'd let you go through this by yourself?"

"I don't know," I said. "I really didn't know."

I suddenly started shaking. Kit bolted toward me and encircled me with his arms. I snuggled into the familiar padded shelter of his chest. "It's okay," he soothed. "Don't think about anything now. Everything's okay."

There's this old Betty Boop cartoon where the dizzy planet Saturn steals the magnet out of the center of the earth, and nothing sticks anymore to the ground. Betty Boop goes floating up, and a cow and a horse go floating up, and Mr. and Mrs. Krazy Kat, and four kittens in a bathtub, and all the houses and trees and the washing on all the clotheslines—everything goes floating up, up through the cotton-candy clouds and off into a dreamy outer space. It was the way I was feeling now, Kit and I and somehow Chloe too, we were all wafting weightlessly and deliciously up into the air. At some time, I knew, we'd have to fall back down to earth, maybe gently, maybe with a crash.

But Kit was right. I didn't have to think about that right now.